Terms AND CONDITIONS

LAUREN ASHER

Bloom books

Published by Bloom Books, an imprint of Sourcebooks
P.O. Box 4410, Naperville, Illinois 60567-4410
(630) 961-3900
sourcebooks.com

Originally self-published in 2021 by Lauren Asher.

Cataloging-in-Publication Data is on file with the Library of Congress.

Printed and bound in the United States of America.
LSC 13

Playlist

The Man – The Killers ♥

I am not a woman, I'm a god – Halsey ♥

If I Ever Feel Better – Phoenix ♥

Glitter – BENEE ♥

Enemy – Imagine Dragons, JID, & League of Legends ♥

Wicked Games – Kiana Ledé ♥

Fallen Star – The Neighborhood ♥

Altar – Kehlani ♥

Slow Dancing in a Burning Room – John Mayer ♥

Trip – Ella Mai ♥

Shivers – Ed Sheeran ♥

Angels Like You – Miley Cyrus ♥

Animal – Neon Trees ♥

Unlearn – benny blanco & Gracie Abrams ♥

Earned It – The Weeknd ♥

safety net – Ariana Grande ft. Ty Dolla $ign ♥

Iris – The Goo Goo Dolls ♥

Daylight – Taylor Swift ♥

Someone To Stay – Vancouver Sleep Clinic ♥

Great Ones – Maren Morris ♥

Marry Me – Train ♥

Paper Rings – Taylor Swift ♥

To anyone fighting an invisible battle.
I see you.

CHAPTER ONE

Iris

t's a crime to celebrate a day like today all by yourself." Cal, my best friend and boss's brother, interrupts me. Despite the rumpled state of his suit and dirty blond hair, he steals the attention of multiple waitresses who pass by our table.

I lock my phone and muster up a smile. "I'm not the one getting married."

His eyes flicker over my face. "No, but you're the puppet master who accomplished the impossible."

"It wasn't that bad."

"Now I know something is wrong with you. Are you...sad Declan is getting married?" His voice drops lower than usual.

A laugh bursts out of me. "What? *No*."

"Then what's wrong?"

My head hangs, and a few spiral curls fall in front of my eyes. I run a hand down my dress to smooth out a few nonexistent wrinkles. The cheery lavender fabric stands out against my brown skin, making me seem far happier than I feel. "I just got an email telling me I didn't get the job."

"Shit. I'm sorry to hear that. I know how hard you worked on the interview presentation."

After the months I spent working on a presentation for the Kane Company's human resources department, they rejected my job transfer. It stings more than it should. While I wasn't exactly shooting for the stars, with an entry-level HR position, I had a good idea with a promising future. One that could benefit count-less dyslexics stuck in a corporate rut. My plan could take the company to the next level, if only they'd give me a chance.

You can try again next time.

My smile wobbles. "I guess it wasn't meant to be."

"That's some bullshit if you ask me."

I laugh. "It's true. At least Declan never found out. Could you imagine if I told him and then I didn't even get the job? He would've never let me live it down."

"He does tend to gloat."

"Hence the party." I point at the ginormous balloon arch with a massive grin.

Cal raises a brow at the flickering neon *She Said Yes* sign. "Understated. He'll love it."

I bat my lashes with faux sweetness. "I simply planned a party like he asked me to. He should have specified what kind of event he wanted."

"Remind me to never piss you off."

"I have a whole plan for the day that happens."

Cal fake shudders. "Where is the wife-to-be?"

"Declan wanted to meet with her before the announcement."

His eyes widen. "Why the hell would you let him do that?"

"Umm…because he hasn't met her yet?"

"Exactly! That's why it's a terrible idea!" Cal runs his hands through his thick waves.

"You think he's going to make her change her mind?"

"Knowing my brother, it wouldn't take much convincing."

"She signed a contract. It's a done deal."

"If you say so…" He shrugs.

"Maybe I should go check on them." I turn toward the elevators.

Cal loops his arm in mine. "No. You're taking the night off."

"But—"

"You're probably right. Declan wouldn't risk losing it all now by doing something stupid. Even he knows when to hold back."

"Now I know you're lying."

He chuckles. "Come on. Let's go inside and wait for Declan. Just think about the way he will try so hard not to scowl and fail anyway. Hell, I don't think I've seen him so much as look in someone's direction without sneering since—" He cuts himself off.

"*Since?*"

He avoids looking me in the eyes. "Since forever. I'm pretty sure his dick is permanently chafed from jacking off every night."

I smack his shoulder with a laugh. "Shut up! He's my *boss*."

"Doesn't make it any less true. I'm surprised said appendage hasn't fallen off from that kind of abuse."

I let out another giggle.

"*Callahan.*" Declan's voice booms.

A few stragglers scurry inside of the ballroom at the sound of Declan's voice.

"He sure knows how to clear a room," Cal says.

Whatever happiness I saw in Cal's eyes dies the moment Declan stops by us with a frown. The air morphs into something cold, with Declan's icy glare threatening to reverse climate change. His massive body blocks my view of the entire lobby. The spotlight behind him only highlights the sharpness in his features, bringing out the darkness in his eyes and the edges of his jaw.

Compared to Cal's golden-boy look of blond hair and blue eyes, Declan reminds me of the deepest part of the ocean—cold, dark, and unnervingly quiet. Like a monster lurking within reach, only a breath away from making someone his prey. From his dark hair to the permanent grimace etched into his face, he gives off a feeling that makes everyone turn in the opposite direction.

Well, everyone except me. Some might say he earned my loyalty through a paycheck, but that isn't the case. We share a mutual respect for one another that has stood the test of time. While our first few months working together were rocky, my commitment to succeeding as his assistant helped pave the way to our relationship today.

Somehow we click although we're opposites in almost every single way. I'm a Black woman. He's a White male. I smile and he scowls. He wakes up early every morning to work out while I wouldn't be caught dead at the gym unless it was to grab a smoothie at the café. We couldn't be more different if we tried, yet we make it work. Or at least *I* do.

I step between the two brothers. "Declan, what are you doing out here? Is it time for the announcement already?"

Declan drags his eyes away from Cal and down toward me. Most people cower under his stare, but I straighten my spine and look at him head-on like my nana taught me.

"She quit."

I blink. "Who quit? The wedding planner?"

"No. The wife. Belinda."

"Bethany quit?!"

Cal dares to look smug.

Declan doesn't bother looking away from my face as he detonates all my carefully laid plans. "Yes. Her."

"This can't be happening." I refuse to believe that he ruined months of my hard work. Finding him a woman willing to marry him and have his child so he could become CEO and earn his inheritance was nearly impossible.

Refusing to believe it doesn't change the facts.

"I hate to be the one to say I told you so…" Cal says.

"This is all your fault." I glare at him.

Cal raises both of his hands up in the air. "No! It's not my fault my brother's attitude is bigger than his dick."

Declan smacks the back of Cal's head. I ignore their bickering as I pace across the carpet, circling around them.

"You should have eloped while you had the chance." Cal drains his glass before stealing my half-finished flute.

"Speaking from personal experience?"

Cal's nostrils flare. His hands ball up at his sides before he takes a deep breath and lets the anger melt off him. He turns his attention toward me. "That is why my grandpa made that

5

inheritance clause in the first place. He knew Declan wasn't ready to become CEO and thought a family might soften him up. I mean, how can someone like him inspire the masses when he always seeks to destroy everyone around him?"

Declan's jaw clenches. Cal raises an eyebrow in a silent taunt.

I point at Cal. "Quit acting like a child and use that big brain of yours to help us out of this mess." Declan's eyes are already focused on me as I turn toward him. "And you stop taking your anger out on everyone else. Your screwing up has nothing to do with Cal and everything to do with *you*."

He only stares at me with that blank gaze I hate more than anything.

Cal scoffs. "Of course he fucked this up. His latest software update didn't include a manual on how to be a decent human being."

"You're both hopeless," I grumble under my breath as I grab my phone and dial Bethany's number. It rings twice before going straight to voicemail. I call again but this time the voicemail picks up right away. "Shit!"

"No answer?" Cal has the audacity to sound amused.

"What did you do?" I hiss in Declan's direction.

Declan picks at a piece of invisible lint on the sleeve of his jacket as if this is the most boring conversation of his day. "She wasn't cut out for the job."

"And what would you like me to do with that information given the fact that we have a hundred people waiting to hear about your engagement to some mystery woman? I'm all ears."

He stares at me with narrowed eyes, and I glare right back at him with my hands on my hips.

Cal makes a loud slurping sound as if to remind us of his presence. "I'm also interested in hearing how this will all pan out. Father will be just thrilled to hear about Declan's failed engagement."

Oh my God. While his father is unaware of Declan's letter from Brady Kane detailing the requirements for his inheritance, he isn't stupid. There's a reason he is a successful businessman after all. I have no doubt if he catches the faintest hint that this engagement is false, he will go running to Brady's lawyer. And if the lawyer believes him, Declan could lose everything.

Think, Iris. Think. I try Bethany's number one more time, hoping a third time is a charm. The voicemail can be heard loud and clear through the tiny phone's speaker.

Cal whistles before making an explosion noise. "That's the sound of Declan's future dying."

"Don't you have somewhere to be? A seedy bar perhaps?" Declan snaps.

"Why pay for alcohol when I can get it for free on your dime?" Cal grins as he dangles his champagne flute in the air.

I try to tune them out as I consider my options.

What can you do? Quit once and for all?

No. I refuse to give up now. Not when I'm so close to helping Declan achieve his goal.

You could call the backup option you have, but Declan made her cry—

"You know, Iris is single." Cal's smile turns sinister. "She could step into the role like a natural since no one knows you better than her."

"No," Declan snaps.

Wait.

Yes.

Me!

It's not like I have much stopping me from stepping in as a substitute. With no boyfriend to speak of or prior commitments, I could easily replace Bethany.

Just because you can doesn't mean you should.

Well, if not me, then who? We are out of time and suitable fiancées.

I open my mouth only to be interrupted by a squeal from Tati, Declan's wedding planner. "There you are! I was wondering where the husband-to-be snuck off to." Tati's high-pitched voice echoes.

"You can't pay for this kind of entertainment." Cal drains my glass before leaning against the table with a smile.

"Where is the fiancée I've heard so little about?" Tati waves her clipboard like a magic wand.

I'm glad I withheld Bethany's identity just in case something like this happened.

You can't be seriously thinking about marrying him. You don't even love him.

I don't need to love him. It's a contract, not a love match.

Declan cuts off my thoughts, "Beatr—"

"Her name is *Tati*, dear." I press my hand against his chest. His body goes rigid, and I give him another pat in a way that says *act naturally.*

His dark brows pull together as he stares down at my hand like he wants to rip it off finger by finger. "What are you doing?" His words come out sharp enough to stab straight through my perfectly crafted exterior.

"Saving you the trouble of having to introduce me and explain our story." I shoot him the sweetest smile I can manage given the circumstance.

Are you really going to do this, Iris? the voice of reason speaks up.

I don't see much of an option here.

This is marriage! It's not something you can just back out of when you get scared.

I shut down every thought speaking out against my plan. It's only a few years of my life.

What about having a child?!

Well, I always wanted to be a mother.

Yeah. In five years!

At least I can get started on my five-year plan a bit ahead of schedule.

I swallow the lump in my throat and turn my attention back toward Tati. I step out of Declan's stiff embrace before grabbing his hand. The muscles underneath his suit bunch up, visibly tightening underneath the material of his jacket.

Great. We'll have to work on his aversion to your touch later. "Tati, I wasn't fully honest with you when we spoke over the phone."

Her smile dims. "Oh."

"I was a bit hesitant about introducing myself as anything but Declan's assistant before meeting you in person. See, I've been working at the Kane Company for quite some time, and you know how easily gossip spreads."

She bobs her head as she clutches her clipboard to her chest. "Of course. I get it."

"I was so scared of what people would think about me dating my boss, but we can't hide it anymore. We don't *want* to hide it." My voice hitches without me trying.

Declan's only sign of distress is the way he blinks at me twice. I've *never* seen him blink twice. Not when a deal he had been working on for two years blew up and sure as hell not when his grandfather died.

It makes me…*unsettled*.

I steel my spine and turn back toward Tati. "We're ready to move forward with our future. There's no reason to keep our love a secret anymore."

Cal gives me two thumbs-up behind Tati's back. *Oscar-worthy* he mouths before prompting Declan to smile with his two middle fingers.

Tati's whole face lights up as she takes in our hands. "Wow! Tonight must be such a big deal for you both then, for multiple reasons." Her eyes drop to my naked ring finger.

"Oh, right. The ring!" I swing my gaze toward Declan's face.

The tic in his jaw is present for everyone to see.

Sorry, Declan, I'm saving you from ruining your entire future, even though it might not seem like it right now.

Declan tugs his hand from my grasp. He pulls out a platinum band with a beautiful solitaire diamond from his pocket. I'm somewhat surprised by the elegant ring. It's nothing like the ungodly monstrosity I chose for his future wife, which only confuses me. Did he pick up the wrong one at the store? I knew I shouldn't have trusted him with something so important, but he insisted.

Tati raises a brow in silent question, yanking me back into the moment.

"I asked Declan to hold on to it since we need to get it resized. The damn thing flew off my finger the moment I threw myself into his arms after he proposed."

"Oh no!" Tati pouts.

Cal slides into Tati's eyesight. "I told my brother it was a bad idea to propose in the middle of a rainstorm, but he insisted it was the perfect moment because Iris loves them."

"I've never seen anyone get down on their knees quicker than him." I wink at Tati and her cheeks flush.

Declan's frown becomes more pronounced, which only makes me laugh.

"The man nearly tore his Tom Ford slacks in half while chasing after that ring. My brother has never panicked like that before, so it's a good thing he found it before it fell down a storm drain." Cal wraps an arm around Declan's shoulders, and Declan promptly shoves him off.

"Did you get all this on video? I'd love to show it to the guests!" Tati beams.

The back of my neck heats. "Oh, no. Declan's proposal was spur-of-the-moment. It was *so* romantic—" I inhale as the devil grabs my left hand, and goose bumps break out across my skin. He traces them as he drags the ring up my finger.

"Oh, look! It fits after all!" Tati claps her hands. I swear she only has two volume settings—loud and earsplitting.

"He must have found some time in his busy schedule to finally have it resized." My cheeks heat.

Declan pulls at the band once, testing the snugness before tucking his hand into his pocket.

I trace the diamond with a finger before giving the ring a

pull. The band doesn't budge at all. I clear my throat and force a smile. "I think it's stuck."

Go figure that Bethany had a smaller finger than mine. Can I catch any breaks tonight?

"In more ways than one." His voice drops low enough for only me to hear it. Something about the depth of his voice sends another chill across my body. He steps out of my proximity, and I take a deep breath.

He readjusts his jacket. "Time to get on with this show."

A show. Nothing more, nothing less. A fake marriage meant to save my boss from losing everything he has worked toward his entire life.

The thought sends a fresh wave of panic through me, much stronger than ever before. I try to tell myself it is only a marriage on paper, but nothing seems to ease the rapid beat of my heart.

Declan's gaze clashes into mine as if he can sense my growing anxiety. My reality sets in like a bad sunburn, and I find my ability to breathe becoming progressively more difficult with each second that passes.

I just signed myself up to help Declan—for better or for worse.

Till death do us part.

CHAPTER
TWO

Declan

I'd like a moment to speak with my *fiancée* in private." The words scrape against my tongue like sandpaper.

Iris's eyes connect with mine. They widen before moving on to Cal in a silent plea for help. While her ability to read me like a polygraph machine makes her effective at her job, it is nothing but an inconvenience now.

Cal opens his mouth. Whatever look I send his way has him backing away slowly.

"See you both inside." He gives Iris a half-assed salute before entering the ballroom.

The wedding planner checks the time on her watch. "I'll be back in five minutes to grab you two. Don't disappear on me again." She winks before entering the kitchen.

My heart beats rapidly against my chest, and I attempt to take three deep breaths to slow the pace down.

You did tell her to find you anyone with two X chromosomes and the ability to procreate. You're the only one to blame here.

I'm beyond the point of no return. Never did I think Iris would resort to this kind of plan without so much as asking me if I would agree. It's a terrible idea that risks everything we have built together over the years.

Calm down.

One…two…

Fuck this.

"What the hell were you thinking?"

Iris doesn't so much as bristle from my tone, although her full lips purse from distaste. "I'm saving your ass, that's what."

"I'm failing to see how that's the case."

"Would you like me to schedule you an eye exam? I hear vision gets worse with age." Her usual joke about me being twelve years older than her falls flat.

My eyes narrow into slits. "Don't test me."

"And don't you dare look at me that way." She places a brown hand on her hip like a battle stance. The diamond on her finger stands out against her darker skin, drawing my attention to it. "If I didn't step in, then you would have had to explain to a room full of a hundred guests why there's no blushing bride-to-be. What would you tell everyone? That she got lost in the mail?"

"No." I grind my teeth together. "Although a mail-order bride seems like a better alternative at the moment."

Her dark eyes damn near *twinkle*. "Face it. You've run out of time and options."

"Clearly." I give her a once-over.

Something flashes behind her eyes before disappearing. She lifts her chin ever so slightly in defiance while staring me straight in the eyes. "Way to make a girl feel special."

"Special is the last word I would use to describe you." It feels far too generic for someone like her.

She lets out a groan as she throws her hands in the air. "I don't know why I thought this was a good idea."

"That makes two of us. What exactly is your motive here?"

"I like you enough to want to save you from yourself. I'm sure it must be a chemical imbalance of some kind, so my therapist will be hearing all about this on Monday."

I blink at her. "Don't tell me you're marrying me out of the goodness of your heart?"

Her dark brows pull together, and she stands taller. "So what if I am?"

"Cut the act. Those ideas only exist in Dreamland films."

Her lips part. "I'm not acting, although your reaction makes me wish I were."

Something about this whole thing isn't sitting right. Why would Iris suddenly volunteer to be my wife after months of searching for a perfect candidate?

Because she didn't want to see you marry someone else, the smallest voice in my head speaks up.

She couldn't… No. There's no way.

Or could it be?

That could explain her erratic behavior. I follow her gaze, finding her staring at the engagement ring. She traces the round edge of the diamond slowly. Dare I say *reverently*.

Oh fuck.

Attraction is one thing. Infatuation is a whole other deadly game I have no interest in playing anytime soon.

My molars smash together. "Are you doing all this because you're secretly in love with me?" The words leave my mouth in a rush. My heart beats hard against my rib cage, fighting for a way out.

Her having strong feelings besides indifference for me isn't something I considered. Hell, I never even *wanted* to think of it for a hundred reasons, but most of all because she's the best assistant I've ever had. Losing her isn't an option. Especially not when she is an essential part of my plan to take over my father's position.

The idea is shattered into a thousand pieces as Iris curls over and lets out the most obnoxious laugh. In the three years I've spent in her presence, I've never seen a crack in her sanity. Who knew all it would take is my ring on her finger to trigger a complete breakdown?

She reaches out for stability, grabbing onto the first thing within arm's length, which happens to be me. Every muscle in my body locks up, and heat travels up my arm like I'm being consumed by flames. I stay ramrod straight as her laugh turns into some asthmatic wheeze.

Rather than feel relieved, I'm somewhat thrown off by her reaction. My stomach sours at her disdain toward loving me.

You'll always be unlovable. My father's voice slithers through my head at the most inconvenient moments, sending a chill across my skin.

I pluck her fingers off my bicep one by one. "Are you experiencing a kind of crisis?"

"No, you fool. And I'm not in love with you." She laughs

again, making the most god-awful wheezing sound every time she inhales. "I'm doing this because we're friends."

"I will never be your friend." *And I never want to be.*

Her lips pull into a frown. "Liar. Friends help friends when they're sick."

"I have no idea what you're talking about."

"Remember the time I had the flu?"

I cross my arms. "I'm still not entirely convinced that was the case."

"So you *do* remember!"

"Only because I had to hire a cleanup crew to ensure every square inch of the place was scrubbed down."

"Fine. What about the time I helped you when you got drunk on a business trip?"

"I never wanted your assistance."

"You were tripping over your own feet and asking me to introduce you to my twin you didn't know about."

My tolerance for vodka is right up there with my tolerance toward people—nonexistent.

"Drunk you is so much nicer. You asked me to tuck you into bed and sing you a lullaby."

"Now I know you're lying. You're one of the worst singers I know." My lips threaten to curve into a smile, but I settle on a grimace instead.

She throws her hands in the air. "Okay, fine. I lied. But I wouldn't have said no if you asked! Because friends help other friends."

I'm tempted to pay any price for the word *friends* to be erased from dictionaries everywhere. I don't have them. I don't want them. And I don't want to be them, especially not hers.

Her raspy laugh turns into a fit of coughs. Before I can stop myself, I grab her tiny purse from the table and shove it into her hands. "Fix that god-awful sound."

She sifts through her bag to find her inhaler. "Concerned about my well-being?"

"Solely for a self-serving purpose."

"Of course. How could I forget." She smiles around the opening of the dispenser before breathing in the medication.

"Let's get a few things straight."

Her brows pull together, and her mouth opens, but I silence her. "Any kindness I showed to you in the past is strictly out of respect for you as my assistant. I don't waste my time on something as pointless as friendship, so if you believe there was anything platonic between us, that falls on you, not me."

Unlike most women who weep in my presence, Iris only shrugs from my harshness. "Silly me for believing you actually could possess any feelings besides disdain toward anyone else. I can assure you it won't happen again."

"I don't feel anything besides a burning desire to achieve my end goal."

She sighs. "There's more to life than destroying your father."

I ignore her as I check my watch, noting we're running out of time. "I need to set some ground rules now."

"Rules." Her eyes widen to their limits.

"Every look." The unsteady beat of my heart floods my ears. Her breath catches in her throat as I cup her cheek. My thumb strokes her soft skin, rubbing back and forth like I could brand my name with touch alone. "Every touch."

Her eyes shut. Every cell of my body burns to retract myself.

To put some distance between us because I shouldn't touch her like this. It blurs too many lines. But I'm useless as I breathe in her coconut scent, and my lungs protest the invasion. "Every single kiss…is nothing but a lie." My lips brush over the corner of her mouth, and my body feels as if it has been struck with jumper cables.

Her eyes snap open as I pull away, a storm clearly brewing in her head. I pocket my hands, appearing unfazed while her chest rises and falls with each ragged breath she releases.

"You—I—wha—" Her speech is as jumbled as her thoughts. I should feel flattered at my ability to incapacitate her, but it throws me off more than anything. My touch shouldn't cause that kind of reaction. Not if she was honest when she said she was only doing this because she considers me a *friend*.

I seek to gain control over the situation again. To throw up some semblance of a barrier around myself. "There is nothing I won't do to earn my inheritance. Remember that when you forget this is only a game to me."

Her mouth opens, but she's cut off by that shrill voice that will haunt me forever.

"All right, you two. The guests are getting antsy to meet the future Mr. and Mrs." The wedding planner interrupts us. She points her clipboard toward the entrance to the ballroom like a military commander.

"Are you ready?" Iris latches onto my hand. Her smile is a watered-down version of the one she offered Cal earlier.

I remain silent, knowing anything that comes out of my mouth will only be a lie.

CHAPTER THREE

Iris

E veryone, please put your hands together for the future
Mr. and Mrs. Kane."

My eyes widen at the DJ's announcement.

So this is how we're going to do it? Just like that?

You're the one who planned it that way. I mentally kick myself
for the obnoxious engagement party. If I had known I would be
the one at the center of everyone's attention, I would have gone
with a simple social media announcement.

My knees wobble as I scan the audience. I straighten my legs
together to stop myself from falling over. The number of designer
clothes all packed into one room is ungodly, and the fake smiles
on their faces have my skin itching.

Declan's eyes collide with mine. It's reflexive at this point, a
single look sharing a hundred words.

"Deep breath." He grabs my left hand, and the heat of his

palm seeps into my skin. It's unsettling how he can tell I'm anxious without me ever expressing it.

You've been working for him for three years. Of course he can tell when you're nervous.

"Iris and I are getting married at the end of the month."

The end of the month? That's in two weeks!

The music stops. Someone coughs. A waiter drops their tray.

We're surrounded by an array of reactions, each one more shocked than the next. I don't blame them. I thought Declan and I had a month to sort out our engagement, but now we only have two weeks.

The silence is deafening. My stomach threatens to dump its contents on the shiny marble floor, but somehow, I swallow back the acid crawling up my throat.

You got this.

"Surprise!" I beam, hoping to counteract Declan's less than exciting display. I rip my hand out of his and throw it up so everyone can see my engagement ring. A million colors bounce off the diamond, drawing everyone's attention toward the symbol of my impending doom.

"Welcome to the family, Iris." Rowan, Declan's youngest brother steps out from the crowd. While most people think he looks like Declan, with his brown hair and dark gaze, I find them distinctly different. Because where Rowan has some hints of humanity peeking through, Declan lacks the same compassion.

Cal breaks through the crowd and raises his drink in the air. "Family therapy is on Thursday nights. Don't be late!"

A few people laugh, and somehow the tension eases enough to make breathing bearable again.

"One hour and we're leaving," Declan huffs under his breath, low, so only I can hear him.

"I was going to suggest thirty minutes, but if you insist."

He doesn't smile, but his eyes light up as they land on me. His chuff of air is practically a belly laugh. We both know we will never make it out of here in half an hour. Not when Declan is the first Kane to get married since Seth over thirty years ago. This kind of announcement is right up there with the prince of England having a child, and everyone is going to want a few minutes with him.

Whatever response Declan has is snuffed out as his father, Seth Kane, parts the crowd like Moses. The intensity of his displeasure could make a lesser man crumble to his knees.

Mine lock into place. I've spent enough time around him to learn he feeds off people's weaknesses.

Declan feigns indifference except for the tiny tic in his jaw. He's a master of hiding his emotions, but every now and then, one appears. A small clench of his jaw. The quick flex of his hand. A narrowing of his eyes before returning to his cool gaze.

"Relax." I lean into him and rub my hand over his pounding heart.

You're not the only one who is nervous. Looks like Declan is more human than I thought.

"Son." Seth doesn't bother acknowledging my presence, as per usual. Since I serve no purpose for him, I cease to exist. Simple as that.

"Father." Declan tips his chin.

They both look eerily similar with their brown hair and empty, dark stares. But that's where their likeness ends. I'm sure

Seth was handsome at one point in his life, but his misuse of alcohol has aged him in a way that Botox can't fix.

"I figure some congratulations are in order." Seth smiles at me for the first time ever. The fakeness pouring off him makes me nauseous. "My son is lucky to have you in his life."

Yeah right. The man knows nothing about me. Even after three years, he still calls me Irene whenever he needs to get patched through to Declan's phone line.

"Save your display for the cameras." Declan wraps his arm around me. While his gesture comes off robotic, I appreciate his ability to try to make this look legitimate. *Try* being the key word. He's stiffer than my nana's cocktails, and those suckers can get anyone drunk from a single cup.

"Fine advice from someone putting on quite the show right now."

Declan's hand grips onto my waist with punishing force. "Just because you're bitter about love doesn't mean the rest of us feel the same way."

He scoffs. "You don't know the first thing about love."

"They say you can learn a lot from others' mistakes, so thanks for that."

There's a crack in Seth's wolfish smile. It's so brief, I almost miss it, but the pain etched into his eyes throws me off.

Don't fall for it. It's not real.

"You know nothing about what your mother and I went through, and I hope you never have to experience something like that during your marriage." Seth turns on his heel and exits the ballroom without paying mind to anyone around him.

So much for appearing like a united, happy family to the public.

Not many things can get under Seth's skin, but the mention of his wife always does it. It's hard not to feel bad for the man who lost his spouse to cancer. But then I remember how much of a dick he was to his sons, and all my pity is wiped away.

Someone new enters our vicinity and calls out Declan's name.

"Let's get this over with," Declan mutters under his breath.

"I never thought I'd see the day when Declan Kane got engaged." The man completely overlooks me as he slaps Declan on the shoulder and whispers into his ear.

Guest after guest comes up to us to offer their congratulations. Each one overlooks me while kissing up to Declan, which adds to the acid growing in the pit of my stomach. My only source of entertainment tonight is watching Declan fake his way through every encounter, but even that loses its novelty after an hour.

You might as well be invisible.

The DJ announces for everyone to clear the dance floor as a slow melody begins to stream from the speakers. I instantly know I'm in trouble.

Declan must pick up on it too because our eyes connect across the room. Usually I would laugh at the tiny tic in his jaw, but seeing as I'm a part of this torture, I can barely find it in me to smile. He walks across the room and grabs my hand.

"Do you know how to dance?" I ask low enough for only him to hear.

"Of course I know how to dance." Although Declan's face remains blank as a white canvas, the way his hand grasps onto mine in a choke hold reveals exactly how he feels about all this.

He hates the attention as much as you.

My whole body feels as if someone set me on fire. A hundred pairs of eyes pierce my carefully crafted exterior, and my anxiety only grows as Declan tugs me toward his body. One of his hands snakes around my back while the other holds on to my trembling hand with enough force to cut off my circulation.

The tips of his fingers skate across the top of my ass. Sparks shoot off my skin from the contact, and I suck in a breath.

"Stop doing that," I say through my forced smile.

"Doing what?"

"Touching me like *that*."

"You're my fiancée," he replies like that explains everything.

His hand retreats, and I release a sigh, only to startle when he yanks me forward so there isn't an inch of space left between us. Breathing is officially optional at this point.

"What kind of slow dancing is this?"

"The kind that has everyone filming us."

My entire face feels molten as I look around the room. "Oh God."

His face nuzzles the top of my head, and I swear I'm practically levitating at this point. For someone who has no interest in being in a relationship, he is doing a great job faking it. It has me questioning everything about us up until this point because where has this man been? And more importantly, why does he keep him hidden?

Why does it matter? This isn't even real.

The thought sobers me, and my stomach sinks with disappointment. This is nothing but an act for everyone else's benefit. I might have gotten caught up in it for a moment, but I need to remember why I agreed to this. This isn't a real relationship. No amount of forehead kisses or intimate touches will change that.

Stick to the program and you won't get hurt.

I repeat the motto over and over again while Declan moves us around to the song. By the end of our dance, I feel stronger than before and ready to separate fact from fiction.

Bring it on.

It takes me another thirty minutes of silently standing by Declan's side before I can finally make it to the bathroom.

I cup some of the cold water from the tap and press it against my cheeks. "You got this, Iris. Don't let them get to you."

Easier said than done. While no one spoke to me besides a quick greeting, they were quick to assess me like a lab rat. The number of women checking out what drink I was sipping and whether my bloated stomach was due to pregnancy or pasta was astounding. I've never been self-conscious about my figure, but the way they were analyzing me had my skin growing hot under my silk scarf.

They don't matter. I roll my shoulders back and touch up my lipstick before exiting the bathroom.

I take a step toward the ballroom before I'm taken off-balance by someone grabbing onto my elbow.

"How much is he paying you?" Declan's father turns me around so I can face him.

I tug my arm from his grasp. "I have no idea who or what you're talking about."

"I'm willing to pay you double whatever he offered to make this engagement cease to exist."

My eyes widen. "Excuse me?"

"You can't be this dense."

"Make sure to speak plainly since I struggle to keep up with high concepts."

"Obviously Declan must have been desperate if he chose you of all people."

The audacity of this man. "I'm a lucky woman. Marrying your son is like a Dreamland story brought to life."

He makes a noise in the back of his throat. "Don't flatter yourself. Declan is only marrying you for his inheritance."

"He's what?" I hitch my voice at the perfect time.

"You didn't know." His brows pull together.

I've got him right where I want him. "What are you talking about? He never mentioned anything about an inheritance." I will my bottom lip to tremble, and the results are miraculous.

"The only reason he put a ring on your finger is because he wants my position. Without you, he has no chance at becoming CEO."

I blink twice. "What?"

His bitter laugh makes me want to recoil. "You can't actually think he wants to marry you for love?"

"If not love, then what for?" My hand presses against my chest, clawing at the material of my dress as if I want to rip my heart out. If Cal were here, I imagine he would hand me a golden trophy for my performance. Maybe Declan would even give me a raise.

"What else? An inheritance. Without a wife and a child, he has no way of becoming CEO."

"Are you serious? What is wrong with you people?" My pitch rises like I might break out into tears at any moment.

He tucks his hands in his pockets. "Unfortunately."

"How did you find all this out?"

His brows pull together. "How I found out doesn't matter."

I withhold the bodily urge to roll my eyes. "Do you have proof? You can't believe I'm dumb enough to take your word over my fiancé's?"

His eyes narrow ever so slightly as if to tell me *yes*, he thought I was that dumb. At least his assumptions about me make this whole conversation that much more victorious.

"He and I had a discussion about all of this when he sought out my advice. I tried to warn him to not go through with this, but he didn't listen."

Boom. I catch him right where I want him. There is no way Declan would ever speak to his father about his inheritance, which means all of Seth Kane's assumptions are based solely on speculation. I almost laugh at my discovery, but I'm not ready to break character yet. I'm having all too much fun playing with Chicago's biggest asshole.

I dab at the corners of my eyes. "Excuse me. I'm just feeling so overwhelmed suddenly."

Mr. Kane shakes his head as if he is truly disgusted by Declan's life choices. He doesn't have two legs to stand on given his history, but he puts on a good show. One almost better than mine. "My son should know better than to play with an innocent woman's feelings. I thought I taught him better than that."

I don't even know where to start with that comment.

Don't let him get to you. He's only trying to scare you into calling off the marriage.

I steel my spine. "There's only one person playing with my

feelings, and I'm staring straight at him. Thanks for all the information though. I'm sure Declan will be interested in hearing all about your attempt to ruin our engagement."

His face morphs into something straight out of a child's nightmare. "You think you're clever?"

"Oh, I know I am."

"I was trying to save you from a loveless marriage, but it seems as if you two deserve each other."

"I sure hope so, seeing as we're getting married."

"He will never love you. He is incapable of it."

"If I wanted some fatherly advice from a deadbeat dad, I'd call my own father." My dig is meant for him and all the shit he put his children through.

His jaw clenches. "This isn't over."

I offer him a beaming smile as a few guests walk past. "I sure hope not. I thoroughly enjoy watching you make a fool of yourself."

I leave Declan's father behind, stewing in the shitstorm he created.

"Your father knows" is the first thing I say as Declan enters the car. Harrison, Declan's chauffeur, shuts the door before entering the private driver's cabin.

His head tilts. "What do you mean 'he knows'?"

"Let's just say he and I had a heart-to-heart after he cornered me near the bathroom."

His look of disgust mirrors mine. "Tell me exactly what he said."

I break down the entire conversation, from the assumptions his father made to the way he offered to pay me double to call off the engagement. Declan remains tight-lipped throughout the whole thing until I finish.

"He has no evidence."

I twist my hands on my lap. "Doesn't mean he won't stop until he finds some."

"Then we will give everyone the show they so desperately want."

"But aren't you worried he might do something irrational?"

His eyes light up with challenge. "I'd like to see him try. There is nothing I'd like more than to tear him down once and for all."

A shiver skates down my spine. "So what's our plan then?"

"*Our* plan?"

I flash my ring finger at him. "This automatically makes you a team player."

The muscles in his jaw clench. "You don't know what you're getting yourself into with this one."

"If Cal's stories are anything to go off of, I think I have a good idea."

"Whatever Cal told you is a watered-down version of the truth."

My brows tug together. "What do you mean?"

Declan's lips smash together, and the silence grows between us.

I roll my eyes. "Well, then. While I appreciate your concern, your father doesn't scare me, so your cautionary tales are a wasted effort."

"You must have a death wish. There's no explanation for your irrational behavior."

I laugh. "Obviously, or else I would have never agreed to marry you."

CHAPTER FOUR

Iris

"Y ou're what?!" Mom's dark eyes go wide. She clasps her hands together to prevent herself from running them through her spiral curls.

"She said she's engaged," Nana replies loudly before slurping on her coffee. Her graying Senegalese twists shift as she readjusts her position on the wicker chair across from me.

"How? Where? To *whom*? Last time I checked, you said you were single!" The brown skin around my mother's eyes wrinkles.

"It's complicated." *Well, that's one way to put it.*

Maybe I wasn't prepared after all for this kind of conversation the day after my engagement party from hell.

"Well, don't leave us waiting here. I don't know how long I'll have on this earth, and with the way you're stammering, you'll be hosting a funeral before a wedding," Nana adds with a serious face. She's probably the reason I could fake an engagement in front of a room full of strangers for as long as I did.

"There's not much to plan since I'm eloping."

"Excuse me?!" Mom's ragged breathing has my smile falling. "No, you are not. You're my one and only baby and I will not let you have some wedding in a back room of a courthouse."

"What's wrong with that? That's the way I got married." Nana actually sounds offended.

"Exactly my point, Mother," Mom says.

"The location was convenient. I took my newlywed ass to Bourbon Street, and your father and I made a night of it."

"I'm well aware of the day I was conceived. No need to rehash that story."

I'm not sure how these two live under the same roof without me mediating anymore. "Do you both want to hear my story or are you more interested in scarring me for life?"

"Story," they both reply.

I go off, telling them about how Declan and I realized our true feelings during a dangerously turbulent flight to Tokyo. Of how I was crying about dying in a plane crash and how Declan kissed me to make it stop. The hardest part of my lie was saying how I kept our relationship a secret for a year because I wasn't sure how things would turn out.

It's funny how that lie is the most believable of all given my track record with men.

"You're trying to tell me that you're engaged to Declan Kane? *Willingly?*" My mother wheezes.

"Is it so hard to believe?"

Mom stops her pacing to look over at me. "No. Not really, to be honest."

My jaw drops. "What?"

Grandma laughs. "Oh, come on. You skipped Christmas last year to spend time with him in Tokyo."

"I was *working.*"

Nana laughs. "*Right.* We all like to work, darling. Some more than others. And preferably more than once a day."

I choke on my coffee. "I thought libidos decrease with age."

"I've got memories to last me a lifetime."

Mom groans. "By all means, feel free to take them to your grave."

Nana howls with laughter.

Mom takes a seat beside me and tugs my left hand into hers. She assesses my ring from all angles. "Are you sure you're okay with this?"

I nod. "Of course."

You're going to hell for lying to your own mother.

At least Declan and you can remain together in the afterlife.

"This seems so…" Mom struggles.

"Out of the blue?"

"*Yes.*"

"It's…special. I really do love him." It takes all my willpower to say the words with a straight face.

She tilts her head. My mother has always gotten the truth out of me, one way or another. I bite down on my lip to stop myself from saying something stupid.

Like the truth?

Oh, shut up. I force my guilty conscience to take a back seat.

"He's your boss."

"I know."

"He's much older than you."

"Is that supposed to be a bad thing?" Nana asks. "Because I only see the positives."

I don't miss a beat. "We can't help who we fall in love with."

Mom sighs. "No. We can't."

A twinge of guilt tightens around my heart like a lasso. She is the poster child of falling in love with someone she shouldn't have, and I was the unexpected result.

She gives my hand a reassuring squeeze. "As long as you're happy, then I'm happy for you."

I nod my head because I'm afraid of what might come out of my mouth instead. If my mother knew the truth behind my engagement, I'm not sure she would be as supportive. She's a worrier. I have no doubt she would be concerned about me tying myself to a man who barely likes me and a baby he doesn't want. She would want more for me than to follow in her footsteps.

My anxious thoughts are intensified as Nana opens her mouth and asks, "So, when do we get to meet him?"

I open my front door to find Cal leaning against the frame.

"You've been avoiding me," he says.

"More like I've been dealing with the fallout of my actions." I give Cal some room to enter my apartment. He instantly makes the space feel ten times smaller. While my apartment isn't much, it's all mine after years of hard work and people doubting me.

He navigates through the minefield of potted plants before dropping onto my worn leather couch. "Why did you do it?"

I take a seat across from him and tuck my knees against my chest. "Because I'm stupid."

"How did you go from breaking up with every boyfriend you had before things got 'too real' to agreeing to marry *my brother*?"

"When you put it that way, it does sound a bit out of character."

He laughs. "What happened to swearing off men forever?"

"Well, forever does seem like a long time when you think about it…"

"Says the woman who thought an ex-boyfriend buying her a spare toothbrush was 'moving too fast.'"

"This is different." Sure, my relationship history isn't the prettiest. I'm always the one to bow out before things get real because fear makes me act first and have regrets later. My patterns aren't the healthiest, but they've prevented me from ever turning into my mother. Because while I love her, growing up witnessing her abusive marriage to my father turned me off from ever putting myself in that position. To love means to lose more than I'm willing to part with.

Cal yanks me out of my head. "Oh, it's different all right. You're getting married. And having a *baby*. As in you are going to make me an uncle."

My stomach rolls. "I know it sounds crazy—"

"That's because it *is* crazy."

I throw my hands up. "Then why did you encourage it?"

"Because I didn't think you would actually go through with it!"

My jaw drops open, but no words make it out.

He sighs. "My brother is the last kind of man you should marry."

A tightness in my chest grows. "Why?"

"Because he will hurt you. It's second nature for him, and it's only a matter of time before you get caught up in the crosswinds."

"It's sweet of you to worry, except our relationship is nothing but a contractual agreement. There won't be an opportunity for him to hurt me."

That's why I agreed to this whole idea in the first place. If I was worried about risking my heart, I would have never said yes. But with Declan's lack of interest in relationships and my fear of commitment, we are a perfect fit.

"*You* could fall in love with *him*."

I laugh until tears spring to my eyes. "Declan and I could be the last two people on Earth and I would still choose my vibrator over him."

Cal's lip curls with disgust. "TMI."

"It's true!"

"Then how do you plan on having a child together?"

"With the help of someone in a white coat." While I haven't reviewed the contract Declan developed, I'm familiar with his expectations for in vitro fertilization.

"Having a child together creates a connection between two people that can never be severed." A dark look passes over his face, and the ache in my chest intensifies.

I swallow the lump in my throat. "I know that."

"I hope you know what you're doing."

I don't. Not in the slightest. But instead of letting the

anxiety swallow me whole, I roll my shoulders back and face my reality.

"Marriage might be hard, but I'm willing to give it my all."

I can only hope that I don't look back at this moment and regret all my choices.

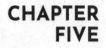

CHAPTER FIVE

I spent the weekend after our engagement party drafting the paperwork, ensuring there was no way for Iris to back out of our deal.

I throw the freshly printed contract against my wood desk. The pastel-pink-colored pages seem out of place against the other documents strewn on the surface.

Iris looks up at me. "What's this?"

"Our marriage contract."

"Why is it pink?"

One would think I asked for her to sacrifice her precious shoe collection based on her facial expression.

"Someone else left it loaded in the copy machine and I didn't know how to change it."

A laugh bubbles out of her. "I don't know what you would do without me."

"Your inflated sense of self-worth is concerning."

"You don't have to pretend to dislike me so much."

"Your first mistake is thinking I'm pretending."

She only grins at the barb. "They say there's a thin line between love and hate."

"Not thin enough," I grumble under my breath.

She laughs some more as she grabs the pink contract.

"Initial at the bottom of each page once you're done reading it." I pass her a pen.

"This contract is about as thick as the Bible." She stares at the stack of pages with a contorted expression.

I remain silent as I lean against my desk and cross my arms. "Is that a problem?"

Her brows draw together for the briefest moment before she recovers. "No, but I'll need to spend my lunch break reading over it."

"Take whatever time you need but that contract isn't leaving this office." There is no way I would risk someone catching a glimpse of our arrangement.

She traces the front page with one finger. "Fine. But I plan on reviewing each page three times just to make sure you're not up to anything suspicious, so don't get annoyed because I'm eating into your precious alone time." Her response flows past her lips without a breath of hesitation.

And she accuses you of lying.

"Spare me the play-by-play and get on with it. I have other things to do." I take a seat in my chair, and it groans under my weight.

"If you pack on any more muscle, that thing is going to split in half one day."

My muscles flex under my suit as I unbutton the front of my jacket. "I'm sure you'd like that."

"Only if I catch it on camera."

I ignore her and unlock my computer. It only takes a few email replies before Iris lets out a noise of protest.

"Is this some kind of sick joke?" Her voice cracks.

"What?"

Her eyes widen to a concerning degree. "You plan on giving me full custody of our child?"

"Is that a problem?"

"Yes! A big problem!"

"I suppose now is the time I mention that the contract is nonnegotiable."

Her chin lifts in defiance. "Then make it negotiable."

"No."

"Then I'll walk."

I don't look away from the computer screen as I reply, "I'd like to see you try."

She rises, throws the contract on my desk, and grabs her purse off the floor. "If you can't be a responsible father, then I am no longer interested in helping you."

"You can't be serious."

"Want to test that theory?"

Fuck. The rules of the game continue to shift without my consent, all because Iris doesn't play fair.

She never has.

"You're going to walk away from a hundred million dollars because of a custody agreement?"

"Money isn't the problem. Your decision is." She turns on her heel and gives me her back.

My control slips with each step she takes away from me. "I'll give you two hundred million."

She keeps walking toward the door, completely ignoring me. The sway of her hips is a silent taunt to grab her. To do *something* other than let her walk away from me and our agreement.

"Three hundred million." Her step falters but she doesn't stop until her hand grips the knob. I press the round button underneath my desk, and the door's locking mechanism clicks into place.

She grunts under her breath. "Open the damn door."

"Not until you sit your ass down and sign the contract."

"*No.*" She jangles the knob, but it's a wasted effort. While the safe-style locks are meant to keep intrusive people out, they're proving themselves quite convenient at keeping my assistant *in*.

I sit and wait for her to tire out. While Iris might have a strong will, mine is ironclad. And with so much on the line, her giving up is not an option, no matter how much she might hate me for it.

She rests her forehead against the door. "What about what I want?"

"You forfeited your rights the moment you became my fiancée."

"Careful, Declan. Your misogyny is showing."

The corner of my lip lifts. "You have no leverage here."

"Consider this my bargaining chip." She flips me off with her ring finger.

"*Cute,*" I reply dryly.

"Either you listen to my conditions, or I'll call the first reporter on my list and announce our split."

My eyes narrow. "Are you threatening me?"

"Me? *Never.*" She bats her lashes. "I prefer the term *motivating.*"

Her brand of crazy happens to draw mine out. "You're a pain in my ass."

"Nope. That's just the same old stick acting up again."

To think I pay her more than any assistant in this building for this kind of treatment.

Because you both know her worth.

I release a disinterested sigh. "Go ahead and list your conditions."

Her heels drag across the carpet before she drops back into her usual chair. The leather is discolored from all the years of her abuse. "I want shared custody—take it or leave it. You're going to be a parent for fifty percent of the time whether you think you want to or not."

"If this is your attempt at trying to use our child to get more out of me, it's not going to work."

Her nostrils flare. "I know this is a difficult concept to wrap your head around given the lengths people go to make you happy, but the world doesn't revolve around you."

"Next you're going to tell me that the Earth isn't flat."

Her nose twitches. "I hate when you try to be funny."

"Why?"

"Because I like you better without a personality." Her eyes are bright, always serving as a mirror straight into her heart.

Her stupid, bleeding heart.

"This is important to me. Like *really* important." Her voice drops so low, I need to lean forward to catch her next words. "I don't want any child to grow up thinking their parents don't love them."

My fist balls up against my thigh. *You had to go and tie yourself to someone with more daddy issues than you.*

Her gaze shifts away from me and off into the distance as if a memory took hold. "I know what it's like to not be wanted by a parent. That kind of feeling isn't one I would wish on my worst enemy, let alone my own child."

As if I could ever be a waste of space like him. I've heard enough about Iris's father from Cal to know I'm nothing like him, but the way she looks up at me threatens my perfectly laid plans. I was never supposed to be contending for father of the year. I've learned through first-hand experience that businessmen don't make good family men, no matter how much they might fake it for publicity reasons.

What's the worst thing that can happen if you agree? You hire a nanny to help raise your child?

My neck grows damp as I consider the consequences of giving in to Iris's demand. I know how this works. One contingency turns into two, and the next thing I know, she will only need to threaten me with leaving to get her way. I expect it from everyone but her, yet I'm not shocked at her ability to use my weakness against me.

Disappointing to say the least.

"One weekend every month." I speak up before I have the chance to stop myself.

She clears her throat. "That's a good start…"

"It's settled then—"

"But no."

"For fuck's sake."

Her eyes widen at my outburst.

Rein it in.

She carries on as if I didn't show a rare burst of emotion. "I don't want to be stuck with all the boring stuff like homework and chores."

"Then hire a housekeeper and a tutor. You can afford it."

She shakes her head. "That's not my point. We should switch off every other week so we can provide a more consistent and stable home. That way we can both be the fun parent."

"I can assure you that I will never be described as the 'fun parent.'"

She rolls her eyes. "Kids are simple. As long as you feed them, play with them, and memorize all their favorite cartoon characters by TV show, then you're instantly the coolest person in the room."

"That sounds like absolute hell."

"At least you'll feel right at home."

I return my gaze to my computer. "Fine. We will swap the child every other week."

"See, I knew you could compromise if given the chance."

"Blackmail works wonders."

She grins. "You would know. It's your go-to tactic."

If only you knew. While Iris is aware of my ability to obtain information about people, she isn't aware of the lengths I'll go to manipulate situations for my benefit. I always get what I want. Iris commanding this negotiation will serve me better in the long run, regardless of her current upper hand.

She lifts a finger. "One more thing."

I don't have a chance to object before she continues. "My mother wants a traditional church wedding."

"No."

"But—"

I cut her off. "We're eloping."

"No, we can't. At least not anymore."

"Let me guess, you'll back out of our arrangement if I don't go along with your plan." Predictable yet effective at getting me to yield.

"What? No. But I'd really appreciate it if you work with me on this. *Please.*" The way her bottom lip trembles makes me regret ever going along with her crazy idea to get engaged.

I hide my surprise. "So this is a request."

"A big one given your view on weddings, but I wouldn't ask you unless it was absolutely necessary."

"You owe me one."

Her eyes glint as she flaunts her ring in my face. "Consider us even."

A noise of disgust gets trapped in my throat. "Sign the contract and get out of here before I change my mind."

She slides the papers toward me. "Sure. Once you make the appropriate changes, including upping the initial payment to three hundred million dollars, then I'll go ahead and sign it."

You little... "You think you're clever."

Her smile only adds to the heat surging through my veins. "I never asked for an increased paycheck, but since you so generously offered..."

Dammit. I cover my small smile with the back of my fist. "Well played."

She winks. "Thank you, sir. You taught me everything I know."

And I regret it every single day.

CHAPTER SIX

Iris

I f I expected my work responsibilities to lessen because I need to plan an entire wedding in two weeks, I was wrong. Pretty much everything is business as usual which is exactly my problem. I'm drowning. In work. In expectations. And in a bunch of pointless questions like what color napkins I want and which style cursive is the best for place cards.

I can't even read cursive.

"I need you to revise this report for Yakura." Declan stops by my desk.

"Again?" I groan. "This is the third time in six months."

He drops a stack of pastel-orange papers on my desk.

"Are you still struggling with the printer? I could show you how it works if you have a second."

He doesn't bother entertaining my question. "I expect to receive your notes by the end of the day."

"*Today?*"

"Is that a problem?"

"Nope. I'll just fit it in between planning our wedding, picking out a dress, and going to a cake tasting tonight." I shoot him a tense smile.

"Perfect. Have it on my desk by nine." He walks past me and toward his private office door.

Have it on my desk by nine. I slam my fingers against the keyboard as I type out my password.

You can do this, Iris. There's a reason you've lasted this long on the job.

My phone lights up with a message from Tati confirming our first dance choreography session for tomorrow afternoon.

Freaking fantastic. Is there anything else the universe wants to throw my way?

"Iris?"

An irritable breath escapes me before I have a chance to catch it. "Yes?"

Our eyes connect. The nerve endings at the back of my neck tingle. I break contact first, ending the strange feeling before it has a chance to spread.

"Thank you for everything."

My eyes snap back to his.

Thank you for everything?! I've never heard Declan express any gratitude without an ounce of sarcasm.

I struggle to find the right words. My silence only adds to the strange tension building between us. Thankfully Declan ends it by entering his office and shutting the door.

I snap out of my stupor and text the only person who could help me process whatever is going on in Declan's mind.

Me: Your brother just told me thank you.

Cal: Rowan? What for?

Me: No. DECLAN!

Cal: What did you do wrong?

Me: Nothing.

Cal: So he actually said "thank you" and meant it?

Me: Yes!!

Cal: Did you hold him at gunpoint?

I laugh as I type out my reply.

Me: No.

Cal: Dagger to the throat?

Me: While the letter opener you bought me is tempting at times, no.

Cal: Shit.

Cal: Maybe you caught him in a good mood.

Me: Was there a global tragedy that gave him the warm fuzzies this morning?

Cal: According to the news, there's a shrimp shortage that has people throwing hands but that's all.

Declan hates shellfish so that can't be it. In fact, there's nothing I can think of that would explain his irrational behavior.

Nothing but the one idea that seems ridiculous enough to make my stomach flip.

He actually meant it.

"Your fairy godfather has arrived with reinforcements." Cal drops a takeout bag on my desk.

"Oh God. Yes." I rip the paper bag open and pull out a sub. "I love you."

"I know."

"Do you mind? I'm having a private conversation here." I point at my lunch.

Cal laughs as he takes a seat. "How are the revisions going?"

"Terrible. I'm not sure what Mr. Yakura wants from us. This is the hundredth time he's sent back our Dreamland Tokyo proposal—this time with one single comment."

Cal leans in. "What?"

"*Something's missing.*"

His brows rise. "Seriously? That's it?"

"Yes! But I can't figure out what's lacking."

"Did you talk to Rowan? He could look at your latest ideas."

I shake my head. "Declan and I met with him a month ago, but it didn't end well."

"Declan's still pissed at him about the whole Dreamland thing?"

Ever since Rowan decided to remain the director of the original Florida theme park, Declan has been icy toward him. It's obvious that Declan is offended that Rowan turned his back on family expectations for the woman he loves. But with Declan trying to develop his own Dreamland park in Tokyo, we might need to try again.

I sigh. "Yeah. I think the pressure from Mr. Yakura is getting to him. We've been working on this deal for months already without any payoff."

"You could find another sponsor willing to sell their land. Many people would kill for a cut of Dreamland's profits."

I shake my head. "Declan insisted it has to be this property. I'm pretty sure Yakura can sense how badly Declan wants it, so that's why he's being so difficult about everything. Maybe he wants a bigger payout."

"Either that or he likes being one of the few people who can make Declan sweat."

I laugh. "Possibly. Doesn't make the rejection any easier to handle though."

"Don't take it personally. Your ideas are great, so it's only a matter of time before he gives in."

"Easier said than done." My imposter syndrome always rears its ugly head whenever we receive another rejection email from Yakura.

As if Cal senses my shift in mood, he perks up. "Want me to help?"

"No, we don't." Declan's voice cuts in. He leans against his doorframe with his arms crossed and his jaw clenched.

Cal tips his chin in Declan's direction. "Hello, Brother. How are you this afternoon? Make anyone cry yet?"

"No, but it's only noon."

Cal turns his attention back to me. "I don't know why you agreed to marry him. He's insufferable."

I shrug. "His personality has grown on me."

"I swear you're suffering from some kind of workplace Stockholm syndrome. There's no other explanation."

Declan drags Cal out of the chair across from my desk. "Get lost. Some of us actually have work to do around here."

"Being the Kane family disappointment is a full-time job, thank you very much. Benefits are shit though."

My laugh makes Cal smile.

"I swear you were only put on this earth to make my life miserable." Declan jabs the elevator button.

Cal fake sniffles. "I finally found my life's purpose all thanks to you."

Declan all but shoves Cal into the elevator once the doors open.

"Bye, Iris! See you at the cake tasting tonight." Cal waves at me while flipping Declan off. Declan doesn't move away from the elevator bank until the doors slide shut.

He turns on his heels and glares at me. "What is he talking about?"

I turn my attention to my computer screen to escape his darkening gaze. "I asked Cal to go with me to taste wedding cakes."

"You didn't think to ask me?"

My brows raise. "Umm...no. You didn't seem interested when I mentioned it earlier."

"I didn't think you would invite my brother."

Oh my God. Is he jealous?

No. That's not right. It *can't* be right. In fact, it feels as wrong as the hint of excitement I get at the idea of Declan reacting that way about his brother.

What is going on with you?

I clear my throat. "He invited himself when I told him I was going alone after work."

Declan's chest heaves as he lets out a heavy breath. "Tell Cal he's not needed anymore."

I shake my head in denial. "No."

"What time is the cake tasting?" He ignores me as he pulls out his phone.

"Why?"

"I'm going. Send Harrison the address." He doesn't leave any room for disagreement as he walks back toward his office. His door clicks shut, leaving me grappling with questions I'll never get any answers to.

"Iris." Something nudges my shoulder.

"Go away. I'm sleeping." I throw my hand out to shove the noise away.

"We need to get going."

"*Ugh*. Now you're bothering me in my dreams too? Will I ever catch a break?"

A deep chuckle in my ear has me bolting upright. My foggy vision clears to find Declan standing beside my desk, wearing the smallest smile known to man.

"We're late." He reaches out and pulls a sticky note off my forehead.

"Late? What for?" I rasp.

"The cake tasting."

"Oh no!" I stand on wobbly legs. "What time is it?" I open my bottom drawer and pull out my purse. I'm quick to shove my heels on despite my swollen toes protesting.

"Ten."

"Ten?! We were supposed to be there at nine!"

He shrugs. "I called and told them we would be late."

I freeze. "*You* called?"

"It took me two seconds."

"Why not just wake me up?"

Silence.

"How long have I been asleep?"

"Two hours."

"Two hours!"

Oh no. The revisions. "Declan, I'm so sor—"

He holds up his hand. "Just send them tomorrow morning."

My mouth falls open. "I didn't mean to fall asleep—"

"Drop it."

"But—"

"You want me to get angry?" His voice sounds far more agitated now.

"Honestly? Yes."

"I'm not a total asshole. I know you have a lot going on," he snaps.

"Stop it."

"What?"

"Stop being so…understanding. It's weirding me out." An irritated Declan I can work with. A nice Declan who doesn't mind me falling asleep on the job and missing deadlines? That kind of unpredictability gives me crippling anxiety.

His jaw ticks. "Let's go. I don't have time for your shit."

Now that reply makes me smile. "Ah. There's the big, grumpy man I know and like."

His voice lowers. "One day that mouth is going to get you in trouble."

I'm not sure what's more dangerous—his unspoken promise

or the way something flutters to life in my stomach from the one sentence.

"I'm in heaven." I sigh before taking in another deep inhale. The different aromas surrounding us have my mouth watering in anticipation.

A bell chimes as Declan enters the dimly lit bakery behind me.

A back door swings open, basking us in bright light as a blond woman about my age comes out. "Welcome! I'm so happy you actually made it!"

"I'm sorry we're late." I wince.

"Oh, please! It's no problem at all. Why don't you have a seat over there and I'll get you some samples?" She gestures toward a small candlelit table for two before disappearing back into the kitchen.

"Isn't this cozy?" I try to break the awkward silence, only to be cut off by romantic music playing softly through hidden speakers.

Declan pulls out one of the chairs for me. The exchange between us is fluid, practiced hundreds of times. Something I realize I have grossly overlooked over the years.

"Thank you."

The wooden chair groans under the pressure of his grip. "For?"

"Always doing that. You know—with my chair." I stumble over the words.

He doesn't say anything as he takes the seat across from me.

…And now I remember why I stopped saying *thank you* in the first place when he does something nice.

"Here we go!" The baker brings out a platter covered in minicakes. "I'll leave you both to try everything out in private. If you need anything, feel free to give me a shout." She scurries away again.

My mouth waters as I scan the tray. "Do you have a preference for what kind of cake you want to try first?"

"Whatever you like is fine." He pulls out his phone and starts scrolling through emails.

"Seriously? Do you ever take the night off?"

"No."

"Then why bother coming in the first place?"

More silence. I'm starting to hate how he closes up whenever I ask anything that requires more than a basic one-sentence answer.

Instead of pulling back, I push harder. "You know what I think?"

"I'm sure you plan on telling me regardless of what I say."

I kick the leg of his chair. While it doesn't move a centimeter, it does draw his attention back to my face. "I think you didn't want Cal to come with me tonight because you are jealous."

He scoffs. "There's no reason for me to be jealous of my brother."

"Really? No reason at all?" I raise a brow in a silent taunt as I dangle my missed call notification in his face.

"Nope." He grabs a minicake off the tray and stabs it with a spoon.

"Great. Then let me FaceTime Cal and have him weigh in on this debate. If you wanted to be friends with us, all you needed to do was ask—"

He steals my phone straight from my hand. "I already told you I don't want to be your friend." His right eye twitches, giving his nerves away.

"Oh my God. You totally do!"

"Stop talking."

But I can't. Not with this precious gem of information at my disposal. "Cal might be opposed to welcoming you into our duo, but I'm sure he would be willing if—"

My eyes bulge as he shoves a spoon full of cake into my open mouth. "I finally found the perfect way to shut you up."

I glare at him as I taste the most delicious dessert I've ever had.

His gaze remains glued to my lips as he drags the clean spoon past them. "All I need to do is keep your mouth permanently occupied."

I graciously proceed to choke.

CHAPTER SEVEN

Declan

I might have jumped the gun when I announced Iris and I would be getting married in two weeks rather than a month. I wanted to make sure she didn't find the first opportunity to back out of our engagement. But now, I have to face the consequences of my actions.

"I expect you to be moved into my home by the end of the weekend." I walk past Iris's desk and toward the door of my private office.

She looks up from her computer screen. "What?"

"You can charge the moving company to my card."

"You want me to move in *this* weekend?"

"Yes."

"But tomorrow is Saturday."

I take a deep breath as I lean against the doorframe. "Your point being?"

She runs her hands down her face and groans. "There's no moving company that is going to be available at the last minute like that."

"They will be for a price."

"But I'd have to break my lease early."

"I'll cover the cost."

"Or I can still keep the place just in case—"

I cut her off. "How do you think it would look to the public if they found out you kept your place 'just in case'?"

Her bottom lip wobbles. "But I love my apartment."

"I'm sure there's a certain charm about living next to active crime scenes, but you'll get over it."

"I live in Hyde Park, not a war zone."

"*Lived* in Hyde Park. As in you are no longer a resident as of tomorrow."

Her eyes narrow. "So that's it? You snap your fingers and I'm supposed to do what you say like some obedient wife, no questions asked?"

"You've been practicing for years already, so there shouldn't be a steep learning curve."

My comment earns me a stress ball launched at my head and one wheezy laugh that can be heard all the way through my closed office door.

Think about your future. My right eye twitches as Iris hauls another potted plant into my house. At this rate, my home is going to be turned into a plant nursery. Spilled soil marks the hardwood floors to serve as a reminder of how my perfectly organized life is being turned on its head.

I walk around three other plants the size of small trees before reaching my front door. Iris speaks to one of the plants in a hushed voice, stroking one of its leaves while apologizing for uprooting its life. She's insane. There's no other way to describe someone who coos at plants like they're children.

At least she'll make a decent mother.

I mute my phone so the head of our auditing department doesn't hear me. "Is that all? You're letting all the heat out of the house." I point at the open front door. On cue, a gust of wind batters against me.

Iris rubs her hands together before blowing on them. "You know, all of this would go a lot faster if you helped me."

"I don't do manual labor."

"Then thank God we're not having a child the old-fashioned way or else I'd be stuck doing all the work."

Any rebuttal gets trapped in my throat, which only makes her laugh.

"You think you're funny?"

"I'd rather be that than a lazy lay." She runs out the door, obviously pleased with herself for stunning me into silence.

I almost forget about the person on the other line until they start speaking. Iris's chaotic presence is already wreaking havoc on my life, and I wonder how I'm going to survive three years of her living here. My whole space is tainted with her shit, from the colorful blankets strewn across my pristine couch to a few framed photos of two women I've yet to meet.

I try my hardest to focus on the conversation, but I'm only half paying attention to whatever is said. My ability to concentrate has been severely impaired ever since Iris's moving truck showed up in my driveway.

Twenty minutes later, Iris drops onto the floor in a heap. "All done!" Her two braids fan out around her, covered in snowflakes. A few spiral curls escaped the tight plaits during the moving process and stick to her face. Her baby-pink winter jacket looks out of place—a complete contrast to my black suit, shoes, and soul.

I scan the perimeter, noting fewer than ten boxes. "You have more plants than things."

She laughs up to the ceiling. "I'm a crazy plant lady. What else can I say?"

"Nothing is preferable."

Her body shakes from silent laughter as she stands. "How does it feel to have someone in your space?"

"Loud."

"Imagine how you'll feel once you have a child running around here and screaming."

"I'll invest in a bark collar."

She blinks. "Please tell me you're joking."

I pinch the bridge of my nose. "Fuck. Of course I'm not being serious."

She lets out a whoosh of air.

"Although a soundproof bedroom doesn't sound like a bad idea."

Her brows jump. "For them or you?"

"Them. Mine was remodeled years ago."

She instantly becomes interested in looking at anything but my face. What I'd pay to hear a second of her thoughts.

Millions. Maybe even *billions*.

"So…" She rocks back on her boots as she assesses her belongings. "How exactly do we go about this situation?"

Right. Stick to the plan.

I grunt as I grab a heavy box off the top of one pile. "What are you carrying in here?"

She peeks at the handwriting on the side of the box. "My high heels."

"They'll look great inside of the fireplace."

She jumps up and tries to swipe her precious cargo out of my hands. "You wouldn't dare."

Destroying her shoe collection would be worth her anger. They've been on my shit list ever since Iris found a loophole in her employment contract regarding workwear. Instead of following the office dress code of neutrals only, she tests my patience with neck-breaking heels and accessories the color of the rainbow.

At least she lives up to her name.

"You should know better than to underestimate me after all this time."

She puts a hand on her hip. "Declan Lancelot Kane. I swear if one single shoe goes missing, I will—"

"Don't call me that," I snap.

She grins. "Would you prefer for me to use the more formal Sir Lancelot?"

"What I prefer is your silence."

She rolls her eyes. "You're no fun."

"This isn't supposed to be fun." Yet it certainly doesn't feel like work.

Exactly why all this is a bad idea.

It's easy to fall into a comfortable rhythm with Iris. Almost *too* easy.

"I swear, you're going to die of a heart attack one day from all this pent-up angst. It's not good for your blood pressure."

I ignore her as I walk toward the staircase. "I'll show you to our room."

"*Our* room?" She trips over her boots.

"I can't have the housekeeper speaking out against the legitimacy of our agreement."

"Right. Of course." She nods with a doe-eyed expression so unlike her usual quick rebuttals.

She's nervous. I give her my back, concealing my small smile as I lead Iris up the grand staircase toward my bedroom. She helps me with the door, and it opens to reveal my favorite space in the whole house. The light blue walls and white furniture stand out against the dark wood floors.

"Wow. It's a lot brighter than I expected."

"Contrary to popular belief, coffins don't make for comfortable sleeping arrangements."

Her howl of a laugh makes my lips twitch in response.

I drop the box near the entrance to her empty closet. "You'll keep your clothes in here."

"But I'm not—we're not—you don't expect me to—" Her eyes dart around the space, not quite landing on anything.

My ability to be the only person who can throw her off-kilter fills me with a burning sense of satisfaction.

"Sleep in the same bed as me?" I finish for her.

Her throat bobs as she nods. "Right. That."

"No."

She gnaws on her bottom lip. "Thank God. That would have been awkward."

"Right." The back of my neck prickles. "In the house, we can act how we want. But in public, I expect you to appear affectionate toward me."

"Are you sure you can stand my touch for extended periods of time?"

"It'll push me to my limits, but I'll make do." I step into her walk-in closet and open the door on the other end.

She halts. "You built a hidden door to another room? In a closet?!"

"Yes."

"But why?"

"Because I was preparing for something like this." The words slip past my lips easily.

"Wait." She holds up her hand. "People prepare for fake marriages?"

"It's to be expected once you reach a certain tax bracket."

Her nose crinkles. "That's gross."

"No. It's life."

She stares at me with parted lips. I turn around and enter the second bedroom. The colors complement my master suite, but instead of blues, the walls are covered in a pale yellow.

"This is beautiful." One of her hands traces the lacy bedspread. The room is large, with its own sitting area, bathroom, and windows overlooking the expansive backyard.

"You can decorate it however you want. I only ask that you keep on top of cleaning since the housekeeper isn't permitted to enter."

She looks up at me. "You've really thought of everything, haven't you?"

"Everything except for you."

"Looks like Iris is making herself at home. I'm sure you love that." Cal assesses one of the plants she added to the corner of our living room. My home has slowly turned into a nursery, with new plants arriving every day to fill empty corners and blank walls.

I ignore him as I take a sip of my drink. "How is the progress on your part of Grandfather's will?"

He shrugs. "What's the rush? It's not like you're becoming CEO tomorrow."

"No, but if I have my way, I will be by the end of the year."

His brows rise. "Does Iris know about this accelerated timeline?"

"She knew the deal when she signed the contract."

His brows jump. "Doesn't mean she's ready to have a child right now."

"Good thing she will have an additional nine months to warm up to the idea then."

A noise gets trapped in the back of his throat. "And here we thought marrying her would humanize you a bit."

"Why would you think that?"

"Because you respect her."

"I do." Her ability to work by my side as a resource rather than a hindrance already puts her leaps and bounds ahead of anyone else. She is quick on her feet and willing to go above and beyond to ensure I'm successful, even if it means marrying me and having my child. I couldn't pay for that kind of loyalty. I tried, but after scaring off multiple fiancées, I'm well aware of how much I need Iris. If she thinks we will become the best of friends because of it, then so be it.

"And we know you are attracted to her."

That is new. "Who is this *we* you keep speaking of?"

"Rowan and I."

"Don't you have anything better to do than gossip about me behind my back? Like, oh I don't know, go find Alana and do whatever Grandpa asked you to do?" Cal avoiding his ex-girlfriend will only last so long, especially when Grandpa put a time limit on his inheritance clause. He needs to reach out to her by the end of the year if he plans on ever obtaining his part of the company shares. After all the grief he has given me about my part, the least I can do is remind him of his lack of initiative.

His jaw ticks. "It's not going to work."

"What?"

"You trying to get a rise out of me because you're feeling defensive about Iris."

"Why would I feel the need to be defensive?"

"You tell me, since you were the one who said you didn't care who you married, so long as they were… How did you phrase it again?" He taps his chin. "Oh right. 'Practical, fertile, and has a face considered proportionate enough to be deemed attractive.'"

My fingers gripping the glass tighten. "I know what I said."

"Didn't seem to age well, did it?"

My jaw clenches. "What's your point in bringing all this up?"

"I mention it as a warning."

I don't speak, instead choosing to take a long sip of my drink.

"You might be my brother, but Iris is my best friend. And while I want you to succeed and become CEO, I won't let you destroy her in your pursuit of whatever you think might make you happy."

I offer him a bored glance. "If Iris is concerned, she can speak to me herself. She doesn't need to send her guard dog after me."

"She's not concerned, but I am."

"If this is what friendship entails, I see why I'm better off without it."

His lips press into a thin line. "Don't break her heart."

A soft chuckle spills out of me. "That should be the least of your worries."

"Of course I worry. You're a coldhearted bastard who doesn't know the first thing about taking care of someone else."

"I helped raise you and you turned out decent enough."

His jaw locks. "We're your blood. You're forced to like us, whether you want to or not."

"Blood doesn't mean shit to me. You of all people should know that."

Taking care of my brothers had nothing to do with our shared DNA. I promised my mom before she died that I would be there for them, and I upheld my end of our deal regardless of the personal consequences.

He looks away with a sigh. "Just take care of her."

My heart pounds harder against my chest as I reassess this entire conversation. A chill makes its way down my spine. "Are you in love with her?" The question comes out far more agitated than I'd like.

His eyes brighten as he laughs. "No."

"For some reason, I'm finding that hard to believe." Based on the way he speaks of her, I would be stupid to think they were solely platonic.

"We kissed once."

Blood rushes to my ears, and I can feel the tips turning red. "You what?" The lethality in my voice draws Cal's eyes back to mine.

"It was a mistake."

"It sure as fuck better be." The glass tumbler beneath my hand shakes from how hard I grip the cylinder.

His lips curve at the corners. "I knew you were jealous."

"As if I could ever be jealous of someone like you."

He winks. "The way you look like you want to murder me says otherwise."

"Torture is my preferred method of revenge, just so you're aware."

He breaks out into a full-blown smile. "If it makes you feel better, the kiss was terrible."

How the fuck is that supposed to make me feel better? I can't get the image of them kissing out of my goddamn brain, no matter how much I try to wipe my mind of the last five minutes of this conversation.

Why does it bother you in the first place?

Because she told me they are just friends.

Right. You keep telling yourself that.

"You're really selling me on the idea of marrying her," I reply with a dry voice despite the anger burning within me.

His chest shakes from quiet laughter. "It had nothing to do with her. I was drunk, and she was lonely. The result was awkward to say the least."

"She was lonely?"

"Of course she is. Her being friends with me should have been your first clue."

"I wasn't aware she felt that way."

"What? Do you expect her to talk to you about it? Unlike the rest of the human population, you *like* being by yourself."

I bite down on my tongue to prevent myself from saying too much. Growing accustomed to something doesn't mean I *like* it. I just learned to prefer it over the alternative option, which includes letting people get too close. What's the point when they always leave anyway?

I take a sip of my drink to wash away the bitter taste of weakness from my mouth. "Kiss her again and I'll enjoy ripping your tongue from your throat."

He holds up his hands. "The only reason I told you about our kiss is so that you can stop thinking I want to make a move on her. I'm not interested in her like that. *Trust me.*"

"Because the kiss was terrible," I repeat back in a voice erased of any emotion.

"Because she was never meant to be mine in the first place."

Damn right she wasn't. Fake marriage or not, Iris is destined to be with one man and one man only.

Me.

CHAPTER EIGHT

Iris

"Oh, fuck off. I can't believe I woke up early for this shit!"

I bolt upright in my bed. It takes me a few seconds before my disoriented brain catches up to the fact that I'm sleeping in Declan's house.

My house.

I run a hand across the crumpled sheets, trying to smooth out the evidence of me tossing and turning all night. Sleeping in a new place is always weird, but sleeping in the same house as my boss? I still haven't fully processed the idea. Maybe because I'm still trying to come to grips with the way my whole life is being turned upside down.

"Another rain delay?! Since when are the stewards afraid of a little summer shower?" Declan's booming voice has me jumping out of bed.

I check the time on my phone and groan. "Six a.m.?" It

should be a capital offense to wake anyone up this early on their one day off.

Declan is all about rules, so maybe it's time I enforce a few of my own, starting with quiet hours between 11:00 and 7:00. I'm quick to take off my bonnet, fix my hair, and switch my pj shorts for leggings before rushing out my door.

Declan's house is a maze of long hallways and empty rooms without a purpose. The only reason I'm able to find him quickly is because I follow the sound of his voice into a man cave.

A massive television takes up the majority of one wall, set up to offer the perfect view from a deep couch I want to dive into. Declan paces the space between the TV playing some kind of sporting event and a coffee table covered in snacks.

"Is that a *mimosa*?" The horror in my voice can't be tamed.

All I can do is gape at him. I can't seem to find any other words to describe the scene in front of me besides *otherworldly*. Mimosas. Donuts. An unlit cigar next to a half-empty bottle of champagne.

What the hell is going on?

Declan halts his steps, and his eyes snap to mine. I bite down on my tongue to make sure I'm not dreaming. The pain is instant, making this moment incredibly real.

Whoever this man is, he must be a figment of my imagination. There's no other explanation for the backward ball cap, athletic pants, and T-shirt speckled in powdered sugar.

I've never seen Declan in anything but a suit. *Ever.* Whether we have a twenty-hour flight or a late night at the office, he wouldn't be caught dead in anything but Tom Ford. I'm tempted to cover my eyes because the man is practically naked with the amount of forearm he's showing off.

"What are you wearing?" His gaze hardens as his eyes scan my body, making me feel inappropriate in a sweater and leggings.

Me? What about *him*?

"You're one to talk. The donuts are supposed to go in your mouth, not on your shirt."

The side of his lips lifts as he brushes the crumbs off his chest. I can't help but focus on how his ridges of muscle shift from the movement. His arms flex, drawing my attention to the veins lining his forearms—

Enough! What has gotten into you?

"You missed a spot." I point to my mouth, showing him where some powder lingers.

Good job. Use your embarrassment to fuel his.

Except Declan doesn't get ruffled. He merely walks up to me, leaving only a few inches between our faces. "Be a good fiancée and help me out."

My lips press together. I could walk away and tell him to go find a mirror, but that would show him I'm ruffled by his presence in the first place.

Which would make things weird.

As if they aren't already.

I lift my hand up to his face and use my thumb to clean the corner of his mouth. His eyes track my every move. Three seconds feels like three minutes with the way he stares at me. Despite my best effort to avoid his lips, my thumb brushes across his plump bottom one. He sharply inhales, and our eyes connect.

His eyes narrow.

He's pissed.

Then he shouldn't have asked for your help!

He probably didn't expect you to grope him either.

Grope him?

Oh. I release Declan's arm from my steel grip like he burned me.

You needed to use him for balance while you stood on the tips of your toes. That's all.

"All good!" My voice comes out like a squeak.

Whatever expression Declan had a moment ago disappears, replaced by his pressed lips and empty gaze.

I distract myself by cleaning up the mess on the coffee table. "Why would you ever willingly wake up this early on a weekend?"

"It's Sunday."

"I don't care if you're Jesus himself, no one should be yelling at 6:00 a.m."

Something on the TV screen captures his attention. He makes a disgusted noise as he throws his hands in the air. "Fuck you, Cruz. No one cares about your shitty start position."

I struggle to reconcile this version of Declan with his usual cold, withdrawn self. "It's like I don't even recognize you right now."

"I can't tell if that's a good or bad thing."

I laugh. "It's a weird thing."

There's a tiny crack in Declan's icy facade as he unleashes the smallest smile. By the time I blink, it's gone.

It's as if putting on normal clothes and eating junk food reminded him that there's an actual human being inside that needs to be let out every now and then.

"What are you watching?" I take a seat on the couch and grab a donut.

"Formula 1."

"Don't they have a race in Indiana or something?"

His heavy sigh of disappointment can be heard a mile away. "You're right. This marriage will never work."

"Shut up."

"Mimosa?" he offers.

I do another slow blink before nodding my head. "Who knew a whiskey snob like yourself enjoys something so frilly?"

"My mom liked drinking them on race days." He says it so casually, like he didn't just talk about his mom for the first time ever.

He drinks mimosas because they remind him of his mom. In all the years I've known Declan, he has never willingly spoken about his mother. The fact that he lost her at such a young age is devastating. I couldn't imagine not having my mom around, scolding me or joking around with me about life. My eyes betray me, and I repeatedly blink until the wetness disappears.

I swallow back the lump in my throat. "Was she the reason you got into racing?"

"No. Grandpa is—or rather was—to blame for that one." His eyes dart away from me and back toward the TV.

"Let me guess, he roped your mother in with alcohol."

"Welcome to the dark side—we have liquor." He passes me a full glass.

My chest shakes from laughter. "So what exactly is happening that has you raging at the TV like a toddler?"

"I'm guessing you've never seen a race before."

"No, but that guy makes me want to." Whoever is being interviewed has my attention. Something about his brown eyes and red race suit has me *definitely* interested in learning all about Formula 1.

"He's married."

"You think he might be interested in polygamy? I've always been good at sharing."

"I'll be taking this back." Declan tries to swipe my mimosa from my hand, but I hold it tightly to my chest.

"No!"

"Stop lusting after Alatorre. It's disgusting."

"Mm-hmm." I pull out my phone and search *Alatorre Formula 1*. The results are promising.

Very promising.

"You're Googling him, aren't you?"

I don't need to look up to know Declan's amused. I'm certain if I catch him in the act, his smile will disappear before I have a chance to truly acknowledge it.

Santiago Alatorre's social media accounts are just as enticing as his Google search. "You know what? I think I have a sudden interest to learn everything there is to know about Formula 1."

Declan rolls his eyes in the most un-Declan-like fashion. "Of course you do."

I understood absolutely nothing about the race except the rush of adrenaline that hits me as Santiago Alatorre crosses the finish line first, much to Declan's disappointment.

"You're just mad my guy won."

"*Your guy* always wins. It's boring as shit watching him be so damn perfect all the time."

"Aw. Better luck next time. Maybe your guy will win if he can actually stay on the track past lap one." I pat his hand with mock sympathy.

"He better, if only to wipe that stupid smile off your face every time they mention Santi's name."

"My, my, Declan Kane. Are you jealous of my little crush?"

"*Little?* You drooled all over my pillow for two hours straight while cyberstalking him."

I drop said pillow and assess it for any evidence. "Liar."

"You disgust me."

I grin. "Same time next week?"

"No."

My smile drops. "Oh." *Way to insert yourself into his plans.*

I just thought—

What? That he might be interested in doing something together on his only day off?

Maybe…

Silly Iris. That's not how this relationship is going to work.

He clears his throat. "There's no race next weekend, but since you weren't the worst company ever, you can join me for the one after."

A spark of something comes to life in my chest that should warn me away from spending more time with Declan. I should take it as a sign to keep my personal life and business life separate, but I don't.

I nod my head and confirm our new tradition.

"I'm disappointed in you." Cal drops into the living room couch.

"What did I do now?" I look up at him from my spot next to the coffee table. Once Declan cleared the space of his contraband snacks, I decided to make myself comfortable and get to work.

Between planning a wedding and working overtime, I can't find enough hours in my day to get everything done.

At least not with our wedding coming up next Saturday.

Cal scans the stacks of papers spread out across the table before scowling. "So this is it? We're back to the same position you were in before you applied for a transfer?"

My heart stops in my chest as I bolt from the area rug and assess the perimeter. The hallways are empty and I don't hear Declan moving around upstairs, so he must be somewhere out of earshot.

After our morning bonding session, the last thing I want him to know about is my little secret.

The one I filed away in the *so not happening* drawer of my brain.

"He left."

"Left the house?" I plop onto the couch across from him.

"He was walking out the door as I was pulling in."

"Oh." I'm not sure why the idea of Declan leaving without telling me anything makes my chest feel all tight and uncomfortable. It's not like I expect him to tell me everything, but a courtesy *I'm going out* would be nice. Especially since I thought we shared a fun moment this morning.

"I'm guessing based on the state of this place that you're not leaving, are you?"

"No."

"Why not?"

"Because I failed."

He shakes his head. "Doesn't mean you can't try again somewhere else. Anywhere else really, so long as they appreciate you."

"Declan appreciates me."

"So long as you do everything he wants."

My eyes narrow. "That's not true and you know it." I don't do *everything* he wants. He might be the boss, but I have no problem standing up to him and sharing my ideas. I'd like to think that's part of the reason I've lasted longer than my predecessors.

"His appreciation is built on contingencies, just like everything else about him."

"What do you expect me to do? We're getting married."

Both our gazes shift toward my engagement ring.

"You could tell him about your ideas."

My head drops back against the couch as I laugh up to the ceiling.

Cal's brows pull together. "What?"

"There's a reason I never told him about my transfer request."

"I know that. But things will be different now. I can guarantee it."

"Because I'm marrying him?"

He nods, which makes me laugh harder.

He shoots me a serious look. "You have something Rowan doesn't have."

"If you say vagina, I'll make you regret not having one."

He winces. "Jesus. I was going to say a marriage contract."

I laugh. "As if that means anything."

"Maybe not yet but give it time. If there is anyone Declan has a soft spot for, it's you."

"You consider this having a soft spot?" I wave a hand over the entire table covered in papers.

"You could quit. Take your ideas and start somewhere fresh."

"I can't leave him right now. Our relationship complicates things."

Cal shakes his head. "No, it doesn't. Actually, if anything, it makes all the more sense for you to leave. It's a conflict of interest to work for your husband."

I sigh. "He needs me."

"He doesn't need anyone. He makes it pretty damn clear every time anyone says so." Cal speaks with a little more of an agitated tone than I'm used to.

"He doesn't even know how to operate a printer on his own."

"He doesn't *want* to know how."

"Why?"

"Because what else would you be useful for?" He grins.

I grab a pillow and launch it at Cal's stupid face.

"For your information, I just caught a mistake on Declan's quarterly report." I point at a misspelled word.

"Children with dyslexia around the world are rejoicing at your success story."

I flip him off with a smile. "I don't know why I ever admitted the truth to you."

"Because you needed a shoulder to cry on after Declan ripped you a new one after your unforgivable typo."

My hands covering my face muffle my groan. "You promised to never bring that up again." It was my first month as Declan's assistant and he nearly fired me for one mistake. I could have confessed the truth to him, but admitting my weakness seemed like a betrayal to myself. Like I couldn't handle the intense work environment because of a learning disorder I spent my whole life trying to fix. So rather than ask Declan for accommodations, I work harder to achieve his standards.

Like reviewing reports on a Sunday.

Why struggle with a work-life balance when I can make my entire life my job?

"You've come a long way since then. Declan even respects you enough to let you lead some of his presentations." Cal's sincere words warm my heart. "But that doesn't mean you should give up your dream because you think my brothers' are more important."

My smile falters. "It's not the right time."

"There's never a right time to make a hard choice."

"How much weed did you smoke this morning?"

"Not enough to be the voice of reason in this conversation."

I glare at him. "I'm not quitting right now, so drop it."

"Not quitting what?" Declan's voice cuts in.

My pulse point flutters at his low, authoritative tone. It takes all my strength to drag my eyes toward Declan's face.

"Yes, Iris, what exactly are you thinking of quitting?" Cal raises a brow, not bothering to hide his smug expression. "Fancy seeing you back so soon, Brother. Forget something?"

Declan doesn't respond, but the two of them share a look before my fiancé's eyes lock onto mine.

"Umm...You see..." I scan the room, trying to spark an idea. A silent commercial for an animal shelter plays on the screen.

"She didn't want to tell you the truth—" Cal starts up.

I jump from the floor and step in front of him. "I'm not quitting until we adopt a dog."

Oh God. Did you really just say that? You have never considered owning a dog in your entire life!

The expression on Declan's face tells me indeed I did.

"A dog," he repeats.

"Oh, yes. Iris *loves* dogs," Cal offers, failing to hide the amusement in his voice.

If looks could kill, Cal would be choking on his own tongue now.

"My mom never let me have a pet, so now might be the perfect chance for me to have one." I mean having a dog might not be the worst thing ever. It could keep me company in this big, empty house.

"You want a dog," Declan states with a strange expression on his face.

An idea of how to get out of this mess strikes me. "Yes. A big, fluffy dog that follows me around everywhere."

"No."

Sell yourself. Don't make him suspicious by agreeing too easily.

"But I'll do everything by myself. I know crate training can be annoying, but I doubt you'll hear them howling over the sound of your snores."

"There isn't a chance in hell I'm letting that happen."

"But think of all the serotonin we could be boosting if we had one."

"My decision is final." He turns on his heel and exits the living room.

"'My decision is final.' What a pretentious ass." Cal's eyes roll.

I drop onto the couch with relief. "You bastard. Why do you do that?"

"You could have told him the truth."

"*Never.*"

"Then I guess don't get angry when you come home one day to a cute puppy in need of a loving home."

I give his shoulder a shove. "Don't you dare! He would kill me if you did that."

"You have to admit that it would be a bit funny for you to adopt a dog when you hate them."

"I don't hate dogs! What kind of monster do you take me for?"

"The kind who actually enjoys working for my brother."

CHAPTER NINE

Iris

"Are you sure about this?" I peek over at Declan clutching onto the neck of the wine bottle with a steel grip.

"My answer hasn't changed since you last asked me three minutes ago." He looks up at my family's apartment building with narrowed eyes.

I've never been ashamed of the neighborhood I grew up in. It might be a far cry from my father's lavish lifestyle, but I was lucky to fall asleep knowing my mom and I were safe and happy without him. Growing up on a Chicago art teacher's salary taught me to be thankful for what I have because there are plenty of kids who have it worse.

"Well, we better get this over with." I lead Declan past the flickering lights of the entry hallway and toward the stairwell.

"No elevator?"

"Only if you want to wait for the fire department to rescue you."

Compared to my heavy panting, he doesn't seem the least bit winded after three flights of stairs.

"Charming place." He assesses the peeling wallpaper and stained carpet with a critical eye.

"Don't judge until you see the inside."

"I'm overcome with anticipation," he replies in a flat voice.

"Jerk." I don't know why his judgment bothers me as much as it does. It's not like he ever minces his words, but would it kill him to be polite every now and then?

Probably. He couldn't even spare five minutes before scaring poor Bethany off.

I grab the knocker and slam it against the door a bit harder than usual. We stand side by side, two stiff bodies unaccustomed to each other's proximity. I swipe my damp palms down the sides of my dress. My nerves seem out of place compared to Declan's cool indifference.

Nana swings the door open. She scans Declan from head to toe before turning her gaze toward me. "I now understand why you're willing to work weekends and holidays for this man. If my boss had looked half as good as him, I would have never quit."

I want to find the nearest sinkhole and jump inside of it. Declan's usually empty gaze is missing, replaced by bright eyes so unlike him, I blink to make sure I'm not seeing things.

He finds this…funny?

Only because he feeds off people's embarrassment.

"I'm Declan. Nice to meet you." He holds out his hand to shake.

"Nice to meet you too." Nana speaks to the expensive bottle of wine. Declan offers it to her, and she disappears into the kitchen.

I look away. My chest shakes from withheld laughter.

"I see where you get your sparkling personality from." The warmth from Declan's body presses into me as he wraps an arm around my waist. Whatever humor I felt toward our situation quickly evaporates, replaced by the uneven beat of my heart.

Guess we are just faking it until we make it here.

Together, we walk inside the apartment. His hand moves from my hip to the small of my back. The way my body burns from his touch makes the gesture seem inappropriate. Not once over the years has Declan made a move to touch me. If anything, it's almost as if he avoided every possible situation that would lead to us getting close enough to have skin-to-skin contact. Maybe that's why I feel thrown off from a simple graze of his palm.

…or maybe I'm suffering from side effects associated with the longest dry spell in Chicago. Only time will tell.

Mom pops her head out of the kitchen. "I'll be out in a few minutes! Make yourself at home, Declan." Mom's cooking makes the whole apartment smell divine.

Declan looks around my childhood apartment in the same way one would analyze a museum exhibit. I'm sure his skin itches to find the nearest exit. Compared to his home, ours bursts with colors, fabrics, and photographs.

"This is where you grew up?" He pauses at each framed drawing I made for my mom when I was a kid.

"Spent most of my life here."

He seems somewhat horrified by that fact as his eyes dart across a water stain.

I speak up. "Although the carpet was in better condition back then."

"One could only hope."

He picks up a framed photo of Mom, Nana, and me at my high school graduation. Tears stream down Mom's face despite her wide smile. We weren't sure if I would ever walk across that stage, but I overcame the challenges and persevered. It only took a repeated grade and hundreds of tutoring sessions to get there.

He assesses the photo in a way that makes me feel like I'm some kind of science experiment. My skin prickles with anticipation as I wait for him to say something. Anything really would suffice compared to his silence.

"I take it you three are close?"

"Depends on the day and if Nana took her meds that morning."

"I heard that!" Nana yells back.

Declan's eyes seem warmer than usual. "I can imagine growing up in a home like this came with its…*perks*."

The way he says it with a scrunched-up nose makes me laugh.

"I never thought I would see the day when my daughter fell in love." Mom cuts into our conversation.

Declan lets out a noise that can be classified as a laugh.

I glare at my mom. "You just love to embarrass me, don't you?"

"You think this is embarrassing? I haven't even offered to show Declan your baby album yet."

"You wouldn't."

Mom only laughs. She wipes her palms across her apron before offering her hand to Declan. "It's nice to meet you, Declan. I've heard so many good things about you."

I point at Mom. "Don't lie. It does scary things for his ego."

Declan's gaze swings between my mother and me before he grabs her hand. He gives it a firm shake. "The pleasure is all mine."

It's as if his grumbling in the car on our way here never happened. *Asshole.*

"Please come and sit. Can I get you a drink?"

We both sit on my mom's retro couch. The flowers are grossly outdated and the complete opposite of Declan's posh home, but it reminds me of Friday movie nights and Nana falling asleep to her Korean dramas.

"Water is fine."

Mom looks sheepish. "Of course! I'll get you a glass. I apologize for my mother's manners earlier. She doesn't leave the house often."

"Only because you stole my driver's license," Nana offers from the kitchen.

"Excuse them. They must be suffering from a carbon monoxide leak or something. They're not usually like this."

Nana pops her head out of the kitchen. "Why lie to him? We're *always* like this."

I give Declan a reassuring pat on his thigh. "Welcome to my family."

I pull my hand away, but Declan sweeps in and holds onto it. The warmth of his palm makes my hand *burn*.

Mom wags a finger at me. "Not yet. He needs to pass the Landry test before he's officially inducted."

Declan raises a brow.

"I hope you like spicy food." Nana makes an appearance, sipping on her wine.

The three of us break out into laughter at the puzzled expression on Declan's face.

Maybe tonight won't be so bad after all.

"Are you okay?" I refill Declan's water cup for the third time in twenty minutes. A damp layer of sweat covers his forehead, and his usually slicked-back hair sticks out in all different directions. He even removed his suit jacket.

The man *never* so much as removes his jacket, let alone rolls up his sleeves. I've tried my hardest to keep my eyes focused on everything above his neck, but the amount of vein porn happening has my eyes glued to his forearm like a homing beacon.

It should be illegal to hide arms like those beneath suits.

Hell, it should be illegal to have arms like those in the first place. They're distracting to the general population.

The scrape of Declan's fork against his plate fills the silence. He glares at the piece of spicy chicken like he wishes he could go back in time and wring the animal's neck himself.

"So, Declan, when did you realize you were in love with my daughter?"

Declan releases the knife in his hand, and it clatters to the floor.

"Aw. You're making him nervous." Nana sips her wine to hide her smile.

These two and their interrogation skills. I'm lucky Declan has understanding people down to a science because I never withstood my family's inquisitions growing up.

"I think part of me always knew she would be the one. It just took a while for the rest of my brain to catch up." His eyes don't meet mine.

I bite down on my tongue to keep myself from laughing. The way he can lie his way through anything is something to be admired. Although it does come off a bit jarring, it seems to do the trick. Mom's entire body melts from his statement.

"Why did you hold back for so long?" Nana asks, not looking as enamored as my mom.

"It wasn't the right time."

Elusive as always. It will help him keep up with his web of lies.

Mom smiles. "Well, I'm surprised she gave you a chance. I've been trying to set her up with one of the teachers at my school but she always declines—"

"Because I wasn't interested, obviously." I nod my head in Declan's direction.

He doesn't so much as look at me. We will need to practice more of these interactions later because his delivery could use some work.

"Iris leaves a trail of broken hearts wherever she goes." Nana raises her glass toward me like I unlocked some achievement.

"No, I don't." I grind my teeth together.

Nana feeds off my embarrassment. "Did you know her last boyfriend proposed to her and she rejected him?"

"Nana!"

"What? I just find it interesting that you are finally willing to settle down. What happened to swearing off men for the rest of your life?"

"Your ex proposed?" Declan's eyes are lighter than usual.

I never admitted to him why I broke up with my ex a year

ago. Declan probably thought we parted ways amicably, but the truth is Richard asked me to marry him.

I declined.

He *cried*.

I thought we were on the same page with everything. It was my fault for not noticing the signs soon enough. The key to his place. A spare toothbrush he left at my apartment. The way he seemed too enthusiastic to offer me an entire half of his dresser *and* closet—valuable space currency in Chicago.

After I broke his heart, I stopped dating. It wasn't fair to lead men on if I wasn't ready for commitment.

Yet you're getting married to your boss, the small voice in my head whispers.

This is different. There are no preconceived notions or expectations. I'm simply doing this to help Declan achieve his goal, and once he does, I can move onto mine.

That's what you've said for years.

"Poor man rented out a nice restaurant and everything for the occasion," Mom adds.

"Ring in a glass of champagne?" Declan asks.

Mom nods. "Oh, yes. Iris nearly choked on it."

I shoot her a withering glare.

"Rose petals on the table?"

"Yes!" Nana shouts. "Red. Her *favorite*."

I *hate* cut flowers because I find them a waste of a perfectly good plant.

"Sounds like everything you love." Declan's gaze captures mine. *What an asshole.* "I wonder what went wrong." His eyes shift back to my mom and grandma.

I despise the way he knows about everything I hate.

"I guess it wasn't good enough because Iris over here flat-out rejected him," Nana replies.

"How unfortunate." Declan's dry tone says everything words can't.

He enjoys every single second of this.

This is not how dinner was supposed to go. My family was supposed to make Declan feel uncomfortable, not *me*.

"Unfortunate indeed." Nana raises her glass in Declan's direction. "Imagine if she had said yes."

"With that kind of generic proposal, it's a shocker that she didn't." He takes a sip of his water.

He doesn't so much as flinch when I stomp on his loafer. I change warfare tactics by dragging my heel up his muscular calf, and I'm rewarded with his sharp inhale of breath. Heat pools in my belly, only to turn molten when Declan clutches onto my thigh.

Stop, his grip says.

Not until you drop the topic, my demure smile replies.

He gives my thigh one last squeeze before abandoning it altogether. The memory of his palm remains pressed into my skin, and I'm hit with a slight chill in his absence.

"Is now a good moment to tell you about the time Iris set a church on fire?" Mom grins.

"I can't wait to hear about this one." Declan doesn't even try to hide the amusement in his voice.

I swear with the way my mom and Nana are acting, it's as if they have never spoken to another human being before.

I sigh. *It's going to be a long night.*

"I approve." Mom grabs my coat out of the closet. Thankfully she kept that comment to herself until Declan went to use the bathroom before we left.

"You better after all the emotional trauma you put me through."

She chuckles. "I hope he can forgive me for the chicken. He was only supposed to eat a few bites, but the man cleared his entire plate. I'm pretty sure I used a whole bottle of cayenne pepper this time."

"I'm still bitter he beat your grandpa's record. That man lost half of his taste buds after I made the chicken for him."

"Do you think he knew it was a test?" I ask.

"He does now." Declan walks toward me with a dark gaze.

Mom presses her lips together to hide her smile.

"To be fair, it really *is* a family tradition." I hold up both my hands in submission.

"Any other traditions I should be aware of?"

"No," the three of us reply at the same time.

Declan's eyes narrow. "I'm having a hard time believing you three."

"At least nothing too dangerous," Nana offers.

His glare makes Nana and Mom break out into fits of laughter.

"We're leaving." He tugs my coat out of my mother's grasp. "Thank you for an interesting meal. I would say it was a pleasure, but I can't feel half of my tongue."

Nana cackles while Mom rocks back on her heels with a

smile. She practically swoons as Declan helps me into my jacket before tugging my hair out from underneath the collar.

I nearly topple over in disbelief as Declan takes his time fixing each button for me. The smell of his cologne permeates my lungs, embedding itself into my memory. A strange temptation to lean in and take another sniff consumes me.

He's doing such a good job convincing everyone around us that he cares, even I believe it for a second. He steps away, and the warmth of his body is replaced by a cold reality.

I *liked* him taking care of me.

The spices from the chicken must have destroyed part of my frontal lobe because there's no way I could like *that*.

Right?

"So, was it as bad as you thought it would be?" It takes me a whole five minutes since we entered his car to muster up the courage to break the silence.

"The food was awful."

I look out the window to avoid showing him my smile. "*And?*"

"And the company wasn't too terrible. Although I could have done without being ambushed near the bathroom."

I bite down on my cheek. "What did Nana say to you in private?" She all but bolted from the table once Declan got up to use the restroom.

"She threatened me."

"No." I muffle my laugh with my hand.

"In graphic detail."

"What did you say?"

"What exactly is an appropriate reply for being told my intestines would make a nice winter scarf?"

"She's been on a Mafia kick lately."

"That explains how she knew a lot about sulfuric acid and the different ways to dispose of a body."

"I did try to warn you about my family. They're a bit…"

"Overbearing?"

I nod. "They worry about me."

"They have a good reason to."

"Why?"

"You got engaged out of the blue to someone who isn't exactly known to be the nicest man in Chicago."

"Now, now. At least you're not the worst."

"I'm sure that really helps them sleep at night."

The self-deprecating way he speaks of himself makes me sad.

"Does the great Declan Kane care about my family's opinion of him?"

His eyes roll. "No. Don't be ridiculous."

"Maybe just a little bit?" I hold my two fingers up to his face, leaving a small gap of space.

He swats my hand away. "I stopped caring about people's opinions of me a long time ago."

I want to ask him why. Heck, I want to ask him a hundred questions after tonight, starting with what made him stop caring about what other people think of him in the first place. But asking personal questions seems like I'm giving him unspoken permission to do the same to me.

I hold my tongue and stay silent for the rest of the ride.

Being curious about Declan would only complicate things, so I'm better off keeping some distance. Living with each other is one thing, but sharing intimate details about one another is a completely different animal. Not that he wants me to know him on a personal level anyway. He has made his stance pretty clear on the matter, and I would be stupid to think this marriage was anything but a convenience for him.

CHAPTER TEN

Declan

I f my grandfather's sole reason for making me get married was to drive me toward the brink of insanity, he achieved his goal. I've officially reached my breaking point, and it only took Iris planning a rehearsal dinner to get me there. Well, her sitting beside me in a body-hugging white gown and the crowd of people waiting inside Chicago's best steakhouse.

"It's not too late for me to tell Harrison to turn the car around." I make one last-ditch effort to cancel tonight's dinner. If it were up to me, we would have gotten married in a courthouse and bypassed all of these *requirements*.

She picks at her pristine manicure. "It's not like I want to go in there either."

"Is this your attempt at making me feel better?" A thoughtful yet pointless effort.

"They say misery loves company." She laughs, and the sound draws me toward her like a siren's call.

My eyes drop to her mouth as I soak in her smile. Her good mood is dashed away with the parting of her lips, and I look up to see what changed. Our eyes connect, making me feel like I was struck in the chest with a lightning bolt. It must zap all my common sense too because nothing else explains me reaching out and holding onto her hand.

She sucks in a breath. "You ready?"

Whatever burst of energy I felt from our eye contact dies at her confusion. I release her hand, and she clasps hers together on her lap.

"As ready as one can be for an event like this."

"Just remember, in two days you will never have to think about throwing a party ever again."

"A lot can happen in forty-eight hours."

"Getting cold feet?" Her eyes light up.

"Frostbite set in about three days ago, but I'll crawl down the aisle if I need to."

She laughs again, and I'm hit with another surge of warmth that scares me enough to open the car door and face the lesser of two evils. Anything seems better than analyzing the weird sense of attraction I feel toward the one woman I can't ever have.

Future wife or not, Iris is the last person I will ever make a move on. She is an integral part of my plan to become CEO, and I refuse to lose my most valuable player for something as fleeting as attraction. Nothing good could ever come out of a temporary fling, so I'm better off being on my own.

Iris and I make our way through rounds of useless conversation. Unlike our engagement party, we are driven apart by our families. There is a reason I always dragged Iris to any event I was forced to attend. Where she thrives in answering people's questions and pretending to be interested, I struggle. Everything about tonight is pure torture. With the endless amount of small talk and my inability to get drunk at my own rehearsal dinner, I can't get out of here soon enough.

To make matters worse, my father showed up to play his part of the doting parent. His fake smile is on full display as he works the crowd with the charm of a cult leader. It's disgusting how many people eat out of the palm of his hand, nearly salivating at the prospect of receiving five minutes of his attention.

I find the darkest corner in the restaurant, observing my father from afar. I'm not sure how much time passes. The dull throb at the back of my head seems to have alleviated during my reprieve, and for that I am grateful.

I take a step out into the light before I'm stopped by Iris pressing her palm against my cheek. "I've been looking for you everywhere. I knew I should have checked the dark and unseemly places first." Her hand lingers, warming my stubbled chin as I look down at her.

"To think you know me better than anyone else."

She laughs, and the sound seems to wash away my last bit of annoyance from tonight.

"How are you holding up?" She removes her hand, but I latch onto it and press it against my chest.

A crease appears between her eyebrows.

"People are watching," I speak low.

She looks around, finding multiple people's gazes homed in on us.

Her lips curve into a small smile. "No wonder you hate going out. This is exhausting."

"Now she finally gets it," I deadpan.

She cracks another smile in my direction. "I never understood why you hated talking to people but now I totally do. Who would want to with a family like yours?"

"If hell were a theme park, they would have lifetime passes." My comment earns me a wheezy laugh.

"How did you survive growing up with so many social climbers?"

"Easy. If you stop being social, there is no ladder for them to climb in the first place."

Her eyes light up. "Well, I better get back to being the cheery one. With you hiding, one of us needs to be present." She tries to free herself from my grasp, but I keep a strong grip.

"Don't go."

What are you doing?

"Why not?" Her brow arches.

A reasonable question if any. Having her by my side feels like the only natural thing about tonight, fake marriage or not. She has a way of making anything tolerable.

"You make tonight somewhat more bearable."

What happened to not needing anyone but yourself?

I'll go back to feeling that way tomorrow. Tonight I accept I am weaker than usual, with hours of small talk pushing me past my limits.

She looks down at our joined hands with a tight expression. "What a glowing compliment."

My thumb brushes the inside of her wrist. "Do you want to hear some more?"

"No."

A small smile forms before I have a chance to kill it. "Why not?"

"I prefer you grumpy and predictable."

"You can't mean that."

Are you flirting with her?

Fuck. Exactly how much alcohol did I drink tonight? I check my one and only glass, finding it still halfway full.

Must be a temporary lapse in judgment given the stress of the situation.

Yes. A slip of the tongue that has nothing to do with Iris and everything to do with my limited patience for people trying to kiss my ass all night long.

"Careful, Mr. Kane. Keep being nice to me and I might start getting used to it." She grins, and a wave of warmth spreads through my chest that has nothing to do with my whiskey.

You hate when people smile.

Except making Iris grin feels like a personal victory.

You're not supposed to be lusting after your paid-per-vow wife's smiles.

I snap out of whatever feelings possessed me. "You're staying with me for the rest of the night." I leave no room for questions.

She seems to ramp up the wattage on her smile. "You're kind of cute when you get all flustered."

"I'm not flustered."

She wraps both of her arms around my waist, drawing me toward her. Our bodies fit together like two interlocking puzzle pieces. Returning her embrace is reflexive, while the feeling happening inside of me is not. There is only one word I can think to describe the contentedness wrapping itself around my heart like a suffocating vine.

Hygge.[*]

"What did you just say?" Iris looks up at me with a contorted expression.

Shit. You said that out loud?

I have two options here—admit the truth or deny it ever happened in the first place.

Deny.

"Nothing."

Except it doesn't feel like nothing. My heart pounds against my chest, and I only hope Iris remains unaware of the betraying organ. A sick feeling overtakes me as I consider my slipup. I stopped using words like that ages ago, after my mom passed. There wasn't a point anymore when the only person who understood me that way died, leaving me behind with an empty heart and a brain filled with useless words.

Yet here you are, using them to describe her.

Fuck.

I run my fingers through my hair, giving my hands something to do besides touching Iris. Nothing good seems to come from that.

---

[*] **Hygge:** Noun, Danish: a cozy quality that makes a person feel content and comfortable.

Iris's arms tighten around me, beckoning me to look down at her. "Is everything okay?"

"Of course." I fight the urge to disentangle myself from her hug. She is growing far too comfortable with them for my taste.

"Great because your father is headed this way and the smile on his face is downright malicious." Iris steps out of our embrace, only for me to tuck her against my side. My hand plants itself against her hip like it belongs there.

My father steps into our vicinity. "Just the couple I was looking for."

Iris mutters something under her breath before plastering on her fakest smile. "Mr. Kane. How nice of you to make it tonight."

I huff at her polite display.

His right eye narrows despite the easygoing smile on his face. "Please call me Seth. We are practically family now."

"You wouldn't know the meaning of the word," I quip.

"Paying for a family doesn't make you an expert on the matter by any means."

"Neither does being an absentee alcoholic who hates his kids."

Iris sucks in a breath.

My father's face turns molten red, and the flush spreads from his cheeks to his neck. "You dare to talk to me that way?"

"Seeing as I just did, yes."

His grin is forced, never reaching his emotionless eyes. "I'm making an effort to be polite and supportive."

"For the public."

"Appearances are everything."

My teeth grind together. I learned that lesson far too many times over the years after my mom died. Because while our house was nothing but chaos in private, to the rest of the world we were the ultimate American family. My private school teachers never questioned the random black eyes or bruises on my skin. They were easily bought like everyone else, feeding into the vicious cycle of my childhood. The one I did everything in my power to protect Cal and Rowan from, even if it meant taking my father on by myself.

"Thank you for coming. I wish we could stay longer and chat, but I want to introduce Declan to my cousin before she leaves."

Iris tugs on the sleeve of my suit, and I follow her without bothering to look back at my father. I'm too lost in my thoughts to notice much else.

It's not until Iris pushes me into a cramped room and flips the light switch that I notice the noise around us is turned down to a manageable level.

I check out our surroundings. "A supply closet?"

She laughs. "I'm sorry. It was the first unlocked door I could find."

"Why are we hiding?"

"Because you looked about two seconds away from blowing up on your father. I thought you might like the idea of getting away from everyone for a few minutes."

Iris always has a superpower of knowing what I need exactly when I need it. She truly is invaluable.

"Thank you." I lean against a shelf of cleaning supplies.

After hours of talking to people, I feel like I can finally breathe again. My temples still throb from overstimulation, but the ache has lessened drastically.

Iris jumps onto a washing machine and uses the lid as a seat. "Tonight has been…"

"Excruciating," I finish for her.

She nods. "If this is the dinner party, I can only imagine how the wedding will go."

"You're the one who wanted a big wedding."

"Only because my mother would kill me for excluding her."

"Then let's elope and invite her along. She can be our sole witness." The statement bursts out of me faster than I can kill it.

Her laugh dies when she catches the look on my face. "You're serious."

I nod, liking the idea more by the second. "We could spin it as a whirlwind idea. I could have us in Vegas in four hours or less."

"We did not go through all this pain to give up right before the finish line."

"It's not giving up. It's changing routes."

She presses her hand against her mouth to muffle her laughter. Her obvious denial of my idea makes me bolder, and I refuse to take her no as a final answer.

I encroach on her space, trapping her against the washing machine. Her eyes get a wild look in them as I step between her legs. The material of her long dress stretches enough to accommodate my size.

I grab her chin, forcing her to look up at me. "Think about it. You, me, and a drive-thru chapel. No press. No frills. No expectations."

"The pinnacle of romance," she replies with a dry voice.

My thumb clutching onto her chin presses a bit harder. "I'll throw in another hundred million to make it happen."

She breaks free of my hold as her head drops back. The laugh she unleashes does something abnormal to my heart rate, the steady beat turning erratic.

"No amount of money can change my mind seeing as my mother would kill me before I have a chance to enjoy it."

My disappointed sigh makes her smile.

She gives my chest a reassuring pat. "If it's any consolation, I hate the idea just as much as you." Her palm burns a hole straight through my chest, directly above my heart.

Her lashes flutter as she blinks up at me, and my attention is split between staring into her eyes and looking down at her lips. Being this close to her does something catastrophic to my self-restraint. I'm not sure whether it's the lack of human contact I've had or desiring something forbidden, but I keep being drawn to her.

"Did you leave the light on in the supply closet again? What did I tell you about wasting electricity?" The knob jangles, and Iris's eyes widen as she looks at me.

"Tell me you locked—"

Iris's hands sink into my hair as she shoves my head to the side. Her lips press against my neck, setting the blood in my veins on fire. She locks her legs around my waist and pulls me closer. Blood rushes from my head to my dick as Iris leaves a trail of kisses down my neck.

Keys rattle against one another as the doorknob twists. Light pours into the room as a couple of servers stare at us with open mouths.

One of them steps up. "I'm sorry—"

"Leave," I lash out.

Iris chuckles against my skin, and I feel the sound straight to my cock. Her laugh is a powerful aphrodisiac I don't have any business relishing in.

The door slams. Iris shoves me away before slipping off the washer. "Well, wasn't that fun?"

My slacks seem to tighten as I consider just how much *fun* that was.

A deep brown hand lands on my arm. I look over to find Iris's mom holding onto me with a shy smile.

"Hi."

"Are you looking for Iris?" I scan the room for her.

"I actually came to talk to you."

Do I have the option to politely decline?

Her smile falters. "I won't take up more than a few minutes of your time. I know you're a busy man and everything."

I see my reputation precedes me.

"Let's go outside." I motion toward the empty balcony and let her lead the way.

I take a deep breath as the doors shut behind us and silence settles in.

"Iris told me you hate these kinds of things." She wrings her hands in front of her.

"Loathe is more like it."

She laughs, and it reminds me of Iris's wheezy one. Like oxygen can't make it to her lungs fast enough.

"How are you holding up with all this?"

"As to be expected for an introvert who hates social gatherings, small talk, and people in general."

"Then why do it in the first place?"

"Because it's expected."

Her braids shift as she tilts her head. "It must be exhausting putting on an image for the public."

"You have no idea."

"I might not know what it is like to grow up in the public eye like you, but I understand having to put on a face for everyone around you."

"You do?" I find that hard to believe.

Her eyes dart toward the city skyline. "I'm sure Iris told you about my ex-husband and his very particular expectations."

I open my mouth but think better of it. In reality, I don't know much about Iris's father besides the fact that he is a deadbeat.

She continues, saving me from having to come up with something to say. "When she told me she was getting married to you, I was excited that she finally met someone who could treat her right. Someone who could prove that love can heal the soul as much as it can destroy it. I've heard the way she talks about you."

Now I'm very curious about this conversation.

"How so?"

She laughs. "It's obvious she admires you, and not just in a romantic way. Your work ethic. The love you have for your broth-ers. The way you gave her a chance to show her worth. For the last one, I can't thank you enough. Truly."

I'm speechless as I stare at her with my lips parted. I don't even know how to process her final comment, seeing as most people are horrified by the way my assistant works more hours than half the executives.

"But of course, like any mother, I worry about her and what

the future holds for her. I don't want her to go through the kind of pain I experienced. I want a better life for her. One that I think you can provide, so long as you promise to always honor her and the vows you make this weekend."

"I can assure you that I will always have Iris's best interests at heart." Even if they jeopardize mine.

CHAPTER ELEVEN

Iris

Y ou look beautiful." My mom tries to blink away the tears brimming at the corners of her dark eyes. She adjusts my veil with a shaky hand, being mindful of my perfectly curled hair. With my vintage-inspired lace gown worth more than a year's rent and shoes that glitter like the diamond on my finger, I feel like a true Dreamland princess.

The bouquet of colorful flowers shakes against my chest.

This is it.

If I had my way, I would have eloped somewhere with only my closest family and friends by my side. But this wedding isn't about me. Hell, it isn't about Declan either, given his preference for a simple ceremony too. Granting my mother's wish for a religious ceremony was the best choice for multiple reasons, but mainly because we need to show the hundreds of guests, including Brady Kane's lawyer, that we're a united front. That we're in *love*.

It takes all the power in me not to scrunch my nose at that idea.

Mom sniffles. "I can't believe my baby is getting married."

"Please don't cry." I couldn't bear it if she did. I'm pretty sure I would crack under the pressure and confess this whole plan if she sheds a single tear.

"It's hard not to. I always dreamed of you finding someone who made you happy."

Something in my chest twinges. "You have?"

She nods. "I was worried I made a bad impression on you when you were a child. That I let my bitterness toward your father get in the way of showing you how to move on despite the hurt."

"Mom—" I want to tell her no, but I can't find it in me to tell any more lies. The truth is, my mother's experience with my father weighed heavily on me while growing up. It changed something in me, and a fake marriage isn't going to fix that. If anything, it only proves what I already know. Love is something that only exists in fairy tales and Dreamland movies. The reality is much bleaker.

As if she reads my thoughts, my mom continues, "Not all men are like your father. It took me a long time to realize that, but I'm glad you learned far quicker than me."

"Right." My voice cracks. I'm about two seconds from falling apart.

She cups my cheek with her hand. "I'm proud of you for finally opening up to someone. For risking your heart knowing all the possibilities—good and bad. You've come so far."

My throat tightens uncomfortably, and I look away to avoid her gaze, afraid she can read the truth in my eyes. There's no way in hell I would ever open myself up to loving Declan. While I consider him a friend, he wants nothing to do with me in that way.

Nana steps out of the bathroom. "Are we done with all the sad stuff now? This is a wedding, not a funeral."

Mom and I burst into laughter, and the moment is gone like it never happened in the first place. But the tight feeling in my chest still lingers long after the topic changes. Conversations about my father always stir up old demons, but today's festivities might as well be a welcoming party for them.

Most girls dream of the day they walk down the aisle. I, on the other hand, always knew I would dread the reminder of growing up without a father. My mother offered to stand in his place, but I wanted to walk alone. I promised myself ages ago that I would just to prove a point to myself that I don't need him. I didn't back then and I sure as hell don't now.

The music plays on cue. Everyone stands and turns their attention toward me. My entire body trembles from all the unwanted eyes assessing me, and I release a shaky breath.

You got this.

I smile beneath my veil, hiding the way my eyes prick from unshed tears. My eyes lift toward my destination. I nearly stumble as I find Declan's eyes locked on me, but I catch myself. Whatever burns in his gaze sends goose bumps across my skin. I'm not sure I have ever seen Declan look at me like this, but it does something crazy to my heart rate.

I march down the aisle like a dedicated soldier reporting for duty. Declan doesn't take his eyes off me, probably to make sure I don't make a run for the closest emergency exit. Something about his gaze today has my stomach feeling light and bubbly.

…or it's because of the last-minute champagne Nana offered me. Because there is no way in hell that my boss gives me butterflies. The idea alone makes me want to cackle up to the roof like a madwoman.

Yeah, definitely the champagne. I've always been a bit of a lightweight.

Declan, like me, stands alone. I'm not sure why he didn't choose one of his brothers to be his best man, but I'm somewhat relieved, given my lack of options for a maid of honor. I don't have many friends. Not because I don't want to, but because I'm too busy working all the time. Cal offered to step in and wear a pink suit for me, but I declined, saying pink wasn't his color. We both know it's a lie. But it seemed better than facing the reality that he is my only friend to speak of.

I stop at the front of the aisle and turn toward my fiancé with a hesitant smile. His jaw locks as his eyes roam over me, making my skin flush under his scrutiny.

His hand traces the edge of my veil. I catch the slight tremble he tries to hide by fisting the fabric. Declan has always hated big crowds. Something about them makes him nervous, not that he would ever confess such a thing to a single soul.

But I know, and the secret makes me smile.

"Relax. Just pretend they're not here," I whisper low enough for only his ears.

He doesn't reply as he lifts the veil up and over my head. Whatever he sees has him blinking twice.

"Is everything okay?" I whisper.

His head does the smallest shake. "You look nice."

Whatever buzz I felt all the way to the tips of my toes dies a quick death.

I. Look. Nice? Is he kidding me? He could have said anything—literally anything—and it would have sounded a hell of a lot better than *nice*.

Screw him. I did not spend five hours in a salon chair, being poked, prodded, and waxed for him to say I look *nice*.

As if Declan can sense my brewing feelings, he grabs my bouquet of flowers and holds it out for someone. Both his hands clutch onto mine, locking me into place. Whatever expression is on my face warrants a warning squeeze. Instead of allowing my anger to get the best of me, I plaster a fake smile on my face and give the priest a nod.

I'll show him nice. *Jackass.*

The priest begins his lecture, but I can barely hear him over the erratic beat of my heart. Declan's hands tighten around mine as the priest speaks about love, commitment, and hardships that will test us. I feel like a fraud for nodding along, feigning adoration. I'm sure to check the back of my dress to make sure I didn't catch on fire for lying in the house of the Lord.

The rest of the ceremony is a blur with an exchange of standard vows. The closer we get to the end, the heavier my breathing becomes. It's not until Declan grabs my left hand in his that I nearly go into cardiac arrest.

"Iris, I offer you this ring as a reminder of my commitment to you, our marriage, and our future. Let it serve as a symbol of my devotion to you, from this day on." Something about his words makes me pause. He could have promised his everlasting love or something equally nauseating for the crowd, but he didn't.

Because Declan Kane doesn't show his cards. Admitting he's madly in love with you in front of a packed church isn't on-brand.

He silences my thoughts as he slides a thin platinum band covered in diamonds up my finger.

The two sentences I mulled over for weeks escape me as I grab Declan's ring from my mom's waiting hand.

"Umm—" *Real smooth, Iris.*

If Declan is annoyed at me stumbling over my words, he does a good job of not showing it. I clutch his left hand while holding onto his ring with the other. "Declan, I give you this ring as a symbol of my promises to you, as your partner and friend. May it serve as a reminder that even during our hardest days, you can always count on me to stand by your side." I slide the band past his knuckle.

Our eyes connect. Something passes over his face. He almost seems angry, but that can't be right? *Sad?* I somehow stop a laugh from escaping me. *No, that can't be true either. Declan has nothing to be sad about.*

As if Declan realizes he revealed a tiny part of himself to our audience, he regains control over the emotions on his face.

And we're back to our regularly scheduled programming.

The priest continues his spiel about trying times and the sacredness of wedding vows. He blesses us, our future children, and everyone attending our wedding.

And then the dreaded moment I blocked from my memory comes to light.

The priest steps backward toward his altar, giving us some space. "I pronounce you husband and wife. Declan, you may now kiss your bride."

My eyes widen. Everyone around us goes silent. I don't have to see them to know they're curious about us. Declan hasn't ever been seen with a woman, let alone kissing one.

My whole body shudders as Declan wraps one hand around the back of my neck. His fingers tighten, and his thumb traces my fluttering pulse point. The world shuts off as my boss leans in toward me, the expensive scent of him washing over me.

My knees go weak, and Declan's other arm wraps around my waist to stop me from falling. He positions me in a way that hides our faces from the audience, keeping our private moment to ourselves.

This is it. He leans forward, and our breaths mingle together. I shut my eyes as his soft lips brush against the corner of my lips.

Wait, what? Not even a whole kiss? It was nothing but a tease meant to appease the masses surrounding us.

He pulls away, leaving only a centimeter between us. His eyes are screwed shut as if he is in pain.

Embarrassment makes my eyes sting. I whisper, "That was hands down the worst kiss in my whole life, and that's saying something given my last ex—"

Declan's lips slam against mine, shutting me up. A buzz that starts from my lips spreads through my body like a brushfire, and I'm lost in the feel of our kiss.

My arms lock themselves around his neck like a lifeline. I feel like I'm lost at sea, drowning in all the sensations consuming me. The press of his chest against me. The weight of his palm burning into the small of my back. The brush of his finger across my neck, so soft it seems reverent.

I'm snapped out of the moment by a roar of applause.

Declan's lips press against mine one last time as if to brand me with his touch. His forehead touches mine, and the sweetness of the gesture has my heart threatening to beat itself straight out of my chest.

What is he doing? More specifically, why are you feeling this way? I have officially lost it. For some reason, this chemical attraction to Declan doesn't quite match my preconceived notion.

While he might be considered cold to the rest of the world, he makes me *burn*.

"They bought it." His rough whisper feels like being doused in ice water. Something about his comment causes a tight ball to form in my chest, growing until it consumes my heart.

His words shouldn't hurt. This is a ruse after all, yet the ache refuses to abate.

Maybe because you bought it too.

CHAPTER TWELVE

Declan

I find it difficult to tear my eyes away from Iris as we walk down the aisle toward the exit of the church. She is the embodiment of elegance and grace, with her smile as dazzling as the new diamond band on her finger. The ring serves as a reminder of her promise to me.

I wasn't sure if we would ever make it to this point. After my failed engagement, I thought we would hit a snag. That maybe Iris would wake up one day and decide this was a huge mistake. But finally, for the first time in two weeks, I feel relief.

The pressure against my chest lessens with each step away from the altar. With one part of my inheritance complete, I only have one more standing in my way of becoming CEO.

Make it through the rest of today before worrying about that.

I twist my wedding ring with my thumb, testing the feel of

the metal pressing against my skin. It doesn't feel as oppressive as I expected. Iris chose a simple band that draws little attention to the eye. Both of our rings get a single message across.

Married.

Two ushers open the doors. Together, Iris and I walk out into the bright sunlight. One of the photographers stops in front of us and yells out our names. I wrap an arm around Iris's waist and pull her against me, ignoring the way she tenses in my grasp.

Her reaction doesn't surprise me, but it still frustrates me. After the heated kiss we shared, I thought she would have gotten used to my touch by now, but I was wrong. She erected another barrier between us instead. The detached look on her face has me testing boundaries. I want to recreate the look on her face right after our kiss, before the reality of our situation set in.

I run my hand down her back, tracing the row of ivory buttons. She does nothing but shoot me a cold smile that doesn't reach her eyes.

I absolutely despise it.

"Tell me what's wrong," I whisper in her ear before tucking a stand of hair behind it.

Her fake laugh grates against my nerves. "Why would anything be wrong?"

I grimace. "You don't look happy."

"Unlike you, some of us can't fake it 24/7." Her voice can barely be heard over a gust of wind.

"What are you talking—"

"Let's get a photo of a kiss before they let the guests out!" the photographer yells.

I grin at the nervous laugh Iris lets out. The click of the camera goes off, catching the moment.

"I think they're coming out now," Iris calls out.

"Then make it quick!" he replies.

I shouldn't give in to his demand, but I'm interested in seeing if our kiss was a one-off or a testament to our chemistry. The kiss I shared with Iris in the church was electric. The kind that shouldn't feel as good as it did, given our circumstances.

The kind I am about to recreate with the hope that the buzz I got after was only a product of achieving the first task of my inheritance.

My arms curl around Iris's back, tugging her against me. Her lips part and her eyes shut as I lean forward. Sparks break out across my skin as our lips touch, and liquid heat spreads through my veins. Kissing her is addictive. Thrilling. So damn wrong I can't help questioning why it isn't right.

She's your assistant.

I nip at her bottom lip to distract myself from the thought. She gasps, and I suck up the sound before it has a chance to be heard by the photographer.

You're paying her to have your child.

My kiss turns more punishing, and she seems to respond well to my desperation. She groans as her arms wrap around my neck. Her bouquet tickles my skin, and I'm surrounded by the smell of flowers and Iris.

The photographer coughs. "All right. I got the shot."

Reality hits me like a fist to the face, and I break away before I tug Iris back against me and repeat our kiss for more selfish purposes than a photo. Our kiss wasn't some fluke or a high I got from completing my grandfather's request. It's far worse than that.

Iris blinks up at me with dilated eyes.

She is affected by you too.

It should fill me with some relief to know she is equally struggling, but I'm far too concerned about the fallout of a discovery like this.

Before I have a chance to wrap my mind around what is happening between us, the doors behind me open. Hundreds of guests pour out of the church. They gather in a circle, suffocating us. I hate the way they batter us with compliments almost as much as I despise the way the crowd grows larger by the minute.

Iris latches onto my hand. "Relax. Focus on me."

That's my issue. I can't focus on anything *but* her.

I can't bear looking at her for longer than a few seconds. The urge to steal her away from the crowd is difficult to ignore, and it wouldn't take much for me to crack.

Remember what's important here.

Iris remains silent as we are both shuffled into the Maybach. I spend the entire car ride to the reception location reminding myself of how acting on my attraction is not possible. Regardless of the two kisses we shared, nothing matters more than keeping things professional between us. We have far too much riding on our positions to be getting lost in a fleeting attraction to one another.

My future is more important than satisfying some momentary urge to kiss Iris. I just need to keep telling myself that.

I hate weddings. They're a cliché excuse for people to drink alcohol on my tab, all while pretending they actually care about my new marriage. They don't. Everyone is solely here because no one would be stupid enough to turn down an invitation to what Iris deemed the wedding of the decade.

Unfortunately for me, I still have three more hours to get through, including cutting a cake right now.

A different photographer from the one earlier calls out for us to look at the camera. "Can I get a shot of you two with the cake?"

"Why did we agree to so many damn photos?" I frown as I grab the silver cake cutter from a server's tray.

Iris smiles up at me. "Because we are going to share snapshots with the world to prove just how much we love one another."

"Why should they care?"

She laughs, and the bulb of the camera goes off. "Because you're a famous billionaire who is in the business of selling fairy tales."

I groan. "Fame is temporary."

"So is discomfort, so get used to it." She presses her hand on top of mine so we are both grasping the knife.

Being near her is the furthest thing from uncomfortable. Rather, the warmth of her touch sends a wave of want through me. I step closer to her so we can both approach the cake.

You're pathetic. What happened to not wanting to get close to people?

I shake my head. I'm not trying to grow closer to Iris, but it's hard to avoid her when everyone keeps pushing us together.

"Declan, a little more smiling please?"

I glare at the photographer.

He gapes. "Never mind." His flash goes off, catching me mid–death stare.

Iris laughs. "I need that one sent to me ASAP."

I shoot her a look, and she only laughs harder. My chest tightens at the sound. Compared to the icy display she put on earlier for our guests, it feels good to make her warm back up to me.

And this is why you need to stay away from her. Because this feeling in your chest?

Merde.

The photographer snaps another photo before I dismiss him. My mood takes a turn for the worse, and I barely pay Iris any attention as we cut the cake. We go through all the motions. She feeds me and I feed her. A few people gasp when she smashes a bit of cake in my face, and I return the favor by shoving a spoonful of cake into her mouth while she is mid-laugh.

Nothing about it is real. I'm detached, but not enough to miss the flicker of hurt in her eyes when I abandon her for the bar. I'm a dick for leaving her to manage the crowd that formed around us. I know it with every fiber in me, just like I know sticking around her is weakening my resolve.

I didn't marry her for love, money, or affection. I married her because I'm a greedy asshole who will stop at nothing to get what I want, even if it means subjecting her to the same fucked-up happily ever after as me. A few kisses and some touching isn't going to change our destiny, so why pretend this is anything but an arrangement?

It's all for the best. At least I tell myself as much as I knock back my first drink of the night.

Alcohol doesn't solve anyone's problems.

My stomach rolls. The feeling has nothing to do with the

drink I burned through and everything to do with the idea of using alcohol to cope. A bartender rushes over to fill my glass, but I push the empty tumbler out of reach.

You're not him.

I step away from the bar before I do something I will regret.

CHAPTER THIRTEEN

Iris

"More shots!" Rowan's girlfriend, Zahra, clutches a bottle of tequila in her hand. She wobbles on her heels, and Rowan swoops in to stabilize her.

My stomach does a little flip at the loving gesture. Watching them interact is nauseating, with Zahra smiling up at Rowan like he hung the moon for her. I'm oddly fascinated by their interactions given my limited exposure to happy couples over the years. Maybe there is some hope after all if someone as grumpy and isolated as Rowan could look at a woman like *that*.

I shouldn't be bitter at my own wedding but seeing as my husband has avoided me as much as humanly possible after we cut the cake, I'm not doing too well. Something shifted in him ever since the church, and I can't help but wonder if it was our kiss.

"What did we say about tequila?" Rowan plucks the bottle out of Zahra's hand.

"That we should never trust a man named Jose." She crosses her arms with a pout and drops into the chair beside me, making the material of her dress poof around her.

Rowan's chest shakes from silent laughter as he pulls up a chair beside Zahra.

Cal grabs the bottle and pours tequila into four shot glasses. "You can't leave a wedding sober. It's sacrilegious."

"You wouldn't know the meaning of the word," Rowan replies.

"My wedding, my rules!" I pass Zahra a shot glass.

"Whatever the bride says goes." Zahra grins as she knocks back her shot. She leans into Rowan and whispers something in his ear. Whatever she says has him swallowing the first shot before pouring himself a second one.

He tucks her hair behind her ear and whispers something in return that has her cheeks blushing.

Gross. I grab my glass and pull it to my lips. Except the rim never touches my mouth because it's stolen straight from my hand.

"I think you've had enough." Declan's rough voice does something to my heart rate.

Cal waves the tequila bottle in Declan's direction. "Come on. Sit down with us and have a celebratory shot."

Declan shoots Cal a scathing look. "I think you've done enough celebrating."

"She's a big girl. If she wants to drink on her wedding night, it's her choice."

"*She's* right here." I stand on my two feet. The room spins around me, and I grab the back of my chair to catch myself. "I'm fine. Stop fussing over me."

"You smell like spring break in Mexico."

Something about his comment has me muffling my laugh with a shaky palm.

His lips pull down into a frown. I take a few wobbly steps toward him before clutching onto his tux so I don't fall over. I use one hand to push the corner of his scowl up into a smile. "There. All better."

"We're going home." Declan's arm wraps around me. The move reminds me of our kiss in the church, which only makes my cheeks hot underneath a pound of makeup.

I pout. "But why?"

"You're intoxicated."

"It's a wedding! *Our* wedding!" I struggle to focus on Declan's three heads. "Hey, why aren't you drunk?"

His three heads merge into one angry version. "Because one of us has some self-control," he snaps.

"It's all Cal's fault!" I blurt out.

"Hey!" Cal throws his arms up.

"He did steal a bottle from the bar. I saw him take it myself," Rowan backs me up.

Declan points at Rowan. "Don't get me started on you."

The way the three of them interact has me raising a brow in Zahra's direction. "See? I told you they never get along."

Zahra smiles. "*Yet*."

"I like her already," I say aloud instead of in my head.

"Let's go," Declan snaps.

"Don't forget to text me! I want all the details," Zahra yells.

I throw her a thumbs-up over my shoulder. Turns out she is the only other person besides Cal and Rowan who knows about the whole sham. Not that I would tell Declan. I'm pretty sure he would murder Rowan for risking our big secret like that.

Declan steers me toward the exit of the ballroom.

"Wait!" the wedding planner yells. "You can't go yet! We haven't even tossed the bouquet!"

Declan lets out the longest sigh ever. My chest vibrates from withheld laughter.

He turns me toward him. "What's so funny about this?"

"You hate every second of this."

"Are we getting off on each other's displeasure now?"

"Like you're one to judge. That's your favorite kind of foreplay."

His reddened cheeks make me smile.

One point for Team Iris.

Tati has the DJ request for all the ladies to gather around on the dance floor for the bouquet toss. Declan holds on to me as if he's scared I might topple over due to my unsteadiness. I imagine he only does so because he wants to make sure people buy our marriage.

So much for forgetting about what he said in the church.

My mom passes me the bouquet with a knowing smile. "I was holding onto it for you."

"You're the bestest mom in the whole wide world."

She shakes her head. "Take care of my girl, Declan. Try to get her to sleep before she enters the drunk-crying phase."

"Tell me she's joking," he orders as my mom walks away.

I giggle.

"Fuck me."

I pat his cheek. "Only in your dreams, sweet husband of mine."

"Did you burn off all your brain cells tonight?"

"Come on!" a woman yells. "Get on with it, you two!"

I turn around, giving the crowd my back.

"One. Two. Three!" I launch the bouquet over my head.

I turn on my heels and almost slip from the rush, only for Declan to catch me and pull me into his firm chest.

Firm chest? Ugh. Maybe you are drunk after all.

The bouquet lands in someone's open arms with a *slap*. I don't recognize the woman who caught it, but the crowd around her squeals as they try to latch onto my bouquet with greedy hands.

"Finally." Declan moves us toward the door before the DJ announces Declan's turn with the garter belt.

Oh shit.

"You've got to be fucking kidding me."

I bristle as he squeezes my hip. Cal slaps a hundred-dollar bill in the DJ's hand as Rowan drags a chair out to the middle of the dance floor.

Cal waltzes over to help me into the chair, being mindful of the layers of lace and tulle swirling around me like a parachute. "Careful, Iris, your husband bites."

An unobservable blush spreads from my head to my toes.

"I hate you both." Declan's eyes move back and forth between Cal and Rowan.

On cue, the DJ plays the most sensual song known to man. My tummy has a thousand little champagne bubbles popping along to the beat, all while my heart rate picks up speed.

Declan bends a knee and settles into a comfortable position in front of me. His left hand shakes again before he fists it, just like it did when he lifted my veil earlier.

Turns out he is human after all.

I tug him out of his nervous thoughts.

"You look good on your knees, Mr. Kane."

"Try to not let it get to your head." The corners of his lips twitch into that usual Declan smile. A flash of a camera goes off, catching the moment.

His hand touches my covered thigh, barely leaving a dent from the layers of material. "This is wrong," he mutters.

"You're right. I feel absolutely scandalized." I speak in an off-key British accent.

His head shakes as a noise that I interpret as a laugh breaks free from him. "You're so drunk."

"No. I'm buzzed."

"What's the square root of sixty-four?"

"Eight, fuck you very much."

He shrugs. "Sober enough."

"For what?"

He doesn't reply as he lifts the fabric of my dress ever so carefully so no one catches a glimpse of me down there. My lungs squeeze, trying to take in oxygen as Declan disappears under my gown.

"Remember, no hands!" Cal calls out, and the crowd hoots and hollers. Declan pops a blind arm out and flips his middle finger in Cal's general direction. A few people laugh while others gasp, probably as shocked as me at Declan's rare display of feelings.

I tune them all out, focusing on the heightened experience. The scrape of Declan's stubble against my calf. The brush of his hair on the inside of my thighs as he parts them with his head. The feel of his teeth grazing the skin around the garter, accompanied by the press of his soft lips as he clamps down around the frilly piece of lace.

I shiver, and a vibration of his throat tells me Declan noticed and *laughed*.

I hate him. I hate my husband so much, he is lucky I don't choke him with the damn thing once he comes back up for air.

Declan drags the garter belt down my leg. He pulls out from underneath my skirt with the strip of white lace stuck between his teeth. With an angry yank, he tugs the material from his mouth and launches it in the air without sparing it a second glance.

"Enjoy your evening, everyone." Declan doesn't bother helping me up from the chair. He swoops me out of the seat and cradles me, full bridal style, adding to the crowd's excitement.

I tap on his shoulder. "Umm, Declan?"

"What?" His eyes soften.

"You're supposed to carry me into the house, not out of here."

He sighs like I'm the biggest inconvenience in the world. "You couldn't walk a straight line out the door in flats, let alone in those shoes."

"Hmm."

His brows pull together. "What?"

"Maybe you care about me after all."

"That's the alcohol talking."

I sigh. "Jose does have a way with words."

His arms tighten around me. "Who the fuck is Jose?"

I grin into the lapel of his jacket. "Nobody important."

"Good, then at least no one will miss him when he's dead."

One might think Declan would soften a bit toward me now that I am officially his wife.

Wrong.

The moment Harrison pulls up in the Maybach, Declan all but throws me in the back seat. I drop into the quilted leather with an *oomph*, and the material of my dress fans around me like a cloud.

"Would it kill you to be gentle?" I peek up at him.

Declan ignores me as he shuts the door in my face. I'm almost positive some of my dress hangs outside, caught in the doorjamb.

"I'll take that as a yes," I grumble.

His elderly driver nearly trips over his feet to beat Declan to his door. Poor Harrison is probably afraid to lose his job based on the scary look on Declan's face. Not that I blame him.

But what triggered his anger? Declan doesn't spare me another glance as he takes a seat, which only adds to the weight pressing against my chest.

"You're acting like a child."

Crickets.

"Are you just going to ignore me the whole time?"

The only reply I get is the revving of the engine as Declan's driver takes off.

"Fine." I go to mess around with the dial to play some music, but Declan shoots me a look that has me pulling my hand back.

After a whole five minutes of silence, my tequila-riddled brain gives in.

"I forgot how fun a wedding could be. It's been years since I went to one."

Declan remains silent as he continues scrolling through his phone.

"It was nice to meet Rowan's girlfriend. She's sweet."

His hand holding the phone tightens. *Hmm. Interesting.*

"I don't know why you don't like her. It's not her fault Rowan chose Dreamland over becoming CFO. You should give her a fair shot at least."

The tic in his jaw makes another appearance, yet he doesn't bother looking at me. *Come on. Give me something to work with.*

"They invited us out to dinner tomorrow night and since we aren't going on a honeymo—"

Declan's head snaps up. "We are *not* going to dinner with them."

"But you've barely spoken to Rowan since he decided to stay in Dreamland. I think it would be nice to spend some time with them while they're in town—"

"I don't pay you to be concerned over family matters."

I clench a fistful of my dress. "Lucky for you I'm doing this for free."

His eyes return to the screen of his phone. "Don't bother. I'm not going to dinner with Rowan and his girlfriend."

"Zahra. Her name is *Zahra*."

"Her name is as irrelevant as her relationship is with my brother."

I can't remove the horrific look from my face. "God, your ability to hold a grudge is terrifying."

"Consider it a lesson to not get on my bad side."

"Lately it's starting to feel like *every* side is your bad side."

"Who knew having a wife would be this good for my ego?" His voice takes on a sarcastic tone.

"It's a wife's job to call you out on your bullshit because the rest of the world sure as hell won't. Not when they're too afraid to speak up around you."

"What part of *we're not a real couple* do you find difficult to understand?"

My chest tightens. I thought Declan and I were falling into a comfortable friendship, but his mood tonight has me questioning if he was only entertaining me so I wouldn't back out of our arrangement.

His words from the night of our engagement come back to haunt me. *There is nothing I won't do to earn my inheritance. Remember that when you forget this is only a game to me.*

Is that what this all was? *A game?* Now that he got his way, there's no reason to play anymore. The idea causes a weird ache in my chest, right above my heart.

I swallow past the lump in my throat. There's no one to blame but myself. Declan was always clear about his intentions, and I stupidly read into our relationship all wrong.

Why do you care in the first place? This isn't even real.

Because maybe somewhere along the way, I forgot that all of this was a lie.

I don't speak to Declan for the remainder of the drive. If ignoring each other were a sport, we would both be team captains with the way neither one of us speaks.

Once Harrison parks the car, I fight my way past pounds of tulle and lace and exit with as much grace as a newborn horse.

"Iris," Declan calls after me.

I don't turn around. I'm too afraid that all my emotions will be written clear as day across my face. "I'm going to bed."

"You forgot your purse."

The urge to stomp my foot hits me but I refrain. "Right." Stupid purse. I knew I should have gone with the wedding dress that had pockets.

I turn back, avoiding his eyes as I pull open the door and search the empty back seat.

"Here." His chest presses against my spine as he traps me between the car and his body. I turn, attempting to avoid skin-to-skin contact and fail. The front of his tux brushes against my bodice, sending a ripple of heat through me.

He offers my clutch. The glittery *Mrs. Kane* shines underneath the overhead lights, looking just as horrendous as the day the wedding planner gifted me the accessory. Based on the expression on Declan's face, he equally dislikes the way his name is flaunted like a show pony. I might not have experienced the same issues as him growing up, but I'm starting to understand him a bit more. Based on the way people treated me at the wedding, becoming a Kane feels like an open invitation for clout chasers and career climbers to have at me.

I stare down at the clutch, which serves as a reminder of my duty. Of the promise I made to Declan to stand by him no matter what.

No matter how much he schemes to get his way.

"Do you mind?" I gesture for him to move back.

He steps out of the way. I attempt to make my escape, only to be held back by Declan gripping onto my elbow. His hold doesn't hurt, but it speaks a silent request.

Stay.

But why?

"Yes?" I ask.

"Is it that bad?"

I look up at him. "What?"

"The idea of becoming my wife."

I swear, the rise and fall of his moods tonight is driving me insane.

"And you care about my opinion all of a sudden? I'm not sure you pay me enough for that kind of service."

His jaw clenches. "Answer the question."

"*No.*"

"Must you always be this impossible?"

"I don't know. Must you always act like an asshole?"

"It's not an act."

I rear back, ripping my elbow from his grasp. "Trust me. It might have taken me much longer than others, but I finally understand why everyone calls you that."

His long blink speaks for itself. "What?"

"The way you treated me tonight—on our wedding night no less—is unacceptable. But I guess you couldn't care less about how or when you hurt other people's feelings, as long as you get your way."

"What I said in the car—"

I hold up my hand. "Don't worry about it. It's my fault for setting unrealistic expectations about us in the first place."

His eyes narrow ever so slightly.

I keep going, wanting to clear the air once and for all. "I never did all of this for love. Obviously." An awkward laugh forces its way out of me. "I only wanted to help you because I thought we were friends. And yes, before you say you never wanted to be my friend, I'm aware it was probably stupid to think that. I've since learned my lesson."

He opens his mouth, but I cut him off. "I realize I don't want to be your friend either. Because getting close to you means questioning your motives about everything, and frankly, that's way too much effort for someone who doesn't seem to like me in the first place."

CHAPTER
FOURTEEN

Iris

I hold my head up high the entire walk to my bedroom. Rather than feel unsettled from my conversation with Declan, I'm hit with a wave of calmness. It seems like we are finally back to where we stood with one another before our whirlwind engagement. Sure, a cake tasting and a family dinner might have been a fun change of pace for us, but that's all it was.

A show for the masses—kind of like a royal tour.

It takes me a whole twenty minutes to undo hours of hair and makeup. I might have ripped off half my eyelashes from lash glue, but it's a small price to pay for finally feeling like myself again.

By the time I get to removing my dress, I almost throw out my back trying to undo the vintage buttons lining my spine.

"Motherfucker." I grunt as I twist and turn in front of a full-length mirror. Nothing works, and I'm stuck staring at my reflection with my hands on my hips.

There's no way you're getting out of this dress by yourself. I let out a resigned sigh as I swallow my pride and exit my room.

My fist knocking against Declan's door echoes off the tall ceilings. I stand there, waiting for him to open up. The pressure in my chest builds as time ticks by. Ten seconds turns into thirty, and before I know it, I'm knocking again. "Declan! I need your help!"

Well, that hurts to admit. If he was sleeping, he sure isn't now. The jangle of the doorknob gives me hope that I won't need to fall asleep in my wedding dress tonight.

Now that's a depressing thought.

When Declan opens the door, I want to run in the opposite direction. My heart rate goes from steady to rapid at the sight of Declan's muscular, *naked* chest on full display.

I choke on my next inhale of breath.

Water droplets trickle down inches of pale muscle before disappearing into a white towel wrapped around his narrow waist. He has V-cut abdominal muscles that point like an arrow to an area I sure as hell should not be thinking about right now. An area that only proves Declan is well-endowed even when not aroused.

Warmth pools deep in my belly. My eyes give him another once-over, and my hands itch to reach out and trace the slab of muscle also known as his stomach.

This can't be happening to me. My eyes snap up toward his face, hoping he missed my temporary lapse of sanity.

He raises a brow at me in silent anticipation.

Oh my God. He knows that you like what you see.

I try to think up a response, but my throat feels dry suddenly.

"You wanted my help?" He stops in front of me.

His help! Right!

"I can't reach the buttons." My voice is far breathier than I'm proud of. Given our argument in the car, I could at least pretend to be disgruntled in his presence.

Declan circles around me like a predator. His muscles shift with each step, and I'm surprised my tongue doesn't roll out of my mouth like a dog as I pant after him.

He drags my wild hair over my shoulder, and goose bumps spread across my skin.

That should *not* be happening.

Anyone with eyes would be attracted to a set of abs. It's evolution beckoning us to choose a mate who can provide for us.

Provide what? Endless stamina and orgasms? I reply.

"There have to be a hundred of them." He tugs me out of my thoughts, and for that, I am eternally grateful.

A laugh escapes me before I have a chance to stop it. "Hundred and twenty according to Nana."

He grunts. "Come inside so I can see them better in the light."

The invitation is innocent, but my body doesn't seem to get the memo as Declan ushers me into his room and toward the light on his nightstand.

"Let me go put some clothes on."

Please don't.

Whatever expression I have on my face makes the corners of his lips lift.

"I'll be back in a second." He walks toward his closet, only to look over his shoulder at the last second.

My cheeks burn from being caught ogling him.

He raises a brow. "It's rude to stare."

"Then don't walk around naked to begin with. Problem solved." *Atta girl.*

He shakes his head and enters his closet without sparing me another glance.

I take a moment to observe the personal objects on his night-stand. A worn copy of *The Great Gatsby* has five different sticky notes protruding from the yellowed pages, neatly lined up next to a remote control for his TV. My eyes widen at the small cactus I bought him two years ago as a Christmas gift.

"Oh my God. It's still alive?" I reach out and grab the tiny *don't be a prick* pot.

"I can manage to take care of a cactus."

I startle at the sound of his voice. "But it's been two years!" And he keeps it on his *nightstand.* I don't have the nerve to ask him why that is, although the urge rides me hard.

He shuts me up by tracing a finger down the base of my spine, right beside the hundred ivory buttons. The pot in my hand trembles as his hot breath hits the back of my neck. My skin prickles in response, and I place the pot down in order to hide the way my hands shake from his proximity.

He starts with the top button, only to fumble. His frustrated grunt makes me laugh.

"You think this is funny?"

I giggle again as he slips again.

"My hands are too big."

I roll my eyes. "Of course they are."

"I'm not joking."

I shoot him a glare over my shoulder. "Well, we need to figure it out because I can't sleep in this."

"What if I cut you out of it?"

"No!" The gown cost fifty-thousand dollars. I can't imagine ruining it just because Declan and his Hulk-like hands can't manage some measly buttons.

He sighs as he tries one last time and fails. "Scissors or a knife?"

"You're joking."

"Would you prefer I rip it apart?"

"Absolutely not!" I push back, forcing him to give me some room. "I'll be back."

I head to my bedroom, open a box labeled *gardening supplies*, and pull out a pair of shears. They still have a little bit of dirt on them, but it doesn't matter. It's not like I'll be wearing this dress ever again, although the option to donate it is not completely off the table.

"Stupid Declan and his massive paws for hands," I grumble under my breath as I walk back into his room.

"Here." I shove the shears against his chest.

He looks down at them. "This is not how I expected tonight would go."

"Disappointed?"

"*Amused.*"

Our eyes lock, and something passes between us. One look sends sparks across my skin and my heart into cardiac arrest. It's as if our outburst in the garage never happened. While I want to be annoyed at myself, I can't help it when it comes to him. He might be an asshole, but I knew what I was signing up for when I married him.

"Get on with it." I turn again and hold on to my hair before he has a chance to move it for me. The less contact we have, the better. I'm already feeling weak tonight as it is.

He grips onto the lace collar of my dress. "Don't move an inch." The cold brush of metal against the base of my neck has me sucking in a breath.

I wouldn't dare. Not with the way my legs are threatening to give out at any moment.

The sound of shears cutting through lace sends another round of goose bumps across my arms. Chilly air hits the skin at the top of my spine, and I press the front of my dress against my chest to prevent it from falling at my feet.

Declan cuts through the fabric slower than necessary, and the blunt side of the shears brushes my back with each snip.

"Almost done." His voice is far huskier than usual.

With a few last cuts, my entire back is on display for him. He chucks the shears on the bed once the job is done. Neither one of us moves, and my anxiety grows with each second that passes. I look over my shoulder to find him staring at my bare back like a puzzle he can't solve.

"Thanks." I attempt to take a step away from him, only to stop when his hand reaches out and skates across my spine. My heart pounds against my chest, threatening to jump out as he stops right above my lacy thong. Lust slams into me like a fist to the face. I can't help choking on my gasp as he traces the edge of my underwear. His fingers brush across my goose bumps, and I suck in a deep breath.

He tugs, and a long, white string snaps. "This was bothering me."

I watch with horror as the thread falls by his bare feet. Of course while I was lusting after his touch, he was thinking about a fucking string. It's horrifying to think I wanted him to be attracted to me.

Tonight is the final wakeup call I needed. No matter how my body might react to his touch, it's only that. A reaction of chemicals responding to pheromones. Nothing but natural selection doing its thing, pushing me to mate with the worst partner on the planet, solely because he's hot and available.

I refuse to let myself fall for his touch again. Because next time, there might not be a string that snaps me out of making a terrible decision.

I acted like a dick last night for a multitude of reasons. The way I presented myself at my wedding was the first misstep in a series of regrets, all because I couldn't get a handle on my feelings. After all these years, one would think I would have mastered the art of not giving a fuck. It's disappointing to know all it took was Iris in a wedding dress to ruin all my hard work.

You won't be making that mistake again.

Not if I can help it. I stayed up far too late last night going over my new approach toward our fake marriage. Whatever happened on our wedding night is in the past. From now on, we will be more careful to avoid putting ourselves in situations that could lead to disastrous consequences.

Like you opening the door in a towel, knowing she was on the other side?

Exactly. Not my smartest move, but I won't make the same mistake twice.

I knock on her bedroom door with my free hand. She yells something indecipherable with a raspy voice, so I rap my knuckles against the wood again. A thud that sounds oddly like a pillow slamming against the door makes me smile to myself.

Iris might be many good things, but a morning person she is not.

I clear my throat. "I was out on my run and grabbed you some coffee."

"From Joe's?"

It is eerie how she knows that. "Yes."

"French vanilla with whole milk?"

My teeth grind together. "Obviously."

Her muffled moan through the door sends a current of energy down my spine. "And extra whipped cream?"

I sigh. "Open your door and find out."

Her laugh trickles through the cracks of the door in the same way it seeps through my chest. I wait a whole two minutes while she does who knows what inside of her room. She finally opens it up, revealing red-rimmed eyes accentuated by smeared mascara. It shouldn't stir up any kind of interest on my end, but the way my blood heats at her faded T-shirt dragging across her mid-thigh makes me question my sanity. It requires an unbearable amount of effort to turn my gaze away from her thighs. I take my time making it to her face, easily becoming distracted by the swell of her breasts pressed against the fabric of her T-shirt.

Snap out of it.

"Here." I hold out her coffee like it carries an infectious

disease. Our fingers brush, sending the faintest buzz across my skin.

Her eyes snap up to my face before she focuses on the coffee cup. "Thanks for the apology drink."

"That isn't what this is."

"Okay. Sure. Whatever helps keep your fragile masculinity intact." The sigh she makes as she takes a sip goes straight to my cock.

"I'll be taking that back now…" I attempt to steal the cup, but she grasps it with an iron grip.

"Don't you think about it! This has to be the best thing I've ever woken up to."

"I see why your past relationships failed." The words slip out of my mouth before I have a chance to think.

Shit, Declan. Where the hell did that come from?

I didn't mean for it to slip out.

Say what you came here to say and get the hell out of here.

"Did you just make a jab at my sex life?" Her voice has a lethal quality to it.

No way in hell am I touching that comment. I press my lips together to avoid saying anything else.

Then you shouldn't have said anything in the first place.

Her gaze hardens. "I think it's time we set some ground rules."

"Rules," I repeat back in a dry tone.

"Yes. *Rules.* You remember ours right?"

"I have a vague recollection."

Her smile could bring a man to his knees. "Let's review. Every look." She drags her eyes across my body like a phantom touch, burning my skin in their wake. "Every touch." It only takes a single finger of hers brushing across my cheek to beckon me forward like a man starved for attention. "Every kiss." This time, she grips my chin roughly, tugging my head down. Her lips brush the corner of mine. It's an exact replica of my kiss at our engagement party, yet this one elicits a whole different reaction from me. "Is nothing but a lie."

I'm rock solid beneath my running shorts. I clear my throat, blinking away the arousal in my eyes before she catches on.

So much for being on the same page.

"Fine. I concede. No talk of exes." I have none worthy of talking about and hers are exactly where they belong.

In the past.

"Great. Glad we are in agreement on that." She sips her drink.

"As entertaining as this conversation has been, I have things to do."

She raises her brow. "Then why are you here? With *coffee?*"

"Because I need to talk to you about yesterday."

"Which part?"

"All of it."

"Well, then. Go ahead." She takes a sip of her drink while scanning my face for emotions.

She won't find any. I've made sure of it.

I start with the hardest subject first. "Our kiss…"

"Kisses. As in plural. Both of which you instigated, just to set the record straight."

My skin burns hot under my T-shirt. "Kisses. As in never happening again."

She smiles. "Fine. You won't hear any objections from me."

146

Fine? I at least expected her to put up a bit of a fight. Based on the way she looked at me last night, I thought she would do something other than stare at me with a smug smile.

Maybe you read her wrong.

"While kissing you was a necessary evil for the public, we no longer need to pretend to be attracted to each other."

Something flashes in her eyes before she recovers. "Good. God forbid you actually have to *pretend* to be into me."

It was a shitty yet effective thing to say. My words do their damage, just like they're supposed to. It's for the best. The way I was compelled to touch her last night, without a single person watching us, says enough.

"Well, now that we cleared the air, I'm going to go enjoy my coffee." She proceeds to slam the door on my face.

Great. That went about as well as I expected.

I knew my father wanting to meet with me for lunch was a trap, yet I willingly went along with his invitation anyway. After his conversation with Iris, I'm interested in determining just how much of a problem he is going to be for me. My intuition tells me nothing about my battle for the CEO position will be easy.

My father's brown eyes swing from the menu to my face. "Any honeymoon plans?"

"No need to act like you care on my account."

He sighs. "I'm simply making small talk."

Bullshit. Every question he asks and all the statements he makes always have an ulterior motive. Because of him, I became an expert in reading between the lines.

"Iris and I are leaving on Friday." At least now we are. I don't care what the destination might be, so long as we go somewhere.

"What about the quarterly budget meeting?"

"I'm sure you can handle reviewing my reports without me. I only get one honeymoon after all." The corners of my lips threaten to rise.

"You seem to find a solution for everything."

I don't miss the double meaning behind his words. "I had a lot of practice picking up after someone's messes over the years."

"Do you even pretend to like me anymore?"

"I find it to be a wasted effort. You hate me and I hate you, so why bother acting otherwise?"

He dares to fake his displeasure. "I don't hate you."

"I find that hard to believe given our past." One I will never forget, so long as I live.

"This is exactly why I respect you more than your brothers. Unlike Cal or Rowan, you aren't afraid to speak your mind."

"We have two very different definitions of respect."

"Regardless, I find your efforts admirable. It's why I consider you a threat to begin with."

"Yet I can't say the same about you."

He chuckles. "I thought I taught you better than to underestimate your enemy."

"Please. If anything, I give you too much credit."

"You might be smart, but you let your need for revenge blind your ability to think clearly. Why else would you marry your assistant of all people? Even I didn't think you were *that* desperate for your inheritance."

Something snaps inside of me. "Talk about her like that

again and I swear I'll make your last twelve months as CEO absolutely miserable."

I can work with him or against him. For the sake of the company, I've been willing to do the first option, but if he continues to insult Iris, all bets are off. She has proven herself loyal time and time again, so the least I can do is defend her from scum like him.

Whatever expression he sees on my face draws a deep chuckle from him.

"Don't tell me you actually care about her?"

I make an effort to keep my gaze blank and withdrawn.

He slowly shakes his head. "To think I considered you my smartest son. What a disappointment."

"Is there a point to this conversation or do you solely speak to hear the sound of your own voice?"

"I'm sure you're aware of why I asked you to come here." His malicious smile puts me on alert.

"You might have to explain yourself given how disappointing you find my intelligence to be."

"Consider this a warning from father to son."

"About?"

"Your grandfather might have provided you with an opportunity to usurp me, but that doesn't mean you will be successful. I don't plan on stepping down without a fight."

"It'll make my victory all the sweeter."

He raises his glass of water. "Let the best Kane win."

I tap mine to his. "He already did."

"I need you to book a trip." I stop at Iris's desk. After spending the entire drive thinking over my father's conversation, I came to one conclusion.

I need to commit to my role as a doting husband—honeymoon included.

Iris looks up from her desktop with a pinched expression. "To Tokyo?"

"No. Pick a place. *Any* place with running water and Wi-Fi."

She looks around the room and under her desk.

"Searching for a hidden camera?"

The faintest smile crosses her lips. "Either that or a wiretap. Just to be clear, I have never nor will I ever take drugs. Whatever green substance you might find in my room is definitely Cal's."

"Funny," I reply dryly.

"Do you ever laugh?" she asks.

"Only when I make people cry."

Her face contorts as she slams a palm against her chest. "Cal is right. You *are* a monster."

"A monster who expects you to have a honeymoon chosen by the end of the business day."

"A honeymoon? Wow!" She looks far too excited about the prospect for my comfort.

"Don't get any ideas. This is strictly for appearances."

"Appearances?" Her grin is snuffed out.

"I'm positive that my father will do everything in his power to delegitimize our marriage. It is up to us to make his attempt futile."

Her lips purse. "By going on a honeymoon? How is that going to solve anything?"

"It proves I care enough about you to take my first vacation in over a decade."

She laughs. "You must live such a sad life if you think sacrificing work for a honeymoon is a declaration of your affection."

"Is it not?" Did she not hear a word of anything I just said? I don't take vacations. Doing so should silence any doubts about our relationship.

Wouldn't it?

"No. It's not."

I grimace. "I'll be the judge of that."

Her eyes roll. "Sure. We can do things your way since you have *so* much experience when it comes to relationships." She mumbles something about *men always think they know everything* under her breath.

I knock my fist against her desk. "Book the plane for Friday."

"*This* Friday?"

"Is that going to be a problem?"

She squeals. "No! Even if it was, I refuse to let this golden opportunity go to waste. I haven't had a vacation in *years*."

"At least you finally get something good out of all of this."

She slaps her desk with a stern look. "You mean there's supposed to be something better than marrying *you*? I refuse to believe it."

I turn and walk toward my door, hiding the grin spreading across my face. Iris is the only person with the ability to make me smile. Not that she knows it. I've done everything in my power to hide how much sway she has over my moods.

CHAPTER
SIXTEEN

Iris

I f someone told me a month ago that Declan would hand me
his black card and tell me to plan a honeymoon, I would have
sent them to the nearest hospital to get their head checked.
But lo and behold, Declan does just that.

"Money is no object," he says before disappearing behind his
double doors.

I squeal as I spin around in my chair.

"Keep it down," he calls out from the other side of the wood
door.

I clamp down on my lips while I grab my cell phone and
text Cal.

Me: Guess who is going on a honeymoon after all.

Cal: How did you make him crack?

Cal: Waterboarding?

Cal: Sleep deprivation?

Cal: Sex???

Cal: Wait. If it's the last one, don't tell me. I don't want to know.

I laugh as I type up my response.

Me: Your father.

Cal: *Pretends to be shocked.

Me: Do you want to help me plan something?

Cal: I'll be there in 15.

"No." I shove a dumpling into my mouth.

"But it's Bora Bora," Cal replies with an exasperated look.

I shake my head. "Sounds boring." Good thing Cal can't see the way my cheeks burn from the lie.

"What is wrong with you?"

More like what *could* be wrong with me if I were to choose a honeymoon location that would require Declan to walk around shirtless and wet all day long. Even I know my limits, and that is one of them. After the little show I got last time Declan was shirtless, it's best we don't test the waters.

Cal uses the computer mouse to scroll through the newspaper article recommending the "Top Ten Honeymoon Spots in the World." "How about Maui?"

I scrunch my nose. "No."

"Fiji?"

"Pass."

"I swear, with the way you're acting, it's as if you don't want to go on a honeymoon at all."

"I do!" *Just not anywhere that might require us to take our clothes off.*

He stares me down. "What about South Africa?"

Huh. Now that is an idea…

"Tell me more."

He looks absolutely horrified by my interest. "You can't be serious. You would choose a safari over Bora Bora?"

"Why not?"

"Because it's not romantic."

I frown. "This might be a honeymoon, but it isn't meant to be romantic."

"Clearly or else you would have chosen something else."

The more Cal pushes me on it, the more I find the idea of going on a safari appealing. Nothing says *hands off* quite like bug spray, motion sickness, and watching animals devour each other. With a busy trip like that, the risk of Declan and I doing something stupid is slim to none.

I throw my napkin on the table and pat my distended belly. "That's it. We're going to South Africa."

Cal groans, and I smile.

Problem solved.

Planning a trip to Africa at the last minute is stressful. I need to juggle Declan's busy schedule, doctors' appointments so we can get our shots, and calling safari lodges to see who has availability at the last minute. I do all this while working from nine to nine every single day.

Declan is absolutely useless when it comes to planning anything, so I'm stuck doing everything on my own. Flights. Travel itineraries. Sleeping arrangements. Everything falls on my shoulders since Declan doesn't care where we go, so long as I post a few photos and make it seem like we are having a good time. His words. Not mine.

Because of his attitude, I don't feel bad booking the most expensive safari lodge on our list. I even book a trip to the salon to get my hair braided—all on his personal card. That's what he gets for being so cold and unfeeling about the whole process. The least he could have done was ask me if I needed any help. Or even thanked me for putting all this together at the last minute, all so he could prove to everyone how we are some happy couple.

It's the smallest things that make people feel appreciated. Not that Declan cares.

I sigh as I stare out the car window.

"What's wrong?" Declan doesn't bother looking up from his phone.

"Nothing. Just thinking about how I need to finish packing for both of us tonight." The lie easily rolls off my tongue. It's not like Declan cares about my feelings on the matter.

Declan remains silent.

"Is there anything in particular that you want me to pack for you?" I ask.

"No." He frowns as he types against the screen.

Is this how my life is going to be for the next three years?

Speaking to someone who is permanently attached to their cell phone?

The emptiness in my chest intensifies as the minutes go on. Declan remains oblivious, and I only sink further into my funk.

What did you expect? To get married and for him to instantly have a change of heart? The world doesn't work like that.

At the very least, I thought Declan would give me a bit of his time, given the fact that I'm his wife now.

Don't go wishing for things that will never happen.

I sigh again. This time, Declan doesn't bother commenting on it. How can he when he is too busy answering the phone and yelling at someone on the other end?

Story of my life.

My phone buzzes in my hand. I unlock it to find Cal's latest text message.

Cal: Did you ever get around to thanking my father for your impromptu honeymoon yet?
Me: I'll be sure to send him a thank you basket when I get back.
Cal: Should I tell him to look out for a faint ticking noise?
Me: Don't ruin the surprise! That's the best part.

Cal responds with a row of laughing emojis.

Declan drops into the captain's chair across from me. The

flight attendant is quick to ask him if he needs anything, but he simply ignores her by tapping on his tablet screen.

"Sir, I'm here to service you in any way you need. Please don't hesitate to ask for anything during the long flight." She bats her lashes at Declan.

Service him? Gross.

Declan remains oblivious to her obvious innuendo. He doesn't bother to look up at her despite the way she stands beside his chair, drooling all over the carpet.

I clear my throat. "Excuse me?"

She doesn't even bother turning in my direction. "The captain said the trip should be a smooth one. I'm curious what made you pick South Africa?"

"I've always wanted to go on a safari." As of three days ago, at least.

She dares to shoot me a scathing look over her shoulder. Is she really going to ignore me while flirting with him? He's wearing a *wedding ring* for crying out loud.

"My husband and I will take two glasses of champagne, please." I lift my left hand in the air to get her attention, and the diamond reflects a rainbow of colors across the ceiling.

She peers over at me with a raised brow. "Excuse me?"

Excuse you. I grind my teeth together. "Actually, you might as well bring out the whole bottle. We're in a celebrating mood."

"You're married?" Her eyes swing back and forth between us before landing on Declan's ring. The way her smile falls elicits my own.

"Get my wife whatever she wants." Declan doesn't look up from his tablet.

My stomach flutters in a way that has nothing to do with flying jitters.

"Of course. Right away, sir!" She rushes to the back of the private jet.

"Right away, sir!" I echo her enthusiasm with a roll of my eyes.

The corners of Declan's mouth lift as he feigns interest in whatever is on his screen.

I glare. "Are you enjoying yourself?"

"I do find your possessiveness entertaining."

"I am *not* possessive."

"Hmm," he responds. His fingers go *tap tap tap* on the screen.

I shift in my seat, and the tips of my braids brush against the small of my back. "Okay, whatever. Even if I was, it's warranted. She shouldn't have flirted with you while you're wearing a wedding ring."

"I see." He drags his index finger across the glass before tapping on the tablet screen.

"What aren't you saying?"

"I'm curious why you feel the need to flaunt your marital status whenever you're insecure."

My mouth drops open. "I am not insecure!"

"I'm aware of your trust issues."

Is he for real right now? He's one to talk about trust issues when the man has a seventeen-digit code to unlock his *cell phone*.

"Is this the part of our relationship where we share our deep-seated daddy issues?" I coo in a joking manner despite the thundering pace of my heart. "Because I'm pretty sure we could spend the whole flight debating who had it worse growing up."

He shrugs. "Defensive as always."

This motherfuc—

Relax. He's good at stirring up people's insecurities and using them to his advantage. Instead of giving in to his taunts, I pull out my phone and busy myself with my email inbox. Sorting messages is a soothing task that keeps my mind numb.

Despite my best efforts, my thoughts drift.

Trust issues? Who is he to call me out on such a thing? Everything about him screams trust issues, from the thirty-page prenup I signed to the way he won't open up despite my knowing him for years.

He readjusts his position in the chair. "You can trust me to remain faithful."

"As if that was a concern," I bite out.

His brow raises in silent question.

"Everyone knows about your sleeping habits."

"And what are they?" His eyes lighten with amusement.

"You don't sleep around and you don't date. Half the company thinks you're gay while the others think you visit a sex club to let off some steam every week."

"I'm disappointed at their lack of creativity." There is a tightness in his voice that wasn't present a moment ago.

"I tried to help them all by spreading a rumor about a woman who secretly visited your office on Fridays, but it only lasted a year."

"Why the hell would you say that?" His neutral expression morphs into something terrifying. If it weren't for the crazed expression on his face, I would be proud to have ruffled his feathers like this. It is no easy feat to get under the great Declan Kane's skin.

I become engrossed in pushing back my cuticles. "It forced people to send me their assignments earlier than usual because no one wanted to interrupt your sexy time for a signature. It was a win-win really. I was able to prepare your Monday briefing reports before the weekend and they earned promotions for their diligent work."

He blinks at me. "You had them believe this for a *year?*"

"Are you proud of me?"

"No."

"You should be. I was so committed to the storyline that I even hired a few women to leave your office at 5 p.m." I waggle my brows.

"Please tell me you didn't charge this to my personal card."

I grin. "Nope. Considered it a business expense."

He rubs his eyes. "Sometimes I feel like I know everything about you, and then you open your mouth and say something like that."

My cheeks heat and I hide my bashfulness with a smile. "Keeping tabs on me?"

"It's expected."

"Because I'm your wife?"

His response is interrupted by the flight attendant showing up with our bottle of champagne. She pops the cork and moves to pour us a glass, purposefully leaning forward. One peek at her cleavage pushes me into action.

I interrupt her. "I got it."

Her face reddens as she places the bottle on the table and leaves.

"Jealousy looks good on you."

"Oh, shut up." I fill the glasses and swipe one for myself.

Declan rewards my brazenness with a deep chuckle so low, I can barely hear it over the hum of the plane's engines.

I smile in return as I lift my flute in the air toward Declan. "To the vacation I desperately needed."

He begrudgingly grabs the other. "And the honeymoon I never wanted."

I tap my flute against his. "Cheers!"

It takes me two whole days to recover from a severe case of jet lag. By the third morning, I am feeling better than ever. My head brushes against my silk pillowcase as I turn on my side and stare out my panoramic floor-to-ceiling windows overlooking the bush. The moon glistens off the surface of our private pool, and I'm tempted to dive in to wake myself up.

I stretch my legs before doing a celebratory wiggle in bed. I haven't had a vacation since before I started working for Declan, so the idea of spending ten days off the grid has me wanting to dance my way through my morning routine.

The sound of my alarm breaks the silence. If I weren't used to waking up early for work, the 5:00 a.m. schedule here would have sucked big time. I'm quick with getting ready given my limited choices of safari-appropriate clothing.

By the time I make it to our living room, I expect Declan to be annoyed that I'm ten minutes late. Except Declan isn't here. I spin around in a circle before making my way through our private villa. His room is located on the opposite side of the place, giving him an equally beautiful view of our pool outside.

A muffled noise comes through the bottom of his bedroom door. I turn the knob and push his door open, finding Declan bent over a desk, looking fresh as a daisy in a three-piece suit. I try my best to ignore the way his ass sticks out, but my eyes linger on his form-fitting pants because I'm not blind. Although the little jolt in my heart concerns me enough to avert my gaze back to his face.

I frown at his attire. "You can't go out like that. The lions will eat you alive."

He ignores me as he scribbles something down on a notepad.

I check the time on my phone. "We're supposed to meet with the ranger in five minu—"

"Sorry, Mr. Kane, what was that?" a woman's voice cuts me off.

He glares at me as he holds a finger to his mouth.

"Just my assistant checking in on me. Carry on, Ms. Tanaka."

Tanaka. Of course Declan would answer a call from Mr. Yakura's assistant. She and her VIP boss are one of the few people who have direct access to Declan's personal line.

Ms. Tanaka spouts something off in Japanese and Declan responds without missing a beat. Watching him shift between languages always impresses me. Whether it is Spanish, Portuguese, Mandarin, or Japanese, the way the words roll easily off Declan's tongue is something to be admired. I've tried to pick up on a few words here and there while listening in on his conversations, but I never had a knack for any kind of words—let alone foreign ones.

While Declan speaks to Ms. Tanaka, I enter his closet and start unloading his luggage. I make quick work of the job since I was the one who packed everything anyway. The suit was a surprise, and I'm somewhat peeved Declan thought to pack it in the first place. We were supposed to be on the same page about all this, including no work.

Because really, what is the point of going through this entire sham of a honeymoon if he is going to work the entire time. That doesn't scream happily in love.

Ms. Tanaka finally ends the call, and I exit his closet with a safari-approved outfit. "Here. Change into this."

"We're not going."

I blink at him. "I'm sorry, what?"

His eyes shift from my face to my trembling arm holding onto his clothes with an iron grip. "Mr. Yakura wants to meet in a few hours to discuss the latest proposal."

"You're joking."

"No. The man is impossible. I'm close to abandoning the land and sending the scouts out to find me a new location."

"But—"

He doesn't let me finish. "I refuse to give up when I'm this close to securing the deal, especially after I promised the board I would follow through on delivering Dreamland Tokyo." He paces the width of his room. His large body makes me feel as if the walls are closing in around me.

I shake my head. "I don't think I'm understanding you."

"He finally gave me some concrete feedback about my proposal and would like to meet to discuss it further—"

"I'm not talking about the proposal!" I throw his clothes on the bed, wishing I could chuck them at his face instead.

Declan's brows pull together. "You're upset."

"No, Declan. I'm disappointed."

"You of all people should understand how important this is to me."

I throw my arms in the air. "That's exactly my problem. I understand your needs even at the expense of my own."

I instantly want to take back the words, if only to erase the scary expression on Declan's face.

"What do you mean by that?"

"I've spent three years of my life making sure you're taken care of, even if it meant sacrificing my happiness to do so," I blurt out.

So much for keeping yourself in check.

His lips flatten, turning the pink color white from the pressure of his grimace.

Abort mission. "Never mind—"

"Is that how you really feel?" he cuts me off.

It takes all my willpower to not break eye contact. "Yes."

"Why?"

His question throws me off. Does he actually care about how I feel? He has never made it a point in the past to check in with me about my needs, and there have been plenty of opportunities. Like the Christmas I missed because he planned a business trip or the hundreds of plans I had to cancel last minute because of some Kane Company emergency.

Over the last three years, my life slowly disappeared until my identity became *Mr. Kane's assistant.*

This is your chance to confess how unhappy you've become with your job. I open my mouth to speak my mind but something in his gaze stops me. The skin around his darkening eyes tightens.

His phone rings, cutting through the silence. The hand clutching onto it hesitates.

He doesn't want to deal with your shitty mood right now when he has more important things he needs to handle.

I put on my best smile that doesn't quite reach my eyes. "Forget it. I'm being extra grumpy from jet lag and waking up earlier than usual for our safari. It's nothing a cup of coffee can't fix."

His phone stops chiming. "Listen—"

"It's fine."

"I didn't expect—" The shrill ring interrupts whatever he was about to say.

"You better get that. Sounds important." I nod my head and offer him a tense smile.

His mouth opens, but I don't stick around. The last thing I hear before shutting his bedroom door behind me is his deep rumble of a voice barking an order at an innocent caller.

Declan, like the complete asshole boss he tends to be under most circumstances, sends me a recorded voice note requesting that I make a PowerPoint just in case Mr. Yakura wants a visual aid for his meeting.

The only visual aid I want is of my hands wrapped around Declan's neck, stopping his airflow.

Okay. Turn it down about ten notches.

Once I rein my temper in, I get back to work. It takes me two hours to create a PowerPoint based on our combined messy notes. What would take a normal person an hour to compile takes me double because I have to triple-check each slide for errors. The last thing I want is for Declan to berate me for a silly typo or incorrect punctuation mark.

After I finish the slideshow, I send Declan a message sarcastically asking if he needed anything else from me. I should have expected it would backfire. Declan throws task after task my way, each more irritating than the last.

Check in with our Tokyo sponsors to make sure they are still interested.

Contact the head of marketing and have him send me an estimated expense report.

Schedule me a last-minute meeting with Rowan before Yakura jumps on the video call.

The more demands he places, the stronger my anger becomes. I'm supposed to have ten days of vacation time. After being denied three years' worth of paid time off, I want my break.

I *need* it.

Maybe you want more than that.

My head drops into my hands as I let out a frustrated groan. While I appreciate my job and the many opportunities Declan has given me, I don't know how much longer I can do this.

Better yet, I don't *want* to do this.

I'm turning twenty-four this year and what do I have to say for myself? Most of my life revolves around Declan and making sure he has everything he needs to be successful. I even married the man so he achieves everything he dreamed of—all because I care about him way more than he could ever reciprocate. He gave me a chance when no one believed in me, and for that, I owe him.

My actions say more about me and less about him. I put my needs aside because I thought it would make me happy to help others. And while it feels great to see everyone else achieve their dreams, it leaves me with a gaping hole in my chest.

Nothing will change unless you do.

Maybe Cal was right. If I keep making excuses for myself, I will never find the right time to take the next big step in my life.

Yet you tried already and failed.

I sigh. Despite all the failures in my life, somehow not being hired for an entry-level HR position stings the most.

So what if you failed? You're never going to accomplish anything worthwhile if you keep to your comfort zone.

But what about Declan? The voice that has had far too much say over my past decisions speaks up. And like always, I listen, pushing aside my thoughts as I get started on Declan's next task.

CHAPTER SEVENTEEN

Declan

There's been something off about Iris ever since I told her we needed to cancel our safari for the day. I thought she would get over her mood by noon, but I was wrong. She only speaks to me through email, despite being a quick walk away from my bedroom, and she avoids all the common areas of the bungalow. The way she ignores me makes me far more frustrated than I would ever care to admit.

I consider checking in on her a few times but think better of it. Whenever she's gotten irritated at work, I've found it best to leave her alone to sort out her feelings. She knows the stakes here, and she of all people knows how much this deal means to me. It would be ridiculous for her to think I would tell Yakura no after the struggle I went through to get him on the phone.

Our meeting time closes in, and Iris still hasn't come to set up the computer. I grab my phone to call her, but it turns out that I don't need to. She walks into the living room with her laptop tucked beneath her arm.

The ever-present tightness in my chest whenever she is around intensifies as I scan her from head to toe. Gone are her usual high heels and dresses, replaced by an all-black outfit that accentuates every dip and curve of her body.

I stand taller in her presence if only to make her notice me. Except she doesn't as she busies herself with setting up the computer for our video call without sparing me a glance.

I somehow resist the temptation to grab her chin and force her to look up at me, instead settling on stepping in her way. "Ready?"

Her hand clutching the charging cable tightens around the cord like a choke hold. "Yup."

Still, her gaze doesn't meet mine. Her lack of acknowledgment shouldn't be a concern for me when I have more pressing issues to handle, yet I am acutely aware of the tension building between us.

I don't like it. Not one bit.

"Iris."

"Yes?" She assesses the log-in screen like it's written in Morse code.

"Tell me what's wrong so we can get on with our day."

She seems to not like my command based on the way she smashes her fingers against the keyboard. "Why would anything be wrong?"

"Quit the passive-aggressive attitude and talk to me." I cover her hand with my palm, stopping her typing.

"You're the last person I want to speak to right now." Her eyes finally slice into me as she steals her hand away.

What I find reflecting in them is not what I expected. She might as well wave a red flag above her head, warning me to stay away. Yet I find it impossible to ignore the way her eyes glisten.

I have come to realize that, while her smile might be my weakness, her damp lashes clinging together will surely be my downfall.

"Were you crying?" My next breath is pinched, the oxygen fighting its way into my strained lungs.

"No."

"You're a pathetic liar."

Her nostrils flare. She stands tall, barely reaching my chin. "You want me to be honest?" Her voice drops dangerously low.

"Yes."

"Even if you hate what I have to say?"

"I can assure you I've heard worse."

For a brief moment, her iciness melts away as her gaze softens. "Don't do that."

"Don't do what exactly?"

"Don't remind me that there's a human being locked up inside of you somewhere."

"What the hell are you talking about?"

Her gaze shifts away from me as she focuses on a far corner of the room. "I—" The chiming notification on the computer screen cuts her off. Her bitter laugh fills the room. "I'll leave you to it then."

Fuck the meeting.

The thought acts like a punch to the throat. My ragged inhale does little to calm me, and my thoughts spiral out of control.

You're losing sight of what's important.

I shake my head, sobering up as I unbutton the front of my jacket and settle onto the couch in front of the laptop. "We'll continue this conversation after." I leave no room for opposition.

"Of course, *sir*." Her snide remark bounces off me. She accepts the call and steps out of the frame.

"Hello, hello!" Mr. Yakura grins into the camera. I try to return the gesture, but the forced smile only makes him laugh.

I don't understand how he can be so damn happy all the time. He reminds me of a golden retriever—all smiles and good times. It's mind-boggling how someone like him, with all the power on his side of the hemisphere, can act the way he does.

Not everyone is a miserable fuck like you.

"No need to smile on my account." Yakura laughs.

"Good. It's not natural." And it requires using one too many facial muscles for my taste.

His chuckle eases some of the tension from my shoulders.

"Where's Iris?" Yakura asks as he scans the room for her.

"Here!" Iris steps behind me, using the back of the couch as a barrier between us. The scent of her, like a warm day at the beach, washes over me. I breathe through my mouth to spare my lungs another deep inhale.

"How are you?" Yakura asks, and some of the tension in my body disappears. Iris thrives under these kinds of circumstances despite my aversion to them. Small talk happens to be my least favorite form of communication, right up there with smoke signals and group texts.

Her smile seems far less forced than mine. "Everything is

great. Same old, same old over here. Just busy working my life away one day at a time."

Our eyes meet through the camera, and mine narrow in silent warning.

"Sounds like you need a vacation. Perhaps even a honeymoon from what I hear." He raises a brow.

Iris's smile drops a fraction before she bounces back. "I see you heard about our news."

"I'm a bit offended I found out the big news from my wife. I thought we were friends." He frowns.

Somehow that word seems to be haunting me regardless of the person. I'm not sure why people are so infatuated with becoming my friend. They would find me lacking in every way, from never remembering their birthday to always leaving their messages unread.

"I sent a wedding e-invitation to your assistant since everything was such a whirlwind, but it must have not made it to you." Iris pouts on command, like the idea of Yakura missing our wedding tears her up inside.

"She must have missed it. I get so many emails each day, I practically take up a whole cloud of storage space."

She waves him off. "No worries. It was spur-of-the-moment anyway." Iris lays her diamond-clad hand on my shoulder, and Yakura's eyes track the movement. I remain stiff in my seat as a burning sensation in my gut surges to life.

"I'd say. I never knew you two were together, although my wife had her suspicions. Part of me is annoyed she was right this entire time."

"Your wife is a smart woman," Iris says.

"How did you two keep it a secret for this long?"

"You know Declan. He always keeps his business and personal life separate."

"Don't I know it. He wouldn't even tell me his favorite color when I asked him."

"Green like a crisp hundred-dollar bill," she responds with a grin.

The urge to roll my eyes nearly overtakes me.

"Is that right?" Yakura's eyes brighten as he looks at me.

"Yes." *No.*

Iris gives my shoulder a pat of approval. Years ago, when Iris asked me about my favorite color, I told her I didn't have one. Naturally, given her frequent bouts of insanity, she adopted one for me. It's become a running joke on her end where every gift-giving occasion includes something green, as if oversaturating me with the color will make me like it.

It doesn't. If anything, it always reminds me of *her*.

"Well, I won't take up too much of your time. But while I have both of you here, I would like to discuss a unique opportunity regarding the Dreamland Tokyo proposal."

This is what you've been waiting for. My breath stalls in my lungs as I wait for him to continue.

"I would like to move forward with the project on a few conditions."

I don't blink. I don't smile. I don't do anything but stare into the camera, wondering how this proposal won him over compared to the others.

What changed?

Who gives a shit? All that matters is he wants to work together.

"Fantastic. The Kane Company would be excited to work with you and turn Dreamland Tokyo into a reality."

He nods. "I am excited as well. But I would like you to iron out a few last details before I present the deal to the board."

"Of course. Whatever you need," I reply despite the tiny tic in Iris's jaw through the camera.

Yakura claps his hands together as he reviews the changes he would like me to address, including Japanese sponsors he wants brought onto the project. "Great. Will it be too much trouble to ask for an updated proposal with a project timeline so I can share it with the company board this Friday?"

The hand on my shoulder tightens around the tendons, but Iris remains quiet.

"No trouble at all."

"Fantastic. I knew you would be up to the challenge."

I'd be an idiot not to. This project is supposed to be my first big move as the future CEO, and I didn't spend the last two years of my life working weeknights and weekends to squander it.

Iris's nails dig into the fabric of my suit. I look up at the computer screen to find her face devoid of any kind of emotion, which is a warning sign.

Her anger is warranted but some things take precedence. Opportunities aren't a matter of luck, but rather hard work and sacrifices. A few more days on the clock won't kill her. She will have plenty of chances to watch animals shit, fuck, and sleep, as long as we accomplish Yakura's request first.

Yakura nods. "I look forward to hearing from you soon."

The moment he hangs up, Iris rips her hand away from me.

"You find me that abhorrent?" I glare at her from over my shoulder.

Her eyes narrow. "You don't want my hands anywhere near your neck right now."

"I didn't know that was your thing."

"Murder?"

"*Kinks*."

Her eyes widen. "You're breaking a rule."

"Which one?"

"No flirting."

"Interesting. Are we just adding rules as we go now?"

"Yes, seeing as there is no how-to manual on faking a marriage."

"Does that make you feel better?" I ask in a bored voice.

Her brows pull together. "What?"

"Putting up a wall between us when things get too real for you."

She laughs, in a deep and wheezy way that borders on obnoxious. "I find it fascinating how you can say that with a straight face given how you treat everyone."

I shoot her a blank look. "I don't treat you like everyone else."

She knows more about me than my own brothers. For her to discount that…it raises my blood pressure.

"You're right."

The tense breath I was holding releases from my lungs. *She finally gets it.*

She continues, "There are moments you treat me great. I'd be stupid to deny that. But there are plenty of times when I feel like I don't matter. That my needs are merely collateral damage in your pursuit of whatever you think will make you happy."

I want to grab her by the shoulders and shake her until she starts making sense. Instead, I keep my hands to myself as I nod. "I see."

"You really don't." She offers me a tight smile that seems all wrong. "I planned this trip thinking we could have fun together. I thought…" She laughs, but it sounds off. "I don't know what I thought honestly, but I'm mad at myself for being surprised that all this even happened. I'm even more disappointed that I thought your work would only be kept to one day."

The victory I felt from Yakura's meeting disappears at her expression. Something about it raises every alarm in my head. "Iris…"

She holds up a hand. "It's fine. I'm going to take a walk."

"No, you're not." We are in the middle of nowhere, surrounded by wild animals and darkness. I don't give a shit how angry she is. I'll be damned if I let her walk out.

She raises her chin with defiance. "I didn't ask for your permission."

The back of my neck heats. "Then as your boss, I'm ordering you to get started on the updates Yakura wants. Time is of the essence."

Her entire body tenses. "Of course. I'll get right on that as soon as I submit my two weeks' notice, asshole."

Oh, fuck. She takes advantage of my stunned state and leaves the suite before I have a chance to stop her. The front door rattles as she slams it behind her.

Good luck trying to undo this mess.

CHAPTER EIGHTEEN

Iris

I wish I could say I'm some bad bitch that was willing to take a nice little jaunt around the safari lodge property. In all honesty, I had every intention of doing just that, especially after my fight with Declan.

But I'm not a bad bitch. Not in the slightest. All it took was some rustling leaves to have me hightailing my butt to our backyard and parking myself on a lounge chair. Instead of making my presence known to the big asshole inside, I kept the lights off. I could lie to myself and say I did it so I could see the stars better, but in reality, I wanted to be alone. He was so adamant about me not leaving to the point of being a complete dick, so I feel like it is only fair.

Well, you did tell your boss you're quitting. That's some bad bitch material that Cal would be proud of.

I groan. That was so stupid on my part. Instead of biting my tongue, I let my anger get the best of me. My phone buzzes for the fourth time since I walked out. Declan's name flashes across the screen, and I sigh as I answer the call.

Be an adult.

"Tell me where you are." His clipped voice rumbles through the phone.

"Out."

So much for acting mature. But seriously, who is he to order me around like that? Has he learned nothing from what happened earlier?

"I swear to God the moment I find you…"

His half-finished threat makes the back of my neck prickle.

What the hell?

"I'm fine."

"You're out in the middle of the fucking jungle."

I coo at him through the phone. "Technically it's called a bush. Not that you would know since you made me plan everything for a trip I can't even enjoy."

"Shut up and tell me where you are."

A soft laugh escapes me before I have a chance to kill it. "This is our exact problem." I keep my voice low just in case he is looming too close to the glass doors surrounding our villa. "You continue to order me around like some disobedient housewife, and I continue to push back."

"If you don't tell me where I can find you—"

"I'm lounging outside by the pool."

Our call disconnects. The pace of my heart increases with each second that ticks by. I clasp my hands together to stop them from shaking, not wanting Declan to pick up on my nerves.

The hairs on my arms rise at the sound of the sliding door opening. I refuse to look over my shoulder at Declan, so I keep my eyes glued to the starry sky despite the burning sensation spreading across my skin from his assessment.

Declan doesn't move for a whole minute. I consider him to be an expert when it comes to torture, given the way he makes me wait on pins and needles while he says nothing. While I have always admired his ability to make people crack under pressure, today I find it unbearable. I almost give in to the temptation to look over my shoulder and check on him, but I stay strong.

The wind conceals my sigh of relief as the sliding door glides shut again. Declan's shoes clap against the wood deck, the thudding matching the staccato of my heart. He lingers close by as if he wants to keep his distance.

I expect him to yell at me. Part of me thinks I deserve it after walking out on him in the middle of an argument. I know it wasn't the most mature thing to do, but I'm only human. While it takes a lot to make me explode, once I do, hell hath no fury like an assistant scorned.

The rebellious part of me stands by my decision, knowing something about him needs to give. I'm not a robot. I have feelings and dreams and a hope that I won't spend the rest of my life assisting him to achieve his goals while putting mine on hold. And if he can't see that, then maybe it's time I move on from my position.

I might have tried and failed before when I applied for a job transfer, but that's what life is all about.

"We need to talk."

My eyes slide from the stars to his face. I open my mouth to speak, but the words seem to get trapped in my throat. I'm not sure what to say. Declan isn't the type of man who wants to *talk*. That alone puts me on edge, and I become unsure of myself.

He takes a seat on the chair parallel to mine. Unlike me, he doesn't lean back, instead choosing to remain in an upright sitting position. The shadows cling to him like a cloak, concealing most of his face. I don't need any light to know he is focused on me. My body does the job for me, sending a shiver down my spine that has nothing to do with the temperature outside.

"I'm sorry." His voice can barely be heard over a gust of wind.

I turn my face away, shielding him from seeing how my eyes nearly pop out of their sockets.

He must take my silence as quiet approval. "I made a mistake."

I might need to take up learning sign language because I have officially lost the ability to speak. Declan doesn't apologize, and he sure as hell doesn't admit when he is *wrong*. That should serve as my first warning that something is off between us.

"I don't want you to quit." His admission hangs between us.

"Why? Because it would suck to find a replacement?"

"No one can replace you."

Who knew one statement could do a whole lot of damage to my heart? It beats harder, as if it wants to respond for me. "I can't do this anymore."

He sighs. "I know."

"I deserve better."

"That was never a doubt."

I tilt my head. "I'm not happy."

His reply doesn't come instantly, like the others. The silence eats away at my calm facade, and I find my fingers tapping against my thighs in a nervous pattern.

"It was wrong of me to make you work on your day off."

I deflect with humor, hoping to ease the tight ball forming in my chest. "Yeah. You're right. It was a total dick move."

The moonlight highlights his small smile, making the whites of his teeth stand out. "You have such a foul mouth."

"Is it just me or do you seem to have an unhealthy obsession with my mouth lately?"

"Who says it's unhealthy?"

Oh. My. Lord. Either Declan is flirting with me or I was murdered by a wild animal and have officially ascended into heaven.

Or hell. Depends on how you look at it.

My toes curl inside of my boots before I have a chance to squash the warmth pooling in my belly.

What has gotten into you? Toes curling? Next thing you know, you'll be swapping out your abstinence card for a healthy dose of Declan's dick.

Stop thinking about his dick!

I clear my throat. "It's fine. All is forgiven." I'll say just about anything to make him go away. There are far too many *feelings* happening inside of me to handle any more of this conversation. Scary kinds of things that I refuse to explore while he assesses me for weaknesses.

He rubs the back of his neck.

Is he...nervous?

No. There is no possible way.

Right?

I'm so mystified at the idea of Declan being self-conscious, I completely miss whatever he says. "What?"

"I called Yakura and told him we wouldn't be able to send him the proposal until we came back from our trip."

I nearly throw my back out from sitting up in my chair. "Why would you do that?"

"Because some things are more important."

Don't you dare ask.

My lips part.

No.

But, I counter.

Who cares why he did it? Asking him about it is a terrible idea. It almost seems forbidden in a way, which I know is ridiculous.

I ignore the strong voice in my head cautioning me away. "What things?"

He deflects. "Did you really mean what you said earlier?"

"You might have to clarify because I said a lot of things."

"That you have spent the last three years compromising your happiness by working for me?"

I release a heavy sigh. "I was angry."

"That's not an answer to my question."

I shoot him a withering glare. "What do you want me to say? I've been working for you for three years already and what do I have to show for it? I have no life, no friends other than Cal, and no future besides helping you accomplish yours. I married you despite all the red flags, and I'm supposed to give birth to a child knowing full well you want nothing to do with them. Of course I'm not happy. In fact, I'm terrified."

That last part hurts to admit.

He blinks. Once. Twice. Three times.

I thought I would feel better after pouring my heart out, but rather, I feel sick to my stomach. Declan is far from perfect in many ways, but that doesn't make him a bad person. He doesn't yell at me or call me names or make me feel uncomfortable. My pay is double the usual salary, and I've been able to save a nice nest egg because of that.

Is he the easiest boss in the world? Absolutely not. He expects just as much from me as he does of himself. His standards are as exacting as his attitude, but that doesn't mean he is unfair. If anything, he pushes me to do better.

And you just admitted how much you resent it all.

My stomach churns. "About what I said—"

"What would make you happy?"

I think being struck by a lightning bolt would have been less shocking than his question. Not once has Declan ever inquired about such a thing, and I'm not entirely sure how to go about answering it. Lots of things could make me happy, but there are very few within his immediate control.

"I—"

"Don't think. Just speak."

I take a deep breath. "First off, I want to be treated like a human being with wants, needs, and feelings."

"Unfortunately, evolution hasn't seemed to work out that little issue yet."

I glare in his general direction. "I'm serious. That means you respect my time, energy, and willingness to go above and beyond to make our fake marriage work. You need to remember that this isn't for *me*. You are the one who screwed up a perfectly good wedding contract with Bethany, and I'm the next best thing. I can be your asset or your enemy. It's up to you to decide."

"Anything else?" Humor seeps into his voice.

"*Are you laughing at me*?"

"Only on the inside."

My eyes narrow into tiny slits. "Yes, actually. There is one more thing. Stop calling Dreamland Tokyo *your* project. We both have spent two years working on that proposal together, and I lost about ten friends and a boyfriend in the process, so whether you like it or not, we're a team. I'd like to be treated as such from this moment on."

He rubs his stubbled chin. "That's a valid point."

I'm not sure whether Declan is appeasing me because he doesn't want to continue pissing me off or because he actually cares about how I feel. I'd like to assume it's the latter reason, but knowing him, he doesn't want to ruin his one shot of becoming CEO. And by making me unhappy, he risks a lot more than losing an assistant.

"Great. So now that everything is settled, I'm going to bed." I stand and take a step toward the sliding door.

"Don't be late."

I look over my shoulder. "For?"

"Our safari tomorrow."

"You want to go?" My pitch rises.

"*Want* is a bit of a stretch. But I am willing."

I grin. "Be ready by 5:00 a.m." I walk across the deck and pull on the handle of the sliding door.

"Iris?"

This time, I turn around and press my back against the glass. "Yes?"

"If you try to leave me again, I'll make you regret it." The slight rasp in his voice does something catastrophic to my lower half.

"Is that a threat?"

"It's a promise." His face remains blank, but his eyes rival the stars above us.

I blink. Somehow I pull myself together and nod before leaving the deck.

Declan's words follow me all the way back to my room, but it's not until I shower and crawl into bed that I realize what struck me as odd about what he said.

If you try to leave me again, I'll make you regret it.

Not quit but leave *him*. Such a strange choice of words for submitting a two weeks' notice, but I believe Declan considers them one and the same. I think he would see me quitting as a slight against him. Maybe he would even go as far as to consider it some kind of betrayal after all these years.

He doesn't need anyone. Cal's voice plays on repeat in my head.

Except maybe me.

CHAPTER NINETEEN

Iris

Unlike yesterday, Declan is already waiting in the main living space for me at 5:00 a.m. *Sharp*.

"You're late," he grunts.

I groan. "By two minutes."

"Here. Let's go." He slaps a Styrofoam coffee cup into my empty hand.

I blink at it. "Thank you?" I take a sip and sigh as the first dose of caffeine hits my tongue.

He makes a noise with the back of his throat. "No need to thank me. Offering you caffeine is solely for my personal benefit. It tends to make you much more compliant."

My jaw drops. "Excuse me?"

He doesn't bother answering me as he exits the bungalow.

"Someone is mighty eager to get going today," I call out to him after grabbing my backpack with all my supplies. The sun hasn't risen yet, so I'm stuck sticking close by Declan's side, using the lamps on the dirt path to guide us toward the meetup location.

"The sooner we get out there, the sooner we get this over with."

"Please keep your excitement to a minimum. I'm afraid the experience won't live up to your hype."

He shoots me a withering glare.

Someone is in a foul mood this morning. One would think I'm taking him to the electric chair with the look on his face. We make our way over to the main lodge, with me sipping my coffee along the walk. Declan seems determined to get to our destination as fast as possible, forcing me to match his speed.

I don't have legs like a giraffe, so I slow to a normal walking pace before my legs give up from exertion. "What's your hurry?"

"They said to be there at 5:15 a.m."

"It's a vacation, not a doctor's appointment. They can wait a few minutes."

Declan mutters something under his breath. I make a show of pulling out my phone and taking a few dark photos of some plants. He hates every second of it. His boots drag across this dirt path, tracking dust behind him as he taps away at his phone.

"What happened to taking the day off?" I ask.

Our eyes clash. Neither one of us looks away.

"I'm here, aren't I?"

"Yeah, with an attitude bigger than the state of Texas."

"I must not be trying hard enough if there's still Alaska to compete with."

His comment makes me curl over and laugh until I wheeze. Most people find him dry, sarcastic, and downright unbearable to be around for long periods of time, but I find him funny. Sarcasm might be considered the lowest form of wit, but I find it the most entertaining. I'm not sure what that says about me though.

I stand and collect myself. "How about we call a truce?"

"A truce?" He raises a brow.

I nod. "Let's spend a day pretending the rest of the world doesn't exist. No work. No Yakura. No regrets. Give me one single day of your time without any of the other stuff bogging us down."

"What do I get out of this?"

Well, that isn't exactly a no. "You get a happy wife who won't suffocate you in your sleep tonight."

"Think about it often?"

My grin makes my cheeks ache. "Depends on what true crime episode I'm inspired by that night."

He presses his lips together, stopping a grin from ever forming. I can imagine he has a beautiful smile, but I wouldn't know. I've never seen it. Not in all the years I've worked for him, despite all my best efforts.

"Fine. But only because I don't think you would survive a day in jail," he replies.

"You're right. Orange is so not my color."

And I swear Declan laughs on the inside.

By the time we make it to the truck area, I've drained the entire cup of coffee and feel much more like myself. The safari driver and guide both greet us. Neither of them complains about us being a whole ten minutes late, and I silently mouth told you so to Declan while they prep the truck.

"Are we the first ones here?" I look around the empty area around our idle car.

The guide looks at me with raised brows. "I thought you knew."

"About?"

"Our tours are meant to be a one-on-one experience so the couples can make the most out of their honeymoon together."

Well, I suppose I must have interpreted the website incorrectly. I look up at Declan and notice the vein above his right eye has appeared. *Great.*

He looks down at me. "At least I don't have to pretend to like people today."

A laugh explodes out of me. The driver and guide look somewhat horrified, so I calm their worries. "He's kidding…"

"I'm not," he replies dryly.

The driver forces a chuckle while the guide looks uncomfortably at me. "We should get going then. The animals wait for no one."

The driver hops in the front seat while the guide settles into the one hanging off the side of the vehicle. Declan gets on the special truck first. He extends his hand for me to grab, and I'm lifted onto the tall platform with ease. His hand tightens around mine, sending a current of energy up my arm.

He releases it like it burned him.

"So, what animals are you most excited to see today?" the guide asks.

"A leopard!" I clap my hands together.

The guide whistles before giving the driver a look.

"Is that okay?" I ask, concern etching its way into my voice.

He nods. "Of course. We do our best to find the leopards, but they're cunning creatures."

"Oh." My smile falls a fraction.

"We'll do everything we can to try to find them."

I nod. "Of course. No pressure."

The guide turns toward Declan. "And you, sir? What animal would you like to see?"

He gestures toward me. "Whatever she wants."

"You don't have a favorite animal?" I ask.

"Seeing as I'm not five, no."

I try to coax an answer out of him. "Come on. I know it was a long time ago, but think back to your childhood. There had to be at least one animal you liked more than the rest."

He shoots me a withering glare. "Elephants."

"*Elephants*?"

His lips twitch. "What did you expect? A lion?"

"Honestly? Yes."

"They're overrated."

"And elephants aren't?"

His eyes shift toward the landscape. "My mom liked them."

My chest tightens from his admission. The lost look in Declan's eyes threatens my control over my tear ducts. Something about the way he speaks of his mother always seems to soften me toward him like magic.

I don't think as I grab his balled-up fist and lace our fingers together. "She had good taste."

A noise gets trapped in his throat before he places his other hand on top of mine, securing it to his thigh. My body vibrates like I touched a live wire.

I look over at the guide. "All right, you heard the man. Let's go find him some elephants."

Declan and I have shared plenty of meals together over the years. While most have been strictly business, there have been a select few where we didn't have a set agenda to discuss. None of those even come close to sitting across from him now without any kind of distraction. No cell phones. No notes to take. Nothing but one another's company to keep us occupied.

But unlike past dinners, today screams romance.

It's a honeymoon. What did you expect?

Maybe something a little more discreet? When they mentioned a dinner under the stars in their brochure, I thought they meant a little sandwich and wine out of a canteen. What they really meant was a full-blown dining experience with white linens and top-shelf champagne.

And flowers. And a bonfire. And enough tension between Declan and me to suffocate anyone within a ten-foot radius.

"So isn't this lovely?" I offer a tight smile.

Declan pulls my chair out before situating himself in the seat across from me. Candlelight dances across his face, bringing out the sharp dips and contours.

My heart beats harder against my chest from the way he looks at me. Our guide breaks the silence as he pops a bottle of chilled champagne for us. For a second, I consider the idea of asking him to join us, with our driver, but he leaves before I have a chance.

"So…" I pour a glass of champagne and chug half of it.

"Why are you nervous?"

I should have known while I studied Declan's tells, he did the same. "I'm not nervous."

"You're chugging champagne like you won a Grand Prix."

I grin. "I heard that's the first step in becoming an F1 WAG."

"WAG?" His puzzled expression is cute.

No. Not cute! Declan and the word *cute* belong together as much as water and electricity. Both equally deadly.

I take another long sip of my drink. "Wife and girlfriend."

He flicks my wedding ring. "This Alatorre crush is spiraling."

"The man has his own charity. One that gives kids free prosthetics, for crying out loud. He is practically begging for the world to fall in love with him."

"I'm aware."

"You are?"

He shrugs. "I sponsor a few kids."

I shoot him a look. "Donating to charity as a tax write-off doesn't count as a sponsor."

The tic in his jaw makes an appearance. "Good thing I don't include it in the paperwork then. Wouldn't want my donation to be null and void." The bitterness in his voice makes me flinch.

Wait. Is he actually a *willing* sponsor? How is that possible? Declan has grumbled about every charity event we've attended over the years, and it took all my power to convince him to go every single time.

His hardened gaze switches from me to the stars above. A vein appears above his eye, and I'm hit with a wave of guilt so hard, breathing becomes difficult.

Shit. Here you are making assumptions about him when he is only trying to talk. I want to slap myself and go back in time if only to replace that look on his face.

"It was shitty of me to assume you were only doing it for a personal benefit."

He sighs, not breaking contact with the sky. "I don't give you a reason to think otherwise. It's not like I'm out here winning any Nobel Peace Prizes."

That he is not. He sure didn't earn his reputation as a heartless businessman for nothing. People think the CEO has all the power, but the man behind the spreadsheets calls the shots. Because if it doesn't make the Kanes any money, then it doesn't serve a purpose, which means it's cut from the program.

Welcome to the Kane Company, where employee wages are as dismal as company morale.

But still, my whole chest aches for him because obviously I have a thing for misunderstood billionaires. "It was stupid of me to say. I'm sorry."

"You know how I feel about apologies."

"Unless they're blood sacrifices made in your honor, don't bother."

The corners of his lips lift. *Got him.* My smile widens, which only makes his disappear before it had a chance to form into something devastating.

"What made you want to become a sponsor?" My question is innocent. An olive branch of sorts. It might be a selfish question, but I don't want to stop the conversation. This is a side of Declan I know nothing about, and I won't forgive myself if he closes back up again because of my stupid assumption.

His gaze slowly makes its way back to me. "I thought Santiago's comeback story was admirable."

I smile, grateful he offered more information. "See! Even you can't resist him! Face it. That man can wrap anyone around his finger, including you."

The corners of his lips rise. "He might have been the reason I donated in the first place, but I continued because of the kids."

"Kids?"

He pulls out his phone and taps the screen a few times. "Here."

I grab onto his phone like a national treasure. The first photo makes my jaw drop. It's one of a redheaded child flipping off the person taking the photo with one metal finger. "Cute."

"That's Freddy."

He knows them by name. My heart threatens to burst inside of my chest.

"May I?" I want to keep swiping through his photos and learn more about the man who hides himself away from the world.

I want to know *everything*.

He nods. I swipe through a set of photos featuring three other kids. Each of them have different prosthetics, with one child requiring four.

I recognize the location of one photo instantly.

"You all went to Dreamland?"

"They did."

Huh. "Where were you?"

"Working."

"You didn't want to go?"

"Does it matter?"

Yes! I want to yell, but my throat dries up and I lose all capacity to speak. The tightness in my chest intensifies, having everything to do with how he sent the kids to Dreamland together without him despite him *wanting* to be there.

I don't know why it makes me sad but it does. Maybe it's because Declan has his eyes set on a position he thinks will be the answer to everything, all while missing out on what life has to offer. And frankly, that's no way to live.

For someone hell-bent on succeeding at everything, he truly fails at life. I want to help him realize that there is so much more to everything than merely existing. That if he spends any more years skipping out on what is truly important, he might regret it later. No. He *will* regret it. I can guarantee it because there will always be some new goal he thinks will fill that gaping hole in his chest. All of them will fall short. It's a vicious cycle driven by one sad fact: he is looking for happiness in all the wrong places.

I spot all the signs I've become personally familiar with.

Then what are you going to do about it?

CHAPTER TWENTY

Iris

Heavy rain splatters against the deck, obscuring our view of the bush. Dark gray clouds block out any sunlight. My faith about going out on today's safari dwindles with each drop of water splashing against the ground.

"Do you think they'll still take us out today?" I ask, unable to stop the hope from seeping into my question.

A lightning bolt cuts through the clouds before a rumble of thunder shakes the glass.

He shakes his head. "We're not going out in a storm like that, regardless of what they say."

"But—"

"No."

I huff. "It's a summer shower. It'll be gone before you know it."

Lightning strikes again, filling the sky with a bright light. He shoots me a look that requires no translation.

"Fine. You're right." My bottom lip juts out as I pout.

"You're giving up already? At least make me work for it." His eyes rival the blinding light outside. The way he stares at me, with quiet challenge, has me wanting to push back.

"Part of me thinks you like picking fights with me because it's the only way you know how to keep me around."

A noise gets trapped in his throat. "Why would I want that?"

"Because I think you *like* talking to me."

"Is anyone else aware of what a narcissist you are?"

"I'm surprised you noticed with how obsessed you are with yourself."

He spoils me with a small smile that gives me the same rush of pride as climbing the tallest mountain. I grin back at him, and his eyes drop to my lips. The warmth in my chest reroutes itself toward a different area of my body.

"Admit it. You like hanging around me."

Now you're flirting with him?

His smile only expands. "I don't exactly hate it."

"Coming from you, that's practically a declaration of love."

He blinks, and I'm hit with the temptation to slap myself.

Ugh. Why did you phrase it like that?

Because you're too busy flirting to use your common sense.

"Well, this is my sign to go jump in front of the nearest moving vehicle." I turn away from the sliding door, desperate for some distance.

Run while you still can.

"What do you plan on doing today?" His question shocks me. I stop and look over my shoulder. "Why are you asking?"

"I'm curious."

"I doubt you're interested in whatever I have planned."

You don't have a plan.

Then I better think of one quick because the last thing I need is to spend more time with Declan. I'm already weak when it comes to him.

"Try me."

Fuck.

"I'll probably watch TV all day until my brain melts."

"Sounds absolutely riveting."

The glass door shakes with another rumble of thunder. I take it as my hint to get out of here before Declan asks me any more questions.

"At least you can spend the day catching up on work. I'm sure it kills you to be away from your computer for more than twenty-four hours." I send him one last smile over my shoulder before I exit the room.

The clapping of his leather shoes against the tile follows me all the way into the living room. I try to ignore him, but he makes it progressively difficult as he parks himself on the couch beside me, leaving only a cushion between us.

"What are you doing?" I frown.

"An experiment."

"Pardon?" I choke the remote control.

"I want to see just how many hours it takes before your brain melts. Strictly for scientific purposes."

Oh my God. Does he actually want to spend time with you outside of staged events and social media propaganda?

"You want to join me?"

"I have nothing better to do."

That has to be the biggest backhanded compliment I've ever received, yet it makes me smile nonetheless. Declan has plenty of things to do. He could spend the day catching up on work that is piling up during our vacation, but he would rather watch TV with me.

A fluttering sensation in my stomach makes me antsy. I shouldn't obsess over something as small as Declan sacrificing his work to spend time with me, but I do anyway. This is a man who will make business deals from his bed with a fever of a hundred and three. Him taking a day off to do nothing but watch TV is huge.

Don't get used to it.

Easier said than done. Because if Declan keeps doing sweet things like this, I might start craving them. And that can only lead to one thing.

Disappointment.

I turn on the smart TV, sign into my streaming service account, and choose my comfort home renovation show, hoping it can ease the anxiety bubbling inside of me. I tuck my legs under me and get comfortable. It doesn't take long for the weight pressing against my chest to lessen, and I'm grateful for it.

By the time the credits roll, I expect Declan to rise up and dismiss himself from the rest of my plans. He remains seated as the next episode starts automatically.

"You don't have to stick around if you don't want to." I offer him an out.

He only replies by grabbing the remote from the coffee table and putting the volume louder.

Well, that answers everything.

He wants to spend time with you.

My skin tingles in response, and I can't help hiding my smile with a throw pillow.

"Another one?" he grumbles before shoving a handful of popcorn into his mouth.

I swear Declan consumes more food than an entire football team. If it weren't for the fact that I manage his schedule so he can make time for working out, I would be concerned about the way he eats his way through my entire stash of snacks in less than four hours.

I hit the mute button, silencing the TV. "Do you have a problem with that?"

"You've watched eight episodes in a row of them doing the same exact thing."

"And I could watch eight more without ever getting bored." I steal back my bowl of popcorn from his lap. There's something calming about watching my favorite home improvement couple renovate dilapidated homes. The episodes are short and predictable, which makes them an easy choice when I'm feeling out of sorts.

"Why?" he asks.

"Because I'm getting inspired."

His brows pull together. "Don't tell me you actually want to do this one day?"

"Of course I do. It looks like so much fun!" Well, at least most of it. I could do without the leaking roofs and sewer issues that seem to pop up out of nowhere.

"They found a family of mice in the last home." The look of horror on his face makes me crack up.

"Nothing adopting a feral cat can't fix."

"I'm allergic to cats." His nose wrinkles.

"Good thing you don't have to worry about that then."

"Why not?" His voice drops.

I laugh and return my attention back to the screen. "Because it's going to be *my* house. If I want a pet cat, so be it."

"Is my house not good enough for you?" His voice comes off flat, but his eyes are anything but.

Where did that question come from and why does his face look like I'm personally attacking him?

"Of course your house is good enough. For now, at least."

"For now," he repeats with a dry voice.

"It's not like we planned on me living there forever."

"I know that."

"You have a very nice house." I backtrack.

"Not nice enough," he mutters under his breath.

Is he actually offended by my comments? The idea alone makes my chest clench. Declan isn't the kind to get offended by anything, but I suppose if I invested twenty million dollars into a home, I wouldn't want to hear negative comments about it either.

I dance between being honest and polite. "It's just that…it's not my style."

"And what exactly is your style then? A forest?"

My chest shakes as I release a loud laugh. "No."

"Then what's the issue?"

"Your place is empty, cold, and devoid of any kind of personality. It might be a house, but it's the furthest thing from a home."

He strokes his stubbled cheek. "That makes no sense."

"Let me try to explain."

"By all means, please do."

I take a deep breath, considering how I can explain such a dark part of my life without diving too deep into my emotions. Declan only knows bits and pieces of my past. Revealing too much could open myself up to growing closer to him, and that's the last thing either of us needs.

"My parents' divorce wasn't the most conventional." I swallow the lump in my throat.

Declan doesn't so much as breathe as I gather up the courage to continue.

"My father—if you can even call him that—was not a good guy. He was…mean." That feels like the understatement of the century, but I can't find it in me to say more than that.

Declan's hands clench against his lap. "Was he mean to you?"

I sigh. "Yes. But not nearly as bad as he was to my mom."

His upper lip curls with a look of disgust. "Don't do that."

My brows tug together. "Do what?"

"Downplay your experience because someone else had it harder than you."

I'm touched by his comment. I spent my whole life telling myself how things could have been worse. I've seen the stats on domestic violence. The way the vicious cycle continues until someone gets severely hurt, or worse, *dies*. Dealing with my father's anger and hateful words seemed like a small price to pay for the future I have now. For the one my mother has too.

Wetness pools at the bottom of my eyes, and I'm quick to blink it away.

Get ahold of yourself.

I muster up a deep breath and carry on, reminding myself of the whole point of this conversation. "Anyway…my mom and I moved out of my childhood house with two suitcases and a thick wad of cash she spent a whole year saving up. She tried her hardest to sell me on the idea of moving into a shoebox apartment with Nana. I spent a whole week crying, telling her I wanted to go home."

"What happened next?" He seems genuinely interested in hearing more, so it fills me with enough courage to continue.

"She taught me how anyone can buy a house, but not everyone can buy a home. With a house, you can buy it, sell it, renovate it." I point at the TV. "But a home is more abstract. It's not a place, but a feeling I can't describe, so you'll just have to take my word for it."

"A feeling," he repeats back with a monotonous voice.

"You know, those pesky emotions you turned off ages ago?"

He frowns. "That sounds like the biggest bullshit I've ever heard."

I laugh. "I knew you wouldn't get it." I have to give him credit for at least listening to my story.

"Only because you're terrible at describing things."

I grin. "Like I said, you'll know it when you feel it."

At least I would hope so. The idea of Declan never finding a place to call home saddens me more than anything about his past.

What are you going to do about it?

I have an idea, but its risks are nothing short of catastrophic. Still, I can't find it in me to stop the excitement bubbling inside of me.

You could be the one to help him make his house a home.

Worst idea ever.

CHAPTER TWENTY-ONE

Iris

Hey." Someone nudges my shoulder.

"Ugh. Let me sleep." I grab a pillow and cover my head to drown out Declan's voice.

"There's something outside you're going to want to see."

"Shh." I tug the blanket I was snuggled into over my head.

Wait. A blanket? I don't remember falling asleep, let alone having the energy to grab a blanket.

"This might be your one and only chance to see a leopard, so if I were you, I'd get up. Now."

"What?" I bolt upright on the couch. The muted TV still plays in the background. Somehow I ended up sprawled out on the couch, taking over my side and the place where Declan sat before.

Huh. Strange.

"Follow me." He leaves me running after him as he exits the living room.

The only source of light we have is the moon shining through the windows. Declan weaves through the house before taking me toward his bedroom.

"This better not be some ploy to get me into your room."

Despite the low light, I can make out the glare he sends my way over his shoulder.

"I'm joking."

"Good because I have no interest in doing such a thing."

Well, then. He doesn't need to sound *so* against the idea.

"Then why are we here?"

"I was in the middle of taking a shower when I noticed something outside." He walks straight into his dark bathroom.

I'm so focused on his story that I slip on a massive puddle. I slide straight into Declan's back, and he lets out an oomph. He struggles to maintain his balance, but his quick reflexes save us both from taking a tumble, although my chest takes a beating after running into pure muscle.

"Why is there so much water on the floor?" I catch the reflection of a trail leading from Declan's shower to the door.

"I was in a rush."

He bolted from the shower for *me*? I don't even know what to make of that knowledge except to concentrate on my breathing so I don't pass out from pure shock.

He doesn't give me a chance to harp on the details of him running out of the shower to come get me. His hand motions me forward, and I grab onto his extended palm. He helps me into the empty porcelain tub that is set up in front of a big window that faces a small river to the side of our bungalow.

"Look over there." He points into the darkness.

"What am I looking for?"

"You don't see it?" He frowns and leans forward.

I laugh. "It's pitch-black."

He squints and points. "Right there. Between the two trees in front of the river."

I try to see what he is looking at and fail. "Nope."

He leans in closer so he can use my hand as an arrow. "Right there."

"Oh my God." I blink again to make sure I'm not seeing some apparition. "It's a leopard!"

"Shh."

Who would have thought we would find one outside our bungalow of all places? We've been on countless safaris and come up empty every single time.

"How did you even see it? It's so dark outside."

"It set off the motion-sensor spotlight. I thought it would run away before I had a chance to come get you, but it seemed more curious than anything. Probably it was thirsty enough to stick around."

"Or hungry enough." I shudder at the thought. Declan and I have seen multiple animals all looming around the river, taking their fill of water. I'm sure some even sleep by it.

I don't know how much time passes, but Declan and I sit together in an empty tub watching the leopard as it prowls around the area. It feels like hours pass us by as the moon slowly begins its descent.

"Did it meet your expectations?" he asks as the leopard disappears back into the bush.

"Yes!" I turn and throw my arms around him. "Thank you for remembering."

His stiff arms eventually return the gesture, and I hold him even tighter against me. Neither one of us speaks. With the way my chest warms in his proximity, I'm tempted to stick around longer.

He clears his throat. "We should get to sleep. It's going to be a long day tomorrow."

My whole face feels like it could catch on fire. "Right. Of course." I disentangle myself from his grasp and jump out of the tub.

Declan stands and follows after me out of his bathroom. I'm careful not to slip on any more puddles, although it seems like enough time went by for them to evaporate.

"Thanks again. For all this."

He says nothing, but the satisfied look on his face speaks volumes. I escape his room and crawl into bed with the biggest smile on my face.

All thanks to Declan.

I drop my empty luggage by the foot of the bed so I can answer my ringing phone.

"Please tell me you're not pregnant."

"I'm sorry? Did you just ask if I'm *pregnant*?" I slam a fist to my chest twice to help me breathe.

"Yes."

"Why?!" I double-check my period tracker app despite the fact that I haven't had sex in months.

"You don't know," Mom whispers, as if she is talking to herself.

My knees shake, so I take a seat on the edge of the mattress. "What happened?"

"There are...stories coming out about you."

"*Me?*"

"And Declan."

My stomach drops. "Send them to me."

She makes a noise. "I think it's better if you don't see them."

Shit. Acid crawls up my throat as I ignore my mother and type my name into the search engine with shaky fingers. The results are horrifying. Each headline somehow seems worse than the last. Buzzwords like fake marriage, baby clause, and gold digger. News articles I can handle, but it's the comment sections that really sting. After the first one claims I don't deserve children because of the mockery I made out of marriage, I exit the internet application. If that's the first one, I can't imagine how awful the rest are.

My social media profiles are no better, with all of them being clogged with people sending me direct messages. Even a few direct *threats*.

My stomach churns. "None of this is true."

Except, isn't it?

I mute my phone and proceed to scream into the mattress.

Mom remains unaware of my breakdown. "Obviously not. I've seen the way you two interact. These soulless people are just looking to ruin anyone so they can sell a few copies."

I have no idea what my mom thinks she saw but I refuse to argue with her. There are way bigger fish to fry.

"What am I supposed to do?" My voice shakes.

"My poor baby." Mom's voice cracks. "I hate that they're saying these things about you. Them calling you a money-hungry…" Her voice drifts off, as if it pains her to finish that sentence.

Don't worry, Mom. It hurts me just as much. The amount of women who wrote nasty comments on my social media posts is nothing compared to the ones who privately messaged me their thoughts. I set my accounts to private, but the stain of their words still lingers.

I'm so close to cracking with each shuddery breath I take.

"Don't let these people get to you." Mom's voice stands firm, and it helps ease the smallest fraction of tension from my shoulders.

"It's a little too late for that," I grumble.

"They're nothing but rumors."

"Except everyone is talking about my marriage, including freaking *Finance Today*." I know I've officially hit rock bottom when the spreadsheet nerds are out to get me.

"They can say anything they want, but that doesn't make any of it true."

Oh, Mom. If only you knew. "But—"

"No buts. These reporters will come up with any kind of story to sell some papers. It's disgusting that they would come after your marriage like this, but I'm not surprised."

Me neither when I come to think of it. The timing is almost too perfect, with Declan and me being unable to do anything about it from here.

With each article I read, my anger intensifies. I know exactly who released these stories into the world, hoping for this kind of reaction. Seth Kane is lucky I'm thousands of miles away from him or else I would give him a piece of my mind.

Or fist.

I don't think anyone could read comments like that about themselves and not feel some kind of emotion toward it. But despite my feelings, I know who I am and what I stand for. Nothing anyone says will change my mind, but it doesn't mean their words still can't affect me.

Unlike Declan, I didn't grow up in this kind of world. I'm not accustomed to having my image plastered all over every celebrity gossip site, picking at everything that makes me who I am. It makes me want to hide away from everyone and everything, but it also makes me want to fight.

"I'm going to fix this." I hold my chin up.

"How?"

I won't allow logistics to kill my motivation. "I don't know yet, but I'll figure it out."

"Oh, baby. You can't change people's narratives. They are going to think what they want based on the facts they're presented with, and nothing you do will change that."

Mom's words cause a lightbulb to shine above my head—as if it was blessed by God himself.

What if I create a story so enticing, they can't help but want to change their view? I *can* control how people perceive us. It might take a bit of work on my end, but it has to be better than the alternative. Because if stories like this continue to pile up, Brady Kane's lawyer will most likely start questioning the authenticity of everything.

No. There is no way I will allow that to happen. I didn't go through all the trouble of marrying Declan so his father could ruin everything anyway. Seth Kane might have won this round, but he has a whole other thing coming if he thinks I'll let a few news headlines hold me back. While his sons have to remain diplomatic around him for the sake of investors and board members, I have no issues getting dirty.

He put a target on his back, and I can't wait to pull the trigger.

CHAPTER TWENTY-TWO

Declan

Disconnecting for the remainder of my honeymoon was a mistake. I have never spent an hour without checking my phone, let alone days.

This is what happens when you take a vacation.

During my time off the grid, someone leaked a story to the gossip magazines saying my marriage was staged. I don't doubt my father was behind this kind of campaign, although it will be difficult to prove it.

I have to give him credit. He was thorough, making sure to include a set of fake documents detailing shit Iris and I never even discussed in our contract. It portrays me as the exact monster the world expects of me. Headlines about a speculated inheritance. Interviews from soon-to-be ex-employees claiming my relationship with Iris came out of nowhere, all because of a clause from my grandfather about giving birth to an heir. There are even sonogram photos of a child who sure as shit isn't mine.

I wouldn't bat an eye at the headlines, but the way they talk about Iris… Now that is simply unacceptable.

You never cared about their opinions in the past…

That was before I had someone worth protecting from the scum of the earth. Iris isn't naive. She knows how the media portrays me and what might have happened if she married me. But this… Even *I'm* horrified at some of the comments.

I tuck my phone in my pocket before I smash it into a million pieces. "Call my lawyer when we land."

Iris looks up from her tablet. "What for?"

"I'm in the mood to make people miserable."

"Can it still be considered a mood if it's a constant state of being?"

I glare.

She holds her hands up in submission. "What's wrong?"

"I'm about to slap half of Chicago with a libel lawsuit."

Her lips form a small O as she nods her head. "Ah. So I take it that you saw the articles?"

I blink. "You know about them?"

She moves her head up and down again as her eyes shift away from mine.

"And you didn't think to tell me?"

Her heavy sigh battles to be heard over the engines starting up. "My mom called me while I was packing this morning and told me about them. I was hoping we would make it through the flight before you read them, but I see it was a lost cause."

"Why didn't you tell me the moment you saw them?" *And please tell me you didn't read the comments.*

"Because I didn't find it worth ruining our last day together with something like this."

"Who the fuck cares about that?"

She offers me a tight smile. "If you're worried about what the lawyer might think, I already have a plan. I refuse to let your father beat us."

Us. Not you. The idea of us working as a team against my father pleases me, but not enough to erase the anger I feel about her putting my inheritance first. "Fuck the plan and fuck my father. That's not what's important here."

She bats her lashes. "My, my, Declan. Are you offended for me?"

"They called you a money-hungry whore." My molars smash together.

"At least they chose a good photo of me for that one. The reporters over at the *Chicago Chronicle* weren't as kind when it came to my secret pregnancy announcement."

"*What?*" I can barely see past the black dots filling my vision as I pull out my phone again.

Iris places her hand over mine. "Don't worry about it."

I should be reassuring her. No one deserves to be talked about that way. While some comments are to be expected, like her only marrying me for a paycheck or my last name, the rest are despicable. They pick apart her looks. Her intelligence. Her *heart.* Each one makes me want to find the internet trolls who said something negative about her and strangle them with their computer cords. I'm hit with a burning desire to erase the first amendment from American history to prevent this from every happening again.

She gives my hand a squeeze, pulling me back from my murderous thoughts. "They're only words."

Inside, I'm seething. On the outside, I'm just as cold and calculated as the articles describe me to be. "I expected a different reaction from you."

What did you really think she would do? Yell? Scream? Cry?

Anything would be better than the current alternative of her trying to reassure me. I don't deserve it.

"I knew all of this would happen eventually." She shrugs as if none of this bothers her, but it's nothing but a lie. Her chin trembles and I find myself fisting my hands on my lap to prevent me from reaching out to comfort her.

Me comforting *her?* I wouldn't even know where to start with something so ridiculous. "I'll handle this."

She raises a brow. "What are you going to do? Defend my honor?"

"At the very least."

Her laugh eases some of the tension in my muscles. "Please don't do something stupid because you're angry."

"I won't."

She lifts a brow. "Or anything that could be deemed a felony."

"Is it still considered a crime if I don't get caught?"

Her eyes brighten, chipping away at the icy block of my heart. "Paying your way out of prison isn't something to show off about."

"What good is having all this money if I have to follow the law?"

"There are so many things wrong with that statement, I don't even know where to start."

"Then don't."

Her nose scrunches. "Moving on. We need to be strategic about all of this. I'm sure your grandfather's lawyer is starting to become suspicious about the legitimacy of everything."

Whatever good mood she brought about a moment ago is wiped away by her comment. How can she think about the lawyer during a time like this? For fuck's sake, there were people making death threats toward her.

"I don't care about the lawyer." At least not right *now*.

She looks at me like I grew a second head. "*Right*. Well, regardless of your current opinion on the matter, I have the perfect plan."

Seeing as her last plan ended up with us being married, I can only imagine how this one will go.

I consider going over to my father's house. The temptation to break his jaw rides me hard, but I hold back. Punching him would only make me feel better for a moment, while destroying everything he loves will have a much more satisfying alternative.

Growing up being raised by someone like him meant developing the same traits because to survive someone like him, I needed to evolve. I learned through painful trial and error to hold my cards close to my chest because to love something meant to risk losing it. I've loved and I've lost, and I despise both feelings equally.

A booming voice outside my office door, followed by Iris's shrill laugh, has me moving to the door and turning the knob. I open it to find Iris and my father in the middle of a death stare contest.

He smirks at me. "Perfect timing. Tell your bitch to heel."

I only manage a single step before Iris's fist flies, slamming straight into my father's jaw. Iris screams as her fist connects with his face. A chill runs down my spine, and I swallow back the acid crawling up my throat at Iris's cry.

He tests his jaw, rubbing the spot she punched with his palm. "You fucking—"

I see red as I lunge for my father, but my attention shifts when Iris lets out a whimper.

"Ow." A single tear slips down Iris's cheek as she checks out her fist.

I don't think as I jump into action. She hisses at me when I try to assess her hand, all while she swipes the tears off her face with her uninjured hand. Something definitely doesn't look right with her pinkie, and she winces as I lightly run my finger over it.

"That doesn't feel too good—" Iris curses as she brushes her thumb across her knuckles.

"That's what you get for thinking you could lay a hand on me."

I swear this man has a death wish.

"Oh, I'd like to lay more than a hand on you, you evil fucker." Iris tries to step around me, but I block her path.

"I'll handle this." I give her shoulder a reassuring squeeze.

Her brows pull together as she shuts her mouth.

"I was coming here to check in on Iris and see how she was holding up after those articles came out. I'm sure it can't be easy being referred to as a mindless slut—"

Bone crunches beneath my fist as I slam it straight into my

father's nose. A deep sense of satisfaction fills me as his head rears back, rolling with the momentum of my punch. Blood gushes down his face and drips onto the carpet.

I grin at the mess.

He tries to staunch the bleeding, but nothing seems to work. "Looks like you're more like me than I thought."

Something dark takes over me. "Get out!" I roar as I lunge at him. My fingers grip onto air as he stumbles backward, tripping over his shoes as he holds his head back.

The pressure in my chest doesn't lessen as he disappears through the double doors. Hopefully he returns to whatever corner of hell he crawled out of before I have a chance to get my hands on him again.

Iris huffs. "Well, that didn't go exactly as expected."

I turn around, finding her hand clutched to her chest. Her twisted expression has my blood rushing to my ears.

"Please tell me that wasn't the big plan you've been working on."

She scoffs. "No. I got a bit derailed, but rest assured, my other idea is foolproof."

"I'll be the judge of that given your current track record."

She laughs before wincing at the hand pressed against her chest. "Ouch."

"Let me have a better look." My pulse quickens as I assess her injury. I'm careful not to touch the skin near her knuckles, keeping mind of the swelling. It doesn't look like an open fracture so at least that is good news. "You're insane. There's no other explanation for why you would punch someone in the face without knowing how."

"I thought it would be like the movies." She flinches as she checks out the damage.

"We need to get you to the hospital to have it checked out." I choke on the words, unable to process the reason I decide to make that call. I fucking despise hospitals.

"No! I'm fine. See!" She wiggles her fingers and recoils.

I'm hit with the urge to go find my father but hold back.

"Why would you punch him?"

Her jaw locks together, and she looks down at her purple heels.

I lift her chin with my finger. "Tell me."

She sighs, and it takes an exorbitant amount of effort not to shake the answers out of her.

"Promise not to do anything illegal if I tell you?"

"No."

Her head drops. "You're not going to be happy."

"I'm never happy." Except for rare occasions. All of which Iris is a part of.

She looks back up at me. Her eyes have a sheen to them that has nothing to do with her injured hand. "He offered me money to…"

"To what?" Every muscle in my body tenses.

"To prevent me from having a baby. *Ever*." She looks away as if she can hide the way her face is a wreck of emotions.

I'm already halfway out the door, body hot to the touch and my head empty of any thoughts besides finding my father and pummeling him into the ground.

I should have known he would try to pull off a stunt like this. Part of me had stupidly hoped he would have some sense of decency left, but it seems he doesn't have a moral bone left in his body. I underestimated just how far he would go to retain his position as CEO. Because without it, he would have nothing to live for. His kids hate him and his wife is dead. Losing his executive position would be the last blow in his miserable life.

Iris grips onto my arm and tugs me back. "Wait!"

"I can't talk to you right now." I can't talk to *anyone*, let alone her.

You're the one who brought her into this mess. What did you expect?

Blood heats beneath my skin. I try to shake her off, but her hold only grows more desperate.

"I need you to take me to the hospital."

I pause, seeing through the cloud of red haze blocking my decision-making. "What?"

Her misty eyes lock onto mine. "I'm in a lot of pain."

Fuck. I release a ragged breath and shut my eyes. "Harrison will take you."

"Please don't make me go alone." Her plea is my undoing.

My plan to send my father into a coma slips away as I shut my eyes and nod my head. "Fine. Let's get you to a doctor."

CHAPTER TWENTY-THREE

Declan

Since Iris is unable to hold a phone herself, I'm tasked with typing everything she dictates. I knew Iris handled a lot, but I didn't fully realize the depth of her job until she had me working through each task with her.

No wonder she isn't happy. The number of emails she has to sift through in a given hour would drive anyone insane. Or maybe I'm just going crazy by sitting this close to her. The smell of her coconut soap is permanently ingrained into my memory as she sits flush against me, pointing at different emails with her uninjured hand.

I can tell her nerves grow stronger as we near the hospital. Her knees bounce up and down as she dictates message after message I need to send, altering my entire schedule for the day.

The work doesn't stop there. After we check in, a nurse

hands us a clipboard filled with pages of information that need to be filled out. Iris stares at it like it might catch on fire at any moment.

"Here." I pass it to her.

Her eyes shift toward the exit. "Will you help me please? I can't write like this." Her voice drops to a barely audible whisper.

"Okay. Tell me your answers and I'll write them down."

Her throat bobs as she scans the first line. It takes her far longer than necessary to read the first question, so I busy myself with my phone.

"Do you mind reading the questions aloud for me? I'm too stressed to concentrate right now." Her overcompensating smile irritates me.

"Are you sure? Some of the questions are probably personal."

Don't be a dick. Just do what she says.

"I don't care." The rigid way she sits in her chair says the complete opposite.

She seems to be one minute away from breaking down, so I concede. I sigh as I grab the pen and get started on the first question. The paperwork doesn't take us as long as I anticipated, so Iris and I sit together in silence. She stares at the exit longingly. The way her eyes dart around the room as she gnaws on her bottom lip makes me feel merciful enough to save her from the anxiety eating her up inside.

"If it's any consolation, I hate hospitals too."

Her head swings toward the direction of my voice. "You do?"

I nod. "Haven't been to one since I was younger."

"Why?"

My chest heaves as I consider the potential consequence of

admitting my reason. I keep my eyes focused on the soundless television playing in one corner. "We spent a lot of time in hospitals while my mom was sick. I grew to resent everything about them, even long after she passed."

Her good hand clasps onto mine and gives it a squeeze. I'm grateful she understands me enough not to ask any follow-up questions. The idea of offering another raw part of myself feels like a betrayal to the years I've spent carefully developing a certain kind of persona.

"I hate them too." Her voice cracks.

"Why?"

She stares down at her swollen hand. "My dad…" She pauses, and I give her hand a reassuring squeeze like she gave me. "Let's just say my mom ended up in the ER a couple times for being *clumsy*."

I take a deep breath to stave off the anger bubbling beneath the surface. "And did you have issues with being *clumsy*?" If she says yes, I swear to God two men will end up floating in the Chicago River tonight.

She shakes her head rather aggressively. "No. *No*."

My rapid heart rate can be heard through my ears. "If you were, you can tell me." While I can't promise I won't do anything about it, I can promise to make him hurt. *A lot.*

The overwhelming sense of protectiveness hits me hard, and I don't shy away from it. There is nothing I hate more than men who use their fists against innocent women and children.

"It never got to that point. Nana made sure of it."

"How?"

"She caught onto the signs and interfered before things got

bad. Used her savings from my grandpa's life insurance policy to help Mom get a divorce and start a new life." A tear slips down her face, and I can't stand the sight of it.

I brush it away with the pad of my thumb, but the damp trail still lingers. A driving force inside of me wants to erase the sad look on her face. "Did Nana's plan also happen to include a jug of sulfuric acid?"

She forces out a laugh. "I think concrete shoes were more in style back then."

I fake shudder. "Remind me to never make Nana angry."

"Forget Nana. You'd have to deal with me." She holds up her injured hand like a war trophy.

"I'm absolutely terrified."

"Mrs. Kane?" a nurse calls out.

Iris doesn't move at the sound of her name.

"That's you." I place my hand on her thigh and give it a squeeze.

She sucks in a deep breath as she stares down at my hand. Her chair nearly tumbles behind her as she bolts out of the seat, throwing her one good hand up in the air. "I'm here!"

The nurse leads us through the emergency room bay. Individual beds line the wall, each area divided by a paper curtain.

The empty bed meant for Iris is unacceptable. Between the person retching behind one partition and the individual on the other side hacking up their lung, I refuse to let her be seen here.

I speak up. "I'd like my wife to be taken care of in a private suite."

The nurse grimaces as her gaze flicks across my body. "This is a hospital. Not the Ritz. Take a seat and wait for the doc like everyone else."

Iris hops on the bed without any complaint, and I'm tempted to grab her and go elsewhere. The nurse doesn't seem the least bit bothered by all the noise happening around us as she checks Iris's vitals and asks some routine questions.

Iris answers each one while chewing her bottom lip raw. This atmosphere couldn't put anyone at ease, least of all her.

The nurse hangs the clipboard at the foot of the bed, and I decide to try again.

"I'll pay whatever it takes to have her seen somewhere quieter. Money is no object."

The nurse only replies by shutting the paper curtain in my face.

Iris laughs while I stare at the curtain, dumbfounded to be treated like this.

"You find this funny?"

She nods, her eyes alight for the first time all day. "Did you see her face when you said money is no object? I think if she didn't put the clipboard away, she would have slapped your face with it."

"It's not my fault she isn't accustomed to how things are done in the real world."

"Wake up, dear. You're living in the real world." She waves around our *room*.

"It's terrifying."

"Come here. I'll make it better." Iris pats the bed.

Doubtful, but I'm a glutton for giving her what she wants lately. Paper crinkles as I sit next to her. I take up most of the bed, giving her little room to get away from me. My thigh brushes against hers. She tries to scoot away, but there isn't enough space.

"Isn't this cozy?" she quips.

She eyes the IV bag with horror before checking out the exit.

"What's wrong?"

She leans closer to me and whispers, "Is now a bad time to admit I pass out whenever someone tries to stick a needle in me?"

My lips lift at the corners. I find the idea hilarious, given her fearlessness in most circumstances. "You're afraid of needles?"

She sputters. "No. I'm not afraid. It just happens to be a bodily reaction I can't control."

"That's good then because the nurse needs to set you up with that IV when she comes back."

"No! Don't tell me that! I thought she was one of the good ones."

I nod, pressing my lips together to prevent myself from laughing.

"She lied to me!" She bolts from the seat and would have tripped over her own heels if I didn't reach out and catch her.

"Careful." I place her back on the bed and decide to stand guard in case she gets any ideas to flee the scene.

Her eyes flit from me to the gap between two curtains, as if she is thinking how she can get past me.

"I'm joking."

She scans my face for the truth before she slaps my shoulder with her good hand. "Asshole! I believed you!"

Laughter explodes out of me like a bomb, stunning her.

"Did you just laugh?"

"No."

"Yes." Someone calls out from the other side of the curtain. "Now, do you mind shutting up? Some of us are trying to get some sleep over here after having our stomach pumped."

Fuck this place and the people in here. "We're leaving."

"Not so fast. You can't leave before I check you out." The doctor strolls in and points at the bed with his clipboard.

Iris remains tight-lipped as the doctor checks her chart. He asks her some questions about how she got hurt, all while staring me up and down like I'm the person she was trying to injure. She is taken away for a few scans, and my breathing doesn't return to normal until the nurse brings her back.

That should be my first sign that things are getting out of hand on my end. I'm inching closer to an emotional minefield without any kind of map, only one wrong step away from exploding.

The doctor checks the scans. "It looks like you have a boxer's fracture."

Her face brightens. "That sounds badass."

I glare at her. "Calm down, Muhammad Ali. I wouldn't count today as a victory by any means."

The doctor's eyes lighten. "Next time, avoid any initial contact on the fourth and fifth knuckles."

"Please don't encourage her."

The doctor shakes his head with a laugh before giving Iris a detailed set of instructions regarding the healing time. I'm skeptical about the whole visit and, given the setting, doubtful about the level of care. I'll be damned if Iris sustains permanent injuries because of my father. My chest tightens at the idea.

"Great! Thanks, Doc!" She hops off the bed, but I hold my arm out, stopping her.

"I'd like a second opinion." The command bursts out of me without any rhyme or reason. Deep down, I know a boxer's fracture isn't the worst thing that could have happened. But things aren't right in my head where Iris is concerned. At least not anymore.

Both of the doctor's eyebrows arch. "For a small fracture?"

"Don't mind him. He tends to be a bit overbearing." She shoots me a look as if I'm the crazy one out of the two of us.

"Okay..." the doctor says.

Maybe I am losing it because why else would I care?

You hate when she cries.

You wouldn't mind murdering someone who hurt her.

You took her to the hospital even though you despise them with every fiber of your being.

The signs all point to one thing: our situation is quickly crumbling, and I'm the only one to blame.

Iris interrupts my thoughts. "I'll be sure to wear the brace for a few weeks and avoid any kind of activities that could aggravate the injury."

"Perfect. And don't forget to schedule a follow-up visit with your physician." The doctor gives me one last look before handing Iris the discharge paperwork. "Nice meeting you, Mrs. Kane."

"Will you help me with this?" She holds out the clipboard with her left hand as the doctor leaves.

I huff as I grab it from her and fill it out.

She checks the time on her phone. "Well, at least that didn't take as long as I thought it would. I'm sure you're dying to get back to work."

That's the scary thing. I didn't think about my job once during our entire time here because making sure she was taken care of was my only concern. I've spent the past fourteen years of my life thinking solely about work, and all it took was one woman to make me completely forget about my responsibilities for a few hours.

As if that doesn't scare me enough, it only takes one glance at her makeshift brace to make my blood burn hot under my skin. I know exactly why her injury angers me more than anything else. It's the same reason I feel an urge to push Cal away from her whenever he gets too close or the way I unexplainably need to see her whenever she is out of my sight for longer than a few hours.

You care about her.

Fuck.

The first stop after dropping Iris off at the office is my father's town house. His assistant let me know he took the rest of the day off due to an "unforeseen illness," so it's not hard to pin him down.

I almost expect him to ignore me waiting at his front door, but I should have guessed that he is too prideful to look weak in front of me.

He opens the door, and I blink at the damage of his face. His nose is a mess of cartilage and bruising, and it feels like I'm looking in a mirror. I don't need to reach out to touch the slight bump on my nose to remember it's there. A bump he caused after a heavy punch and too much alcohol. My stomach rolls from the realization that I'm no better than him, lashing out with fists when provoked.

You won't make the same mistake again. You can learn to be better.

Despite my reassuring words, I find it hard to battle the chilling realization.

"I doubt you came here to stare at your handiwork, so get on with it or get off my damn porch."

"I came by to drop something off." I slap a thick file against his chest.

I have one for every person in my life. Secrets are as good as any currency, and I happen to be filthy fucking rich, all thanks to the private investigator I have on retainer.

He opens the file before shutting it not a minute later. "I see."

"Take your time and have a good look. I'm particularly fond of the reports from previous teachers going into detail about your abuse, although the hidden hospital visits for broken bones are particularly compelling. There's a USB attached to the back that includes some videos of our more public altercations as well, just in case you want some visual context of what's coming if you mess with Iris ever again."

"Why are you showing me this? Why not go out and share it with everyone so you can take over my position?"

I release a bitter laugh. "Because I don't need to resort to your level to steal your position, but I'm willing to do so if you ever pull a stunt like today ever again."

"You would ruin our family's reputation for her?"

"We aren't family. You made sure of that the moment you told my wife to get her tubes tied, you fucking monster." My hands clench by my side, but I hold back from throwing another punch. I'd rather use words as a weapon than my fists.

"I'm trying to save you the mistake of having a child with someone purely for an inheritance. You should be thanking me."

Deep breaths, Declan. Deep fucking breaths.

"If I catch you talking to Iris again, whether about business or not, I'll release this to the public. No questions asked. No second chances. I don't care if you need to use a damn smoke signal to get in contact with me, so long as you leave my wife out of it."

"You'd publish this even if it makes you look weak?"

"That's the thing, *Father*. I spent plenty of years thinking I was pathetic because I couldn't fight you back, but I eventually realized the only weak man here is the one staring right at me. In one way, I guess I'm glad Mom is dead because at least she doesn't have to face the disgusting excuse of a human you've become." I turn, feeling his burning gaze following me all the way back to my car.

CHAPTER TWENTY-FOUR

Iris

Declan has been abnormally quiet ever since our trip to the hospital yesterday. I try to pry him away from his foul mood with a few comments, but it only seems to make him frown like I'm some nuisance.

If possible, the next day back only gets progressively worse. I can't type with my right hand, so I'm limited to pecking individual keys with my left index finger. I'm tempted to throw my keyboard at the wall after only half an hour of working on a spreadsheet. Instead of resorting to violence, because we all know how that went last time, I text my knight in shining Armani.

Cal strolls into the office thirty minutes later. "I always thought it would be Declan who showed Dad what it felt like to be on the receiving end of his parenting style, but it turns out you did the favor for him."

My chest aches for the children who grew up with such a

cruel father. If only I could go back in time and throw a real punch.

Cal's gaze narrows. "Don't look at me that way. I don't have nearly as many daddy issues as the other two."

"That's because you have a whole host of other problems."

"It makes me layered."

"No. It means you need to seek therapy."

He laughs as he pulls out the metal chair across from me. "I've been there. Done that. Turns out if you're not interested in changing, they can't help you much."

I shake my head. "Imagine that."

He grins. "So I heard you needed my services."

"Depends. How flexible are your plans over the next few weeks?"

"For you? Consider them canceled."

I release a sigh. "I seriously owe you one. I can't get much done with this brace when it takes me twenty minutes to type a single paragraph."

"You're going to regret asking for my help."

"Probably, because you can't focus for shit, but I'm all out of other options. I'm not about to spend hours next to a temp. At least this way you can make my job slightly more bearable."

"You sure know how to flatter a man."

"Declan doesn't seem to have a problem with it."

"Because, most days, he can barely be classified as human, let alone a man."

Oh, he's all man all right. I've seen the evidence in vivid detail.

Cal shudders at whatever expression is on my face. "Oh God. Whatever put that look on your face needs to go. *Now*."

Declan's mood deteriorates over the next few days. I'm almost hesitant about introducing my plan, but after all the work I put into it, I can't go back now.

"Why are we stopping?" Declan reaches out to press the driver's call button, but I stop him.

"Welcome to phase one of Operation Fake Dating."

He turns in his seat and stares at me. "What are you talking about?"

"This is my plan. Together, we're going to squash any doubts about our marriage, starting tonight."

His lips curve downward. "With fake dating? What does that even mean when we are *married*?"

"It's simple really."

"I'm burning with anticipation here," he deadpans.

I ignore his mood. "I planned a few public outings to make sure we are seen by anyone who is anyone in Chicago."

"You lost me at public outings." He reaches for the call button, but I latch onto his hand to stop him.

I release him instantly, afraid a torrent of butterflies might take flight in my stomach if I touch him for longer than a second. "I know you want to stay hidden away in your suburban mansion, but avoiding the press isn't going to solve any of our problems."

"It's worked before."

"I'm sure it has, but are you willing to bet your twenty-five-billion-dollar inheritance on it?"

I'm surprised he can get any words out with the way his teeth grind together.

"No."

"I'm going to need you to trust me on this one."

He remains silent, so I take it that he is willing to hear me out.

"I booked us a reservation for two at La Luna with a table overlooking the river. It took a lot of finagling to get one at the last minute, but I know a guy."

"Does his name happen to be Benjamin Franklin?"

I grin. "Bribes work wonders. You taught me yourself."

It feels good to return to our regularly scheduled programming—even if it is only for a night. With him ignoring me for days, I kind of missed our back and forth.

"Why did it require a bribe in the first place? You could have told them it was for me."

"You think that highly of yourself, don't you?"

He shrugs, and I roll my eyes.

"For your information, name-dropping wouldn't have worked here because I had a very special request that required some monetary motivation."

"I'm hesitant to ask, but I feel legally obligated to as your husband."

I laugh as I clap my hands together, leaning more toward evil genius rather than angelic. "Our table happens to be right next to the *Chicago Chronicle*'s lead gossip columnist's."

His spine straightens. "Now I'm intrigued for a very different reason."

I glare. "I didn't go through all this trouble for you to blow it by doing something stupid."

He releases a heavy sigh. "How can you be sure they're here tonight?"

"I'd tell you, but then that would make you an accessory to the crime."

He shakes his head and looks out the window, but I make out a faint smile in the reflection. "You expect me to sit next to someone who called you a brainless babymaker and do nothing about it?"

"Aw. You actually sounded insulted for a second."

He mutters something under his breath.

"Listen up. The plan is simple. We go to dinner, have a drink, and pretend we're in love."

"Because we're fake dating," he replies back with a robotic voice.

Finally. "Right! Now you're getting it."

"Dating you would be…"

I cut him off, growing more nervous with each judgmental stare he sends my way. "Painful. I don't need you to tell me twice."

His lips press together as he stays silent, scanning my face like he's taking an MRI of my soul. "Yes. Painful is exactly how I would describe this situation." His voice is devoid of all emotion, and a chill spreads across my skin.

I swallow back the uncertainty and steel my spine. "Great. Now that we're on the same page about all that, are you good to go? They'll give away our table if we don't show up in the next five minutes."

"I'm only agreeing to this scheme because you broke a few laws to make it happen."

"If I ever get caught, it's a good thing I have you to bail me out of jail."

"Who says I wouldn't be in there with you?"

My grin might make my cheeks hurt, but his small smile causes my whole chest to ache.

Well, that shouldn't be happening.

Avoiding your feelings doesn't make them any less real.

Oh, shut up.

Plan a fake date, they said. *It'll be easy.*

Said no one ever.

The hostess, who is now five hundred dollars richer thanks to me, guides us to the table located right beside the reporter. That's all I can think of as Declan's mask of indifference slides in place and his palm finds the small of my back. The warmth emanating off him bleeds into my skin, and I'm tempted to shimmy closer to him.

"Anything else I can get for you, Mr. and Mrs. Kane?"

The redheaded reporter looks up from her menu. A flicker of surprise passes over her features as her eyes scan Declan from head to toe.

I shake my head as Declan replies for us, "No, thank you."

Declan's hand breaks contact with my back as he pulls out my chair. I take a seat, and he pushes me closer to the table. Unlike other times, he doesn't step away, but rather he leans forward.

His lips brush against the shell of my ear as he whispers, "You better be right about this."

I shiver. "Have a little faith in me."

"I'm a bit hesitant given your track record." He chuckles, sending those butterflies in my stomach on fire.

"I take offense."

"Forgive me." His teeth graze the tip of my ear, sending another current of energy through me.

Is this part of the show? I'm extremely confused until I catch Declan's eyes connecting with the reporter's.

I release a pent-up breath as Declan pulls away and drops into his seat across from me. The weight of his stare presses against my chest like an anvil, making each inhale progressively more difficult.

I look past him only to lock eyes on the reporter. She types away on her phone, completely ignoring her date.

Something tells me she is taking notes.

Time to put on the show of your life. "I wish we were still on our honeymoon."

Go along with it, I say with my eyes.

"I do too," he says, without an ounce of sarcasm.

Huh. Does he actually mean that or is he lying to appease our audience? The first thought makes me push for more. "Why?"

"Because it turns out vacations aren't the worst thing in the world."

"Told you!"

His lips curve at the corners, but he remains quiet.

"What changed your mind?"

He leans in. "Not having to think about anything but which way I wanted to fuck you next."

My sharp inhale isn't staged. Neither is the way my heart beats like a war drum against my chest. My eyes flick between his burning gaze and the reporter's flushed face.

"What are you doing?" I lean in and whisper with a forced smile. Although my gaze is locked on Declan's, I can feel the reporter's eyes tracking my every move.

He reaches out and tucks a braid behind my ear. "Selling a story," he whispers.

"Then settle down, Romeo. This is a romance, not a porno."

The way his eyes brighten has nothing to do with the candlelight. "Fine." He grows bolder with his touches as his thumb traces my bottom lip. It sends a rush of warmth through my body.

"So, I was thinking…" I speak louder, gaining the attention of my target.

"That can never be a good thing."

I laugh as I shove his shoulder. "Shut up. We both know you actually like my brain."

"I like your heart more."

For someone who sucks at using anything but grunts and orders to communicate, he sure knows how to make my insides melt from a single sentence.

Except it's all a lie. "That's…sweet."

His lips press together in a thin line. I wonder if he does it to stop himself from laughing aloud.

"Anyway…I thought we could do something fun this weekend."

"Define *fun*."

"I want to host a little family get-together."

His eyes speak of a hundred unspoken promises. There is no way he will go along with this plan, but it's fun to pretend for the reporter's sake.

"What kind of get-together?" he asks through gritted teeth.

"An F1 watch party!" This time, my smile is genuine. The idea seems like the perfect way to help Rowan and Declan get over their disagreement. Plus, I would love to spend more time with Zahra, even if it's only for a couple of hours.

"No."

I frown. "Why not? Rowan will be in town for a budget meeting, so it's the perfect time for all of us to get together."

He avoids my gaze as he assesses his menu. "That's our thing."

The way he says it makes my body buzz. "If you had it your way, everything would be *our thing* so that you never had to share me with anyone else, you territorial caveman."

"I'm glad you finally understand. It took you long enough."

Through the corner of my eye, I catch the reporter smiling at us.

"You can turn it down a notch. We're married now. No one is going to swoop in and take me away from you. Although…"

"*Don't.*"

The reporter scoots her chair a few inches closer.

"I would leave you for one man and one man only."

He raises a brow. The reporter nearly tumbles out of her chair from the way she leans forward to hear us.

I throw my hands up in mock surrender. "Okay, maybe two men. Absolutely three tops!"

He sighs. "This list of F1 drivers seems to be growing by the week."

"It's all your fault."

"I'm well aware of my shortsightedness. Trust me when I say I regret it every single day."

My smile turns flirtatious. "You're cute when you get all possessive." I don't mean it, yet his nostrils seem to flare regardless.

"Not sure you'll be feeling the same way once we get home."

A blush spreads from my cheeks down my neck, unbeknownst to him. I expected Declan to entertain a fake date because his reputation needs it, but I didn't think he would elicit all these reactions from me. My body doesn't seem to understand his promises are nothing but fake. Hell, my brain is having a hard time making sense of the way his eyes seem to darken, the blacks of his pupils eating away at the dark brown irises.

I swallow the lump in my throat and pray I can make it through a few more of these. Deep down, I know it isn't real, but my body seems to have a hard time understanding his words are nothing but empty promises.

I should have known going on a fake date would be a bad idea, but I don't have many options. The only thing I can control is how much time I interact with him. Because if tonight is any hint at what the future might look like, I'm not sure I have the power to resist him. At least not when he says and does things that make my heart race and my skin flush.

So what happens if our fake dating game turns into more? I'm too afraid to answer the question, although I think I have a good idea.

Sex. Love. And heartbreak.

CHAPTER TWENTY-FIVE

Declan

I thought Iris's idea of going on a fake date was ridiculous until I actually sat down and realized I have her undivided attention for at least two hours. It reminds me of our honeymoon and the dinner we had together. Except this time, she is solely focused on putting on a show while I'm more interested in getting to know her. Not the person she is during work hours or the hidden glimpses I get when she lets her guard down, but the real her.

I take advantage of the reporter's bathroom break to press her for more information. "If you didn't have to work, what would you do on weekends?"

She rears back. "Like if I had a day off?"

"You have Sundays off."

"I'm usually too dead to move by then, so I prefer vegetating in my bedroom. I'll only come out for water and food."

"Why?"

"Because I'm exhausted. Working for you sucks up all my energy so by the time I get to the weekend, I'm running on fumes."

This conversation is quickly taking a turn back to work, and for once, I have no interest in speaking to Iris about business.

"Fine. What would you do if you weren't tired or working?"

She laughs. "Honestly, I have no clue. The things I used to do don't really apply anymore."

"Like?"

"Grabbing brunch with friends. Spending the whole day movie hopping. People watching at the zoo. The options are endless really. I'm pretty easy to entertain, so long as it isn't anything that requires much thinking."

"When's the last time you did any of that?"

She looks up at the ceiling. "Huh. Cal and I went to the movies a couple months ago."

"Together?"

"No. We went to separate theaters and called each other afterward to discuss the plots." She laughs. "Of course we went together. Who else do I have to go with?"

"A boyfriend?"

"After the last one ended in a rejected proposal, no."

A pity. "What about a friend?"

"Cal is my friend."

"Another friend? Preferably of the same gender?"

Her laugh comes out sad. "I don't have any more of those."

"Why not?"

She looks down at her plate. "Turns out people stop inviting you places when all you do is say no."

"Why did you say no?"

"We lived two very different lifestyles. Most of my friends had nine-to-five jobs and worked only five days a week. At first, I tried to keep up with them, but eventually I was burning myself out. I had to choose between my job and my life, and we know how that went." She motions toward me.

The look on her face stops me from asking anything else. A strange feeling in my gut comes to life, and I can only label it as one thing.

Guilt. It's my fault she has no friends. Well, none except for Cal and me, that is.

You're the one who told her you don't want to be her friend.

My stomach churns as I consider how I rejected her friendship. With so few left, I'm sure she takes them very seriously.

That's why she helped you in the first place. She really does consider you a friend.

Except I don't want to be her friend. Not when she elicits all these feelings inside of me that are nothing close to platonic.

Who said you can't be both?

I should have never ordered another drink after our empty plates were removed from in front of us. The amber liquid serves as a reminder of my moment of weakness. Iris was ready to go the moment the reporter paid her bill and left, but I was the one who wanted to stay.

The thought alone pains me more than I ever care to admit. I take a sip of my drink, only allowing the smallest amount of liquid to slip past my lips. Iris seems somewhat perturbed at how I make an ounce of whiskey last longer than all her past relationships combined. I'm selfish for keeping her out this late on a weeknight, but I can't help it. Watching her speak about topics besides work is fascinating.

She talks until she's breathless, filling the silence I have grown accustomed to with her endless chatter. Every subject we touch on she talks about with passion and intrigue.

A dilapidated house she saw while driving home that seemed perfect for a renovation. How much fun she has visiting her mother's classroom. Her plan to attend Nana's cornhole championship coming up next week at church.

I didn't even know there was such a thing as cornhole championships, let alone that Nana was the reigning champ.

I'm thoroughly enjoying my time with Iris, to the point that I don't want it to end.

"Are you almost done?" Iris shatters my thoughts with the stark reality.

"With?"

She glares at my drink. "Your overpriced glass of whiskey."

"I can afford it."

"You have the same bottle at the house for half the cost."

But would I have the same company? Probably not. The thought of drinking alone tonight seems unbearable. I've spent an entire lifetime by myself, and while it was never a problem before, it is slowly becoming intolerable.

"I'm enjoying the view."

She glances out the window. "Says the man who hasn't even looked outside once."

"That's not the view I'm talking about."

Her eyes find their way back to mine. I'm startled when she drops her head back as a laugh explodes out of her. It's rough and raspy, drawing the attention of multiple patrons. Warmth rushes through me at the sound despite knowing her amusement is at my expense.

By the time she looks back at me, her eyes have a watery shine to them and she can't seem to take enough deep breaths.

My hand tightens around the glass as I take another chug. "What the hell was that?"

She dabs at the corners of her eyes. "The reporter left. You don't need to pretend anymore."

"I'm not pretending."

"That's...*concerning*."

"I don't see it as such."

"No."

"*No?*" What the hell is she even talking about?

"No." She speaks with a firmer voice this time. "That's not how this is supposed to go."

"How exactly is this *supposed to go*?" I won't admit I'm confused, but damn, I feel it. Everything about her confuses me. From the pinched feeling in my chest whenever she laughs to the draw I feel toward her at all hours of the day.

"We work together."

"And?"

Her deep sigh echoes the one building inside of me. "We have a deal."

"Are you stating the obvious solely to annoy me?"

"Of course not. I'm simply pointing out the stakes. There

is far too much riding on our *relationship* for us to screw it up because we're horny and confused."

I don't miss the way she says *we*, although I think *she* did.

"I'm not confused. Far from it, actually. I know exactly what I want."

"And what is that?"

"You."

The way she laughs makes me want to stifle it with my lips against hers. I settle on latching onto her hand, which sobers her enough to stop laughing at my expense.

She tries to rip her palm out of mine, but I hold on.

"This has to be some kind of sick joke."

The muscles in my jaw ache from the way I grind my teeth together. "How so?"

"You can't want me. Not like that at least."

"Why not?"

"This isn't meant to be anything but a contractual obligation."

"It's what we say it is." I trace over the diamond on her finger, drawing a sharp breath from her.

Her eyes widen. "Oh my God. Are you actually suggesting that we hook up?"

I've always been a straight shooter—to a fault. "Yes."

"Why?"

"Because I want to."

Her bitter laugh sends a wave of uneasiness through me. "Then I'm sure it will be extremely difficult for you to accept that my answer is no."

"Why waste time denying what we both already know?"

"Because the last thing we need is to further complicate things."

"Hate to break it to you, but our relationship is nothing but complicated."

"No, Declan. Our relationship is nothing but a facade."

Her words land their blow, and I'm struck speechless as I process her words. She stands and grabs her purse. The small smile she shoots my way feels all kinds of wrong. I don't want her to leave. That much I know is true, yet she doesn't seem to acknowledge the silent plea in my eyes.

"I think it's best if we pretend tonight never happened. For both of our sakes." She bends down to kiss my cheek, and she might as well have burned the impression of her lips onto my skin. "I'll meet you in the car. Take your time."

A tightness in my chest grows with every step she takes away from me. I hate the feeling sprouting inside of me like a weed, tangling around my heart like a vine, almost as much as I hate Iris walking away from me.

Tonight might not have gone like expected, but I am not the kind of man to admit defeat.

I plan. I act. I conquer.

Iris might have rejected my first offer, but I will rise to the challenge and prove just how good things can be between us if she were to give me a chance.

Our marriage might be fake, but these feelings burning inside me are anything but. It's only a matter of time before I make her mine. She just doesn't know it yet.

The car isn't even parked before Iris escapes the garage.

Harrison opens my door with his lips pressed together.

"How long have you been married?" I exit the car and button my jacket.

His head rears back like I have never spoken to him before. We might not be confidants, but he has been my driver since before I ever had a license. Of course I interact with him. He even has my personal number, strictly for coordination purposes.

"Forty years and counting." He smiles to himself as if the idea pleases him.

"Willingly?"

As opposed to what? A contractual agreement like yours?

He laughs. "She might say no if you asked her."

My head tilts. "Why?"

He looks at me as if he's questioning my IQ. "Because marriage is hard, and apparently I'm not the easiest person to get along with. Plus, I snore."

A laugh gets trapped in my throat. "Makes sense." I turn toward the door, but Harrison's words stop me.

"Mind if I offer you some advice?"

I sigh and look over at him. "Only if you feel that it's absolutely crucial."

His eyes wrinkle at the corners as his lips turn up into a small smile. "You might have gone about all the steps in the wrong order, but that doesn't mean you can't restart from the beginning and try again."

The back of my neck prickles like tiny needles driving into my skin. "You know."

"Of course I know. I've been driving you around since before you could reach the pedals. If you owe me anything, it's to not insult my intelligence like that."

"You signed an NDA."

He gives his head a shake. "I'm not interested in selling your story. If I was, I would have taken the money your father offered me and retired with Gerty to a sandy beach in Mexico."

My mask of indifference slips. "He wanted to pay you?"

"That's not the point."

"How much?" I tuck my clenched fists into my pocket.

He shuts the back door. "Also not the point."

"Why wouldn't you accept his deal?"

"Because I wasn't about to give you one more reason to hate the world."

"You should have taken the money because nothing you could ever do would change my opinion about humanity. I can guarantee it."

"Probably not, but there is one person who might."

My body goes rigid underneath my suit. "Not possible."

He releases a deep belly laugh.

"Am I missing something amusing about this conversation?"

He wipes his eyes with a handkerchief. "It's comforting knowing that the smartest man I've ever met is an idiot like the rest of us when it comes to women."

My brows tug together. "Do you even care about keeping your job anymore?"

"You could try to fire me but we both know Iris would hire me back first thing tomorrow morning."

I glare at him, which only makes him smile.

"I was only trying to offer you some advice because something told me you might need it. But I see that isn't the case, so have a good night, sir." He tips his hat and turns back toward the car.

249

"Harrison," I call out before I can stop myself. Since I already embarrassed myself, I might as well take advantage of his advice.

He pauses. "Yes, Mr. Kane?"

I must be having some kind of mental crisis because nothing else explains what I do next.

"What would you do if you're attracted to a woman who wants nothing to do with you?"

He laughs in a way that makes me feel like I'm missing the second half of a joke. "Mrs. Kane can say what she wants, but she's interested in you. I've seen it with my own two eyes."

"With or without corrective lenses?"

He taps his thick-rimmed specs. "The bifocals don't lie."

"Regardless of what you've seen, she claims otherwise."

"Oh, I'm sure she does. But that's where you come in."

"And do what exactly?"

His frail lips break out into a genuine smile. "You chase."

Harrison's words linger at the forefront of my mind as I walk up to my bedroom. I have spent my entire life chasing after anything I want, so while the concept isn't anything ground-breaking, my desire to do so with Iris is new.

Bullshit. You've always been interested in her.

Except my thoughts never went past just that. *Interest.* Pursuing Iris was never an option before, but there is no way I can continue on the same trajectory. I will drive myself mad fighting the urges threatening to consume me whenever she enters the room. Lately, I seem to be driven by the burning sensation in my gut.

I rip off my tie and dump it on my dresser before making quick work of my button-down. I chuck it in a corner of my bathroom, along with my pants.

I hoped a shower would calm me down, but I was wrong.

My mind wanders, making up an entirely different scenario of what could have happened after our date if Iris were willing to take me up on my offer. To me cornering her and kissing her until she loses the ability to do anything but drag me toward my room.

I try to avoid touching myself. My hand is nothing but a temporary fix for a lifelong problem. One that has plagued me for years, never quite scratching the itch I crave.

My cock lengthens as I imagine Iris exploring all of me with her hands. Of how she would be greedy with my body, raking her nails across my flesh.

I grab my hardened cock with my right hand. I promise myself this is the last time I'll use my hand, but I know it's a lie. A hiss escapes me as I pump it once before rubbing the bead of arousal at the tip. My mind conjures up a series of sounds Iris might make when my hands grip her hips. A moan when my tongue strokes against hers. The sharp hiss as I scrape the hollow of her neck with my teeth. Her breathy groan when my fingers embed themselves into her ass like I could brand her skin with the marks of my fingertips.

My hand grips my cock like a vise, each angry tug sending a shot of heat down my spine. It's easy to fantasize about what could happen between us if I push her to accept her new reality. How Iris would beg me to take her right then and there like a mindless animal.

I picture her touch turning desperate as I memorize her body with my lips. Of her returning the favor, learning every dip and curve of me with the tip of her tongue. My arousal leaks from the tip as I consider her nails digging into my skin with each thrust of my cock. I'd wear her tiny half-moon marks like a proud battle scar, knowing what I did to earn them.

Heat spreads through my veins that has nothing to do with the hot water streaming down my body. I slap my other palm against the tile, trying to support my weight as my legs tremble. The burning sensation becomes unbearable as my yanks become sloppier.

The bedroom fantasy shifts to her catching me in the shower, touching myself like this. Her hand would replace mine as she looks up at me with her big brown eyes. The way she might hesitate as she grips me, learning how to please me the way I like.

Only a taste, she would whisper before getting down on her knees and taking me in her mouth.

It wouldn't take much to push me over the edge. A few slow licks up my shaft. The hollowing of her cheeks as she sucks on my cock until she chokes. Her moan as I grip onto the back of her head and shove myself down her throat, making her scratch at my thighs for reprieve.

The illusion is shattered as my release hits me. Spots darken my vision, and hot cum shoots out. It splashes against the tile before being washed down the drain. I jerk my cock, taking my anger out on the softening shaft.

My breathing is ragged by the time I'm done. I lay my head against the tile and curse to myself, knowing damn well I will never be satisfied until Iris is mine.

Not even close.

CHAPTER TWENTY-SIX

Iris

It takes three days for the reporter to publish a story about us. I had hoped the results would be promising, but she exceeded my wildest expectations.

"I told you!" I slam my phone against Declan's desk.

He grabs it and reads over the article outlining how an insider learned about a hidden side of Declan Kane. Turns out, the coldest man in Chicago happens to have a soft spot for one person in the whole world.

Me.

The way the reporter describes our relationship is something out of a movie. Whispered secrets by the candlelight. Stolen glances when one of us was looking the other way. A kiss under the stars, with both of us completely oblivious to the world around us.

He frowns. "That never happened."

"It's a gossip column, not the *Wall Street Journal.* They're not here to present the facts."

"It's a wonder they're still up and running with that mentality."

"Because articles like ours already have a million reads and counting. The advertisement money alone must keep them afloat."

His eyes widen. "A million? It was published an hour ago."

I grin as I drop into the chair across from him. "I told you it would work."

"I never doubted you to begin with." He speaks with such sincerity, my chest twinges with a silent reply.

I deflect with humor. "Liar. You totally did."

"It's human nature."

"No, it's *your* nature."

"It's gotten me this far."

"No. That's all thanks to your last name being on the building," I tease.

"*Our* name."

I roll my eyes. "For now."

"Quick to get rid of me already, *Wife?*"

Somehow, one word seems to cause a rush of warmth from my head to my toes.

Danger. Red alert. DEFCON 1 activated.

So I do what I always do when Declan stirs up feelings inside of my chest that have no business being there.

I escape.

Turns out I can only avoid Declan for so long when we live in the same house. It doesn't take him long to find me, struggling to drain a pot of boiling water with only one hand.

"Are you trying to end up in the emergency room again?"

I'm not given a chance to explain as he swoops in and grabs the pot from me.

He glares. "If you wanted my attention, this isn't the way to get it."

My mouth drops open. "I am *not* trying to get your attention." On the contrary, I was trying to avoid it at all costs—third-degree burns be damned.

"Then what are you doing?" He drains the pasta without me having to ask.

"Cooking." I grind my teeth together to prevent myself from saying more.

Why is it when I'm the one who doesn't want to talk, he can't seem to help himself? The injustice of this all is not lost on me.

He places the empty pot back on the stove. "I can assure you boiling pasta isn't cooking."

"Can you go away please? I'm trying to eat in peace." Dealing with him at work is one thing, but having him in my space, acting holier than thou, is not how I want to spend my night.

You're just mad because you like having him around.

He lingers like a shadow as I scoop a large helping of noodles onto my plate.

"You should have asked for my help."

I bristle. "I don't need your help."

"Could have fooled me with the way you were holding on to that handle for dear life."

"Don't you have somewhere else to be? Perhaps there is some riveting documentary about spreadsheets or expense reports you can go fall asleep to?"

He laughs, and it feels like the clouds parted and heaven graced us with a miracle.

Oh, Iris. This is how it all starts.

I recognize the warmth seeping through my chest as he smiles at me.

I hate it. I love it. And I can't seem to stop myself from craving more of it.

He smiles. "I actually came down to eat."

"Great. I'll leave you to it then." I drench my noodles with pasta sauce before stepping away from the counter. I'll clean the mess up later once Declan goes away.

"Or you could stay."

"What?" I blink.

"I never said you had to leave."

Shit. If I leave, it makes me seem unequipped to handle him for long spans of time without adult supervision.

Probably because it's true. It's one thing to spend time around him in an office; it's a whole other thing to interact with him in the confines of our home.

I shake my head. "Oh no. I had plans to eat upstairs anyway."

His eyes drop to the napkin and shiny cutlery I set down. When he looks back up, his eyes seem to brighten. "Do I make you nervous?"

"No," I say too quickly.

His grin widens.

No wonder the man doesn't smile often. The world

wouldn't stand a chance against him if he were to use them more frequently.

He opens a cabinet and grabs an empty plate before loading it with a healthy amount of noodles. "If it makes you feel better, we could talk about work."

My horrified expression can't be masked. "How is that supposed to make me feel better?"

"Because it's normal."

"Doesn't make it right!" I laugh.

The skin around his eyes tightens. "I concede. No talking about work."

"Fine. But only because you seem pathetically in need of some company." I drop onto the barstool with defeat. During the limited time Declan and I have interacted in the house, we have never eaten together. He seems to always busy himself in his office while I cook a sad meal for one. And unlike our fake date, this feels intimate. At least significantly more intimate than eating in a restaurant full of people for show.

He situates himself beside the place mat I put out for myself.

"So…" I grab my fork.

His eyes reflect his amusement as he lets me stammer through the silence.

"I don't like this game you're playing."

"And what game is that?" He clutches his fork and twirls it in his pasta. His elbow touches mine, and I suck in a breath at the sensation shooting up my arm.

"You know damn well what I'm talking about."

"I'm drawing a blank." He spreads his thighs, and one of them brushes up against mine.

I shoot him a glare as I lift my fork. "Touch my leg again and I'll be forced to take physical action."

His head drops back. Declan's laugh is a weapon of mass seduction, and I'm its biggest target. It's rough and unpracticed, and it makes a tingle shoot down my spine.

I melt into the stool, allowing the sound to wash over me like a warm summer day. A sense of pride hits me at making someone like him laugh like this in the first place, given just how much he resists it. It feels like my own kind of superpower and a secret I plan on protecting.

Declan sobers, snapping back into reality as he takes a bite of his dinner.

"How is it?"

"Tastes like it came out of a box."

I laugh. "I've never been much of a cook. By the time I get home, usually I'm lucky if I'm motivated to boil some water."

"I could cook tomorrow if you're interested."

My mouth drops open. Is this conversation even really happening?

"I didn't realize you knew how to cook."

"Imagine if I didn't. I'd be eating boiled noodles for the rest of my life like someone I know."

"Three years."

His brows pull together. "What?"

"For the next three years. Not your life."

"Right." His voice is devoid of emotion.

I nudge him with my elbow. "But I'll still take you up on dinner tomorrow. I don't think I could stomach another night of pasta anyway."

"Out of all the things you could use me for, you go with my cooking skills?"

"I don't see why not. It's not like you have much else going for you." My comment earns me a death glare.

"You sure know how to make a man feel special." His lips curve, throwing me back to the night when our whole lives changed.

"Special is the last word I would use to describe you," I repeat his words from our engagement party back at him.

His gaze holds mine hostage. "What word would you use then?"

"It's improper."

"All the better."

I shake my head. "I'll pass."

"Then ask me what word I would use to describe you."

I really shouldn't, but curiosity wins out. "Fine. What word?"

There's something about the way he looks at me when he says it that makes butterflies take flight in my stomach. "*Yuánfèn.*"

I blink. "I'm sorry. Was that even *English*?" I'm already at a severe disadvantage when it comes to the language I speak every day, let alone foreign ones.

He seems privy to some joke with himself. "No."

I pull out my phone and try to search the word based on my spelling, but I must be butchering it big time.

"Can you say it again for me? *Slowly.*"

He says it again—this time with a phonetic breakdown of consonants and vowels—which would be easy enough for anyone *but* me to spell out. My fingers hover over the keys, and I try my hardest to spell the word he said, but the only thing that comes up is *you ahn phan.*

"Want my help?" His voice drops low, making me feel helpless.

I want to throw my phone at the nearest wall. Tears fill my eyes, but I blink them away. Showing weakness in front of Declan is like waving a red flag in front of a bull. I refuse to do it.

"Whatever. It's probably a curse word anyway." I clutch my phone with a death grip as I hop off the barstool.

"To you, it might be."

His joke lands on deaf ears. I'm too far gone to do anything but walk away before I admit something I'm not ready to share.

"Hey. Where are you going?"

"To bed." I don't bother looking back at him.

"What's wrong?" The scrape of his stool pushes me into action. I take longer strides. I'm halfway toward the stairs when his hand latches onto my elbow.

"What happened back there?"

I can't look him in the eyes as I respond. "Nothing. I'm just tired." I tug my arm out of his grasp, and this time, he lets me make a smooth getaway.

I take the stairs two at a time, all while Declan's eyes burn a hole through my back. It's not until I'm in the comfort of my room that I let it all out. I grab a pillow, shove my face in it, and let the tears fall.

I cry for the girl who was bullied all throughout her schooling. The one who became a running joke in class and was called every awful name in the book. Tears fall for the version of me that was ridiculed by her father until her mother had to intervene, only to see her get destroyed by his equally vicious words. The same person who made a working woman out of herself despite all the people who told her she would go nowhere in life because she couldn't even read.

I spent most of my life trying to prove people wrong. It took years of tutoring to get to the place I am now, and I won't let one setback throw me off.

So what if I couldn't spell a stupid foreign word? My disorder might be a part of me but it doesn't *define* me. Not anymore at least.

My phone buzzes against my comforter. I unlock it to find a new message from Declan. The fact that he sent a one-word text doesn't shock me given his preference for using five words or less in all our conversations. It's the content that surprises me, and not because it takes me three tries to finally make out the word.

Declan: *Yuánfèn.*

I consider ignoring it, but curiosity wins as I pull up my search bar and type the word in the box with shaky fingers. The results are mind-blowing.

Yuánfèn: A predestined infinity.

Turns out Declan likes to casually switch to a foreign language whenever he wants to avoid saying how he really feels. Because there is no way he would tell me to my face that he thinks I'm his *destiny*.

I think carefully about my next message. It takes me some time to find the perfect response for how I feel, and my search history is filled with variations of *words that have no English translations*. I copy and paste the word I found that describes exactly how I feel and press the send button.

Me: *Kilig.**

I throw my phone across my bed and don't touch it until the next morning. It's not until I get dressed and put my makeup on that I have enough courage to open Declan's message.

Declan: *Merak.*†

I copy and paste it straight into the search bar, only to drop my phone against the bathroom counter and shatter the screen.

A perfect symbol of how Declan is wrecking my plans, one by one.

Declan and I barely speak throughout the next day. I keep to my area and he keeps to his, with neither of us rehashing whatever the hell happened last night. I'm thankful that he doesn't. Together we are dancing on a fine line, and neither one of us wants to take the plunge.

It's complete *mamihlapinatapai*‡ between us, with stolen glances across the conference table with no intention of seeking more. At least not for me. Although Declan sure is trying. His latest strategy to rope me in with foreign words that have no direct English translation seems to be working. Now I spend my

---

*   **Kilig:** *Noun, Tagalog:* a feeling of exhilaration or elation caused by an exciting or romantic experience.

†   **Merak:** *Verb, Greek:* to do something with pleasure.

‡   **Mamihlapinatapai:** *Noun, Yaghan:* a look shared between two people, each wishing that the other would initiate something that they both desire but which neither wants to begin.

breaks looking up new words and adding them to a running list I have, just in case Declan tries to outdo me with one.

I never thought I could have this much fun with words, but Declan seems to be keeping me on my toes. He has already sent me two words today, neither one romantic like yesterday, but each make me laugh based on our context.

The first message nearly outed me for texting in the middle of his father's biweekly board meeting presentation. I'm not sure what Declan was thinking by sending me a text of the word *backpfeif-engesicht.** I choked on my water as I searched the word and found out it means something along the lines of a face that badly needs a fist. I'm convinced there is no other word more fitting for Declan's father, although I can't pronounce anything beyond the first syllable.

It turns out Declan does have a funny side. He just happens to be so nerdy, I need Google to help me figure his jokes out. To be honest, it's kind of fun. The words are so difficult to pronounce that I don't even feel the need to stress over them. It's the meaning behind them that matters.

If I continue down this path, I foresee myself slipping further into uncharted territory with Declan. So while I can have fun, I need to keep my guard up, because a few funny messages don't translate into anything more than what it is: two people who can never be more than friends, no matter what.

"Why do you keep smiling at your phone?" Cal pauses his typing to look over at me.

---

*   **backpfeifengesicht:** *Noun, German:* a face badly in need of a fist.

Shit. "No reason." I tuck my phone away in a drawer.

You were smiling? Pull it together and stop rereading text messages like a lovesick teenager.

"*Right.* Exactly how stupid do you think I am?"

"Are you sure you want me to answer that?"

His withering glare reminds me of an angry golden retriever. "I find it interesting that my brother has been equally invested in his phone today. During a board meeting no less."

Deny. Deny. Deny. "I have no idea what you're talking about."

"Really? Because anytime he put his phone away, you picked yours up."

"Purely circumstantial evidence at best."

"Except I was sitting right next to you. I saw his name flash across your screen twice within five minutes."

I wag my finger at him. "It's rude to read other people's messages."

"I couldn't care less about whatever nonsense you two weirdos text each other. I care more about your feelings."

His comment draws a chuckle from me. "Your worries are misplaced."

"What kind of best friend would I be if I didn't warn you away from my brother?"

"Fair point. Except you're forgetting it's my job to know everything about your brother. There's very little you could warn me about that I wouldn't already be aware of."

"That's exactly my worry. You know everything and still volunteered to marry him."

"Because I care."

"But have you ever asked yourself *why* you care?"

"Because…" I could fill in the blank with so many responses, each equally questionable from Cal's perspective.

Declan gave me a chance to learn from my mistakes when other bosses fired me within a week for "careless" typos and an inability to work fast enough. He pushed me to try harder and think of the big picture, which helped me build enough confidence in myself. Unbeknownst to him, he helped me grow into a woman who believed in herself, and for that, I owe him so much.

Cal sighs. "It's okay to like him. I'm not telling you that you shouldn't, but I want you to be prepared for the worst-case scenario."

"And what's that exactly? That he breaks my heart?"

"Worse. He makes you fall in love with him."

CHAPTER TWENTY-SEVEN

Iris

Things between Declan and me seem to be escalating. It has been a week since I had the brace removed, and Declan has yet to pull back. With each day that passes, he seems to grow more insistent about spending time together. Whether it's eating dinner with one another or him working on his tablet while I watch an episode of TV in front of the fireplace before bed, I can't seem to shake him.

I never thought he would want to willingly spend this much time with me. While it might not bother most people to grow close to their fake husbands, it feels like I'm losing focus. Like I'm forgetting the reasons I thought we would never make a good couple in the first place.

If I were being really honest with myself, my thoughts have slowly started drifting away from friendship and right toward a big red flag known as infatuation. I'm not talking about the physical kind either. More like the soul-deep attraction that tempts the broken part of me to open up fully to him, regardless of the consequences.

It is terrifying to think I might willingly let him come closer.

Not like you have a choice with this evening's plan.

Even if I wanted to avoid him, tonight's fake date would make it nearly impossible to do so.

I knock my fist against his office door.

"Come in."

No one man should have the power to make my heart beat harder within my chest with a few words. I take a deep breath before walking into his domain. After days of limited contact, I feel starved for his attention.

Starved for his attention? Maybe you do *have workplace Stockholm syndrome after all.*

Our gazes collide, and neither one of us breaks away. His gaze moves from my face, down my body, before lingering on my lime green stilettos. The straps wrap up my legs, making me feel every bit like a Roman gladiator despite the dainty little bow at the end. His stare stirs something deep within me, making heat pool in my belly.

"What do you need?" His rough voice snaps me out of my daze.

I lift my chin, preparing for a fight. "We have another fake date planned for tonight."

"A fake date." The way his lips curl at the statement fills me with trepidation.

"You know. Because we need to look like a happy couple?"

"Right. God forbid we actually *feel* like one, right?"

Oh. My. God. You need to get out of here.

I let out an awkward laugh. "Anyway…your tux is dry-cleaned and ready for tonight. Be ready at 7:00 p.m. sharp."

I turn toward the door but halt when he calls out after me.

"Not so fast."

My throat closes up as I rotate on my heels and look back at him. "Yes?"

"Where are we going?"

I regain my composure. "The charity gala at the Walton Hotel."

"A charity gala?" His nose scrunches with disgust for the briefest second, and it makes me smile.

"I'll make it worth your while."

"How so?" He leans back in his chair, his cold mask slipped back into place. Except his eyes can't hide what burns beneath the surface.

Poor man thinks I'm trying to seduce him. The thought makes me laugh to myself, which only makes his gaze darken as it drops to my lips.

"Your grandfather's lawyer will be attending."

"That isn't the answer I was searching for."

My eyes roll. "Of course not."

"If you wanted to make it worth my time, you should have gone with something a bit more…*tempting*." He strokes his stubbled chin, and my heart picks up its pace.

"I'm confused. Is there supposed to be something more enticing than earning your inheritance?" I choose to play coy because the alternative seems risky based on the look on Declan's face.

"You and I both know what I want."

"I don't want to hook up with you," I blurt out.

Oh God. Why did you say that?!

"Who said anything about hooking up?" He stands and buttons his suit.

Deep down, I know if he gets near me, I won't be able to control myself. His penetrating gaze incapacitates me, and I'm unable to take a single step toward the door as he rounds the corner of his desk. I stand like an innocent lamb awaiting slaughter as he eats up the distance between us.

"I want to strike a new deal." He reaches out and cups the back of my neck.

Goose bumps spread across my skin. "I'm not open to negotiating."

He shrugs as he says, "*Strikhedonia*.*"

He robs me of my reply as his lips slam against mine. My eyes remain open, shock making me unable to process everything happening all at once. Declan must sense my inability to connect because his teeth drag across my bottom lip in a silent command to pay attention. One of his arms wraps around my waist, trapping me against him as he kisses me. My body shudders from a simple scrape of his teeth.

I shut my eyes and relish the sensation of his lips against mine. His fingers gripping my neck tighten ever so slightly as my lips part with a sigh. His access to my mouth isn't taken for granted. He explores like a man on a mission, using his tongue as a brand onto my very soul.

Everything about his kiss is selfish. The way his fingers embed themselves into my skin. The feel of his tongue against

---

* **Strikhedonia:** *Noun, Greek:* the pleasure of being able to say "to hell with it."

mine, stroking, testing, *owning*. The way he destroys any semblance of normalcy with a single thrust of his stiff cock against my stomach.

I think I'm dying.

I think I'm *soaring*.

I'm hit with wave after wave of emotions, with each pounding against me without any sort of reprieve. I don't understand what's happening.

Maybe you don't want to.

I grow frustrated with my mixed emotions. My skin tingles and burns all at once, driven by some primal need to gain control. I thrust my hands into his hair and tug at the roots. He soaks it up like a man starved, and my lips stifle his moan.

He likes you touching him. His hands run down my curves before gripping onto my hips. He breaks our kiss, and I nearly groan with protest before his lips follow a path toward my throat. His tongue traces my fluttering pulse point before sucking on the skin. I buck under him, only to push myself farther into his firm length.

Oh God. I realize that I must have said the words aloud because he laughs against my skin. The sound that got me into this mess makes something snap inside of me, and I all but shove him away. Both of us are breathing hard, staring into one another's eyes.

The way he looks at me...it makes me feel alive. Powerful. *Desired*.

I can't handle the weight of his gaze, so I scan the rest of him. Bad idea. The outline of his aroused cock pressing against his pants makes my mouth water. I'm hit with a sense of want that is so strong, it has my breath catching in the back of my throat.

Half of me wants to run while the other half wants to drop to my knees and get a better look. It's the sane half that wins.

Go. Go. Go.

"I need to answer the phone," I rasp.

"I don't hear one ringing."

The temptation to kiss that stupid smirk off his face rides me hard enough to wake me up. I power walk my way toward his door without sparing him another glance.

"Iris—"

"Be ready by seven." I slam the door behind me, but not quick enough to miss him saying *fuck* under his breath.

Music blasts from my minispeaker as I sing my way through my makeup routine. While Declan hates galas, I love them because I don't mind getting lost in the glitz and glam for a night. In the past, whenever he invited me as his guest so women wouldn't approach him, I would spend the whole week finding the perfect outfit.

Tonight is no different. I take extra time applying my makeup and painting my nails. I somehow shimmy into my floor-length gown, being mindful of not catching my braids on the open zipper. Despite my efforts, I can't seem to reach the zipper. I'm shoved back into the memory of my wedding night. Except unlike before, I don't mind asking Declan for a little help, so long as he is fully clothed.

A knock on my door saves me from having to travel far for his assistance.

I grab the knob and tug the door open. "Hey."

Declan leans against the doorframe, his hair perfectly styled and his tux molded to his muscles as if it were sewn straight onto his body. The only thing unkempt about him is the way his bow tie lays undone against his shirt.

You had to go and marry one of the most handsome men in all of Chicago.

Screw Chicago. More like the most handsome man in all of the *world*.

I want to drown in his whiskey-colored eyes and never come up for air. There is something about the way he looks at me that seems to strip me bare, ridding me of any sensible thoughts. Some men look like a dream. Others a nightmare. Declan happens to be a lethal combination of the two—beautiful in a way that should terrify me. Emphasis on the *should* because if anything, I yearn for more. Especially after our kiss earlier.

"You look…" He pauses.

"If you say *nice*, I swear I'll make your death look like an accident."

"*Devastating.*"

My throat tightens with emotion. "Are we back to using English words to describe our feelings?"

His eyes *glitter*. "Only for tonight."

I break eye contact first, unable to withstand his stare.

"Are you ready?" he asks.

"Almost. I just need your help with something first." I turn and pull my braids over my shoulders, revealing my exposed back. "I can't reach."

My cheeks heat as I think back to our wedding night.

Somehow, I continue to land myself in this position without even trying.

He doesn't move to help me, so I glance over my shoulder to see if he is still there. His eyes are transfixed on my back. They trace the length of my spine like invisible fingers before stopping at the dimples.

"Declan?"

His eyes snap back to mine. "I got it." He steps forward and reaches out his hand. Instead of grabbing onto the zipper at the bottom, his knuckles graze the base of my neck. A shiver racks my body as he drags his fist down my back. The way he draws out the simple task makes me regret ever asking him for help in the first place.

Why didn't you choose a dress that doesn't have a zipper?

I suck in a breath as the tips of his fingers hover over one of my dimples. My neck heats as Declan releases a heavy sigh, and the silky material of his tux brushing against my bare arms sends another current of energy through me.

What is going on?

The drag of the zipper fills the silence, and all too soon, his warmth pressing against my back disappears.

He readjusts my hair for me, and my heart gallops in response. "We should get going."

"Hold on. You forgot this."

His brows pull together as I step forward and grab the ends of his bow tie. I pull on one side before passing the longer end into the neck loop. He releases a shuddery breath as my fingers brush his skin, and I look up to catch his gaze fixed on me. The way he looks at me feels…

Devastating.

I hurry through the rest of the steps before I do something crazy like pull his lips down to mine. "There." I readjust the sides so the knot is centered.

I move to step away, but he grabs my hands and holds them hostage against his chest. "Thank you."

My slow blink gives me a moment to process. "It's just a bow tie."

"I mean for everything. The fake dates…"

"The broken laws."

"And noses."

I laugh. "That was all you."

His lips curve into a seductive smile that makes my knees *tremble*. He reaches out and traces my cheek with his thumb, and my stomach does a betraying little flip that terrifies me.

No matter how tonight goes, one thing is clear: Declan isn't going to back down. If anything, our kiss made him bolder. I'm not sure how I am going to survive tonight without doing something stupid.

God help me.

Declan and I make it to the gala without kissing, fighting, or talking. It isn't until he steps out of the car and holds out his arm for me to take that he finally speaks.

"How long do we have to stay here?"

I clutch onto his hand and exit the car. "We haven't even gone inside yet."

He huffs. "You know how I feel about these things."

"I might know *how*, but not *why*."

His eyes seem to roam over me before landing back on my face. "I have my reasons."

"Do they have anything to do with you painfully pretending you like other people for two hours straight?"

"If only it were that simple."

"What would you do if you didn't have me around to save you from hours of small talk?"

"Death by a butter knife would be most appropriate given the setting."

I lean into his side as I laugh. He wraps his arm around my waist, and I look at him with wide eyes and a smile that has yet to fall. His lips part as if he is about to say something, but our moment is cut short by a flash of a camera bulb. Someone shouts Declan's name. It sobers me enough to take in our surroundings and the different people mulling about the red carpet, interviewing each person who walks by.

I give him a reassuring pat on his chest. "Let's get this over with. The sooner we go inside, the sooner we get to leave."

"You don't need to tell me twice."

I laugh again, and his hand on my waist tightens.

Does he like my laugh? The idea seems comical given Declan's preference for silence.

My theory is proven correct later on when I break out into another fit of laughter and Declan's hand squeezes my hip in response. A rush of happiness hits me as I come to grips with my revelation.

Interesting. Very interesting.

CHAPTER TWENTY-EIGHT

Iris

It doesn't take us long to spot Brady Kane's lawyer. He would be hard to miss given his boisterous voice and equally loud embroidered tux.

Declan makes a move to walk over to his corner of the ballroom, but I tug him back.

"We should play it cool and wait for him to come to us."

The ice in Declan's whiskey glass rattles as he takes a long sip. "You want us to wait and do what, exactly?"

I awkwardly laugh before taking a deep chug of my wine. "Talk?"

He grimaces.

"So how was work today?"

He shoots me a glare. "You were there."

"I don't follow you around 24/7. There are plenty of things I might miss, like you struggling with a printer or harassing an innocent employee because they forgot to use Arial font in an email. I mean, come on, what did Times New Roman ever do to you?"

His scowl deepens. "It's not my fault they can't follow simple directions."

"I think you'd be surprised at how motivated people are to do a good job when you rein in the attitude."

He looks away with a huff.

I grin. "You know, as the future CEO, you will have to learn a couple things about leadership if you want to be successful."

"I know how to lead."

"Do you, though? Because there is a big difference between giving orders and leading a company."

He drags his eyes back to mine. "If my alcoholic father can do it, I'm sure I can't screw up too badly."

I take a sip of my drink as I consider my next statement. "But don't you want to be better than him?"

His jaw clenches. "Of course."

"Then what do you want to do when you become CEO?"

"What do you mean?"

"What's your next goal once that happens? Where do you feel your father has been lacking?"

"It would take me years to repair all the business relationships my father has damaged."

"Because you suck at kissing ass?"

His withering glare makes me laugh. The tightness around his eyes softens, all while his lips press together as if he wants to stop himself from matching the smile in his eyes.

He wants to smile because of you!

My brain might overload from all the sensations happening inside of me at the thought of Declan smiling because of *my* laugh.

"Look who it is!" A wrinkled hand clamps down on Declan's shoulder. "I heard you were here tonight." Brady Kane's lawyer grins.

Declan doesn't bother trying to smile, and the brightness from before is replaced by cool indifference. "Leonid."

The lawyer shudders, making his head of gray hair shake. "Please call me Leo. You know how I feel about formalities."

Leo turns his eyes toward me. "And is this the wife I've heard some whisperings about?"

One of Declan's arms snakes around me before tugging me flush against him. "Iris, this is Leo. He was my grandfather's best friend."

Best friend? Why didn't Declan mention that tiny detail during our thousands of exchanges about the man?

Probably because he doesn't have best friends, so he doesn't think it matters.

I refrain from sighing.

Leo holds out his hand for me to shake. I take it, and he pulls me out of Declan's arms and right into his chest. "We will be having none of that. We're practically family."

Are we, really? Did I miss the part where this man showed up to our wedding?

Leo must read my mind or at the very least the expression on my face. "I'm sorry I couldn't make it to your wedding. I was off the grid for a month while hiking Mount Everest, and by the time I came back, I heard you two had already tied the knot."

If he seems wary of our marriage, he doesn't show it.

"*You* climbed Mount Everest?"

"I might look old, but I sure don't feel it." He taps his heart with a grin.

"Says the man who called an emergency helicopter to rescue him after he thought he could compete in the Tour de France," Declan replies.

"It was your grandfather's idea. Bastard always wanted to show off how fit he was. I've always hated cycling."

Something flashes in Declan's eyes, and it makes my chest ache. I reach for his hand to give it a squeeze. The move is instinctual, yet I still blink at our interlocked fingers with surprise.

Leo catches the whole thing with a smile. "But enough about me. I want to hear all about you two."

"There isn't much to tell." I smile.

He wraps an arm around Declan's shoulder and guides us to a table. "Nonsense. But first, we need a toast to celebrate your marriage. Is vodka good with everyone?"

Declan's groan catches in the back of his throat, and I can't help the giggle that escapes me.

Leo can't stop smiling as his eyes bounce between the two of us. "Do you prefer something else?"

"No. Vodka sounds great." Declan speaks through gritted teeth.

My body shakes from quiet laughter, and Leo shoots me a look before he leaves us to go find a bottle of vodka.

"I fucking hate vodka." Declan drags his chair closer to mine. He wraps his arm against the back of my chair like we do this all the time. His arm brushes against the back of my neck, sending a rush of goose bumps across my arms.

"Are you cold?" He frowns at me.

I only nod, afraid my voice would betray how I really feel about his proximity.

He stands and shimmies off his jacket. "Here."

He gestures for me to scoot forward. I comply, jaw gaping as he slides the material over my shoulders. It smells like him—clean with a hint of spice. Without looking too obvious, I take a second sniff, allowing the scent of him to filter through my lungs.

My cheeks heat as I catch his eyes zeroed in on me. The inner voice in my head chants to keep him away. That nothing good could come from me entertaining the budding attraction forming between us.

The inner voice wins, all but shoving his kind gesture out the window. "Who knew you would be good at all this?"

"Good at what?" His lips tug downward.

"Your whole thoughtful-husband routine could fool *me* if I'm not careful." I gesture at the tux jacket threatening to swallow me whole.

His eyes darken. "Not everything is a fucking act."

I flinch at the bite in his voice.

Isn't this what you wanted?

Sure I do. Him being nice isn't part of the protocol.

There is no protocol. That's your issue.

Neither of us tries to fill the tense silence, and I can only pray Leo returns to us soon with enough vodka to make his Russian ancestors proud. Anything to save me from this achy feeling growing in my chest.

My prayers are answered as Leo slams the bottle of clear liquor on the tablecloth a few minutes later.

"Here we go." He crooks two fingers at a waiter who places three empty glasses beside the bottle.

"It's a family tradition to toast to the newlyweds."

I nod and grab the full glass Leo holds out for me.

Leo slaps Declan's shoulder as he places a glass in his hand. "If your grandfather were here, he would have probably had this whole speech written, so I'll just have to improvise." He lifts his own tumbler. "Marriage is like going on a road trip with the person you want to spend the rest of your life with, except you have no map or fancy GPS system to help you out. You might not always agree on what music to play or which direction you should go. I can guarantee there will be moments you want to rip your hair out—or each other's. Just like there will be times that test you, where you think that maybe things would be easier if you hitch a ride with someone else. The point is, life is going to throw a lot of things at you. Stuff like flat tires, dead ends, and mechanical issues. But you can either make the most of the journey with one another or cry about never getting to your destination. No one can make the right decision but you."

He calls *that* improvising? I've never heard anyone describe marriage in such a raw way like that before. Declan's gaze clashes into mine, and I wonder if he feels the same. Because no matter what our intentions were when we signed the paperwork linking us as husband and wife, we agreed to a road trip together.

Leo taps his glass against ours. "To the newlyweds." Declan and he both bring their tumblers to their lips, but I can't do anything but blink at mine.

I don't know if I will ever be ready for a marriage like Leo describes. Sure, I might be married to Declan to uphold a legal contract, but that isn't the same as what Leo shared. His version requires trust and someone without an SUV worth of baggage.

I don't need to ask Declan how he feels. His intentions are written clear as day across his face—a snapshot into his heart that I know he reveals only for me.

I'm not ready to commit to a road trip. At least not the one he clearly wants. If I did, I would have said yes to my ex when he proposed.

Declan isn't him. Not even close.

My heart pounds within my chest, like a trapped bird trying to fight its way out of its cage. One thought batters me, over and over, as I sip my drink in silence.

I might have made the biggest mistake of my life by marrying Declan.

Fuck me.

CHAPTER
TWENTY-NINE

Declan

ris stands the moment Leo excuses himself.

"Where are you going?"

She can't even look me in the eyes as she replies, "Bathroom."

I rise and grab her hand, forcing her to glance up at me. "Is everything okay?" I hate asking the question almost as much as I hate the haunted look in her eyes. Desperation claws its way up my throat, beckoning me to keep her at my side.

"Sure." She offers a tense smile. "Do you mind calling Harrison to come pick us up while you wait?"

I nod.

"Great. I'll be back in a second." Her body remains rigid, spine straight as an arrow as she crosses the ballroom and disappears around a corner.

I consider what might have spooked her, and I can only assume it has something to do with what Leo said. She seemed fine before he went off talking about marriage…

Did it make things too real for her? It's plausible, given her aversion to love. She has made her feelings on the matter crystal clear, and I've gone along with it because it's what she wanted. It's not like it is any easier for me. After watching my father destroy his family after my mother died, I didn't want to put myself in a similar position. Everyone I love always leaves anyway. Why bother letting anyone close if there is no guarantee they will ever stay?

But are you going to spend the rest of your life alone because you're too afraid to get close to someone? It's still the same loneliness no matter how you paint it.

The back of my neck heats, and I turn to find Iris's eyes focused on me. A few men stop and stare at her, and it takes everything in me to ignore them as I walk across the room.

"Is Harrison downstairs wait—"

Her question is cut off by me pulling her into my arms.

"What's gotten into you?"

"Leo stopped by and asked if we were sticking around for the auction. I told him yes."

You're a bastard for lying to her.

I'll feel bad about it tomorrow. Tonight, I'll take advantage.

She groans. "Why would you do that?"

"Because I don't want to give him any reason to think we only came here for him."

She sighs as she wraps her arms around me. "Is there a specific reason you're hugging me?"

"I thought I saw someone I know."

Will you ever stop lying wherever she is concerned?

Only if I ever grow a conscience. Given the number of lies piling up around me, I doubt it would be during this lifetime.

"Did they go away or do you plan on holding me all night?"

Well, if I have an option…

You don't.

I sigh as I reluctantly release her only to grab her hand. "Let's dance."

"Is this the vodka talking?"

I shoot her a look. "It was one glass."

She laughs. "That's all it takes. You don't even like to dance."

I don't release her hand as I lean in and whisper in her ear, "Keep making a show in front of everyone and I'll make you regret it later."

A shudder runs through her, and I trace the goose bumps on her arm with a single finger. "That's promising."

Her mouth opens and closes repeatedly as I lead her toward the dance floor. I wrap an arm around her waist, and she responds by locking her arms behind my neck. Our faces are only a few inches apart as we rock in circles to the soft music playing through the speakers.

"If you wanted to dance with me, all you had to do was ask. No need to use empty threats to coerce me."

"Your mistake was thinking they are empty." I allow myself to smile.

She sucks in a breath, her eyes not leaving my lips. My fingers graze the soft curve of her ass. A groan gets trapped in my throat as she jolts forward to avoid my fingers, all to run right into my now hardening cock.

Her wide eyes blink up at me. "Please tell me that's a phone in your front pocket."

I throw my head back and laugh myself hoarse. By the time I come back for air, I find her eyes transfixed on me. Hers and a few others around us, all acting like they have never heard a grown man laugh before.

"It's a shame you don't laugh like that more often."

I lift my hand and cup her chin. "Maybe I finally have a reason to."

Her face softens, and her body melts into mine. "Stop looking at me like that."

"Like what?"

She escapes my question and my grasp all at once. I let her get away with it, only because she presses her cheek against the front of my tux, bringing her body closer to mine.

When the slow song bleeds into a fast-paced one, Iris squeals. I move to escape the dance floor, but she tugs on my hand and drags me back.

"I love this song!"

"Why am I not surprised?" I pretend to rub my ears in pain.

She laughs as she begins jumping up and down like a madwoman. I'm nearly knocked unconscious when she throws up her arms and sways her hips to the beat. I catch a few men staring at her rolling her body to the music, and my glare scares them off.

"Let's go sit," I snap.

"Please. One more song." She grabs my hands and drags them toward her hips. "Watch me."

I can't do anything *but* watch her. I'm entranced as she shimmies her body to the beat, keeping her lower half only an inch apart from mine. The way she dances isn't meant to be erotic, but I find myself growing aroused.

She smiles up at me. "You're not dancing."

I'm not sure I'm even *breathing*.

She laughs as she wraps her arms around my neck and tugs me closer. "Move your hips to the music."

I try and fail, which makes her break out into another fit of laughter. If that's the reward I get for looking like an idiot, so be it.

She turns around and places my palms back on her hips. "Copy me."

Her rasp of a voice can barely be heard over the thud of my heart. I snap out of my trance and swivel my body like hers, matching her movement. Heat courses through my body as we both move to the music. Her ass grinds against my cock, and I groan into her ear.

"Now you got it." She laughs as she steps out of my embrace.

My hands mourn the loss of her touch as she goes back to dancing. Her eyes shut, and she gets lost in the music. I don't bother trying to dance. I'm far too immersed in the way she moves to care about anything else. Everyone around us moves to the beat of the song until the last note plays, and the crowd disperses, ending the moment all too soon.

"That was so much fun!" She takes a step toward the tables, but I pull her back.

"Not so fast."

Her lips gape. "You want to keep dancing?"

I clutch onto one of her hands while my other finds the small of her back. "Yes."

"I thought you always hated dancing at these things."

"That was before."

"Before what?"

"Before I could do this." I pull her against me and place a soft kiss against her lips before retreating.

Keep her wanting more.

Her sharp inhale makes me grin into her hair. My skin buzzes as she grips onto me and we find our rhythm, two bodies swaying to the music. The song changes and people pass us by, but neither of us dares to end the moment.

The only time we step away from the dance floor is to get more drinks and partake in the auction I have no interest participating in. All it takes is Iris squealing at the prospect of a trip to Mexico for me to become an active bidder, with me raising my paddle to outspend everyone in the ballroom.

Iris wraps her arms around my neck and kisses my cheek when the auctioneer announces our paddle number. I don't have a chance to process her lips against my skin before she pulls away and settles back in her chair.

Fuck it. I become invigorated by the smiles she sends my way. Some people try to outbid me for whatever catches Iris's attention, but I outmatch them every time. By the time the auctioneer steps away from the podium, I've spent over fifty-million dollars solely for the rush I get whenever Iris smiles.

It doesn't take much convincing on her end to drag me back onto the dance floor once the auction ends, although I make a pit stop at the bar to get me through it. We keep dancing until the final song plays and we are the last couple in the room. I regrettably let her go, only for her to limp a couple feet. She doesn't protest as I wrap an arm around her and take the brunt of her weight.

"I think my feet need to be amputated." She flinches as she loses her footing.

I don't think as I haul her over my shoulder, bringing her ass to my eye level. "Problem solved."

"Declan!" she shouts into my back. "What are you doing?!" She rams her small fists into my spine, and I grunt.

"Being a gentleman."

"More like a caveman! Put me down right now! This is so embarrassing."

"No one is here to see you." The lack of bags makes my job of finding her clutch that much easier. I pass it to her so she can hold on to it while I walk.

Her head lifts as she assesses the empty ballroom. "Where did they all go?"

"Home."

"Then why are we still even here?"

"I lost track of time."

She gasps as she checks her phone. "It's midnight!"

"You'll make it home before you turn into a pumpkin, princess."

"That's not even how the story goes." Her laugh is muffled by the material of my tux as I carry her out the door.

"Close enough."

"You're a disgrace to your last name."

I smack her ass for that comment.

"Did you just spank me?!"

My hand burns to do it again if only to hear that little gasp she makes when my palm collides with her flesh. She returns the favor and smacks my ass *hard*. I almost drop her from the shock of it all, but I recover with a laugh.

"Ugh! You weren't supposed to like that!"

I collect myself before walking through the lobby with Iris hauled over my shoulder. The bellhop gives us a look as he opens the door, and I tip my chin in his direction.

A random passerby takes a photo as they catcall, and Iris flips them off.

"I hate you so much right now." She huffs.

Harrison's eyes widen as he opens the door of the car for me. "Sir. Is Mrs. Kane all right?"

Iris waves. "All good. Although I can't say the same about my husband once we get home."

She rarely calls me her husband, but when she does, it sends a rush of warmth through my body.

Harrison laughs as Iris pinches my ass.

"Do you mind? I'm starting to feel dizzy."

I unceremoniously dump her in the back seat before circling the car and dropping into mine. Harrison takes off down the road. Iris stares out the window, watching the Chicago skyline pass us by as we drive out to the suburbs.

I spend the entire car ride playing out different scenarios of exactly what might happen when we get home. By the time Harrison parks the car, I am buzzing with anticipation.

My thoughts are dashed as I turn to look over at Iris. Her body leans against the door, and her eyes remain shut as she breathes deeply in and out.

She fell asleep.

After all that talk on her end about getting payback, she couldn't even stay up to seek retribution.

"Should I wake her, sir?" Harrison peeks through my side of the car.

"I got her." I step out and walk around the trunk. I'm careful to open her door slowly so I can catch her before she falls out.

She doesn't stir as I tug her into my arms, cradling her the same way I did on our wedding night. Somehow, she remains fast asleep as I walk us through the house and up the stairs. I struggle to open her door without dropping her, but I am able to configure myself in a way so I can turn the knob.

Her door hits the wall with a soft thud. I make my way toward her bed and place her on the mattress. She tucks her hand under her cheek and curls into herself, uncaring about her dress or makeup.

I hate the idea of waking her up, but I doubt she wants to go to bed dressed like that. It can't be comfortable.

"Iris." I give her shoulder a subtle shake.

Her hand flies straight to my face. I release a whoosh of air as I duck, somehow missing her palm before it connected with my cheek.

"Iris. Wake up."

She groans. "Shh, Declan. Stop talking and do that thing with your tongue again."

My pulse thunders in my veins, matching the quickening of my heart rate. Is she...dreaming of me? I blink, trying to wrap my head around Iris having a dirty dream about *me*.

She lets out a soft whimper that I feel straight to my cock. I consider the consequences of waking her up and showing her what the real deal feels like, but I think better of it.

Start small and be strategic.

Making a move on her tonight would be anything but smart. No matter how much I want to, I need to go about this in a way that won't spook her. Her previous failed relationships are proof of what happens when people come on too strong, too fast.

I didn't spend this long chasing after her for me to squander it because I couldn't control my dick. My patience will be rewarded soon. It is only a matter of time before she comes crawling to me, and I plan on making her work for it.

Starting tomorrow.

CHAPTER THIRTY

Iris

The morning after the gala, I wake up in a designer gown, smudged makeup, and a serious case of *how did I get here* syndrome. I wiggle my sore feet, noting a few blisters that weren't there yesterday.

I sigh as I grab my phone from my nightstand. "Shit!"

I nearly fall out of bed when I see the time. Curses fly out of my mouth at the unread text message Declan sent hours ago. I unlock my phone with a shaky finger, only to release a breath of relief at the text.

Declan: No work today.

No work today?! I read his message twice to make sure my brain isn't acting up again and rearranging all the letters.

I clutch my phone to my chest and do a little twirl. The idea of having a Saturday all to myself makes me want to break out into a whole song and dance like a Dreamland princess. I swear I could touch the stars with how high I feel right now.

While I shower, I comb through the memories of last night. Leo and his toast. Declan and I dancing until midnight. Him carrying me around like a sack of potatoes because my feet hurt.

The last one makes me smile to myself like a complete loon.

Oh, Iris. What have you gotten yourself into?

I try to come up with answers as I make my way downstairs for breakfast, yet I can't seem to find one. I'm not sure what is going on. The marriage I signed up for is nothing compared to the reality. Declan wasn't supposed to be nice. He sure as hell wasn't supposed to do all these different things that stir up a longing in my chest I've never felt before. Even during my most serious relationship, I didn't feel anything close to the giddiness that overtakes me when Declan does something completely out of character.

I try to block out the thoughts by blasting music through my earbuds. It seems to work temporarily, and I dance my way into the kitchen while singing along at the top of my lungs.

What I find has me halting my steps. One of my earbuds pops out, the blaring music barely audible over the sound of Declan chopping vegetables.

Excitement is fast replaced by skittishness as Declan glances up at me with eyes full of heat. What did I do to earn *that* kind of look?

"You're here," I reply after what feels like a whole minute of us staring at each other.

"I am." He turns back to the cutting board and resumes chopping vegetables.

"You're taking the day off too?"

Chop. Chop. Chop. "Not exactly."

"Oh." A heavy sigh escapes me.

"I planned a fake date for us."

I blink. "I'm sorry. Did you just say you planned a *fake date*?"

His lips twitch. "I did."

"Wow. That's…unexpected."

"We need to be out the door in the next hour."

I cock my air gun and pretend to take aim. "Who's the target?"

His lips press together. "I'll tell you after."

"Why not before?"

"I want you to act natural."

All right… "And you telling me who we're trying to impress could compromise that?"

"Yes."

"Wow. They must be pretty important if they inspired you to plan something."

His hand grasping the knife tightens. "I'm capable of planning a date."

"Sure, you're capable, but that doesn't mean you actually want to."

"Who says I don't?" His question is far too loaded for me to handle without coffee.

So, instead of pushing Declan for more info, I help him with breakfast. With the way he keeps touching me while moving around the kitchen, one would think we live in an apartment the size of a shoebox instead of a mansion. I try to ignore the way a thousand sparks shoot off my skin whenever his body brushes against mine. Every time I sharply inhale, his lips seem to curve at the edges. I swear he does it all on purpose.

I can barely concentrate on cooking, which results in a half-burnt omelet. Sure, it might not look like the most appetizing meal, but it should get the job done. Calories are calories, am I right?

"Do you mind?" I snap when his chest brushes against my back.

"Your technique could use some work." He assesses my breakfast with a scowl.

"Fine, Mr. Food Network. Why don't you show me how it's done?"

"Did it hurt to swallow your pride?"

"Eh. I've swallowed worse."

His nostrils flare.

Iris: 1. Declan: 0.

I smile as I take a step backward and hold out the spatula, expecting him to take it. The breath is knocked out of my lungs as he crowds me against the stove, clutching onto my hand holding the spatula.

"I prefer a more hands-on learning approach." His hips press against my ass.

"Says the same man who used to tell me to *figure it out or find a new job* whenever I needed help."

He replies by nipping at the skin of my neck.

My next sentence comes out ragged. "What are you doing?"

"Helping my wife."

My throat bobs. "You're growing a bit too comfortable with that nickname for my liking."

"I use it to remind you of your place."

"And what's that?"

"Mine."

My cheeks burn, along with the area below my waist. He ignores my sudden shyness as he pours the mixture with his free hand, trapping me in place between both of his arms.

"Your first mistake was pouring too much in the pan at once." His hot breath hits my neck, eliciting goose bumps across my body.

The eggs sizzle, matching the way my insides feel as his chest brushes against my back. I never thought cooking could be considered an erotic experience—at least not until Declan. The man makes cooking eggs seem like a kind of foreplay.

I swallow past the lump in my throat. "What's next?"

He carries my hand gripping onto the spatula toward the hot stove. "You let the eggs cook."

It's a simple task, yet he holds my hand hostage as we gently push the eggs over and over until the top surface of the eggs has thickened. Each minute feels like an eternity with the way he holds onto me. He seems to be drawn toward the curve of my neck, and he kisses me twice before dictating the next set of directions.

"Now you fill one side with your toppings."

"Not both?"

His deep chuckle rattles my bones. "Greedy as always."

"More like famished."

"That makes two of us," he replies huskily as he presses his hips into my ass.

That's definitely *not* a phone in his pocket this time. I can tell that much.

"I think we're talking about two different hungers here." Somehow the words make it past my tight throat.

His thick length presses against the seam of my ass, telling me exactly how he feels about *cooking*. He pulls away all too quickly, taking his warmth with him as he adds some space between us. I don't understand his reaction.

Why do you care? It would only complicate things even more.

I care more than I would ever admit.

Because you want him too.

It is a tough fact to admit. I do want him. I want him really freaking badly, yet I don't know how to go about pursuing something like that. And more specifically, I'm not sure exactly *what* it is that I want to pursue. Casual sex seems almost as complicated as proposing that we try something more. Either option would blow our whole plan to hell, and I'm not sure I want to do that either. My options seem as hopeless as my ability to hold off on our attraction.

If Declan is aware of my inner panic, he doesn't reveal it.

"Be ready in thirty." Declan gives me one last look before he grabs my shitty first attempt at an omelet and walks out of the kitchen.

I grip the counter and take a few deep breaths.

How the hell are you going to survive a fake date today when you feel like this?

Declan grabs a pair of keys hanging on the wall.

"You're driving?"

He spins the keys on his index finger. "I gave Harrison the day off."

"I'm not sure what we did to deserve this kind of treatment but I'm here for it."

Declan doesn't comment as he walks up to a shiny vintage convertible that looks like something out of a spy movie.

My mouth drops open. "This is our ride?"

"Yup. Get in before we're late."

I'm stupefied as he circles around the hood and opens the passenger door for me.

"Wow. This is so cool!" I walk over to my side and drop into the seat, completely speechless as I trace the leather. Declan shuts my door before walking back around to the driver's side. He puts the keys in the ignition, and the engine revs to life as he puts it in first gear.

I sigh. "The things I would do to get a chance to drive this car."

He laughs. It's rough, deep, and steals all my capacity to breathe. "You can get me to do many things, but driving this car isn't one of them."

"Let me guess. It's a *man's car.*" I roll my eyes.

His previous smile is wiped clean off his face. "More like a woman's. My mother's to be specific."

I feel like someone stuck me in the chest with a knife and twisted it. "Your mother's?"

His Adam's apple bobs. "I thought I'd take it out since I haven't run it in a month."

He takes it out every month? My chest aches for the man who keeps the memory of his mother alive through her car. I can tell Declan cares based on how much the car is taken care of, from the polished leather interior to the perfectly waxed exterior.

I can't think of anything to say, my tongue thick with emotion.

The image Declan portrays to everyone is nothing compared to the one he hides from the world. While he isn't anything close to perfect by any stretch of the word, he is still human. He hurts just like the rest of us.

We take off down the driveway before he stops to open the gate. He rambles, and I smile because I have never seen him stumble on his words.

"She probably loved this car more than she loved my father—which if you knew them before she got sick—was a lot. Not sure what she saw in him, but I suppose he was different with all of us before she died."

I don't miss the way he talks about his parents before she got sick. As if her illness changed the dynamics of everyone's lives, including Seth's. My lips turn down, and I hate myself for the ounce of sympathy that bubbles to the surface of my heart for the man who is as vile and ruthless as they come. Somehow love seems to humanize the worst souls.

"Will you tell me more about her?" It's a loaded question. One that I'm not sure is fair to ask in the first place, but I can't help myself. I want to know more about the man who takes his mother's car out once a month as if she might return at any minute and ask for it back. I want to know about it all.

He sighs, and I just know deep down in my heart that he is about to turn me down. For some reason I can't bear the thought, so I do something stupid. Something so incredibly stupid I'm sure I will regret it tomorrow. But I'm too enraptured by his story to care about what might happen.

"What if we make a deal?"

The corners of his lips lift. "I'm open to negotiations."

"What's something you want?" I drop the bomb back on his lap. I'll let him be the one to decide what he wants most and then see if I'm up for the challenge.

"I want an equal exchange…" He pauses, and my breath stalls in my chest.

Another kiss? A real date? *A blow job?* The options are endless really. A warmth travels from my head to my toes at the thought of what he might choose.

"What do you have in mind?"

"I'll tell you about my mother if you tell me about your learning differences."

If my life had a soundtrack, this is the moment the DJ scratches the record, making me feel like a total dud. The air escapes my lungs like a deflated balloon. What the hell kind of deal is that? And more specifically, how the hell did he find out?

I cross my arms and throw up a barrier. "Who told you?"

"No one."

"Bullshit. Was it Cal?" I'm about to tell Declan to pull over and let me take over, solely so I can go find Cal and rip him a new asshole.

He shakes his head. "I found out on my own."

"*How?*"

"I knew the signs."

A bitter laugh escapes me. "You expect me to believe that? Exactly how gullible do you think I am?"

His face softens. "My mom was the same way."

"Your mom? The same one who was a history major?"

He clutches onto the steering with white-knuckled fists. "Just because she struggled with reading doesn't mean she hated it."

I feel like a dick for assuming otherwise. To be fair, I'm struggling to keep up with all this information. There is no way I can process Declan knowing about my dyslexia and his mother struggling with the same disorder all in one conversation.

"I should have known you would figure it out."

"There was no reason for you to hide it in the first place."

I clench my fists against my lap. "You don't get to judge my choices."

"I only want to understand them." The softness of his voice tears me up inside.

I stay silent.

"*Please.*"

I release a shaky breath. Declan doesn't say *please* ever, so it makes me weak enough to open up about my past.

I stare out the window. "I spent my whole life feeling different than everyone else. First, it started with teasing and being made fun of. Little things like teachers calling me lazy or classmates gossiping about how I was stupid. I was held back a year, which led to more embarrassment because all my friends moved on to the next grade without me. Eventually kids got bolder. Their words became harsher and their actions meaner. It didn't take long for someone like me to start believing those words, especially when your own father called you a disappointing idiot every day." My voice cracks.

Declan reaches out and forces my fist open so he can lock our fingers together.

"It was a self-fulfilling prophecy. With my parents' divorce and all the stress with that, I stopped caring about class despite my mom trying her hardest to get me into tutoring. Nothing was working, and I think she was losing hope too. My shame and anxiety kept growing until I would cry every day before school. I shut down with everyone, so my mom took a chance and found me a therapist so I could open up to someone about what was happening."

His hand gives me a reassuring squeeze.

"With my therapist's help, I started building myself back up and found projects I was good at that had nothing to do with school. That's where my plant obsession started. Turns out I had a calling for bringing my mom's dead plants back to life."

"I thought therapy was supposed to fix our problems, not create more of them."

The tension in my chest eases as I laugh. "It helped. One plant turned into two, and eventually I started building a whole collection. My therapist called it a coping strategy."

"I suppose it can be considered a better solution than drugs."

Our eyes connect, his filled with a lightness I wish would remain for long spans of time. "Once I got the emotional stuff down, I was much more open to tutoring. It took a while, but I finally started succeeding in school."

"And then what?"

"And then I graduated high school with a lot of help. I wasn't ready to commit to a university yet after all the difficulties I went through in school, so that's how I ended up at the temp agency you partnered with."

"And then you drew the short stick and had to come work for me."

My nose scrunches. "You went through assistants like one would go through underwear."

"It's not my fault they didn't meet my expectations."

I shake my head. "Whenever you fired someone, the remainder of us were forced to drop our names into a hat. I was lucky up until that point, but then—"

"You were chosen," he finishes for me.

I nod. "I showed up to your office on Monday knowing I wouldn't make it to the end of the week. But then…"

"What?" His eyes darken.

"I could just tell in your eyes that you expected me to fail."

"And?"

"I spent my whole life having people look at me that way. Something snapped in me when you told me to not bother unpacking my stuff since I would be gone by the end of the week. It lit a fire under my ass. I was ready to do whatever it took to prove to myself once and for all that I could achieve anything I wanted, starting with my job."

"Weren't you afraid?"

"Of course I was. Your reputation was as terrible as your track record with assistants, but I knew nothing you could have said to me would have topped any of the shit I grew up hearing as a little kid."

The steering wheel creaks under the pressure of his palms. "If I had known sooner, I would have held back on some of the things I told you—"

My laugh cuts him off. "Please. We both know you would have fired me if you realized my struggles."

His jaw tightens. "That's not true."

"Why not?"

"Because if my mom were alive, she would have been ashamed of me for doing something like that."

My chest feels as if he cut it open with his words alone. "Is that why you kept me all this time? Despite the errors and typos and slower turnaround times?" My voice sounds so small and unsure—a perfect match to how I feel with Declan stirring up all these emotions.

He draws a slow breath. "I kept you because you're fantastic at your job. You always rose to whatever challenge I threw your way, whether it was a part of your job description or not. There wasn't a single time I felt like your differences got in the way. If anything, I think it made you ten times better at your job because you thought differently than me. Just look at the Yakura deal. He would have never accepted the proposal without your additions to my model."

A swell of emotion lodges itself in my throat. "Oh."

"I might be cold, rude, and distant, but I'm not blind. My whole job is about evaluating assets and it turns out that you're my biggest one."

I never thought someone talking finance to me would be so heart-wrenchingly beautiful.

He gives my hand another squeeze as if to remind me of our connection. "There isn't anything I wouldn't do to keep you by my side."

"You don't need to try too hard. I am your wife after all."

"Even if you weren't, I won't give you up." The little smile on his face does something crazy to my heart rate.

I never thought someone like him could be capable of such sweet words. "Who knew you were such a nice guy underneath your grumpy exterior?"

"Don't go telling anyone else or they'll be disappointed to find out it's only for you."

Looks like the reporter *was* right. Declan does have a soft spot for me after all.

"Why?"

"*Forelsket**." His raspy whisper makes me feel like he shares a secret I can't decode.

"Spell it for me." I pull out my phone.

He shakes his head as if it can erase the tiny smile on his face. "Some words aren't meant to be translated."

"That's such a lie! All your words have translations."

"Correction. Some words aren't meant to be translated by *you*."

I cross my arms. "Where did you learn all these words anyway? There's no way you know all these languages."

He turns his head back toward the road. "It was a game my mom and I played together when I was a little kid."

My throat gets scratchy at the thought. "How?"

"I was always bad at expressing my feelings, way before my mom ever got sick."

"You? No. I refuse to believe that," I say with absolute seriousness.

His glare makes me laugh.

"She taught me how some people need a hundred words to express a single thought, while some people only need one word to share a hundred thoughts."

"I never thought of it that way."

His eyes become distant. "It became our secret code. If I was feeling a certain way, she would ask me for my word."

---

* **Forelsket:** *Noun, Norwegian:* that overwhelming gut-rush euphoria exclusive to the beginnings of falling in love.

My bottom lip quivers. "What made you start using them again?"

He turns and looks at me. "Not what but *who*. We both struggle with words in our own ways. Me with expressing them, and you with reading them." His explanation makes each word he shares feel even more meaningful.

The burning sensation in my chest intensifies, betraying just how much my heart wants to throw caution to the wind. It scares me more than I care to admit, so I stick to a safer question. "What made you choose untranslatable ones?"

"They started out in English but eventually once my brothers started picking up on it and started copying me, I switched gears. There was no way they could say *kyoikumama*, let alone spell it."

"Always against sharing, ever since a young kid, huh?"

"You're an only child. You can't even begin to understand what it is like to grow up with siblings always stealing your stuff and copying you."

"I wish! That seems a whole lot better than spending your entire life alone."

"The silence must have been nice."

I laugh. "It got old fast. If everything goes my way, I plan on having enough kids to fill a whole house so they never have to grow up feeling the way I did."

He shoves the gear stick a bit harder than necessary. "Kids?"

"A whole minivan if I'm lucky."

"I didn't know you wanted a big family." A vein in his neck throbs.

"You never asked, and I didn't think it mattered."

"Why not?"

"Because we only agreed to one child."

"What if that weren't the case?"

I feel shocked by his question. "What exactly are you suggesting?"

He pauses, clearly thinking of a response before shaking his head. "Nothing."

Nothing? I want answers, but my fear of his response stops me from asking any questions. And with the way he shuts down, I know that I'm not going to get them today anyway.

Maybe it's for the best.

CHAPTER
THIRTY-ONE

Iris

There is no way Declan's target happened to go to the Chicago Botanic Garden on a Saturday. After our whole conversation in the car, I know he planned this for me. Not that he would ever admit it. So rather than call him out on it, I go along with the whole charade. I'm far too excited about visiting the garden to ruin it by calling Declan out on his lie.

The garden is my favorite place in the entire world—sorry, Dreamland. I have so many fond memories here, dating all the way back to my childhood. My mom, Nana, and I would come here together after my Saturday tutoring sessions. Mom and I would visit all the gardens while Nana would huff and puff about her busted knee, only to be easily swayed by the pretty flowers and champagne popsicles.

I laugh as Declan grabs a map from an information stand. He doesn't ask for my help, and I don't bother offering it. While

I know every corner of this place, watching him assess the map like we are exploring uncharted territory is far too entertaining to pass up.

He locates our current position on the map. "Is there a certain strategy to all this?"

"Strategy? It's a garden, not a chessboard." I laugh.

"Fair point. Then is there something in particular you want to see first?"

"Shouldn't we go wherever the person you came to see is?" I push my lips together to prevent giving myself away.

"I don't know where they are." He says the lie with such ease, it unsettles me enough to push for more.

"You know, if I knew what they looked like, it would make this process a little easier. How else am I supposed to know when we need to pretend?"

Declan shuts the map, pockets it, and grabs my hand. "We don't."

Sparks shoot up my arm from the contact. "So, what? We just act like a couple the entire time?"

"Exactly."

I fake groan. "But this place is huge. It could take hours before we find them."

"Maybe even more." He doesn't release my hand as he leads us toward the start of a trail.

I give him another opportunity to confess. "They must be pretty important if you're going out of your way to subject yourself to walking around a garden for hours while holding my hand."

"You have no idea."

I turn my head away so he doesn't catch me smiling at his lie.

Declan wraps his arm around my waist as if we touch like this all the time. What happened to the man who struggled with touching me only two months ago? Because it seems like that version of Declan is long gone, with him using today's fake date as an excuse to touch me however he wants.

I'm so lost in obsessing over his embrace that I almost miss my favorite part of this whole place.

"Ah! Stop!" I pull back on Declan's arm.

Declan halts, and I stumble from the momentum.

"What happened?" He checks the perimeter.

"You're walking so fast that we almost missed my favorite part."

He looks around, missing the greenhouse during his scan of the bushes behind us.

I point with my free hand at the glass structure.

"You want to go in there?"

"Yes! It's the best place!"

"A greenhouse?"

I smile. "Is there something wrong with that?"

"I'm just surprised you prefer that over the outdoors."

"I'll show you why." I all but drag him through the doors. Instantly, we are hit with a gust of humid air. Fans spray a warm mist across all the plants, and we are caught in the crossfire.

A crease appears in between his eyebrows. "Why is it so muggy?"

"Because they need to recreate the tropical climate."

"What for?"

It excites me to know more about a topic than Declan, and I delight in the fact that he doesn't know everything after all.

"Plants like these would never normally survive the seasons here. Without a greenhouse, they would most likely die, especially in Chicago."

He follows me as I walk through the rows of short palm trees.

"Is that the reason you keep all your plants indoors?"

"Do I need a better reason besides to annoy you with them?"

His glare makes me laugh to myself.

"Living in an apartment had many perks, but a greenhouse isn't one of them. Not enough space." I lead him toward the small pond at the back of the greenhouse. "You know how you have different words to express your feelings?"

He nods.

"Plants have different meanings too." I gesture toward the lotus flower stems peeking out of the murky water. "These are my absolute favorites."

"Why?" He pockets his hands and stares at me head-on without a flicker of emotion.

"Because it amazes me how the most beautiful flower can blossom from the worst conditions." I check out my reflection in the murky water. "It seems silly to relate to a flower—"

"It's not."

I look up to find his eyes focused on me. The warmth reflecting in them encourages me to open up without worrying about the consequences. "I spent a long time underestimating myself, only to realize I needed to make it past the bad stuff and find the light."

"Is this the reason you liked visiting the greenhouse?" He stops beside me to get a closer look at the flowers.

"The main one."

"Any others?"

"You're looking at it." I spin in a circle with my arms extended, and my hands brush against a couple of leaves.

His lips press together in a poor attempt to hide his smile. "You're a crazy plant lady."

"Please. I haven't officially earned that title until I have a greenhouse of my own."

"Do you want one?"

"A greenhouse?"

"Are the pesticides in here getting to your head or are you just struggling to comprehend what I'm asking?"

"Maybe I'm struggling because of *what* you're asking in the first place."

His chest heaves from a deep breath. "Would you like a greenhouse?"

"In your backyard?"

"I think we can start calling it ours, seeing as you live there too."

My mouth opens before shutting again. "You're offering to build me a greenhouse?"

"If only to save me from tripping over potted plants in the middle of the night when I want a goddamn glass of water."

"Of course. How silly of me to think you wanted to build one to make me happy."

"Anything I do is solely for my benefit." But his grin says the exact opposite.

The warm feeling from his smile follows me as we keep walking through the greenhouse. I take the time to explain all the different plants to Declan. For someone who always seems to be taking the lead, he doesn't seem the least bit bothered about following me.

As we step out of the greenhouse and blink up at the sun, Declan asks, "Where to next?"

I point toward the trail that will take us around the lake. "That way."

Together, we walk hand in hand like it's the most natural thing in the world. Declan asks me questions about different plants and I answer them, getting far too excited about topics like the difference between tropical and semitropical. He asks silly questions, half of which I'm sure are done purposefully to make me laugh.

Seriously, there is no way I willingly married someone who doesn't know the difference between a succulent and a cactus. He seems confused about how all cacti are succulents but not all succulents are cacti, and I spend a good hour in the Arid Greenhouse with him, explaining everything I know about the different plants. Not once does he seem bored despite my non-stop chatter.

Declan, a man who doesn't speak for longer than five-minute spans of time, spoke to me for hours. The idea makes me far giddier than it should.

It's not until the sun begins to set that Declan steers us toward the exit.

"So, did you ever find them?"

"Who?"

I lift our interlocked hands in the air to remind him of our duty. "The reporter we came here to pretend in front of."

"No."

"I knew it! You can stop lying now."

"Lying about what?"

"We didn't come here so a reporter could see us, did we?"

His eyes lighten. "Why else would we come here?"

"Because you wanted to take me out on a date, but you didn't want to admit it was that in the first place just in case I rejected you, so you made up this whole elaborate story so I wouldn't ask questions."

"Is narcissism genetic or is our child safe from that awful personality trait?"

The way he says "our child" sends a wave of *something* through me that I refuse to acknowledge. "Depends. If we're going based on paternal history, they are screwed from the start."

He reaches out and runs his thumb across my bottom lip. "Hopefully they inherit their mother's selflessness instead."

I officially raise the white flag as I stand on the tips of my toes and kiss him.

CHAPTER THIRTY-TWO

Iris

We sit in silence during the entire drive back to the house. I'm not sure what to say, and Declan looks about one comment away from fucking me in his mom's car, so I stay quiet.

My heart rate reaches a critical level by the time he drives into the garage, and I'm out of breath as he pulls me out of the car and straight into the house.

He moves so fast. One moment I'm blinking up at him, the next I'm being pushed up against a wall. My spine tingles from the momentum.

"Tell me what you want." His crazed expression does something insane to my insides.

My heart thuds against my chest, my pulse thundering with each beat. I lose all ability to speak. The way he stares at me, with his jaw clenched and nostrils flaring with each ragged breath, makes me shiver.

"I'm not sure."

He lets out a groan as he steps away.

I miss his warmth instantly. "Declan—" I reach out to touch him, but he grabs both my wrists and locks them above my head.

"You haven't earned the right to touch me yet."

"And you have?"

He traces the column of my neck with his free hand, and my whole body lights up like a firework. "I'm not scared to claim what's mine."

"I'm not afraid." Not anymore. I'm done with the back-and-forth. The uncertainty is driving me crazy, and it isn't fair to him. He planned a date for me and pretended it was a fake one just so I would go. I don't think anyone has done something so sweet for me ever.

"Prove it then." He releases my wrists.

"*Strikhedonia.*" I no doubt butcher the pronunciation, but it seems to draw a genuine smile from Declan nonetheless.

I wrap my hand around the back of his neck and drag his lips toward mine. Unlike our first kiss, Declan lets me take the lead. It's tentative at first. Nothing but a few soft presses of my lips against his, each becoming progressively more desperate on my end. He doesn't make a move to touch me, and my skin itches for connection. His silent challenge to prove how much I want him plays in the back of my mind as I trace his bottom lip with the edge of my tongue.

I never thought I would crave his touch as much as I do at this moment, and I find myself growing irritated with how much control he exudes over the situation.

That won't do. The tips of my fingers tingle with the need to touch him *everywhere.* My hands grow bolder as I drag my fingers down his shirt, straight toward the bulge beneath his pants. He releases a shuddery breath as I trace the outline of his length. I use the opportunity to tease his tongue with mine, and the results are miraculous.

He groans as his palm finds the back of my neck, locking me in place as he ravishes my mouth. I rub the palm of my hand against his cock. His kissing grows more uncontrolled as I make quick work of undoing his belt and zipper. Our tongues tangle together, stifling his moan as I slip a hand inside his pants. He sucks in a breath as I trace the tip of his cock. I swipe at the bead of arousal with my thumb before rubbing it in circles across his head.

He bites down on my bottom lip, drawing a metallic taste in my mouth.

I giggle to myself as I withdraw my hand and pull back. "How was that for proof?"

The hand around the back of my neck tightens, and his thumb presses against my thundering pulse point. His chest rises and falls with each ragged breath. Goose bumps spread across my skin as he opens his blown-out eyes and turns them on me.

"I'm not entirely convinced."

My lips part. "You're so full of—"

I'm cut off as he hauls me over his shoulder, stealing me before I ever have a chance to run.

"Are you kidding me? We're back to this again?" I pound my fists against his back.

He turns toward the stairs. "I want to conduct a more thorough observation."

"Are you insane?"

"When it comes to you, that was never a question."

I laugh as he carries me up the million steps. "You know I can walk right?"

"Acutely. That doesn't mean I'll let you."

I laugh. "Why not?"

"You're a flight risk."

"Am not!"

"If I had it my way, you would wear an ankle monitor so I could always know where you are."

My eyes widen. "That is absolutely terrifying."

"Tell me about it. I've already looked into GPS chips for our child."

Our child. Those two words seem to have my heart in a choke hold today.

"Thinking about becoming a father often?" I ask with a shaky voice.

"More than I should."

The idea of him considering fatherhood doesn't scare me as much as it should. I knew what I was getting into when I signed the deal, but it seems like such a contrast compared to the man who needed to be manipulated into shared custody rights.

Oh, Iris. What are you going to do now?

Declan seems to answer for me as he enters his room. I cling to his shirt with sweaty palms, desperate for something to ground me.

My world turns right-side up as he throws me onto the bed. I let out an oomph as my back slams into the mattress, and all the air is knocked out of me for a completely different reason than being flung. Declan's hands grip onto my thighs as he drags me toward the edge of the bed. The material of my dress slides up, and the hem skates dangerously close to my underwear.

He stops and stares at me in a way that makes me feel like he is picking me apart, piece by piece. "Let's play a game."

"You and your damn games. I swear it's like you were deprived of fun as a child."

His lips twitch as he slides his palms up my thighs. They tremble beneath his touch, and I press them together to hide their shakiness.

"You'll like this one. I promise." He makes quick work of my sneakers and socks, and they thud against the carpet like stripped battle armor.

I rise up on my elbows. "What are the rules?"

His eyes bleed to black. "There is only one."

"That seems easy."

He *tsks* as he drags my dress hem a little higher. My breathing comes out harsher, and that seems to only encourage him.

"Beg."

I shoot him a glare. "If you expect me to beg for your cock, you have another thing coming."

One side of his mouth lifts into a smirk. "Who said anything about my cock?"

"Then what exactly do you want me to beg for—"

Declan's fingers grab onto the edges of my thong and drag it downward. He takes his time, turning the removal of my clothing into an event. I can barely take his drawn-out touches and the burning glances.

"I don't like this game." I groan, growing impatient with each passing second.

He tugs my dress up higher and parts my thighs. "I'm sure I can change your mind soon enough."

Any reply I might have made is stolen as he presses his palm against my chest and shoves me backward. He drops to his knees and drags me toward his face.

Oh God. A sight like that could bring a woman to the brink of orgasm alone. With the way my lower half throbs, it wouldn't take much to pull me over the edge. Especially not with the way he stares at me. It scares me as much as it enthralls me, and I dance between the two as his fingers part me for him. My entire body buzzes as his tongue darts out, teasing me. I arch my back in response, and my thighs squeeze his head between them. His chuckle makes my clit vibrate. My fingers grip onto the comforter as he destroys my ability to think of anything but his tongue diving into me.

I don't think I've ever been this turned on in my life. Everything about him is sensual, from the way his nails dig into my thighs as he teases me to the way he groans against me when I sigh. All is lost the moment he slips a finger inside me. His lips wrap around my clit, sucking to the point of pain. He stops every single time I near my peak. I curse him in the same sentence I praise him, and that only seems to make him draw everything out.

No man has ever made me feel *devoured* like this. I want him to make me stop hurting as much as I want him to never stop fucking me.

I nearly crack and beg for him to finish what he started but I hold out. If he expects me to break, I'll make him work just as hard to prove a point.

I won't yield for him. Not in a boardroom and not in the bedroom.

Declan rises to my challenge with vigor. My sensitive clit aches, begging for mercy Declan won't give. I'm a mess as I thrash against the sheets. He takes his time, pushing me close to my breaking point before pulling back. My frustration grows until I give up, and one word earns me the keys to paradise.

"*Please.*" My cheeks are damp from tears I wasn't aware had fallen.

His chuckle sends another wave of arousal through me. "You put up a good fight. You'll be rewarded for that."

I moan as he slips a second finger inside, crooking the two so they glide against my G-spot. The way he sucks on my clit combined with the torture of his fingers shoves me off the edge.

My body shudders as Declan continues fucking me with his tongue. He plays my body like his favorite instrument, drawing out my orgasm for as long as possible. I expect him to stop as I come down, but his movement only grows more desperate.

My voice is hoarse as I scream out his name, and that seems to drive him *wild*. His fingers grip onto my ass as he pulls me forward, driving his tongue into me like I wish he would do with his cock. I clutch onto his hair and tug at the strands. He groans, pressing his thumb against my swollen clit. The way he circles the flesh has me climbing until I chase my second orgasm like a shooting star.

Declan abandons my clit and pulls me into his embrace. He sucks up my cries as his mouth latches onto mine, drawing another shaky breath from me. My lips part and he brushes his tongue against mine, making me taste just how much I want him. His fingers grip onto the back of my neck, and his thumb strokes my rapid pulse point.

His kiss becomes less frantic as I come down from my high. He switches from punishing to apologetic, with the slight trace of his tongue across my bottom lip becoming my undoing.

I feel light-headed, like a high I have yet to come down from. "Are you sure you're a virgin?"

He gives my pussy a slap. "What did you say?"

I gasp. "I'm kidding!"

"Just because I haven't been with anyone in a long time doesn't mean I forgot how things work."

"Why haven't you? Been with someone, I mean?" I never should have asked the question. I knew it was a bad idea, yet I couldn't stop myself, as per usual around Declan lately.

"It didn't feel right."

"Because you were obsessed with me?" I stroke the fire in his eyes with verbal lighter fluid.

His lips press against mine. "That's narcissistic of you."

I grin. "It must be contagious around here."

He kisses me until I'm completely boneless, waiting for the next step.

What *is* the next step?

"Shouldn't we discuss what happens next?"

He grabs my palm and presses it against his jeans, right over his rock-solid cock. His lips trail a line of kisses down my throat.

I rub his erection with my hand before retreating. "So what? We have sex?"

He nips at the sensitive skin at the hollow of my neck. "Not everything needs a plan."

"But—"

He drags his hand up my body and caresses the edge of my breast. "Do you want this or not?"

It feels as if he placed a loaded gun in my hand. "This will complicate things."

"I can guarantee it." His touch grows bolder as he traces my sensitive nipple through the fabric of my dress. "Now that we settled everything, do I have permission to fuck you?"

"You seem far too excited by the prospect."

He grins in a way that makes his whole face light up. I commit his look to memory so I can obsess about it later. His body presses me into the mattress as he leans forward. I wrap my arms around his neck and kiss him until I can't take it anymore. Until I'm dizzy and desperate for more.

My hands shove at his chest. He takes his weight off me and stands.

"What—"

I cut him off as I stand and grab the hem of his shirt. "Off," I order.

He complies with my command, revealing a chest of pale, muscular flesh. I sigh at the sight. His body deserves to be a national monument. If I didn't suffer from an insane amount of jealousy, I would nominate him myself.

"Like what you see?"

I smirk. "Depends. Is it all for show or do you have the stamina to back it all up?"

He shoots me a lopsided grin I feel straight to my heart. "I swear you like stirring me up."

"Only because I like unraveling you so much more." I run my hands down his abs, tracing each curve with the tips of my fingers.

He shudders as my hands reach to remove his belt. I slide down onto my knees, and a hiss escapes him.

"Relax," I say with the utmost confidence despite the rapid beat of my heart. I'm quick to shove his jeans past his thighs, revealing the bulge straining against the material of his briefs.

The outline of his cock makes my mouth water. I become crazed as I tug his briefs down his legs, not stopping until his cock bobs in front of me. A bead of arousal leaks from the tip. I've lost all sense of self as I lick him from the base of his shaft all the way to the tip, tracing my tongue over the pearly white drop.

Rather than grip my head, he clutches onto my chin and forces me to look up at him. "This is better than anything I could have imagined."

My cheeks burn. "Think of me often?"

"Regrettably."

I'll show him regrettably. I grab one of the bows holding up my dress and tug on the string. Our eyes remain locked together as I move onto the next strap, pulling at the strand until both sides of my dress fall. The material puddles around my lap like a halo.

His eyes widen as they drop to my chest.

"Eyes up here." I snap my fingers and point them at my face before taking his cock in my mouth.

He hisses as I alternate between sucking him off and tracing his shaft with the tip of my tongue.

"Did you think about this?" I reach out and cradle one of his balls, earning a groan before I take him in my mouth again. He pushes his cock farther down my throat. I've felt powerful in many situations, but nothing compares to the high I get watching Declan lose himself in the pleasure of my touch.

"Or how about this?" I take him deeper than ever before while sucking in long drags of air to prevent my gag reflex. The salty taste of him coats my tongue, and I suck at his tip to get another taste.

"More like I think of this." He pulls away, taking his cock with him. My mouth falls open as he swoops in and throws me back on the bed.

He makes quick work of discarding my dress, leaving me blinking up at the ceiling, naked and waiting. I slide across the comforter as he drags me toward the edge of the bed. My limp legs hang over the side, dangling as he shoves them open.

He slips a finger inside me, dragging it back and forth before adding another. "Who knew you liked sucking cock that much?"

I rise on my elbows. "Driving you wild seems to have an addicting quality to it."

Based on the smile on his face as he turns away from me and grabs a condom from his nightstand, I think he liked my answer. One can only hope I'm rewarded for my honesty.

I watch him slip the condom on his shaft, and I'm hit with another wave of admiration for him. Knowing he is willing to put aside his goal to get me pregnant makes my whole chest ache.

He steps between my legs again and lines himself up at my entrance. My breath catches as he drives forward, slamming his hips against mine. Tears prick my eyes from the burning sensation of him stretching me.

He wraps my trembling legs around his waist, and I hiss at the tightness.

"I hate you," I say through gritted teeth.

"I look forward to fucking the lies right out of you." The look of hunger in his eyes sends a shiver down my spine. His nails dig into my hips as he withdraws, only to slide into me again. The air is knocked straight out of my lungs as his tempo shifts to something I can only describe as insatiable.

His onslaught destroys any sense of control I have over the situation. He throws one of my quivering legs over his shoulder before adding the other, changing our position so I can take more of his abuse.

A burning desire in my lower half intensifies with each slap of his hips against mine. I claw at the sheets. His chest. His thighs. Anything to ground me as he memorizes my body like a language only he can translate.

His pumps never cease, and my orgasm starts to build inside of me. He runs his thumb across my clit before drawing small circles with the pad. I detonate like a bomb, warmth exploding in my chest as he shoves me over the edge of no return. My eyes slam shut, only to snap open again as he pinches my clit.

"Look at me." The rough whisper of his command sends another round of liquid fire through me. I shatter around his cock without breaking eye contact. My release seems to spark his. His fingers dig into my flesh as his cock drives in and out of me like he is a man possessed. He groans, fingers tightening around me as his head drops back and he comes. The sight of him unraveling devastates any last hope I have of keeping him at arm's length.

I found my newest addiction, and it happens to be my fake husband.

CHAPTER THIRTY-THREE

Declan

"Why did you use a condom?" Iris asks as she tugs a clean T-shirt of mine over her head.

I busy myself with digging through a drawer. "I wasn't about to kill the moment by asking if you wanted to try for a baby."

She laughs. "I appreciate the thought, but I know what I signed up for."

"So, what, us having sex is just a way for you to fulfill your end of a contract?" My tone carries more bite than intended.

"I never said that."

"Then what?" I snap.

"I mean, I know we agreed to having a child via in vitro, but if we are attracted to each other, then maybe…" Her voice drops off.

Is she fucking kidding me? If we are *attracted* to each other? The way she minimizes our connection makes me want to throw her back on the bed and show her how *attracted* she is to me. It's bullshit is what it is.

You're angry at yourself because you're developing feelings and she isn't.

Fuck yeah, I'm angry. I hate this discomfort growing in my chest with each ragged breath as much as I hate the way she is the one person I can't control.

I slam the drawer shut, which makes her wince. Her reaction only adds to my already deteriorating mood.

Rein your temper in before you do something you regret.

I'm quick to throw on a pair of sweatpants and a T-shirt before grabbing my wallet.

"Let me explain." She grabs onto my arm, but I shrug her off.

"I don't want your explanation."

What I want is silence and some time to think by myself because something I'm doing isn't working. I chased. I conquered. Yet she still won't acknowledge the obvious feelings growing between us.

"Where are you going?" She follows me down the hall.

"Out." I don't look back at her as I barrel down the stairs.

"It's late." Her voice edges on the side of panic as she follows behind me.

I *almost* turn around, but I can't. Not when I feel like *this*. I don't even know what this even is, but I want to claw at my chest until I have the ability to rip my useless heart out.

"Don't go. Not like this." She grasps my chin in her hand and forces me to look at her.

"Tell me why you don't want me to go."

"It doesn't feel right." Her reply is instant.

"Why?" I press.

She bites down on her lip and glances away. "Because you're upset."

"Try again."

One more chance and then you're walking away.

"Because I don't want you to go."

"Better, but not good enough." I lean forward and kiss the top of her head before walking out of the house.

She doesn't stop me again, although I wish she had.

I drive around Chicago without any destination. The empty feeling in my chest only intensifies with each mile I put between Iris and myself, much to my frustration. I don't want to be away from her, but I don't want to be around her either. Not when I feel out of control and one sentence away from destroying all the progress I've made up until this point.

I refuse to give her another reason to question our relationship, even if she doesn't know we are in one in the first place. But how do I convince my wife by contract that we are meant to be together by choice?

The question plagues me for a whole hour. Nothing I come up with seems to be good enough, and I always circle back to the same issue.

I'm hopeless and desperate by the time I knock on Cal's door.

He opens it not a minute later. "I was wondering when you'd show up."

"She called you."

His lack of a smile is the only confirmation I need. "Whatever you did, go back and fix it."

"Why do you assume it's me that did something wrong?"

"Are you seriously asking me that question?"

"Fair enough."

He sighs. "Come on in. You look like you could use a person to talk to."

I walk past him and enter his apartment. He keeps the place pristine, a complete opposite of what anyone would expect given his wreck of a personal life.

"Do you want a drink?"

"Water's fine."

Cal acts like a good host, bringing me a glass of water and a tumbler of my favorite whiskey. "Thought you could use both."

"You don't even like whiskey."

"No, but I like my brother. *Sometimes*." He grabs the bottle and places it down next to the tumbler just in case.

I pick up the water and leave the whiskey on the coffee table. Alcohol will only make matters worse, and I need a clear head.

"While I'm flattered you came here to seek out my advice, I'm not sure I'll be able to help much."

"Because?"

"Iris is my best friend. I'm not going to help you if it means hurting her."

"I'm not trying to hurt her, dumbass. I'm trying to show her that I care about her," I snap.

Cal's eyes widen. "Holy shit."

These are the moments I wish life had a rewind button.

"You care about her? *Really?*" The mystified look on his face reminds me of the day I told him Santa wasn't real.

I press my lips together to avoid saying anything else.

He grabs my glass of whiskey, takes a sip, and unceremoniously spits it out, straight back into the same cup.

To think we are related.

"Well, this changes things."

"How?"

"I thought you would make her fall in love with you, not the other way around." His head drops back as he laughs, his voice hoarse.

"I never said anything about love."

He only laughs.

My teeth grind together. "Are you done?"

"I'm sorry. It's just too fucking good. You married her thinking she would make your life easier, only to realize you like her. A lot."

Cal makes me feel like I'm the punch line of some joke.

"I don't know why I thought coming here was a good idea." I stand.

"Wait." He holds up his hand. "I'm sorry. It was shitty for me to laugh at you when you're obviously going through a hard time."

Except his eyes *twinkle* from withheld laughter.

"I'm leaving."

He blocks my exit. "Stop. I'll help you."

I raise a brow. "I'm starting to doubt you even know how."

"You might not like my advice, but if you're willing to try it, then I think you'll be happy with the results."

"I'm listening." I sit back down.

"Iris isn't much different from any other woman. She has wants, needs, and fears."

"To think I thought you would be helpful."

He glares. "If you want her to fall in love with you, you have to prove to her how you're different from all the men she has dated before."

"That can't be too hard. They were all disgustingly average in every single way."

"Unfortunately for you, you fall into the same category."

My frown deepens. "I highly doubt that."

"You can either argue every point I make or you can shut up and listen to someone else for once."

I do one slow blink.

"There was always something that held her back from going all in, but the reasons all stemmed from the same issue."

"Which was?"

"They never fully earned her trust."

"All I've done is given her reasons to trust me."

"Your whole relationship is a lie."

I glare. "No, it's not."

"I'm not the one you need to convince."

"What do you suggest I do?"

"Easy. Start with the truth and go from there."

"What truth?"

"The fact that there is probably a part of you that has been in love with her for a long time, way before you ever signed a marriage contract."

There he goes again with the L-word. It could explain my

insane need to keep Iris close and protect her from harm's way. The way my chest feels all tight when she is gone. How my heart beats faster whenever she is in the same room as me. My intense need to mind my words so I don't hurt her.

Shit.

I am falling in love with Iris. The signs were all there, and I ignored them because I didn't truly understand them.

Instead of an intense wave of panic at the idea of loving Iris, I feel calm. Love, I can work with. I might not know how, but I'm willing to learn. For her and *only* her.

I switch my water for the whiskey. "I feel like I'm going to need something stronger for the rest of this conversation."

Whoever said *the truth will set you free* is a dumbass. My legs feel weighed down by invisible cement blocks as I walk inside the house. I throw the keys on the counter and make my way toward the stairs, only to change paths toward the bright light on the other side of the house.

A lamp in the corner of the living room basks the space in a low light.

Iris, still dressed in my T-shirt, lays sprawled out on the couch with a blanket covering the bottom half of her body. One of her hands still clutches onto her phone as if she is waiting for a call.

She stayed up for you.

I instantly regret my decision to turn off my phone after she called me the first time. It was a rash choice made in the heat of the moment, but it was clearly the wrong one.

I lift her carefully in my arms, being mindful not to wake her with any sudden movements. She mumbles something before snuggling up to my chest. My chest tightens as I look down at her, wondering how the hell I ended up married to a woman like her.

You know how.

My teeth grind together as I let out an agitated breath. Iris's head bobs with the movement, but she doesn't stir.

I carry her up the stairs and toward my room. Somehow, I'm able to get her tucked into bed without waking her up, although she mumbles a few things in her sleep about her mom.

I shower before crawling into bed and tugging Iris against me. I intertwine her legs with mine, securing her to my body so she isn't able to escape in the morning.

CHAPTER THIRTY-FOUR

Iris

I wake up sweating and unable to move anything but my head. Somehow, I ended up in Declan's bed, trapped by his arms *and* legs.

The audacity of this man is unrivaled. I try to escape his grasp, but it only seems to make things worse. His arms tighten around me as he mumbles something unintelligible into my hair.

"Declan." I push against his chest.

"Shh." He kisses the top of my forehead before releasing a soft sigh.

"Wake up." I shove him a bit harder, and that seems to do the trick.

He blinks up at the ceiling before looking at me. "Good morning." His arms remain locked around me, equally as irritating as his legs securing me to his side.

"You can take your *good morning* and shove it up your ass."

He laughs, and I'm instantly peeved from the way the sound warms my insides like alcohol in the dead of winter.

"Is there a reason I'm in your bed?"

"Because I wanted to be able to do this."

My back hits the mattress right before his lips press against mine. The kiss is a complete contrast from yesterday's desperation, and I find myself growing frustrated with how controlled Declan appears. It's soft, sweet, and far too tame after the kind of sex we had.

How can he kiss me like that after walking out on me? Blood rushes through my ears, making the tips hot.

I shove at his chest. "Get off."

"No can do."

"What?"

"I'm holding you hostage until you hear me out."

My mouth drops open. I try to budge, but he created a cage with his limbs.

You fell for the oldest trick in the book.

Instead of kissing him, I should have been trying to get out from under him. Declan had me completely dickmatized, goddammit.

"Stop fighting and give me ten minutes."

"You don't deserve ten seconds, let alone ten minutes of my time."

"How about ten words then?"

I laugh. "I'd like to see you try."

"I am falling in love with you, Iris Elizabeth Kane."

I blink up at him. Either I am still sleeping or I must have not heard him correctly because there is no way Declan Kane just admitted that he is falling in love with *me*.

Absolutely no fucking way.

Right?

I squeeze my eyes shut as if that can erase the words from my memory. "You're joking."

"I'm not."

"This is just another part of your game." I try to push him away, but he doesn't budge.

"It stopped being a game for me a long time ago."

"You're lying."

His brows pull together. "Ask me why I hate when people use Times New Roman instead of Arial."

"Are you serious right now? What does that have to do with any of this?"

"Because I chose it for *you*."

"I'm sorry, what?"

"I read somewhere online that sans serif fonts are easier for people with dyslexia to read, so I changed my requirements. Forced everyone else I oversee to switch with me or else they would face my wrath. All because I wanted to help *you*."

Emotions clog my throat, preventing my ability to reply. What can I possibly say that could compare to *that*?

Declan doesn't give me an option as he continues. "Want to know why I kept the cactus?"

I nod.

"Because it was the first time someone got me a present that made me laugh."

If hearts could melt into puddles, mine would be liquified right about now.

His eyes dart away from my face. "Ask me why you were denied the job transfer."

No.

There's absolutely no freaking way.

"Tell me you didn't."

His lips press into a thin white line. "I couldn't let you go."

"I can't believe you right now." I push at his shoulders but it's as effective as moving a boulder.

"For what it's worth, I'm not proud of it."

"You sabotaged me." My voice cracks.

His face softens. "I'm sorry."

"You're sorry? I spent months on my presentation, perfecting it to the point of obsession, only to be rejected because you were too selfish to let me go? Who does that?"

"Someone who doesn't understand the first thing about loving someone, but is willing to try if you give me a chance."

"You want me to give you a chance after everything? Do you think I'm stupid?"

He winces, and a bit of my anger fades away at his vulnerability.

"Intelligence has nothing to do with this."

"Easy for you to say when you're not the one who feels like a fool."

"Really? Because based on your reaction today, I'm feeling pretty damn foolish for ever admitting that I'm falling in love with you." He slips off the bed, leaving me feeling chilled to the bone.

"Declan…" I reach out, but he takes a step back.

My eyes sting from his rejection. It *hurts*.

"I'm not asking you to love me back. I don't expect that and I'm not sure if I ever will because I'm the furthest thing from lovable. I'm selfish, rude, and don't know the first thing about being in a relationship with someone. But that doesn't mean I'm not willing to try for you if you let me."

How am I supposed to be angry at him when he thinks he is *unlovable*? A pain rips through my chest at the thought of him talking about himself this way.

I slide off the bed and walk straight into his chest. His arms stay plastered against his sides, so I grab them and wrap them around my waist.

"Just because you make selfish *choices* doesn't mean you're a selfish *person*. At least not completely." The man protected his brothers from their alcoholic father for years without any kind of payback. If that isn't a selfless sacrifice, I don't know what is.

"Your logic is half-baked at best."

"So is yours, seeing as you called yourself unlovable."

His body tenses. "I'm stating facts."

"I don't know what bullshit your father told you over the years, but it's not true. Your brothers love you."

"They're obligated to."

"No one is *obligated* to love someone else. Blood or not."

He takes a deep breath. "You're right."

I smile up at him. "I could get used to hearing those words."

He reaches up and cups my cheek. "Give me a chance and I'll tell you them every single day."

I sigh and look away. "I don't know."

"Tell me what's stopping you."

"You don't do relationships."

"Good thing I'm married then."

I shake my head. "Our marriage isn't even real."

"A scrap of paper doesn't define what we are. Feelings do, and mine are a hundred percent genuine."

I avoid his penetrating gaze. "What if my feelings are telling me to run?"

"It's cute you think you can outrun me, but I'll give you a head start just to make things interesting."

I stammer. "Do you always have an answer for everything?"

"Not for the one that matters most." The way he looks at me stirs up something deep inside of me.

Longing.

I want to give him a chance, regardless of the potential fallout.

You might get hurt.

I might, but I might miss out on something special because I'm too afraid of the *what-ifs*. I'm done being that person. Even if it means getting hurt, I'd rather try and fail than never try at all.

I stand on the tips of my toes and press my lips against his. He holds me tight against his chest, as if he is afraid of letting me go.

I pull away, only to clasp onto his stubbled chin. "This could be a disaster, but I'm willing to try."

He shuts me up by pushing his lips against mine, sealing our new deal. The way he kisses me is different than any time before. He cups my face with the palms of his hands as his lips mold against mine, teasing me until I feel dizzy. His thumb brushes across my cheek back and forth, and heat rushes down my spine, straight to my belly. He makes me feel cherished. Protected. Loved in a way that makes me never want to come back down to reality.

I could spend forever being kissed like this and still feel like it isn't enough. While Declan might not be the best with words, his kiss says it all.

He is falling in love with me. No translation necessary.

CHAPTER THIRTY-FIVE

Iris

The next weekend, I wake up to absolute chaos downstairs. I roll out of Declan's bed, run to my room to get dressed in something other than one of his T-shirts, and freshen up in the restroom.

It doesn't take a super sleuth to find out where all the noise is coming from. I make my way through the house, following the sound of Cal's voice.

"Look who finally decided to join us!" Cal claps his hands as I walk into the living room.

"What is going on?" I check out the usual spread of donuts, mimosas, cigars, and other contraband materials.

Declan doesn't bother answering me as he stares at the TV. With the way he analyzes the black screen, one would think it were actually turned on.

"Your husband here invited us over to watch an F1 race."

"*Us?*"

"Rowan and Zahra are late, as per usual." Cal grabs a donut and demonstrates what he thinks they're doing.

"They're coming *here?*"

"Surprise?" Cal looks over at the man in question.

"The batteries are dead." He announces before leaving the room. If I expected any answers, I'm not about to get them from him.

"He really didn't tell you?"

"No. It must have slipped his mind." *Or he wanted to surprise you.*

My heart could possibly burst from the reality that Declan planned this all for me. I dropped the idea after he protested it, so knowing he went out of his way to plan it anyway...

It makes me want to kiss him.

Or fuck him.

Or kiss him *and* fuck him.

Cal holds up the sparkling apple cider bottle with a scrunched nose. "Do you have some exciting news to share with me or is this an insult to injury?"

I laugh. "I'm not pregnant."

Declan reenters the room. "Not yet at least."

My whole body feels about twenty degrees too hot. The way this man looks at me makes me wonder if it's possible to get pregnant via intense staring and palpable longing. Inquiring minds want to know.

"Well, that's my cue to go find something stronger to drink. There's no way I'll get through being the fifth wheel without wanting to chop my own dick off."

Declan shoots Cal a withering look as he leaves the living room.

"So…" I start.

He uses the now-working remote to turn on the TV and find the right channel.

"What's the real reason you planned this all?"

His back muscles shift underneath his T-shirt. "*Gezelligheid**."

I pull out my phone and stare at the search bar with a pinched expression.

"*G-E-Z-E-L-L-I-G-H-E-I-D*." He spells it out slowly without me even asking.

"Where did you learn this one?"

"During my month studying abroad in the Netherlands."

I laugh when the page loads. "*Cozy?* That's why you did this?"

He shakes his head. "It's more than that. It's about creating a place where people can relax and feel happy."

"Since when do you care about making people happy?"

"I couldn't care less about anyone else's happiness besides your own."

My chest aches from his confession. "That has to be one of the sweetest—but extremely fucked up—things anyone has ever said to me."

"Fucked up how?" He seems genuinely confused by my statement.

"Because you should do nice things because you want to, not because you think it would make me happy."

---

* **Gezelligheid:** *Noun, Dutch:* the warm feeling of being surrounded by loved ones; the state or fact of being cozy.

"I *want* to make you happy, so therefore, I do nice things."

Well, I can't exactly debate his kind of logic on that one, especially when it makes me want to kiss him until we're both breathless.

I bite down on my lip. "What happens when what makes me happy goes against what you want?"

His gaze darkens. "Then I'll convince you otherwise."

My head tilts. "That's not how relationships work."

"We aren't a typical relationship, so therefore, the same rules don't apply here."

"There might be a time in your life when you can't convince me. What then?"

"When it comes to you, I'm not opposed to using any means necessary."

"Including torture?"

He cups my cheek and draws me toward him. "Is it still considered torture if I let you come?"

"I've unlocked a sexed-up monster."

He laughs as he pulls me into a searing kiss that makes my toes curl. With the caress of his tongue against mine, our conversation is erased from recent memory.

The doorbell rings, and Declan hesitates to let me go. He tugs me back toward him for one last kiss.

The doorbell chimes again, and I laugh as I leave a scowling Declan behind to go answer the front door. I throw it open to find Rowan and Zahra standing hand in hand on the porch.

Zahra looks over at me with a smile. "Hey!" She doesn't give me a chance to say anything before she barrels into me and throws her arms around my torso. "I'm so excited to hang out with you!"

"Me too," I wheeze.

Declan's shadow seems to make everyone freeze in place.

"Declan." Rowan tips his chin.

"Thanks for coming over." He holds out his hand for Rowan to take.

Rowan's lips twitch as he ignores it and throws an arm around his back and gives him a pat. "Your threats made me curious."

"Threats?" I ask.

Declan doesn't pay any attention to my question as he shoots Rowan a death glare.

Rowan turns his gaze toward me, and a smile brightens his whole face. "I'm going to thoroughly enjoy this all."

"Are you a big fan of F1?"

He looks at Declan as he responds to my question. "The biggest. I love watching people crash and burn."

"That's horrifying." Zahra smacks Rowan's arm.

Declan's jaw ticks.

"Well, as fun as this whole pissing contest is, some of us came here for the mimosas." Zahra loops her arm in mine and drags me away from Declan and Rowan. "Lead the way."

I keep an eye on them over my shoulder. Declan shoves a finger into Rowan's chest as he encroaches in his space. Rowan doesn't seem the least bit bothered; instead, he's laughing and saying something I can't make out from this far away.

Zahra pats my hand. "Don't mind them. Rowan has been out for Declan's blood ever since the whole Dreamland debacle happened. It was only a matter of time before they hashed everything out."

I'm not sure a simple conversation will solve everything, given how upset Declan was when Rowan chose moving to Dreamland over helping him with the company.

I turn back toward Zahra. "You know about that?"

She laughs. "Oh yeah. Rowan told me after he decided to stay at Dreamland."

"Wow."

"As much as I love that he did that, I'm not one for family drama, so I'd rather they fix things sooner rather than later. For Rowan's sake at least. He pretends he doesn't care about Declan being angry, but I know him. He loves his brother."

"If it means anything, I think Declan misses him too."

"More like he misses picking on his baby brother."

Cal steps out of the living room. "Declan found someone else to torture now, so I think we're safe from his wrath, so long as Iris puts out."

I choke on my inhale. "Who said anything about that?"

"I caught you kissing earlier."

Zahra's eyes widen. "You kissed him."

My cheeks burn as I look away.

"Oh my God. We need to talk. Now." She drags me toward the stairs, but I make a quick detour so I can grab two mimosas. I have a feeling we are going to need some alcohol for this conversation.

Zahra and I make our way to my room with our drinks in hand. For the first time since I moved into the house, I finally use the sitting area by the huge window.

"Nice room. It's a lot different than what I expected," she says as she looks around.

"The dungeon is being cleaned so this was the next best thing."

She laughs. "Sorry. I tend to talk out loud sometimes and forget my manners."

I take a sip of my drink. "Don't worry. I'm sure you're curious about everything."

Her whole face lights up. "Yes! I've been dying to ask you about your fake marriage, but your wedding didn't seem like the most appropriate place."

"For legal purposes, I have to tell you not to repeat this conversation to anyone."

She snorts. "Does that spiel actually work on any of your friends?"

I shrug. "I wouldn't know. Besides Cal, who already knows everything, I don't have any."

Her bottom lip juts out. "That's sad."

I sigh. "It's old news."

"Is it?"

"I thought we came up here to talk about my marriage." My deflection would make Declan proud.

She clinks her glass against mine before taking a sip. "Touchy subject. Got it."

I instantly feel bad for being snippy. "Sorry. I don't mean to come off rude."

"Don't worry about it. I'm not here to judge you."

"Not even a little bit?"

"What for?"

I look around my room. "You don't find my situation a little...weird?"

Her chest shakes from silent laughter. "Not at all. If anything, it's kind of romantic, seeing as he invited us over here to spend time with you."

"That in itself is confusing."

"How so?"

"I asked him a while back and he told me he didn't want to."

Her lips form an O. "I see."

"Feel free to share your thoughts."

"There isn't much to it. You wanted something and he made it happen. At least he's a quick learner. It took Rowan months to realize he actually cared about my feelings more than his own."

I laugh. "Whoa. I didn't say anything about feelings."

Her eyes roll. "Come on. You must know he has some kind of feelings for you."

"He told me himself that he does."

"Then what's the problem?"

"Me." It pains me to admit it, but it's the truth. I'm not sure if I will ever be in the position to fully trust someone. Maybe I'm too broken.

"Oh. It all makes sense now."

"What does?"

"It's normal to be afraid of something new. I was like you—scared and unsure about dating a man again after I was burned badly."

"You were?" I wouldn't associate her positive energy with someone who struggled to trust anyone.

"Oh yeah. I went through a rough breakup with someone I thought I was going to marry one day. Turns out he was cheating on me with one of the Dreamland princesses."

"Ouch." I wince.

Her smile falters. "At the time, it felt like my world was ending. But now I realize it was the best thing that could have happened to me."

"Because you found Rowan?"

She shakes her head. "Because I found myself."

"I feel like I'm going to need a lot more than a mimosa for this kind of conversation."

She laughs. "Too deep for a Sunday morning?"

I nod. "Way too deep."

We break out into a fit of laughter. We move on to safer topics that have nothing to do with my relationship with Declan. I'm grateful he planned today's family gathering, solely because I got to spend more time with Zahra and hear another person's opinion on my marriage. While Cal means well, he isn't exactly a guru when it comes to relationships. Hence his resistance to contacting Alana despite him needing to for his inheritance.

Speak of the devil, he throws open my bedroom door with a dramatic flare. "I hate to interrupt this bonding session but the race is about to start and Declan's getting antsy."

"He's just annoyed he has to talk to you for twenty minutes straight."

"Watching him fumble through small talk that has nothing to do with work or our inheritances is far more entertaining than I thought."

I lock arms with Zahra. "Let's go put Declan out of his misery."

Cal scoffs. "I know you're biased because you're his wife, but the man has been miserable ever since the day he was born."

Zahra winks. "I have a feeling that's about to change."

CHAPTER
THIRTY-SIX

Declan

It only takes one email to ruin my whole year.

"Iris!"

She comes running into my office with my brother on her tail. "What?"

I don't even bother asking what he is doing here. Knowing him, it has everything to do with avoiding his responsibilities.

"Did you see Yakura's latest email?" I slam my finger against the mouse, shutting the email browser before I have a stroke.

"No. What happened?"

My entire face feels like it's on fire. "He received a call from my father."

"*Fuck.*" Cal wipes his face.

My thought exactly. "Yakura's threatening to pull out of the project."

She drops into the chair across from me. "Why?"

"He didn't go into any specific details, but his sentence about how *our goals don't seem to align* was as good of a hint as any."

It doesn't take a genius to understand what happened. With my father's personality and his desperation to remain CEO, I have no doubt he went out of his way to make my project seem inadequate. Because in the end, the Kane Company bottom line doesn't matter so long as he remains in power, even if it means ruining a deal that could make us billions.

He wants to make me look weak and inexperienced compared to him, and this is the best shot he has at destroying whatever credibility I have with the board thus far. The executives know how hard I have been working on this project. If it falls through, the blowback could be detrimental to my transition.

"We can fix this. I'll reach out to Yakura." Iris rolls her shoulders and tips her chin up. She has a unique ability to command the situation and ease the growing tension in my shoulders.

"And say what? 'Sorry my dad's a dick. He didn't mean it,'" Cal offers.

Her brows scrunch together. "Of course not. What do you take me for? An amateur?"

"Then how do you plan on winning him over?"

Iris turns toward me. "We show him how our goals align."

"Do we even know what those are?" Cal's head swings back and forth between Iris and me.

My face is as blank as my thoughts. I thought Yakura's goal

was to build a park worthy of his land, but that doesn't seem to be the case.

"I have an idea but I don't know if it's a good one…" Iris's voice trails off.

"This doesn't sound promising." Cal grimaces.

I shoot Cal a look that tells him to keep his mouth shut. "Go ahead."

She perks up at my obvious interest. "When we initially introduced the idea of building Dreamland Tokyo, Yakura's first question had nothing to do with profits. I found it strange that someone as successful as him wouldn't care about how much money he stands to make."

"What did he ask about?" Cal leans toward Iris.

"If we could make Dreamland Tokyo happen before he was too old to enjoy it with his grandkids."

"I don't remember that," I reply, drawing a blank on that part of the meeting.

Her eyes roll. "Of course you don't. You were too focused on pulling up the next slide discussing expected proceeds."

"So he cares about his family," Cal says.

She nods.

"We're screwed. There's no way Declan can work with someone like that."

"I disagree. Because while your father might be clever, he missed one tiny detail."

"What?"

"Me." Her smile rivals the sun.

Fitting because it burns away that last bit of remaining anger I have toward my father. In its place, I am filled with a newfound sense of hope. I can convince Yakura to stick with the project so long as Iris helps me. She can appeal to just about anyone's humanity—mine included.

Cal whistles. "Someone thinks mighty highly of herself."

I want to smack the back of his head but hold back. I'd hate to waste his last brain cells with something impulsive.

"I know my strong suits, and picking up after Declan's messes happens to be a personal strength of mine."

"So what's your plan then?" my brother asks.

"Easy. We show him exactly what Dreamland has to offer." Her eyes seem to sparkle.

"How do we do that?" I lean back in my chair and consider her idea.

"We take him to where it all started and show him what he would be missing out on if he walks away from this deal."

"Are you suggesting we take a family trip to Dreamland?" Cal asks.

She nods, and his smile is wiped clean off his face. I feel the same way. Unlike Rowan, neither one of us wants anything to do with the park. Every memory of our life with our mother is attached to the place. The only times I've gone have been strictly for business, and I've been sure to keep it that way.

"How is this supposed to change his mind?" My voice comes out rougher than intended.

"Yakura is a family man. We need to show him how, unlike your father, so are you."

Cal's laugh grates against my nerves.

"What's so funny?" My teeth grind together.

"The idea of you playing a family man is too good to pass up. You can count on me to be there."

"Who said you were invited?" She looks at him like a bug beneath her shoe, and I could kiss her for it.

He waves a hand down his body. "I'm part of the promotional package."

"Not happening," I respond for her.

He looks over at Iris for help and she shrugs. "He's the boss."

Forget kissing her. I could fuck her for standing by me instead of Cal on something like this.

"I don't like you two ganging up on me." He rolls his eyes.

She gives his hand a pat. "It's in your best interest. You hate business talk anyway."

He sighs. "You're right. Still fucked up though when you're my best friend."

"And he's my husband. Don't make me choose between you two."

My world seems to tilt as she says the words. The weight behind them nearly knocks me on my ass, and I grip the handles of my chair in a choke hold.

"You two in love is disgusting." Cal's lip curls.

She laughs. "No one said anything about love."

The way she laughs his statement off feels like someone pierced my chest with a serrated knife. My chest burns equally strong as my gut churns.

Give her time to come around.

I've seen the way she looks at me. There is no way she doesn't love me, even if she hasn't processed it yet.

"There's a chance he might not even say yes," I grumble

355

underneath my breath. I'm almost hoping that's the case if only to avoid visiting Dreamland.

"After all this time, you still doubt me?" Iris actually looks somewhat hurt by the idea.

"It's not you that I'm worried about," I amend. It's everything that going to Dreamland will stir up for me.

"Leave it to me."

Iris drops a stack of papers on my desk. "Here."

"What's that?"

"Next week's travel itinerary. I already went ahead and cleared your calendar, that way we have enough time to get acclimated to Dreamland before Yakura visits."

Holy shit. She fucking did it.

Did you really doubt her in the first place?

No. Of course not. Although I was worried about the damage my father caused and how Iris would overcome such a challenge, I never doubted her.

I grab the stack of papers and flip through them. The first packet includes information about our pilot and our Dreamland schedule, from a park walk-through with Rowan and Zahra to meetings with the different creative teams on the property. She even secured a private office for me to work out of.

I scan the next packet which includes everything on Yakura. From all his preferences to an entire family tree, there isn't a single stone Iris left unturned. "Please tell me you went about this plan the legal way."

"That depends on if you consider it illegal to hijack Yakura's travel plans to the Grand Canyon and pay someone to ground his plane in Florida."

I pinch the bridge of my nose. "You didn't."

She laughs, and it does something strange to my heart rate.

"Of course I didn't! Although I'm flattered you think I could pull off such a stunt."

"I wouldn't put it past you to accomplish anything you put your mind to."

Her smile wavers. "Don't go saying sweet things to me at work."

"Why not?"

"Because it makes me want to do something inappropriate."

I lean back in my chair and throw her papers on the desk. "Like what?"

She wags her finger. "Nope. I'm off-limits during business hours."

Blood works its way straight to my dick. "We could call in sick."

What the hell are you doing by suggesting both of you should skip work?

She laughs. "It's the middle of a workday, and you have a meeting with the head of park development in ten minutes."

I check the time on my computer. "Clock is ticking then." I press the automatic lock button underneath my desk, and the clicking sound makes her brows rise.

"What are you—"

I latch onto her hand and pull her straight onto my lap.

"You've lost your goddamn mind."

"Then I hope I never find it again." I slam my lips against hers, silencing any protests. An electric feeling sparks across my skin as she kisses me back with enough intensity to make my head spin. Kissing her feels like I cheated my way into heaven, and I plan on soaking up every second of it.

We break apart as she straddles my lap. My head drops back against the chair as she presses herself against my cock, swiveling her hips in a way that drives me wild with want. I grip onto her hips with a choke hold to keep her pressed against me. She kisses her way down the curve of my neck before sucking on the spot that makes my hips buck forward.

A wet spot gathers in front of my pants from the way she rocks back and forth against my stiff cock. I'm mindless as I push her up and down, switching directions and making her moan as she grinds into me from a different angle.

The shrill ringtone of her phone threatens to kill the moment. She pulls away, but I don't release her hips from my grasp.

"I have to get that." Her husky voice sends a fresh wave of arousal through me.

"Let it go to voicemail." I grip her chin and pull her mouth back toward mine.

She turns her head at the last second, giving me her cheek. "It could be important."

"Not nearly as much as this." I help her onto her feet before turning her toward my desk. "Bend over and put your hands on the desk." I press my palm into the small of her back and push.

She must sense my self-control wavering because she does what I say without asking any questions. Her palms flatten against the wood as she leans forward, making the hem of her dress lift to an enticing height. Her sharp inhale fills the silence as I run the tips of my fingers up the back of her thighs. I lift her dress, revealing the globes of her ass.

"Did you wear this for me?" My dick is rock-hard underneath my slacks as I play with the lacy strap of Iris's green thong. If it wasn't my favorite color before, it sure as hell is now.

She turns her head so she can properly glare at me over her shoulder. "Your narcissism is showing again."

"How so?"

"Green is *my* favorite color."

"Since when?"

"Since way before you adopted it as yours." Her laugh feels like being basked in sunlight.

I shake my head and regain control over the situation. "You know what I think?"

"Feel free to keep it to yourself."

Iris sucks in a breath as I drag my fingers up and down her thighs.

"I think you hoped something like this would happen."

Her eyes are two glittering orbs of brown. "Quite the assumption on your part."

"So you don't want this?" I tease the damp triangle of material before retreating, and she stares at me with a look of murder in her eyes.

"I wouldn't go *that* far."

I chuckle as I grab onto the strap of her thong and drag it down her legs. She lifts each foot for me, and I bend down to retrieve it.

Her brow arches as she looks over at me pocketing her thong. "I never pegged you as the souvenir type."

"Why would I need a souvenir when I can have you anytime I want?" I nudge her legs apart one at a time. She bites down on her lip to stifle her moan as I drag my index finger across her slit, collecting her arousal. My heart pounds in my ears, growing louder with each second that passes. I sink a finger into her only to withdraw it a second later, making her hiss.

She pushes her ass out. "Please."

"Please what?" I step out of her reach, and she grinds against the air.

"Make me come."

Her death stare turns into one of lust as I thrust two fingers inside of her. My cock aches to replace them, and my movements grow desperate to match. Her teeth dig into her bottom lip, quieting her moans. I press my thumb against her clit and rub it in slow circles. My fingers brush against her G-spot, and her knees buckle as she clutches onto the desk for stability. She unravels, her legs dropping out from underneath her as she comes.

She is completely dazed as I undo my belt buckle and pull down my pants. I'm quick with putting on the condom, ignoring the way my chest tightens at the idea of disregarding my duty for her.

It's only a matter of time before she comes around to the idea. Give her time.

I push my erection against her opening. She bolts upright, but I push her flat against the desk.

I lean forward and press my chest against her back. "I could come at the sight of you, ass up, facedown, and wet for me."

"That would be quite disappointing, to say the least."

She releases a sharp breath as I push her hair aside, revealing her neck. I kiss the spot that seems to drive her wild. She bucks under me, pushing the tip of my cock into her. I bite down on the inside of my cheek to stop my groan, although my eyes roll back into my head. Never have I felt this kind of connection to someone else. Over the years, I forgot what it felt like to desire someone. To be driven by the need to possess them in every single way.

I have a meeting in five minutes and I'm too busy fucking her to prepare for it. In fact, it turns me on to consider them waiting outside, listening to how good I make Iris feel.

Iris doesn't seem pleased with my lack of action as she uses the edge of the desk to push backward, and I sink farther into her.

I grip onto her hips. "You're not in charge here."

"Oh, honey. I've always been in charge. You just were too caught up in yourself to realize who was running things around here." Her wide grin steals my ability to breathe.

I ram into her, and her gasp of air makes me smile.

"You were saying?"

She *laughs*.

It stirs the wild side of me that I keep under lock and key. I withdraw, only to thrust back into her with punishing strength. Her dilated eyes still reflect amusement, and it drives me feral that she doesn't seem the least bit fazed by this connection. Desperation claws against my chest to show her who holds the power between us.

I take out my frustration on her body. My hands grip onto her waist as I ram into her over and over again. Her breathing becomes more ragged, and her grip on the edge of the desk slips along with her control.

You're not in charge here, my ass.

A knock against the door makes Iris's eyes widen.

"Mr. Kane? I wanted to let you know I'm here for our meeting at three."

I lean forward and press the pad of my thumb against her clit. "Talk."

"Hi, Mr. Davis. We'll be ready in a few minutes." Her cheery voice doesn't match the arousal in her eyes.

She attempts to shift away from me, but I hold her in place.

"What are you doing?" she whispers.

"You're not dismissed yet."

"Asshole."

I withdraw my cock and trace the seam of her ass with the tip. "Does that mean yours is on the table?"

"I will murder you with a dull pencil if you try."

I shrug. "Pity. Maybe next time."

I smile as I slam back into her without warning. Her gasp fills me with pride while the trembling of her legs makes me crazed. Fucking Iris is quickly becoming my favorite pastime, where each round feels like a battle of who will surrender first.

A tingle shoots down my spine as I fight off the urge to come. I work hard for each gasp and moan that makes it past her lips, and I feel victorious as she comes around my cock. Her legs give out, and I hold her up as I thrust into her over and over again until I find my own release.

The relief is all-consuming, filling my vision with black spots as I come. She claws at the desk as I ram into her one last time. My own legs threaten to give out, but I refuse to withdraw yet. I don't want to kill the connection, regardless of who is waiting on the other side of the door.

I lean over and kiss her neck. "Remember this when you

think you're in control here."It's a bullshit statement on my part. I lost control weeks ago, and now I'm nothing but a slave to the sensations she stirs up inside of me.

"I'll never look at this desk the same way again." She sighs.

"Says the woman who doesn't have to work next to a set of claw marks from now on."

She swipes the wood chips away like that changes anything. "At least it'll stir up some good memories for you."

"That or a hard-on."

"Why not both?" She laughs, and I smile against her skin, loving the way I elicit that kind of reaction from her.

Fucked. You're absolutely fucked.

CHAPTER THIRTY-SEVEN

Iris

We finally made it to Dreamland. The smell of fresh-baked cookies makes my mouth water. Our three-row golf cart flies across the brick pavers, easily navigating the empty streets. We pass by smiling employees, decked out princesses and princes, and shops prepping for another busy day in the park.

My excitement only grows as we near the massive princess castle in the middle of it all.

Declan places a palm on my bouncing thigh. "Are you okay?"

I grin. "Just excited."

His forehead wrinkles as he frowns.

"When was the last time you visited the park?" Zahra turns her body so she can look back at us.

My smile falls. "We've traveled here once for business."

"You've been to Dreamland one time, and it was for *business*?" Her face is one of absolute horror.

Declan's hand on my thigh tightens in a silent *look at me* gesture, but I don't. I don't want to see the pity on his face.

I consider lying but think better of it. "My mom didn't have enough money to get us tickets. With flights, hotel, and admission fees, you could buy a month's worth of groceries for the same price as a trip here."

"What does your mom do?"

"She's an art teacher."

Zahra grasps onto Rowan's arm. "We need to offer teacher discounts. And children of teacher discounts. And discounts for adults who have never been to Dreamland as a child."

He shoots her a look. "At that rate, we won't make any money."

"There are grown adults out there who have never been to Dreamland, Rowan. Now is not the time to be stingy."

He looks over at Declan for help, but Declan is solely looking at me.

"I didn't realize you had never been here before."

I shrug. "You never asked."

The hand on my thigh squeezes harder. I shift my gaze toward Declan, and the look on his face sends a shiver down my back.

"Would you like to check out the park?"

"For work?"

"No. For fun."

The idea makes me laugh. "You hate this place."

"I'm willing to pretend that I don't for a day."

"What about prepping for our walk-through with Yakura?"

"The park will still be here tomorrow. We can talk business then."

Heat spreads through my chest. I wrap my arms around his neck and give him a squeeze. "I'd love that."

Declan speaks up to the rest of the group. "Plans have changed."

Zahra squeals with delight, and like that, our day is completely altered because Declan declared it so.

All for me.

Zahra is the best tour guide ever. Turns out she has been a part of Dreamland since she was a child, so she knows everything about the place. With her knowledge and Rowan's ability to help us skip any lines, there is nothing stopping us from exploring the whole park in a day. Well, nothing but me. I try my hardest to keep focused, but I am distracted every few feet by the different flower and plant displays. The array of colors captures my attention, and I can't help stopping each time to check out the perfectly designed topiaries of different Dreamland characters.

Declan looms over me like a shadow, assessing my every move.

I turn toward him with heated cheeks. "What?"

"I should have known you would care more about the plants than the rides."

"Because look at this! It's art!" I throw an arm up at the sculpture of Iggy the Alien, Brady Kane's iconic first character. The entire thing is made up of trimmed green leaves and a ball of wire.

"Art?" His voice has a hint of amusement despite his blank face.

Zahra bounces over to us. "You know, if you're interested, we could take you to check out the horticulture department."

My eyes widen. "Really?"

She smiles. "Sure. It would be no big deal."

"Oh my God. I'd love that!"

"With the way you keep taking photos and gawking at their plants, they'll probably feel like rock stars."

"That's because they *are* rock stars."

She pulls out her phone and taps away at the screen. "Do you have any free time tomorrow? The head of the department is going to be there and would be happy to show you around. They might be a little busier than usual because they're prepping for the Flower Festival, but they'd love to show you the behind-the-scenes action."

I gasp. "The head of the department wants to show me around?"

Her chest shakes from withheld laughter. "Yes. Said so himself." She flips her phone so I can see the text chain with my own eyes.

Declan clears his throat.

Shit. This isn't a personal vacation, remember? Today is already enough of a deviation from the protocol. The last thing Declan needs is me becoming distracted by things that aren't important right now. I can come back and visit Dreamland whenever, but we only have one shot to convince Yakura to work with us. Plants can wait.

I shake my head. "Um. Actually, tomorrow doesn't work for me. Tell him I'm sorry and maybe next time I can make room in my schedule for a visit."

Her smile falls. "Oh. No worries."

Declan tugs on my elbow. "Why are you saying no?"

"Because we have our walk-through to prepare for. Yakura will be here in a couple of days and we need to be ready for anything he might throw at us."

"It's not going to be anything different from what you've seen today."

I frown. "But we're a team."

"I'm sure I can survive a few hours without you while you go check out some plants."

"Please. During work, you can't go thirty minutes without finding some reason to stop by my desk."

"I like giving you verbal instructions."

"Why?"

"Do I need a better reason than I like watching the way your eyes light up with defiance?"

"You're such a liar."

His right eye twitches. "I did some research on how people with learning differences like yours do best with verbal and written instruction."

My knees tremble. "Anything else you learned?"

His arm wraps around my waist, which is probably best seeing as my legs are about two confessions away from giving out.

"Voice notes or phone calls work best."

I laugh despite the tight ball of emotion forming in my throat. "Here I was thinking you just hated texting."

His lips lift the slightest bit at the corners. "I do hate texting. Don't trick yourself into thinking it had anything to do with you."

"Shut up." I laugh as I give his chest a shove.

His arms don't budge, although his lips curve up into a smile. "Zahra, you can go ahead and schedule tomorrow's activities. It might be hard for her, but Iris can survive a day without me."

I stick out my tongue. "Please. I don't think you've spent a whole workday without me for three years."

His voice drops as his dark eyes capture mine in a trance. "And I don't plan on doing so anytime soon."

I snuggle against Declan's chest as he throws the comforter over our entwined bodies. I'm grateful he takes initiative because my muscles are aching after going around the entire park *twice*.

I trace mindless patterns on his chest. "Thank you for today."

"You don't need to thank me every time I do something nice."

"I read somewhere that reinforcing good behavior increases the likelihood of it happening again."

"There are better ways to reinforce good behavior." His raspy voice turns my insides into bubbling lava.

"As tempting as sex sounds right now, I don't think I can move a single muscle."

"I'll do all the work."

"Who knew you were so proactive?"

"They say practice makes perfect, so I'm trying to fit in all the lessons I can get."

I laugh so hard, I'm afraid I might pee if I don't stop. "You don't need any more practice. Trust me." For someone who has avoided women for God knows how long, Declan sure knows what he's doing in the bedroom. Or office. Or shower. Pretty much anywhere that has a surface to fuck against is no longer safe.

"My ego thanks you, but I'm talking about practicing for a baby, not sex."

My eyes widen. We haven't talked about condoms ever since our conversation a couple of weeks ago when Declan walked out on me in the middle of our argument. Neither one of us has dared to broach the subject, so we haven't stopped using them.

"Are you suggesting…" My voice trails off. I can't even get the words out.

"I'm ready whenever you are to get started on your little soccer team."

"Who said anything about a soccer team?"

"You did."

"What? When?"

"If I'm not mistaken, I believe you said you wanted a whole minivan of kids."

I'm not sure I'm even breathing as I speak up. "But we only agreed to one child."

"Plans change."

"You didn't even want one child. How do you expect me to believe you want a whole soccer team now?"

"I do because it would make you happy."

"That's not why people should have children. They're a life-long commitment—"

He presses his lips against mine to shut me up. "Exactly."

"But—"

He kisses me again, and my body melts into the mattress.

"We could have one kid or five, so long as you only have them with me. I'll give you the minivan life, solely if you want it."

"What if I'm not ready? What if this is all too much all at once and I can't handle a new relationship and a new baby?"

His throat bobs. "Then we wait."

"Even if it means holding off on you becoming CEO?"

"Even then."

I'm hit with a wave of emotion so strong, my eyes glisten. A single tear slips down my face before landing on the pillow beneath me. Never in a million years did I expect to hear those words come out of his mouth.

He kisses me until my lips tingle and my legs tremble around his waist. Our clothes land in a pile on the floor next. When he reaches for a condom on the dresser, I cover his hand with mine and shake my head.

"Are you sure?" He looks down at me with a pinched expression.

I nod, afraid to speak. He groans as he kisses me, this time with enough heat to set my lips on fire. His movements are unhurried as he touches my body like it's the very first time.

I feel cherished as his lips kiss a path from my mouth to my chest. He draws my nipple into his mouth, teasing the tip with his tongue. I jolt from the zing that shoots down my spine. His throat vibrates against my skin as he laughs, but his amusement disappears as his mouth returns to torturing my breast. He moves on to the other, focusing all his attention on pushing me to insanity.

I rub against him, trying to seek relief. Pressure builds inside of me from just him sucking, licking, and nipping at my breasts, but I'm not able to find my release.

I groan from frustration and pull on his hair.

"Someone's impatient."

"Someone's about to finish this themselves if you don't keep moving."

His laugh fills me with a different kind of warmth than the one bubbling in my lower belly. He crawls down the bed, making a mess of our sheets as he spreads my legs wide. Our gazes stay locked as he sinks his tongue inside of me. My back arches, but his hand holds me flat against the bed as he fucks me with his tongue.

Will it always feel this good?

His chuckle sends another vibration up my body, and I realize I must have said it aloud.

"Only with you." His fingers tease me, working in unison with his tongue as he draws my pleasure from me with each thrust. His thumb rubs against my clit, and I groan as my orgasm hits me.

Declan doesn't stop until I lay helplessly on the bed, splayed out and waiting for him.

"You're beautiful." He crawls over me and cups my face. His hands shove my legs apart even wider, giving him room to settle between them.

"I could spend the rest of forever with you and it still wouldn't be enough time to finish everything I have planned for us."

"That's a lot of plans."

"Let's start with this one first."

I shiver as he lines his cock up at my entrance. He drags the tip back and forth, collecting my arousal with each swipe. His shuddery breath fills me with pride.

I wrap my legs around him, encouraging him to continue.

"Are you sure about this?" His voice is hesitant.

"Only if you are."

"I don't deserve you. Never have and never will, so long as I live."

"You are worthy of good things."

Our eyes don't leave one another as his cock fills me inch by inch. We both shake as he seats himself inside of me, and his eyes screw shut as he takes a deep breath.

"Fuck," he speaks between gritted teeth.

Fuck is right. I'm afraid he might not move again, but he seems to get better control over himself and starts to pump in and out.

With each snap of his hips, I climb higher. His movements are crazed. Uncontrolled. Primal in a way I've never experienced before. My head spins from all the sensations happening at once. A feeling of weightlessness takes over me, and it feels like I am having an out-of-body experience.

Declan seems to be right there with me. His eyes are pitch-black as he drives into my body like he owns it, leaving bruises where his hands hold me in the right position for his pleasure. It makes me feel used in the best kind of way.

He angles me just right so his cock slides against the spot that has me gasping for air. His thumb finds my clit again, and it only takes a few slow circles to have me explode from ecstasy.

He fucks me through my orgasm until I'm writhing underneath him again. When he finally reaches his climax, he releases a groan I feel straight to my clit. His hips don't stop moving as he comes inside of me. He drops down on his elbows, careful not to crush me as he kisses me once before laying his forehead against mine.

Neither one of us wants to move and break the moment. So we stay there until he is forced to pull out, and part of his release spills out.

"Shit." He seems starstruck as he swipes some of his cum and uses it as a lubricant against my clit.

I sigh as a tingle shoots all the way down to my toes.

"That has to be the sexiest sound I've ever heard." His husky voice does something powerful to my libido.

I thought he would be done with me already, but he keeps touching me until I'm desperately reaching for him again.

The second time he enters me, his movements are slow, sweet. *Loving*. He apologizes for his earlier brutality with soft kisses and a reverent touch. I've never felt so loved in my life, and it has everything to do with the way he looks at me as he fucks me this time around.

He kisses my neck, shoulders, breasts, forehead. Not even my soul is left untouched as he whispers foreign words in my ear. I have no idea what they mean, but the way he says them sends goose bumps across my skin.

"*Daisuki*[*]." His deep thrust makes me gasp.

"*Szeretlek*[†]." He presses his lips against my forehead. My pulse flutters at the gesture, sending a rush of pleasure all the way to my toes.

"*Ich liebe dich*[‡]."

Our gazes connect. The way I shiver has nothing to do with his touch and everything to do with the way he looks at me.

I might not be able to recite foreign words like him, but I understand tone and body language, and whatever he says makes my heart feel so full, it might burst.

You're falling for him.

For the first time ever, I'm not afraid of love. If this is what it feels like, I'm willing to try, consequences be damned.

---

[*] **Daisuki:** *Japanese:* I love you.

[†] **Szeretlek:** *Hungarian:* I love you

[‡] **Ich liebe dich:** *German:* I love you.

CHAPTER THIRTY-EIGHT

Declan

Of course, the one day that Iris takes off is the day everything turns to shit.

"We have a problem," Rowan says the moment I pick up my ringing phone.

"What's wrong?" I readjust my tie in the mirror.

"Yakura just showed up at my office."

"Fuck." I grab my wallet off the dresser and stuff my feet into my shoes.

"It gets better. Guess who came with him?"

"No."

"Father is waiting in the lobby with him. Get over here. *Now*."

I don't have a chance to panic as I rush out the door of my hotel room. I'm quick to pull up Iris's number and call her.

It goes to voicemail, so I dial again. She picks up on the fourth ring which is unlike her.

"Hey!" She laughs at someone talking in the background. "Give me a second."

Someone boos, and it sounds an awful lot like Zahra. I'm hit with a twinge of guilt. Am I really going to drag her away from Zahra so she can come help me pick up after my father's mess? It's not her fault he keeps screwing around with our plans. And to be honest, I don't want her anywhere near him. Not because I don't think she could control herself, but more so because I don't want him to use her to get to me. He has already hurt her enough.

"Miss me already?"

I open my mouth to tell her about what is happening, but I stop myself. I think back to our honeymoon and her reaction to being forced into working on her day off.

I've spent three years of my life making sure you're taken care of, even if it meant sacrificing my happiness to do so.

No, I can't make her leave now. She has already sacrificed enough for me, and it's not her fault my father won't stop his attack against me.

I take a deep breath and accept my choice. "I was calling to check in on you. How is it?" I press the elevator button and wait.

"It's like the Chicago Botanic Garden on steroids. They have fifteen greenhouses. I already got lost *twice*!"

She sounds so damn excited, and it solidifies my plan. I can't rip her away from her day. Not when the only option I have is to throw her into a family feud she doesn't deserve. It's the last thing I want for her. My father has no limits when it comes to Iris, and

I refuse to subject her to that kind of abuse after everything she has been through in her life.

"Sounds like we need to invest in that ankle monitor."

"I wish you could be here." The wistfulness in her voice makes me feel even shittier about today.

"I do too." If I didn't have a mountain of responsibilities, I could take the day off and spend it with her. A normal man would.

Except you're not a normal man.

It's better to get used to this kind of feeling now because it's only going to get worse once I become CEO.

Zahra calls out Iris's name.

"Zahra is asking if we are still on later for dinner with your brother?"

"Only because you manipulated me with sex to get it."

"You weren't complaining last night."

"I'm saving it all for later."

She laughs. "Be good to your brother today."

"I'm making no promises."

"Declan…"

"Fine. But only because you told me to."

The elevator dings and the two doors slide open in front of me. "Shit. I gotta go."

"Me too. We're visiting the Flower Festival floats next. I'll send you pictures!"

Her excitement is contagious, and I smile to myself knowing my decision is the right one. There is no way in hell I'm stealing her away from that opportunity. I might not be a normal husband, but that doesn't make me a stupid one. At least I hope not.

"Have fun," I say before the call cuts out.

It feels good knowing at least one of us will have a good day today. Even if that someone isn't me.

Mr. Yakura showing up a couple days early is a problem I can handle.

My father deciding to come along so he can make amends is a whole different issue. One I'm wary of from the get-go. While I might not know every part of his plan, I'm smart enough to put the pieces together. It doesn't require much effort, given the way I walk in on my father speaking to Yakura about moving up the timeline.

The bastard wants to steal my deal.

Rowan shoots me a look that says *You need to fix this.*

"Mr. Yakura."

The older man looks over at me with a smile. His white hair is perfectly styled, and his usual suit is replaced with a bright Hawaiian shirt and khakis.

"Declan. Just the man I was hoping to see."

I hold out my hand and he shakes it. "What a surprise."

He grins. "I was just telling your father here how I was too excited to wait any longer."

"Where is your wife?"

He waves me off. "I didn't want to bore her with the little details, so she and I will be exploring the park together tomorrow. She's the whole reason I agreed to this meeting in the first place. It's not like she would ever let me turn down a trip to Dreamland."

I'll have to have Iris send her a special gift of some kind to express my thanks.

"We can get you VIP passes," my father speaks out.

I shoot daggers at him, and he ignores it with a smile.

Yakura raises a brow at my father. It's the smallest gesture, but it fills me with newfound confidence.

They're still not on good terms. No matter what kind of timeline my father wants, Yakura isn't biting.

It looks like my deal isn't lost yet.

I release a genuine smile. "So, are we ready to get going?"

Yakura waves his hand toward the front door. "After you."

Rowan and I share a look that tells him to keep my father occupied by any means necessary. He nods, and I roll my shoulders back.

At least I have one person on my team today because I already know I'm going to need him.

My father doesn't let me get away with being the leader for long. After I show Yakura Story Street and the entrance to Princess Cara's castle, my father steps in with something I wasn't even aware of.

"I'd love to show you a hidden part of the castle if you are up for some steps."

Rowan looks over at me and shakes his head.

Shit.

"I'm sure it can wait until after we circle around the park."

My father's smile brightens. "Might as well knock it out of the way while we are here."

Yakura seems wary of my father but nods.

Rowan pinches the bridge of his nose.

Fuck.

My father navigates the group toward a hidden entrance of the castle. He motions for Rowan to use his key card to open the door, and my brother complies while shooting me an apologetic look.

My father and Yakura walk up the steps first, so I hang back with Rowan as he shuts the door. I don't want to leave my father alone with Yakura longer than necessary, but I need to be fully informed before I can plan my attack.

"What is he doing?" I whisper as my father and Yakura disappear around the first corner of the stairs.

"Showing him the hidden tower."

"*What hidden tower?*"

Rowan's eyes dart toward the empty steps. "The one Grandpa had built for Grandma before she passed. Since she never got to see it, he never showed it to anyone else."

Yakura is a sucker for sad stories. All my father needs to do is capitalize on the story of how his mother never had a chance to see the park become what it is. Yakura will eat it all up given his passion for developing a park he can enjoy with his family while he is still alive.

You're fucked. "And you never thought to mention this story during the countless conversations we had about this place?"

"I didn't think it mattered."

"Obviously you were wrong, which seems to be a trend lately," I snap.

I told myself I wouldn't bring up his decision to move to

Dreamland anymore, but I can't help it. Anger makes me stupid and vile.

A nasty personality trait you picked up from the one man you can't stand.

Rowan frowns. "Don't lash out at me because you're pissed."

"Pissed doesn't begin to cover how I feel right now. You had one job to do. To think you gave up everything for this position and you can't even do it right. What a fucking disgrace."

It's a shitty shot at him and his choice to stay here. I'm not proud of letting my anger get the best of me, but I can't find it in me to stop. Not when I might lose out to my father of all people.

"Fuck you and fuck your walk-through." My brother slams his key card against my chest before leaving out the door we came through. "Find your own way around the park, asshole."

I tell myself that it is fine and how I don't need him. That if I can't secure a deal with Yakura by myself, then I don't deserve the position of CEO to begin with. Those thoughts are the ones that push me to take two steps at a time.

It's time I prove to myself that I have what it takes to usurp my father. It might not be an even playing field, but that will only make my victory all the better.

I let my father have his moment. Just like I anticipated, Yakura is moved by the story of my grandmother and her untimely passing before Dreamland ever opened its gates. My victory is slipping past my fingers with each of my father's tugs on Yakura's heartstrings. He is good at telling people what they want to hear. While I picked up on the skill after watching him pull the same trick on every person in his path, his mastery over people's emotions is unmatched.

My father gloats as we make our way out of the castle. I'm grateful he waits to rub it in my face until Yakura excuses himself to use the restroom.

"You thought you could plan this impromptu trip without me finding out?"

"It's not your deal."

"I'm the CEO. Everything about the company is mine."

I keep my fists hidden away in my pockets. "Except this one won't start until *I'm* CEO."

"Not if I can help it." His smile is genuine, which is all the more infuriating. He thrives off my shortcomings.

"You didn't even want this deal."

"I didn't until you thought you could blackmail me and get away with it. I'll thoroughly enjoy ripping this project away from your fingertips, only to show you what a pathetic excuse for a CEO you would make."

I was a fool for thinking I could make it through this process without Iris. There is no way I can manage my father's manipulative strategies and Yakura's needs at the same time.

I'm quick to pull out my phone, but I hesitate over the call button.

Are you really going to ruin her day yet again?

I don't have much of a choice. Without her, I might lose the deal.

But if you steal her away again, you might end up losing all the progress you've made.

Screw it. If there is one person I can count on to fix this, it's her.

"Calling your wife for help?"

I completely ignore him as I hold my ringing phone up to my ear.

He chuckles to himself. "You're a pathetic excuse of a man if you need your wife to help save the day."

He tries to goad me, but I refuse to go for it. I'm no less of a man because I admit I need Iris's help. She is the one who understands Yakura best, and I'd be foolish to think otherwise. Even if it means stealing her away again.

She answers on the second ring. "Hey. I was just thinking of you while checking out a—"

"I need you."

"What's wrong?"

I instantly feel guilty for the worry in her voice. "Yakura and my father stopped by ahead of schedule."

"Oh." Somehow one word carries more disappointment than an entire speech.

I consider telling her to forget about it, but she doesn't let me get a sentence out.

"Send me your location and I'll find you."

CHAPTER THIRTY-NINE

Iris

My shoulders drop as I end the call. I can't ignore the guilt that hits me straight in the chest, knowing Zahra planned this whole day only for it to be ruined because of work.

Another plan has come and gone because of working for Declan. I know it's not Declan's fault his father pulled a stunt like this, so it makes me upset to even feel that way in the first place.

I can't erase the growing pressure in my chest at the thought of canceling another plan. I like Zahra. Canceling on her feels like a repeat of how I lost countless friends—all while working for Declan.

It's not his fault you don't set boundaries. Cal warned you that something like this was bound to happen, but you stayed anyway.

If I were working for anyone else and they called me on a day off, I would say screw it. With Declan, I don't have a choice.

I release a heavy breath. My feet drag across the pavement as I reenter the greenhouse.

Zahra waves me over. "Check this out. They've been waiting six years for this one to bloom. Six!"

I look at the Titan Arum with a frown. "I'm going to need to take a rain check on today's plans. I'm so sorry, but something came up."

Zahra's smile drops. "Oh no, are you feeling okay?"

I shake my head. "I feel… Frankly, I don't know how I feel."

I'm disappointed about today. It feels like I'm falling into the same pattern as always.

"Can I help?"

"You can by telling me how I can get back to Dreamland. Seth showed up and I need to go help Declan before something happens."

"Seth is here?" Her gaze darkens.

"And Mr. Yakura."

"*Together?*"

"I have no idea how that happened, but I don't doubt Seth was behind it."

"Well, we can't just let him take over, can we?" She blazes a trail straight out of the greenhouse.

Zahra calls someone's name and asks for a pair of keys. A random worker throws them at her, and she starts a small golf cart that still has a few plants in the back.

"You're driving me?"

"You need to get to the park somehow, don't you? I hope you didn't think I'd let you walk all the way there."

"Thank you." I slide into the bench seat and Zahra presses a foot on the pedal.

"That's what friends are for."

"Aren't you upset I have to cancel?"

She shrugs. "We can come back another time."

"I'm so sorry again."

"No need to apologize. I get it. Things pop up for Rowan all the time at the last minute."

I sigh. "Does it ever upset you?"

She laughs. "Oh yeah. Sometimes I want to take his phone and drop it in the nearest toilet."

I laugh. "But you don't."

"Only because of sheer will and a parting orgasm from Rowan before he goes to fix whatever crisis popped up."

"I guess that's one way to pacify a partner."

"You have no idea. If you asked Declan, I'm sure he would be happy to oblige with the same policy."

I sigh. "I guess."

She nudges my shoulder with hers. "What's really wrong? Something tells me it has nothing to do with orgasms."

"It's just that…" My voice drops off.

She stays silent, weaving the golf cart through curvy sidewalks and underground tunnels. I try to think of how to phrase my feelings, but they sound small in comparison to the stressor. As Declan's partner, I should drop everything to help him. I understand that and am more than willing to. But I'm worried what might happen if it continues on as a pattern.

"I struggle with not feeling upset at him for things like this. Being his assistant is great, don't get me wrong, but it's exhausting.

I'm worried things will only get worse once he's CEO. I can't help wondering how it could tear us apart as a couple, adding resentment that shouldn't even be there if I weren't his employee as well as his wife."

"And if you have a baby…"

"There's no way I could be pregnant and keep up with his crazy schedule. I'd spend more time asleep on my desk than I would spend working at it."

She laughs. "Do you plan on finding a replacement sometime soon?"

"I'm not sure… I haven't considered it since I thought about transferring jobs."

"It could be nice to give it another thought, especially if you're more serious as a couple now. Sometimes what feels wrong in one moment can feel perfectly right later on."

"He won't want to let me go."

"He might not, but it's to be expected. I hear you're amazing at your job and really kick-ass."

My smile wobbles. "Thanks, but it feels like my ass is the one being kicked right now."

"Sometimes life is like that. Not every plan can work out the way you want it to." Zahra slams on the brakes and the golf cart screeches to a halt.

"This is the closest I can get you to his location without actually driving where guests can see me."

"Thank you so much."

"Thank me by kicking Seth's ass." She shoves my backpack into my hands. "Go! Take the back alleys so you can avoid the crowds."

She doesn't have to tell me twice. I'm nothing but shaky limbs and protesting lungs as I chase after the little blue dot that marks Declan's location. I don't stop running until I find Declan, Yakura, and Seth all talking. Well, more like Seth is talking and Declan looks about one minute away from shoving him into the nearest fountain a hundred feet away.

Mr. Yakura's eyes land on me. "Iris!"

I can't respond as I keel over, slapping my hands against my thighs as I take in a few deep breaths. My breathing doesn't seem to get any better, and my throat feels like someone wrapped their hands around it and hasn't stopped squeezing.

I stare at two dark shoes stopping in front of me.

"Where's your inhaler?" Declan's voice seems rough and on edge.

It makes me bristle.

"Your inhaler, Iris." His tone has a bit more bite to it.

I point at my tiny backpack in between wheezes. He makes quick work of finding the red canister amongst all the Dreamland junk I've collected over the last twenty-four hours.

"Here." He uncaps it before passing it to me.

I go through the motions, and my breathing becomes easier as the medicine makes its way through my system. Declan steals it back from my hand and packs it away.

I rise up and look over at Mr. Yakura with a shy smile. With the way his eyes shift from Declan to me back to Declan again, he seems almost smitten by his overbearing display.

It was kind of cute. I'll give him that and *only* that today. Even though he is acting like a total ass right now, not even bothering to look at me as he stares down his father with a scowl.

"I was wondering where you were." Yakura pulls me in for a big hug.

I catch Seth shooting lasers at me from afar, and I give him a little wave with my free hand.

"Where's your wife?"

He releases me from his embrace. "She stayed at the hotel. Had I realized you would be joining us, I would have brought her along."

"What if we go get her?"

His whole face lights up. "Are you sure? I wouldn't want to put anyone out by changing our plans."

"Nonsense. We can't spend the day at Dreamland without her. It wouldn't be right."

He winks. "This is why I like you."

Seth stares at me like an enemy he wants to destroy, so I welcome his challenging gaze with one of my own. It's his fault Declan and I were put in this position in the first place.

And I don't plan on forgetting it.

CHAPTER FORTY

Declan

I thought having Iris along would solve my problems, except it doesn't. If anything, it only adds an extra complication to my already failing plan.

Her idea to bring Mrs. Yakura along? Great in theory, but she is just another pain in my ass. She stops every twenty feet to stare at something, which only slows us down. And by slowing us down, it gives my father more opportunities to lead the discussion. Iris tries to move her forward, but she becomes immersed in every damn flower, child, and sign in our path.

Herding Mrs. Yakura is about as successful as gathering a bunch of stray cats. It doesn't help that her husband seems to encourage her, with his attention span split between my father, me, and his wife.

I take another deep breath as Mr. Yakura pulls to the side with Iris and his wife to check out another topiary. They act as if they have never seen a shrub before.

"Doing okay, son?"

I swear I'm about one comment away from grabbing him by his tie and choking him with it.

Breathe.

I try to use my usual phrases to calm myself down, but each time I try, it only seems to make matters worse.

"I'm fine."

He chuckles underneath his breath. "You can give up at any time and I'll take over to secure the deal. I'm even willing to give you credit and put in a good word for you during our next board meeting."

"Shut up."

"I'm trying to help you. While I'd be happy to finish this off and secure us a new park, all it would take is one misstep from me and the deal is good as dead."

My teeth grind together. "You shouldn't even be here."

"You should have mentioned that to your wife then, before she set up an automatic email letting everyone know where you were this week."

"You're lying."

He smirks. "Go ahead and check your phone. I'll wait."

I pull it out but stop myself. His tricks aren't going to work on me.

"I don't believe you." Even if she did send out an email like that, it doesn't mean my father could connect me all the way back to Dreamland.

"I take it you don't want to accept my offer to help finish this once and for all?"

"Over my dead body."

"No parent wants to bury their child, but I suppose I'm willing to make an exception."

"I don't have time for this shit." I push past him and walk toward Iris and the Yakuras.

"I was telling them all about the greenhouses we have on the company property a few miles away from here." Iris smiles up at me.

"Great. I doubt they're interested in going there though," I speak between gritted teeth.

Her smile drops before she recovers. "So, I was wondering what you both would like to see next?"

"Roller coasters," Mrs. Yakura says at the same time as her husband replies, "Nothing that causes back pain."

Great. I have to choose between giving Mr. Yakura permanent nerve damage and pleasing his wife.

Fan-fucking-tastic.

My father and I spend the afternoon battling for Mr. Yakura's attention. He consistently interjects himself as if to remind us that he is still a part of the group, and Yakura falls for it. He wants to know about our family, our history with the park, and what it was like growing up with a grandfather who created the biggest fairy-tale empire in the world.

I jump in and respond to some questions before my father has a chance, although his years of experience give him an advantage. Yakura seems pleased with my responses. But then again, he seems equally interested in what my father has to say. Maybe even more so.

This wouldn't be a problem if he weren't even here to begin with. A problem my assistant caused by creating a damning automatic message insinuating I was at Dreamland. My father is no idiot. He knows exactly what a trip to Dreamland means, and it has nothing to do with visiting Rowan.

Since I didn't believe him, I check my email. There are multiple ones from employees where I automatically replied back saying I would be out of town for business at Dreamland.

My father wasn't lying after all. Iris fucked up astronomically, and now I'm stuck trying to fix the mess she made.

As if she senses my darkening mood, she tugs on my sleeve. "I need to use the restroom."

I'm hesitant to leave my father alone with the Yakuras, but it seems like I don't have much of a choice as Iris drags me away. She leads us toward the nearby restroom area, out of sight from the others.

"This isn't going well."

"Really? What gave it away?" I ask with a dry voice.

"This doesn't feel right. I think we need to step back and regroup before it explodes in our faces."

"I'm not about to run away from something difficult because it doesn't *feel right*." My voice carries a bit more bite than intended.

Her brows pull together. "Your father is up to something."

"I appreciate your concern, but I didn't ask you to come here so you could waste your time analyzing my father, seeing as he wouldn't even be here if it weren't for you."

"What?" She rears back.

"He told me about the automatic email replies you set up for me."

"So what? I always do those. It's company policy—"

I cut her off. "What good is company policy if I might not have a damn company to run in a year because of this?"

She winces.

Calm down before you say something you'll really regret.

I take a deep breath and try to recalibrate, but with how everything is going today, I feel beyond flustered. All because my father found out about my trip from the one person I trusted to handle all this.

Now isn't the time to get into it with her.

I shut my eyes to avoid looking at her face. "I think you should go." It was a mistake to drag her into this.

"You're joking."

"It's for the best. You're nothing but a distraction that I don't have time for right now."

Her mouth drops open. "A *distraction*? All I've done is try to help you."

"Your job description says you're supposed to alleviate problems, not cause them."

She takes a step back like I physically slapped her. "That isn't fair."

"Neither is life. Get over it."

Her eyes have a sheen to them that wasn't present a minute ago. "I think you're making a mistake if you keep going today. If I were you, I would end it, circle back tomorrow, and see if you can meet with Yakura privately. He is more observant than you give him credit for."

"As much as I have appreciated your input up until this point, I'm the boss. I can determine whether or not I should continue."

"We're supposed to be a team."

"We are, but every team has a leader, and it's not you."

She sucks in a breath. The noise acts like a needle against the pressure building inside my chest. I'm hit with a strong wave of guilt.

Be better than him.

I reach out to cup her cheek, but she steps back.

"No. You don't get to touch me right now."

Her rejection slices against my thinning resolve. "So, is this how it's going to be? You're going to punish me whenever you don't get your way? What's next, withholding sex because I did something stupid like comment on your job performance?"

Her eyes narrow. "That's not my issue with you and you know it."

"Then what *is* your problem?"

"You don't trust me—not entirely that is. If you did, then you would listen to me because I've spent two years helping you build this project from the ground up. I don't want you to ruin it because you're not thinking rationally. Today isn't about beating your father or trying to talk over him. It's about showing Yakura that you will put family first, regardless of your personal feelings because it's in the best interest of the company."

"I trusted your shitty plan and you *failed*, so don't lecture me on trust when you're the one to blame for my father being here in the first place. If you were as good at your job as you say you are, none of this would have ever happened."

Her eyes widen and she takes a step back but stumbles. When my arm shoots out to help her, she flinches.

Fuck.

Fuck. Fuck. Fuck.

The regret is instant, like a bullet to the heart. It's one thing to lash out at my brother because I'm pissed, but it's another to talk to Iris this way.

Say something.

I wish I could go back in time and make better choices because the look on her face guts me. Absolutely makes a wreck of my insides to the point of physical pain. "Iris, I shouldn't—"

She laughs. It elicits the same reaction as nails running down a chalkboard. I reach for her again, and I think she must be in shock because she lets me hold her.

"I never thought I would be on the receiving end of your temper, but I should have known that being your wife wouldn't save me from that kind of treatment. If anything, it makes it ten times worse."

"I didn't mean it. I was angry about the situation with my father and took it out on you."

She stays silent, so I kiss her. Her arms hang by her sides which only increases my desperation. I want her to do something—anything really, so long as it takes away this feeling growing in my gut.

"I'm sorry," I mumble against her lips. Something wet and salty hits my lips, and I break away from our kiss to find a few tears streaming down her face. I brush them away, trying to erase the evidence of my words, only to find more in their wake. It's like trying to fix a leak with duct tape. Nothing works to stop the tears from breaking free, and they only make me more frustrated.

"Please don't cry."

Her brows tug together as she looks up at me with glistening eyes. "You're not laughing."

"What?"

"You told me you laugh when you make people cry." Her voice cracks.

I'm a mess inside. She doesn't even seem to be looking at me but rather through me. Her glistening eyes serve as a window to her soul, and what I find is devastating. A beautifully broken soul who happens to be a mirror of mine.

You hurt her.

I feel no better than my father, wielding words like knives out of anger. While it might not leave the same kind of wounds as fists, words can do more damage than anything.

To think you've tried so hard to prevent yourself from becoming like him, only to realize you're an exact copy.

She doesn't meet my eyes as she sniffles.

Maybe even worse.

Based on the way I feel, it sure seems that way.

I pull her against me, this time kissing the top of her head. Except her usual sigh is absent. She doesn't melt into me the way she always does, and my worry only intensifies.

"Let go of me," she rasps as she pushes against my chest.

I release her like she might catch on fire if I hold on to her for a second longer. The way she looks at me...it feels like she took her nails and sunk them straight into my chest.

"We can talk this out."

She takes a large step back as she wraps her arms around her like a hug. I want to be the one to console her, but how do I make her feel better when I'm the one that hurt her in the first place?

"I've been called a failure by many people in my life, including my own father, yet none of them seemed to have made it hurt quite like you just did. I trusted you."

My stomach rolls as I am unable to escape the sick feeling plaguing me.

"I'm sorr—"

She cuts me off. "The last thing I want to hear right now is how sorry you are. I can't believe I came here thinking you needed my help, only to end up being blamed for all of this. What a joke. The only two people to blame here are you and your father. Him for being an absolute dick and you for following in his footsteps, lashing out at me instead of taking personal responsibility."

I take a step forward, only for her to take a big step backward. My hand drops back to my side. "Don't go."

She shakes her head as she takes another step away from me. "We're supposed to be a team."

"I don't want to be on your team. Not anymore."

A punch to the face might have hurt less than the way she looks at me like I'm below her.

"I'll be better."

"Funny. That's what my father always told my mom too, right before he hurt her all over again."

Her final blow lands exactly like it was meant to. I try to take a few deep breaths as I think of something to say, but I struggle to come up with anything worthy.

She takes advantage of my stunned state and retreats to a hidden exit out of the park without sparing me another glance. I'm torn between chasing after her and going back to the group. Leaving Iris alone after knowing how upset she is seems unconscionable, yet I can't exactly leave the Yakuras in my father's hands. Not after how hard Iris and I have worked to make this happen.

You can deal with Iris later, once all of this is done.

It seems like the best idea, yet I struggle to make my way back to everyone. Each step away from Iris feels like I'm trudging through quicksand.

You did not spend two years of your life working on this deal to lose it now. Pull yourself together.

I return to the group, ignoring the weight pressing against my chest with each step away from Iris. For the sake of my future, I need to shelve my emotions and push through. It seems simple in theory until Mrs. Yakura asks where Iris is.

"She wasn't feeling very well."

My father's eyes gleam, and I can't stomach looking at him without feeling an urge to shove him away from me.

"Oh no. Does she need help getting back to your hotel?" Mr. Yakura offers.

I shake my head. "She didn't want us to stop our tour for her."

"Are you sure? We could—"

I cut him off. "I'm sure."

"Hopefully she feels better." Mrs. Yakura smiles.

If the look on Iris's face is a small inkling of the pain she feels, I doubt she will for a long time.

I made sure of that.

CHAPTER FORTY-ONE

Iris

D id I expect Declan to attack me like he did after I went out of my way to drop everything and help him when he asked? No, but damn did the surprise hurt almost as much as the things he said about me.

Your job description says you're supposed to alleviate problems, not cause them.

My throat closes up. How dare he talk about me and my job description like that. I can't believe I spent three years of my life fixing his problems whenever they arose, only for him to cut me down to nothing the moment I messed up.

If you even did mess up.

Regardless of if I did, Declan should have never spoken to me like that. He used my insecurities against me until I was left standing before him feeling just as broken as ever before. I've been on the receiving end of his verbal lashings before but never like this. This one felt personal in a way I never want to experience again.

You can only get angry at yourself. You're the one who let him in to begin with.

What was it that Declan used to always tell me?

Oh, right.

Learn to use your words as weapons because they can be stronger than any fist.

I feel like a fool for giving him the perfect ammunition to use against me. A tear slips free, and I swipe it away with the sleeve of my shirt.

Instead of wallowing in self-pity during the bus ride back to the hotel, I call the pilot and ask him to prepare the private jet for takeoff. I might be a failure, but I'm still a Kane, so Declan can fly commercial for all I care if he wants to get back to Chicago within the next day. I'm not staying in Dreamland for another hour after the way he spoke to me. The park feels too small for both of us right now, and I'd rather get the hell out of here. At least that way I can wrap my mind around everything he said without anyone trying to sabotage me, talk down to me, or make me cry. Knowing my husband, he might do all three if I stick around.

Running is what I'm good at. Staying and dealing with problems that hurt like a bitch, on the other hand? Hard freaking pass.

Screw him and screw his stupid deal. I deserve more than him hurting me to save face, especially after all the sacrifices I made for him.

The bus drops us off at the hotel. I don't know how long I

have until Declan gets back to the room, so my panic forces me into action mode. If I'm lucky, Mr. Yakura will keep Declan and his father discussing contracts for hours. Maybe even *days*.

Except the thought doesn't make me happy like I would expect. Rather, it drives me to a fresh round of tears as I consider Declan choosing to secure the deal over coming after me. After everything he said, one would think he would want to fix things right away if they really mattered to him.

I'm so screwed up in the head about everything that I can't even tell whether it's selfish or not to wish for something like that.

I shake my sadness off and get to packing. The whole suit-case looks close to bulging but somehow my belongings stay put.

I throw my hotel key on the nightstand, write a quick note, and leave the room without looking back. Turns out my worries about Declan coming back to get me were misplaced since he never bothered to show up. Instead of feeling relieved, I'm hit with another wave of despair.

Of course he didn't show up. Declan's priorities will always align with the company no matter the cost. He has been trained since a young age to work like that, and I was willing to be second best because his love is worth it.

Was. His love *was* worth it. Not anymore though. I could live without feeling like he took my heart and shattered it into a million pieces.

You're nothing but a distraction that I don't have time for right now.
He did apologize right after.

Yeah, so did my father after saying the ugliest things to my mom. I learned from her mistakes and don't plan on falling into the same trap.

You need to get out of here.

I hope Declan gets the deal. Not because I'm petty or mad, but because I want it to be worth everything he lost to get it—the option of earning my love included.

The concierge desk calls me a cab to take me to the private airport. By the time I get there, the cabin door is open and the plane is ready for takeoff. I get out of the cab and stare at the plane. I'm hit with an ounce of doubt, wondering if I should turn around and go back to the hotel.

Are you really going to leave him? What if he needs you?

His voice from earlier comes back with a vengeance.

Every team has a leader, and it's not you.

I shake my head, clearing any lingering doubts.

You're not going back. Not after he spoke to you like that.

I roll my shoulders back, climb up the stairs to the jet, and take the seat across the aisle from our usual spot. The staff on the plane is limited to a single flight attendant who offers me drinks and snacks. My stomach churns at the idea of eating anything at the moment, so I decline.

Somehow, I hold myself together during the entirety of the flight. Harrison picks me up at the airport, and he is kind enough not to ask me where Declan is. I'm not sure I could handle his question without crying. The way he looks at me makes me wonder if he knows something happened, but he stays quiet as he helps me with my luggage. He drops me off at Cal's place before taking off.

Up until this point, I've been numb and strictly on survival mode. Sure, I shed a couple of tears, but I didn't truly allow myself to consider everything Declan said until I knock on Cal's door.

He opens the door. "Hey. What are you doing back here so soon?"

Tears leak from my eyes before I have a chance to blink them away.

"Oh shit." He pulls me into his place and shuts the door.

His arms wrap around me, holding me up so my legs don't give out. My tears turn into full-body sobs. He listens to me while I recount everything that happened today, with him only interrupting to ask a couple of questions.

He doesn't speak until I stop. "He's an idiot for telling you all that crap. The only thing that was shitty about today was his attitude."

I pull away and wince at the tearstained spot on his shirt. "He said I failed."

"*He* failed *you* the moment he lost control like that. No one should talk to you like that, least of all him."

I sniffle. "He was so mad at me."

"I don't give a fuck how he felt. It doesn't make any of it okay."

My head hangs. "I made a mistake."

Cal grabs my hand and drags me toward the couch. He disappears before returning with a tissue box, some headache medicine, and a glass of water.

"Thank you." I look up at him with a wobbly smile.

His frown deepens as he assesses my face. "It's the least I can do seeing as I'm the one that encouraged him to chase after you."

"It's not your fault."

"I knew he didn't deserve you."

I wince, remembering the moment Declan said the same thing. "I—"

"Don't make excuses for him. The things he said are unacceptable, especially after everything you shared with him."

I take a deep breath. "Do you mind if I stay here tonight?"

"Guest room is all yours for as long as you want it."

I sigh. "I can't hide out here forever."

"You can do whatever you want. Declan isn't your keeper."

"I know but I need to be mature about this."

"Oh, like he's one to talk about maturity right now."

"We're married. One fight isn't going to change that."

He lets out a deep exhale. "No, but it might change the way you approach your marriage."

"I know." I twist my hands on my lap.

He drops onto the couch next to me. "Everything is going to be okay."

"Is it? Because it sure as hell doesn't feel okay. He didn't even come after me after everything he said. He just let me walk away like I didn't mean anything to him, all because a deal is more important than me." A loan tear slides down my face before landing on my lap.

"He fucked up. There's no easy way to put it."

"What am I supposed to do?"

"*You* don't need to do anything. He's the one who messed up, not the other way around. I know you're used to always picking up after his messes, but sometimes you can't fix everything for him."

My throat bobs. "What if he doesn't fix it?"

"Then he was never worthy of you in the first place."

CHAPTER FORTY-TWO

Declan

My father and I continue to compete for Mr. Yakura's attention. Rather than go with Iris's advice, I choose to fight back harder, proving I'm the best candidate to bring Dreamland Tokyo to life. My father meets my every stride. He makes promises I'm not even sure he can uphold, although he appears mighty confident in the manner. I can tell it's getting messy. Mr. and Mrs. Yakura try to keep their smiles wide and their eyes bright, but I can only imagine how exhausting all this is.

Iris warned me to end it, but I didn't listen.

No. I trampled all over her instead because I was too pissed to think clearly. After working so damn hard to earn her trust, I threw it away at the first sign of adversity. There is no one to blame but me. Not my anger. Not my father. And definitely not Iris, although I'm sure I made her feel that way.

A dark cloud of emotion follows me through the rest of our walk-through. I can't shake the feeling that I made a huge mistake by continuing on with the rest of my day despite Iris's advice. The more time that passes, the less I'm sure my choice to stay was the right one. My doubt has nothing to do with my father stealing Mr. Yakura's time, but more so to do with the idea of me hurting Iris and letting her walk away. The urge is stronger than ever to leave them all behind so I can go find Iris.

I can't stop thinking of the things I told her when I was angry. It was one thing to call her a distraction, but it's a completely different issue to doubt her ability to do her job. I know she is capable of everything and more, yet I tore her down like she was worth nothing. I'm not proud of the way I told her how the plan she made was shitty. But nothing feels worse than telling her she failed. I chose my words out of anger without truly thinking of the impact they could have.

It's not until we make our way back to the entrance of the park that Mr. Yakura pulls me aside. My father's eyes track us even as we step out of earshot.

"Declan. Is everything okay?" He looks up at me with a big smile as bright as his ridiculous neon shirt.

"I'm fine."

"I couldn't help noticing how you've been much quieter since Iris left. While I appreciate you spending the day with us, we would rather you be with your wife if she isn't feeling well."

If you even have a wife to go back to.

"She wanted me to see this through." At least I think so.

His smile falters. "I expected as much. She was rather persuasive on the phone when she was setting up this entire trip for us. I almost felt bad for inviting your father along, knowing the two of you aren't on the best of terms."

Wait, what? "Repeat that."

"I was the one who invited your father to join us here. Why else did you think he would show up?"

"When did you do that?"

Mr. Yakura tilts his head. "The same day Iris called to schedule everything with my assistant. I wanted to make sure everyone could make it here for the announcement. It's a shame Iris won't be here though. I know how hard she worked on putting all this together and I hate the idea of leaving here without telling her that this decision had nothing to do with her."

With the way my stomach rolls, I'm about one confession from throwing up. Iris had nothing to do with my father coming here. Sure, she set up an automatic email telling people I would be visiting Dreamland, but my father knew about the trip way before she created that.

Fuck.

I made a colossal mistake. One done out of anger and irrationality, all because I thought I could blame everyone else for my failure except *me*.

"Why would you do that?"

"I was curious about how you and your father worked together. Turns out my theories were right."

Fuck him and fuck my father. If Mr. Yakura wants to work with him, then fine. If he wants to work with me, great, although I'm not too certain I even want to work with him anymore. Not with the way he played me. I'd rather work with honest people who aren't out to manipulate me.

He holds his hands up. "I can tell this news upsets you. I promise I didn't mean for you to take any offense. My intention was solely to better understand the family dynamics before I made a decision to work with either of you."

"And let me guess—you don't want to."

His lips press together. "It's not that I don't want to, but your relationship with your father is complex. I can tell there is a lot of animosity between the two of you, although both of you try to pretend it doesn't exist. It became more apparent once Iris left."

If you had listened to her instead of shooting her down…

I take a few deep breaths to slow down my thoughts.

You're a fucking idiot, Declan. A stupid idiot who drove away the one person in your corner because you wanted to prove you had what it took to finish a deal.

"Did you even come here with the intention of signing a contract?"

"I did come with an open mind. My wife and I were both rooting for you, but I see there is still a lot you need to overcome. You're young, Declan. Young and ambitious and passionate enough to have what it takes to be a leader one day. No one is discounting that, although I'm sure it might feel like that because of my decision."

My temple throbs from the building pressure behind my skull. "I see."

"I doubt you want to hear this from me, but if you don't mind, I want to give you advice from one CEO to a future one."

I take a deep breath to stop myself from snapping. "Go ahead."

He releases a sigh as if he was actually nervous I would say no. "You're only as strong as your biggest fear. Take your father for example: he is afraid of being powerless, so he will go out of his way to ruin his own child's success just to feel strong and relevant. It will be his greatest downfall one day—I can guarantee that. So choose to learn from him and his mistakes before it's too late for you. Embrace your fears and grow from them or spend the rest of your life fighting them at every turn."

I try to stop myself from speaking but lose the ability to control my words. "What's mine?"

He laughs. "Go do some soul searching and find out for yourself. I can't just give you all the answers. That's the whole point of life."

Mrs. Yakura calls his name, and he looks over his shoulder and holds up a finger.

"One last thing." He turns back toward me.

As if this entire conversation can't get any worse. "What?"

"Come back and talk to me when you feel the time is right. If the gossip articles my wife reads are correct, then maybe it's sooner rather than later. Hopefully you have yourself sorted out by then." He winks.

I have no idea how he knows, but I can tell in his eyes that he suspects something.

"Go take care of your wife. Tell her I'm sorry and that I hope she understands." He gives me one last smile before he and his wife leave the park.

I watch them disappear behind the gates, so I miss my father walking up to me.

"How does it feel to lose something you worked two years on?"

"Not nearly as pathetic as you must feel going home to an empty house, knowing you only have your miserable self to keep you company. I'll see on Monday."

His shoes clap after me. "Where are you going?"

"I'm done here. I tried and I lost. If you'll excuse me, I'm going to get my wife and get the hell out of here."

He grabs my arm and I rip it out of his grasp.

"Don't touch me," I seethe.

"We're not done here."

"If you're looking for some kind of big reaction from me, you're not going to get one. Not anymore."

"Really? I guess I'll have to wait for Monday then when you have to present your failure to the board."

I shrug. "It doesn't matter what they think about me. Half of them think you're a piece of shit and they still kiss your ass because of your last name. So long as I have my inheritance, their opinions of me aren't worth shit."

"And you consider this proving yourself? It makes you look like a pathetic option for CEO."

"Maybe, but it doesn't matter, does it? Grandpa made sure of that."

"I will fight you every step of the way on this."

"You can sure try, but I'm not planning on fighting back. I'm done. You're a lost cause I refuse to spend any more energy on. I'd rather redirect it to what's important like my wife, kids, and brothers. You made your choice to be a miserable fuck, but that doesn't mean I have to." I walk away before I say anything else.

Mr. Yakura wanted me to consider my biggest fear and I was staring right at it.

I don't want to become my father.

I've spent my entire life striving to be better than him, to the point of following in his same footsteps to usurp him. I spent far too much of my time trying to destroy him when I should have been focusing on what's important.

I don't plan on making the same mistake. Not anymore.

I return to the hotel expecting to find Iris in the room, but discover it empty of all her things. Did she get another room because she wanted to avoid me? After what I said, I wouldn't blame her. But if she thinks I'm going to have her sleep somewhere else, she's mistaken.

Couples fight. We can get through this. But first, I need her to listen to me.

I check my messages, but none are from Iris. My heart beats harder against my chest as I call her cell phone and it goes directly to voicemail.

"Shit." I throw my phone on the bed, and it bounces against a piece of white paper that blended into the comforter. I'm almost afraid to turn it over but suck it up. The message is my worst fucking nightmare.

> Consider this my informal resignation letter. Formal notice will arrive on your desk this Monday at 9 am.
> —Iris

I crumple the paper before chucking it in the trash bin. I'm not letting her quit because we got into one fight about work, no matter how much she might want to. My words were harsh, uncalled for, and out of line, but that doesn't mean she can quit without giving me a chance to make it up to her.

But first you need to find her.

"Shit."

CHAPTER FORTY-THREE

Declan

I can't find Iris anywhere in the hotel. The only other place besides the park that I think she would go to is Rowan's place.

I take a deep breath and knock on his door. The light above me turns on before the door swings open, revealing Zahra on the other side. She looks bright and cheery as always—like she gets her energy straight from the sun. I don't know how my brother can stand it.

"Have you seen Iris?" I don't bother with pleasantries.

"Umm, shouldn't she be with you?"

I turn around and walk down the steps, not wanting to waste any more time.

"Hey! Wait!" Zahra chases after me.

I speed up.

"Stop!"

I don't.

The sound of flip-flops smacking against the ground makes me grind my teeth together. I ignore Zahra calling after me, only to be stopped by my brother on his way back from his run.

He pops an earbud out as he scowls at me. "What are you doing here?"

Zahra stops beside me, trying to catch her breath. "Has anyone told you that you have very long legs?"

"Why are you chasing after my brother?"

"Because I wanted to talk to him, but he didn't want to be caught."

Rowan raises a brow at me. "Care to explain why you are running away from my girlfriend?"

I take a deep breath. "I don't have time to chat. I've wasted enough of it as it is."

"Then make time."

"I'm trying to find Iris."

"Good luck with that."

I take a step forward. "Do you know where she is?"

"I'll tell you if you do what Zahra asks and give her a few minutes of your time. It's the least you can do after acting like such a dick to me earlier, don't you think?"

My jaw clenches. "Fine. Speak." I look down at Zahra.

"Can we go inside first? I need a glass of water."

My short fuse burns down to nothing as I follow them back into the home I spent most of my youth vacationing at. The memories slam into me as I take in Mom's porch swing, still hanging in the same spot years later.

"It's my favorite place in the whole house." Zahra shoots me a small smile.

Of course it is.

I ignore her as I walk through the front door. The place hasn't changed besides a fresh paint job and more modern furniture. There's still a doorframe by the kitchen that has our height marks over the years, with me being the tallest.

"It's pretty weird coming back here after so long, huh?" Rowan leans against the kitchen counter, observing me as I take it all in.

"How do you stand living here?"

"It reminds me of some good times."

"That makes one of us."

The corners of his lips lift in a silent reply.

"Would you like anything to drink?" Zahra pops her head into the fridge.

"Water is good."

She pours me a glass before getting one for herself.

"So, would anyone like to tell me why I'm being held emotionally hostage here?"

Rowan looks over at Zahra and she only grins. "I lied when I said I had something to tell you. I was only hoping to stall you for as long as it took until Rowan got back so you both could talk this out once and for all."

Rowan shakes his head as he looks up at the ceiling. "You're a pain in my ass."

"I know, but you love me for it." She kisses his cheek before disappearing up the stairs.

"She's smart."

"She's a meddler is what she is. She hates when we fight, especially when it's over my choice to stay here."

"You told her about earlier?"

"I tell her *everything*."

I take a sip of my water. "Interesting." Safe to say Zahra probably thinks I'm the biggest asshole around.

He grabs a glass and fills it to the top with water. "How did the walk-through go?"

"Why are you asking?"

"Because I care."

"Even after I lashed out at you?"

He sighs. "Love isn't conditional. I know Father made us believe that, but just because I get angry at you and vice versa doesn't mean I don't love you or care about you. Even if you do act like an idiot most of the time."

"Who knew Dreamland would turn you into such a sappy fuck?"

"Dreamland and the people in it." He smiles in a genuine way that reaches his eyes, and I can't remember the last time I have ever seen him look this happy. Maybe never.

No one can control falling in love, and he happened to find it in the last place I expected. It's time I accepted it and moved on for both our sakes. I've been punishing him for seeking out what makes him feel fulfilled, all because I felt like he betrayed me. I held on to the idea of him abandoning me like everyone else to manage my father and all the expectations that come with the company. Rather than support him, I held his happiness against him just like my father did countlessly throughout our lives.

You're no better than him.

It is a sour feeling to realize the man I have spent my whole life resenting is the one I am slowly becoming.

It's not too late to start making better decisions.

My mouth feels dry no matter how much water I drink. "I've made some mistakes."

Rowan blinks but stays quiet.

"I've said things I'm not proud of. Made threats, talked down to you, pushed you away because you made a decision I didn't like. As your big brother, I'm supposed to set the example. Be the bigger person. Make the best choices. Stay strong no matter how much I'm being beaten down. Except all I've done is show you what not to do. Instead of letting you become your own person, I was trying to shove you back into a mold you didn't fit into anymore. It was selfish of me, and I'm sorry."

"Wow." He blinks.

There isn't much else I need to say. From now on, I plan on being better. The end.

I stand. "I better get going."

Rowan grabs a set of keys from a bowl on the counter. "Let me drive you to the airport."

"Airport?"

He chuckles. "Iris took the jet back to Chicago earlier."

"She *what*?"

"Looks like you're flying commercial tonight. You better buy a ticket before you lose the chance."

I'm still trying to wrap my head around the fact that Iris is in Chicago right now.

Why would she stay? You never gave her a good reason to after the way you spoke to her.

I swallow back the lump in my throat. "I fucked up."

"It's nothing some good groveling can't fix."

"Groveling?"

"Get in the car and I'll explain." His grin is worrisome.

Well, shit. This is going to be an interesting car ride.

Does groveling include mentioning to Iris how I rode a commercial flight for the first time in a decade solely so I could get to her sooner? Because if so, then the middle economy seat I was subjected to buying at the last minute was worth every excruciating minute, seeing as I was stuck between a toddler who wouldn't stop talking and a mother holding a crying infant.

My ears are still ringing by the time I make it back to our house. Harrison opens my door, and I get out. I don't think to ask him about Iris until I walk into a silent, dark house.

"Iris?" I call out as I walk through the halls filled with her plants.

No one answers back. I search the whole house twice before I come to the conclusion that she isn't here.

"Fuck." I pull out my phone and call Iris. Not surprisingly, she doesn't respond.

I dial Cal's phone number next, but he doesn't pick up.

Me: Is Iris with you?

He doesn't answer right away, and I'm not interested in sitting around. I might as well drive to his place while I wait.

Less than thirty minutes later, I park outside his apartment and decide to call him again. He finally answers, but his voice is gruffer than usual.

"What do you want?"

I see Iris got to him first.

"Where's Iris?"

A door shuts in the background. "She's sleeping."

"At your place?" My teeth grind together.

"I don't think it matters much to her so long as it isn't yours."

"Put her on the phone."

"She doesn't want to talk to you right now."

"I want to hear her tell me that herself."

"Man, just listen to me. Take the night to cool off. Both of you are too emotional to deal with one another right now."

"Fuck this." I hang up the phone. I'm not about to let Cal tell me how to handle my wife. They might be friends, but I'm her husband. She belongs in our house no matter how upset she might feel right now. Couples talk issues out. They don't need third-party mediators to handle their shit for them.

Cal's doorman holds the door open for me. I press the elevator button and wait, tapping my loafer against the floor until the doors slide open. The ride to the top is quick.

I knock my fist against Cal's front door. "Open up."

"Motherfucker." I hear him grunt before the door swings open.

"Go home," he seethes as he shuts the door.

I block it with my foot and throw it back open. "Where is she?"

He shoves me, and I stumble back.

I blink. Cal pushed *me*? He doesn't touch anyone, much less throw his weight around because he is pissed. The only time I've ever seen him do such a thing was on the ice during high school hockey games, and it was a part of his sport.

He jabs a finger against my chest. "She doesn't want to deal with you right now."

"So what? You know what's best for her?"

"One of us has to, seeing as you sure as hell don't. I knew you weren't capable of taking care of her. I freaking knew it and I still helped you, thinking maybe you were really starting to change. That maybe you really did love her."

"I *do* love her. Not that I owe you any explanation."

"No, Declan. Clearly you don't if you called her a failure like every other disappointing fuck in her life."

"Shut your fucking mouth."

"Why should I? It's not like you ever do the same."

My jaw tightens. "I made a mistake."

"A mistake?" He laughs. "You belittled your wife until she felt as worthless as you. You made her feel small, useless, and insignificant—all because you care more about your job than the person you claim to love. So all I can say is congratulations, Declan. You spent your whole life protecting us from our father only to become just like him."

"Fuck you." I bite down on my tongue and taste blood.

He salutes me with his middle finger before slamming the door in my face.

Nothing feels worse than returning to the house without Iris. Defeat presses against my shoulders, making each step feel more difficult than the last. I drag myself inside the dark house that is as silent as a tomb. What used to bring me comfort only fills me with dread now, especially knowing what I did to earn it. I'm stuck replaying my brother's words to fill the silence.

You called her a failure like every other disappointing fuck in her life.

You belittled your wife until she felt as worthless as you.

You spent your whole life protecting us from our father only to become just like him.

It's the last one that hurts the most. To hear how Cal thinks of me...

It makes me want to rage. Not because of the sacrifices I've made, but because he is right. If I don't check myself, I will become just like my father. It's not like he started out as a cold bastard either. It took him time, and heartbreak, to get to a dark place faster than most.

You can be different. It's not too late.

I release a deep breath as I move toward the kitchen. After my flight from hell and my brother's conversation, I have no energy to cook anything, but my grumbling stomach demands some kind of nutrition.

I sift through the pantry, turning over different items before settling on Iris's favorite.

Pasta straight out of a box.

The pressure in my chest intensifies as I consider all the times she cooked for me over the weeks. It might not have been gourmet, but I didn't care so long as she kept me company.

Company I no longer have because I drove her away.

I set up two place mats without thinking much of it. It takes me a whole ten minutes before I realize my mistake, and my throat tightens to the point of difficulty breathing. I try to eat but everything tastes like cardboard to me.

The churning in my gut gets progressively worse as I dump my half-finished plate of pasta in the sink and go upstairs. No matter where I go, I can't escape my mistakes. Even my damn bedroom isn't safe. The memories of Iris assault me the moment I enter, with her perfume lingering in the air.

Her hair tie on the dresser. Some random heel left abandoned in a corner during a hookup. A framed photo of us on our wedding day, with her smiling up at me while I scowl at the camera.

I grip my chest, wishing for the tightness to stop. My hands tremble and I take a few deep breaths, trying to curb the anxiety attack before it starts.

You never deserved her.

No. I didn't yet I wanted her anyway.

I miss my wife. She belongs next to me, complaining about how I like to cuddle although she secretly loves it. I'd do anything to hear her groan about my alarm clock in the morning or for the grumpy kiss I get before I crawl out of bed to go work out.

I slide under my comforter after my shower and stare up at the ceiling, surrounded by the smell of Iris's coconut body wash. No position feels comfortable without her.

You're fucked.

I turn over for the third time and stare at the cactus she bought me two years ago.

Don't be a prick.

I'll try. Just for her.

I arrive at Cal's doorstep at 8:00 a.m. with a coffee in hand, ready to talk to Iris. I'm running on limited sleep and a lot of caffeine after an endless night of tossing and turning.

My brother opens the door wearing a suit and tie, which is out of the norm given he doesn't even have a job to go to.

"Where are you going?"

"Work." He shuts his front door and locks it.

"Since when do you have a job?"

"Since you needed an assistant."

My mouth drops open. "What?"

"Iris isn't coming in today."

"Like hell she isn't. Her two weeks haven't even started."

He laughs. "Maybe you should check your email."

I frown as I pull out my phone and scan my inbox. "You're kidding me."

"Nope. She's taking a two-week vacation, starting today."

"No, she's not."

He actually grins. "Are you giving me a ride to work or not?"

"Why are you enjoying this?"

"Because it's nice to watch someone finally put you in your place. Did you really think you could talk to her the way you did and expect her to go into work for two weeks?"

My molars smash together. "I want to talk to her."

"She'll speak to you when she's ready."

"Then I guess I'll be the one to do the talking then." I steal his keys straight out of his hand and unlock the door before he has a chance to grab them.

"Dec—"

I slam the door in my brother's face and turn the deadbolt before he has a chance to get in.

"Open the damn door!" He pounds his fist against the wood.

I throw his keys on the side table before following the music straight toward the kitchen. Iris's eyes immediately latch onto mine.

"What are you doing here?"

"I brought you coffee." I step close enough to pass her the cup.

She stares down at it like it might be poisonous. "You came here to bring me *coffee*?"

"No. I came here to talk to you. Coffee is merely a bribe for your time."

"I don't want your bribes. Not anymore."

"Fine. Maybe later." I place it on the counter.

"Should I even ask how you got in here?"

"I stole Cal's keys and locked him out."

"Declan—"

"I miss you."

"It's been less than twenty-four hours since you last saw me."

"The addiction gene runs strong in my family. Take pity on your husband."

She only scowls at my joke. I refuse to lose hope, although the way she looks at me makes me question it for a moment.

"I miss you so damn much, I don't know what to do with myself. The house is too quiet and the bathroom is far too clean. Even pasta doesn't taste the same without you cooking it."

"I don't cook. I boil. That's a big difference according to you."

"Come home. I'll cook every day for the rest of our lives so long as you agree to not leave again."

Her eyes shut. "No."

I take advantage of her guard being down and walk up to her. Her chin fits perfectly within the palm of my hand, and I stroke her cheek with my thumb. "Please. I'm miserable without you."

She blinks up at me. "I'm not ready."

"What do you mean *you're not ready*?" The sick feeling in my stomach returns stronger than ever as she pulls out of my embrace. I don't stop her, although every cell in my body is pushing me toward her like a magnet.

"I need time to think."

"What's there to think about?"

"You. Me. *Us.*"

"What about us?"

"Whether or not there was even an *us* to begin with."

My chest aches from her confession. Instead of lingering on the pain festering inside of me like sepsis, I choose to ignore it. "You signed a contract."

"Our deal never said anything about being in a real relationship. You yourself called it a game."

"This isn't a fucking game and you know it." The idea of her thinking that makes me want to rage, but I hold back. I've done enough damage as it is.

She shakes her head. "I don't know what to believe anymore."

"So what? You just want to go back to how things were before we fell in love?"

Her eyes dart away, and it's written clear as day across her face. *That's exactly what she thought.*

I release a bitter laugh. "Go ahead and take your time, but nothing is going to change the fact that you and I are inevitable."

It takes a ridiculous amount of self-control to step away from her, but nothing good will come if I keep pushing her on this. She wants her time, and I plan on giving it to her. So long as it happens according to my rules.

Cal drops off Iris's official resignation letter at 9:00 a.m., exactly like Iris promised. After everything I went through to prevent it from happening, she is leaving anyway.

All because of you.

Cal hovers in front of me.

I look up from her letter. "Yes?"

"Are you going to sign it?"

I clutch onto her resignation letter with my two fists. "I plan on it."

He raises a brow and motions toward the paper.

"You can go back to your desk now."

"And miss all this internal conflict and angst? What do you take me for?"

"A dead man walking."

He grins. "Watching you struggle to cope with all this is far too entertaining to pass up, especially given how miserable you made Iris."

"Can you please leave me alone? I'm not in the mood."

His brows jump, and I realize my break in character. I *asked* him to go.

Ever since I entered the office, I've been stuck in a constant state of heartburn. No amount of meetings or busy work can steal my mind away from the conversation I had with Iris this morning.

I pass by Cal's desk instinctively, half expecting her to be there, only to remember she won't be returning. I'm so used to her being around that I'm not sure how to handle her absence.

"This is for the best." My brother pulls out Iris's usual chair, but I point to the other one.

He shoots me a look as he drops into the one opposite of Iris's seat. "She's not coming back. Saving her chair won't change that."

"She's still my wife. That chair is hers regardless of her occupation status, so use the other one."

"*Is* she still your wife?"

"Get out," I seethe.

He shrugs. "I'm just asking."

"No, you're looking for a fight."

"Maybe I am. At least that way we can settle this. I don't like working with all this tension around us."

"There is nothing to settle. This is between me and her, regardless of whatever impression you might be under."

"She came to me *crying*, Declan. I'm not going to sweep that under the rug because you decided a little too late that you made the wrong choice and you want her back."

My fists clench against my lap. "I'm not doing this with you."

"Then sign the paper and I'll leave."

I grab an ink pen to sign her resignation letter, but stop myself. My hand hovers above the blank signature spot.

Cal clears his throat. "If you really love her, then this needs to be done."

"Even if it feels wrong?"

"Of course it feels wrong. You've both been codependent on one another for far too long."

"At least all that rehab I paid for taught you something." Even if it didn't keep him away from drinking again, at least he learned a thing or two about bad habits.

He flips me off. "This job shouldn't be the thing that keeps you together just like it shouldn't be the reason that drives you apart. So if you want a chance at a successful marriage, you need to let her go as your employee."

I press the pen against the page and sign my name beside hers.

"Here." I shove it away from me before I have a chance to shred it.

"It'll be okay."

"It sure as fuck doesn't feel okay. Not when it feels like I'm losing her before I ever even had her to begin with," I snap.

His face softens. "It's not too late to get her back."

"How do you know?"

"Because for some goddamn reason, she loves you despite all the reasons she shouldn't."

"She never told me."

"What?"

"She never told me she loved me." My voice drops.

"That doesn't mean she still *can't*." He leaves my office with Iris's signed resignation letter.

I pull out my phone before I can stop myself. I'm not going to go back on my deal to give Iris space, but that doesn't mean I need to be silent while doing so.

I pull up our chat and text her a single word to express how I feel.

Me: *Litost.**

I include a photo of her empty chair to express the suffering I feel at the reminder of how lonely I am without her.

She doesn't respond. I didn't expect her to, but it still makes my chest heavy anyway.

I try to get back to work, but my mind keeps drifting back to my relationship. My brain can't seem to concentrate on any actual work, no matter how hard I try. Instead of pushing myself, I shut

---

* **Litost:** *Noun, Czech:* a state of agony or torment.

my computer off and spend the rest of my workday thinking of how exactly I can get Iris back.

Cal's words from earlier seem to echo in my head.

She loves you despite all the reasons she shouldn't.

But what if I gave her all the reasons she should?

CHAPTER FORTY-FIVE

Iris

I spend my first vacation day doing absolutely nothing. It should be incredible and everything I hoped it would be, but I can't get past the fact that I quit my job. And in a big way, I feel like I quit Declan too.

I stare up at the ceiling for what feels like hours, trying to decide what to do. The urge to check in on Cal is almost as strong as the desire to reply to Declan's message. How could I not after he sent me a photo of my chair and a word that translates into something along the lines of *feeling miserable*?

I don't know what to do with all the feelings hitting me all at once. While I feel angry at Declan for how he acted at Dreamland, I feel equally guilty to know he is suffering because of me. I'm not the kind of person who likes holding grudges. They make me nauseous, irritable, and anxious to the point of needing a Xanax.

I try to distract myself by updating my résumé. I'd rather

make myself useful instead of wallowing in my feelings, although the task is more emotionally draining than I thought as I review my job history as Declan's assistant. I stop scrolling at my least favorite section of my résumé titled *Previous Education.* It remains empty, with only a mention of a high school diploma I earned.

The shame I usually feel knowing I never went to college isn't present anymore, which shocks me. I spent years avoiding conversations with other employees about my degrees and what my qualifications were. My self-consciousness about my lack of experience plagued me, so I worked to show everyone around me that I wasn't a failure.

Declan's previous words hurt for a multitude of reasons, but maybe the biggest one has nothing to do with him. Because deep down, I am a failure, but not in the way people assume of me.

I failed to face my fears. Instead, I spent years tying my worth to my position, and now that I don't have it, I feel lost. I put off going to school and played it safe. And even when I took a risk and applied to the HR department, it was still me trying to stay within my comfort zone.

I avoided going back to school because I was scared of failure. And instead of facing that fear, I fell into a rut. One that has been going on ever since I graduated high school at nineteen. The same one that will continue to happen so long as I keep allowing my past insecurities to rule over my current decisions.

You're not that girl anymore. You don't need to prove your worth to anyone but yourself.

That's the thing. I am finally ready to prove that the only limitations I have are the ones I set for myself.

I close my browser and open up a new one so I can search

for local universities. If the old me could see me now, she might have a heart attack. Never did I think I would willingly apply for a college degree.

You think that would give her a heart attack? You married your boss for an inheritance that isn't even yours.

I shove thoughts of Declan aside. If I want to get anything done today, the last thing I should be doing is thinking about him, no matter how much I want to.

I pull up a fresh Excel document and get started on a new pro-con list focused on schools, programs, and tuition costs. After that, I create a task list of things I need to do before I can even apply, including studying for the SATs.

By the time Cal comes home from his first day of work, I'm sure of one thing: I'm going back to school.

My phone buzzes with a new message. I swipe it off the counter and unlock the screen to find it's from Declan.

Declan: *Saudade.*

A photo loads of our kitchen island. My place mat is set up beside his as if I might show up at any second to join him while he eats his pasta. This is the third night in a row he's sent me a similar photo, each with a different word all following the same kind of theme.

Longing. Sadness. Regret.

Maybe Declan isn't the only one suffering from *saudade*.

---

* **Saudade:** *Noun, Portuguese:* a feeling of longing, melancholy, desire, and nostalgia.

From the way my chest aches as I obsess over his text, I'm hit with the urge to go home.

Home.

Shit. Since when did his house start feeling like *home*?

Since you started falling in love with him.

My throat tightens, and I struggle to take deep breaths.

"What's wrong?" Cal walks into the kitchen.

"Nothing."

"Declan sent you another message?"

I sigh. "Yes."

"Have you answered him yet?"

"No." Although I want to. I really freaking want to, but the rational part of me holds back, asking questions that stop me.

What if he messes up again?

What if he is only chasing after me because he wants to earn his inheritance?

What if I choose to fall in love with him despite all the warning signs, knowing he could hurt me all over again?

My head is a mess with questions that have no real answers.

"Do you want to talk to him?"

I avoid eye contact as I answer. "No."

"You miss him." He states it like a fact.

"Of course I miss him. I miss him so damn much it makes me sick to my stomach because I feel guilty for wanting him in the first place."

"Then why don't you speak to him?"

"Because I trusted my heart before and look where it got me. Now I'm doubting *everything*. If this is what love feels like, then I don't want it because it really fucking hurts." My eyes fill with tears.

Cal pulls me into a hug. "Everything is going to be okay."

"How can you be so sure?" His chest muffles my reply.

"Because if Declan loves you half as much as you love him, then he will stop at nothing to make this right."

After my breakdown yesterday, I decide to visit the one person who understands me most. Maybe my mom can help me get a better understanding of the emotions plaguing me. Although she doesn't know the whole story about my marriage, she knows enough about relationships to help me understand mine.

Her classroom hasn't changed over the years. It still smells like old paint with a hint of glue, and it reminds me of afternoons spent coloring while she ran her after-school program.

"Well, isn't this a surprise." She returns my hug with a squeeze.

"I wanted to see you."

"What happened?" She shoots me the same look she always does when something is up.

"Nothing…"

She laughs as she pats one of the classroom benches. "Sit." She passes me a piece of blank drawing paper and a pack of colored pencils.

This is how things always worked between us. *Color and confess* she would always call it, seeing as she always got me to break down eventually.

"As much as I love you stopping by to see me, I can't help but wonder why."

"Do I need an excuse to come visit my mother?"

"Seeing as you haven't visited my classroom for three years, yes, you do."

I sigh.

"That bad, huh?"

My head drops as I stare down at my hands. "Declan and I got into a fight last week."

"Ah. I assumed as much."

"Things got a bit too real and honest, if you know what I mean."

The few wrinkles by her eyes tighten. "He said some things that hurt you."

I give her an abridged version of our fight, mainly focusing on our issues with work and how that bled into our personal life.

"I can't help but wonder..." My voice trails off as I consider how to phrase my worry.

"Whether he might turn out to be like your father," she finishes for me.

"Yes."

She puts her hand over mine, stopping my coloring. "It's a normal fear after everything you've witnessed between your father and me, but you need to understand that couples fight. It's a part of any healthy relationship. That doesn't mean the other person should ever talk down to you or intentionally hurt you, but people make mistakes. This isn't going to be the first or last time Declan says something he doesn't mean in the heat of the moment. But so long as he is sorry—and I mean *truly* sorry—then you need to learn how to forgive him."

"Easy for you to say."

She gives my hand a squeeze. "Learning how to forgive is just as important as asking for it in the first place."

CHAPTER
FORTY-SIX

Declan

L   ike clockwork, I send Iris another message in the morn-
    ing. I attach a photo of us at the Botanic Garden with a
    word that describes the exact yearning I feel for her.

Me: *Sehnsucht.*

I stare at my phone screen for far longer than I should, waiting for a reply that never comes. My heart shrinks in my chest
with each ignored message.

You can either get upset or move forward with the plan.

I take a deep breath, shut down my computer, and lock up
my office.

  Sehnsucht: Noun, German: longing, desire, yearning, or craving.

"Where are you going?" Cal looks up from the computer.

"I'm taking the rest of the day off."

"What?"

"Please cancel my appointments for the remainder of the workday. I won't be available."

"All *eight* of them?"

"Is that a problem?"

"No, but—"

"Great. See you tomorrow." I make my way toward the exit before stopping to look back at my brother, whose mouth is still hanging open. "Thanks for helping me out. I know you don't have to, but I appreciate you stepping in for Iris nonetheless."

"I'm doing it for Iris. Not you."

"I know, which is why I appreciate it even more." I leave the office with my head held high and ready to push my plan into action.

Harrison and I drive around all of Chicago as I search shelter after shelter for the perfect dog. Iris was specific about her requirements, and I don't plan on screwing them up. My enthusiasm dwindles with each shelter that comes up empty, and by the tenth one, I'm losing hope.

"Maybe we can try again tomorrow, sir." Harrison holds the car door open for me.

I release a heavy sigh. This is an integral part of my plan, and I'm already failing. How hard can it be to find a big, fluffy dog who will follow Iris around everywhere?

Damn near impossible it seems.

I pull up my phone and look up the next shelter on my list. "Let's try one more and then I'll call it a day."

Harrison drives me to the last one. It's not in the best part of town, so I don't plan on staying long since Harrison and the Maybach might not be here by the time I get out.

A bell rings above me as I enter the building. The only employee in the place doesn't look up from her magazine.

"Hello." I stop at the counter.

She blows a bubble with her gum before popping it. "We're closed."

I check the sign on the front. "You're still open for another thirty minutes, so try again."

Her eyes widen before narrowing, as if she recognizes me from somewhere but can't pin down where. "How can I help you?"

"I'm looking for a big, fluffy dog that has separation anxiety."

"That's oddly specific."

"Tell me about it. Do you have any dog that fits my description?"

"Umm…not that I know of."

The last ounce of hope drains from me. I'll regroup and try again tomorrow once I've had a good night's rest. Or at least as good as I can get with Iris on the other side of Chicago, sleeping in my brother's apartment.

I knock my hand against the counter. "I see. Thanks for your time then."

"Do you want to take a look out back just in case?"

I open my mouth to say no, but I think better of it.

You did drive all this way. You might as well go check out the place while you're here.

"Fine. Lead the way."

She shows me to the back room. Kennels line the walls, stuffed with dogs and other animals all waiting for a new home. Some cower in the corner of their cage as I walk past them while others hiss or bark in my direction.

"See any you like?"

"No." All of them are either too small, too well groomed, or too scary to be deemed appropriate.

A dog barks from the farthest cage.

"What's that?"

"That pen is reserved for the dog being prepped for euthanasia. He's probably a bit anxious about being separated from everyone else."

"You plan on killing him?"

"We don't have enough room or money to house all of them, so once they reach a certain amount of time pending adoption… you know."

Jesus. I take a step toward the final cage. Two dark eyes look up at me, barely observable from behind a mop of white and gray hair covering him.

"What breed is this? Polar bear?"

She comes over and checks the nameplate. "They think he's an Old English sheepdog. Hard to tell without DNA testing."

He looks old all right. Based on the card, his estimated date of birth was more than five years ago. That's practically ancient in dog years.

"Can you let him out?"

"Are you sure? He's a bit…restless." With the way her eyes keep darting around the room, one would think she requires some kind of taser wand to handle a dog.

"Just open it up."

She shrugs before unlocking the cage. The dog barrels out like a bullet before slamming into me. I try to catch myself but end up falling flat on my ass as the dog licks my entire face from chin to hairline. It's absolutely repulsive, yet I can't help laughing when he repeats the gesture on the other side of my face, leaving no area unlicked.

"This one is being put down tomorrow?"

"First thing in the morning."

The dog whimpers as if he can understand the conversation. He takes a seat on my lap like a small dog, only to crush my cock beneath his weight.

I push him off me and stand. "No one wanted to adopt him?"

"Nope." She reviews his card again. "Oh, look. He suffers from abandonment issues and doesn't like being left alone for more than a few hours at a time. If he is, he might tear into your favorite couch or pee on your rug."

Great. Mystery solved.

He blinks up at me like he silently promises to be on his best behavior. I'm having a hard time believing him based on the way he drools all over my shoes like he wants to make them his new favorite chew toy.

"I think that's the closest thing I'm going to get to separation issues."

"So you'll take him?"

"Sure. Get me the paperwork."

I'm now the proud father of a clingy dog who will most likely destroy my home before Iris ever has a chance to come back to it.

Perfect. Just perfect.

The next day, I show up to work with the dog who has yet to be named. After he destroyed my favorite loafer while I was out on my evening run, he can't be trusted around nice things. Bringing him to the office is a temporary solution. One I need to fix soon, once I find the appropriate doggy day care to train him.

"What is that?" Cal stops by my office door.

"A dog." I don't look up from my computer.

The dog barks in reply. He tries to break free from his leash attached to my desk but fails.

"I see that, but why is it here? In your office?"

"He has attachment issues."

The dog barks again in agreement.

"Is he yours?" Cal takes a hesitant step toward it.

"And Iris's."

"Tell me you didn't get her a dog because you thought it would make her happy."

"Okay. I won't."

He rubs his face. "Shit."

"If you're going to judge my plan, you might as well get back to work. I'm already stressed as it is." Between fielding new temps for Iris's position and sorting through the rest of my plan, I'm spread thin.

"What even *is* your plan?"

My eyes narrow. "Why do you care?"

"Because I'm your brother and I feel obligated to help you before you do something drastic."

"Is there something considered more rash than adopting a dog?"

"I sure as hell don't want to find out." He pats the dog's head.

I glare at him. "I thought you were angry with me."

"I am, but I want what's best for Iris, even if that happens to be you."

"Thanks a lot for the backhanded compliment, asshole."

He shrugs. "Like you need any more self-esteem boosting."

"Seeing as my wife wants nothing to do with me, I could use all the help I can get."

"Who knew you being in love would make you this pathetic?"

"If you think this is pathetic, wait until you see what I have planned next."

CHAPTER FORTY-SEVEN

Iris

"Are we almost there?"

When Cal asked me to go on an errand with him, I thought he meant a quick trip to the grocery store. We have long passed the grocery store and any sign of civilization.

"Yes." He taps the steering wheel to the beat of the music streaming from the radio.

"It feels like we've been going around in circles for hours."

He laughs. "It's been thirty minutes. *Max.*"

A lightning bolt cuts across the sky. "It's about to rain."

"How convenient," he replies with a dry voice.

"Are you going to tell me what you have planned or are you sticking with the element of surprise on this one?"

"I'm not the one surprising you."

"*What?*"

He pulls over and unlocks the doors. "Get out."

"Are you joking?"

"Unfortunately not. Although I'm sure you wish I were."

I don't move a muscle. Cal hops out of the car and circles around the hood to open my door. "Come on."

"We're in the middle of nowhere."

"Stop being dramatic. We passed a Starbucks ten minutes ago."

"Why are we even here?" I'm too shocked to do anything but follow him out of the car.

"Just give him a second."

"Tell me you didn't set me up." I look around, trying to find the *him* Cal speaks of.

My comment goes unanswered as Cal jumps into his car and does a dramatic U-turn away from me. His tires squeal as he accelerates down the road, leaving me choking on car exhaust.

"What the hell?" I grab my phone from my purse and dial his number.

The dick sends me straight to voicemail.

I start talking the moment it beeps to leave a message. "You better have a good reason for ditching me like this—"

My rant is cut off by a car driving down the road. I've seen enough crime documentaries to know nothing good comes from hitchhiking with a stranger. I search the perimeter for somewhere to hide, except I'm surrounded by flat land and a few pieces of garbage. "Fuck. Cal, I'm going to kill you tonight in your sleep. Dead or alive."

As the car gets closer, I realize it isn't a car at all, but a white minivan. One that looks awfully similar to those serial killer vans everyone warns women to stay away from. My heart pounds harder against my chest, fighting for a way to get out.

I cross my fingers and whisper, "Please don't be an ax murderer. Please don't be an ax murder—"

I startle at the sound of a horn followed by a loud bark.

"Need a ride?"

My eyes widen at the sound of Declan's voice. "No fucking way." I bite down on my tongue and a metallic taste immediately floods my mouth.

I guess this is really happening.

Declan steps out of the vehicle wearing his best suit. "I have somewhere I need to be, so if you want a ride, you're going to need to hop in." He leans against the hood of the car like this isn't the weirdest situation ever.

I open my mouth to ask why Cal set me up, only to be cut off by a clap of lightning.

He raises a brow. "So are we going or do you want to get electrocuted?"

I stomp my way toward the passenger side and open the door. "Drop me off at Starbucks down the road."

"I'm going in the opposite direction."

"Then make a U-turn." I take a seat before the sky opens up above us.

He doesn't answer me as he shuts my door with a small smile.

"What—" My reply is cut off by a dog barking.

I check out the back seat and find a massive dog attached to some kind of animal car seat. He is covered in fur from head to paws, and I can barely make out his eyes due to his giant poof. I'm surprised he can even fit in the back seat based on the sheer size of him.

"Whose dog is that?" I ask when he opens his door.

"Ours."

"Ours?!"

The dog barks with a reply.

I'm not even going to touch that comment. Instead, I search the directions for the nearest Starbucks on my phone. "Take me here."

He completely ignores my map as he turns in the opposite direction.

"Declan!"

"I know I don't deserve it but give me ten minutes of your time."

I'm thrown back into the memory of the last time he asked for ten minutes but gave me ten words instead.

I am falling in love with you, Iris Elizabeth Kane.

The memory makes me compliant enough to keep quiet as he drives us down the road. Gray clouds part above us. Rain falls against the windshield, and Declan is forced to turn on the wipers to see clearly.

The dog whimpers at the sound of thunder. "What made you get a dog?"

"You said you wanted one."

My mouth drops open, and no words come out.

"It took me eleven shelters to find the one that fit your exact requirements, but somehow I pulled it off. I just hope you like him because there is no way he is ever going back to that god-awful place. They would have put him down if it weren't for me."

A laugh bursts out of me before I can swallow it. When I made up the story of the dog, I never really thought Declan would actually go out and find one for me. Let alone adopt one that is the size of a bear.

"Why would you do that?" My voice cracking mirrors my resolve.

"Why not? You wanted it, so I made it happen."

"And the minivan?"

"I thought we might as well have one ready to go for all the kids you want one day."

My vision turns misty. "You can't possibly mean that."

"I do, and I plan on showing you." He stays silent as he presses a foot on the accelerator.

The rest of the ride is a bumpy one. I'm grateful when Declan stops the van before I throw up from carsickness. He parks us in front of an old farmhouse with boarded-up windows and a porch that looks about ready to collapse. With the way he gets out of the car without an umbrella, I could almost forget it's *raining*.

He doesn't seem the least bit bothered by it as he opens my door and holds out his hand. "Come with me."

I blink up at him. "It's raining."

"I know. That's kind of the point." He grabs onto my hand and tugs me out of the car.

Raindrops splash against my skin. Declan leads me away from the car, although we don't make it very far before he stops in front of the worn-down porch. Water clings to his hair, skin, and clothes. I'm not sure I look any better with the way my T-shirt is plastered against my body. I'm tempted to seek shelter on the porch, but the wood looks warped and decayed from years of neglect.

"What is this place?"

"One second."

"Sure, I'll just wait while I catch pneumonia."

His hand gripping onto mine tugs and rotates my stack of rings until they both slip off.

An unbearable tightness in my chest intensifies as I check out my ringless finger. "Wait—"

Declan pulls out a ring box from his jacket and gets down on one knee. His face remains a blank canvas, completely devoid of any visible emotion as he looks up at me.

My heart pounds against my chest as he latches onto my left hand.

"What are you doing?"

"Proposing to you in the middle of a rainstorm in a Tom Ford suit."

Oh. My. God.

No way. There is no freaking way he is recreating the story I made up.

Right?

Wrong. He pops open the ring box, and I gasp. Even without the sun shining down on it, I can tell he bought the most beautiful emerald ring I've ever seen.

"Iris."

"Yes?" I drag my eyes away from the ring and back toward his face.

His hand holding onto mine *trembles*, and I know it has nothing to do with the rain. I give him a reassuring squeeze. He mumbles something that sounds like *here goes nothing*, and my chest caves in on itself at his display of vulnerability.

"*Ya'aburnee.*" As in *you bury me*. A rough translation for the

---

* **Ya'aburnee:** *Arabic:* "You bury me."

way I want to leave this world before you because I can't imagine having to go through a single day without you in it. If this last week was a preview of that kind of life, then I can assure you it isn't a life worth living. You're my wife and my best friend. The future mother of my children and the one place that truly feels like *home*. You're the woman I want to spend the rest of my life with, not because you signed a contract, but because you love me enough to stay without one.

"I want to be the kind of man who is worthy of a woman like you—if it's even possible. I promise to work every damn day to make sure you don't regret marrying someone as miserable as me. Because when I'm with you, I'm not miserable at all. You make me happy in a way that makes me afraid to blink just in case it all disappears." The vulnerability of his words tugs at every single one of my heartstrings.

"I'll give you anything you want—anything at all—so long as you give me a chance to make you as happy as you make me. A dog. A family. A *home*. I want it all. These are my terms and conditions, take it or leave it because I'm not open to negotiations."

"Only you could make a proposal sound like a business acquisition and get away with it."

"Marry me," he orders with a smile that could make me agree to just about anything.

"I *am* married to you." My tears mix with raindrops, and I'm not sure where one begins and the other ends.

"Marry me for real this time. No contract. No inheritance. No expectations other than for you to love me despite all the reasons you probably shouldn't."

He doesn't say anything else as he looks up at me. Emotions

flicker across his face like a mood ring, switching from happiness to fear. The heavy rain slowly turns to a light sprinkle as I stare at him.

To marry him again means to trust him with my heart, knowing he can break it. It means giving him a fair chance to learn from his mistakes and become a better man in light of them. Marriage isn't easy but neither is life, and I can't imagine doing either without Declan. Luckily, I don't have to.

"Yes." The response comes out as a whisper, so I speak firmer, "Yes. I want to marry you."

My legs tremble from the smile on his face as he slides the new ring up my finger. The diamonds surround the green gemstone like sun rays, shining as the sun finally beams down on us.

"Those were the most excruciating thirty seconds of my life."

I laugh. "Serves you right after everything you put me through."

He stands and pulls me into his arms. His lips slam against mine, stealing my ability to breathe as he kisses me with every ounce of love in him. Declan's embrace feels like coming home. My toes tingle and my chest warms, and I get all excited as his lips press softly against mine in a silent apology.

Our kiss goes on for what feels like hours. By the time we break apart, both of us are soaked to the bone although the rain has officially stopped.

The way he looks at me sends another shiver down my spine. I take a step back, knowing what a look like that means.

I clear my throat. "Are you going to tell me what we're doing out here in the middle of nowhere?"

"Showing you our new home."

"Our new *what*?" I gape at the house. I use the term loosely, seeing as the place looks like it has been abandoned for years.

"Let me show you something." He clutches onto my hand as we circle around the back of the house.

"No. Freaking. Way." I blink.

He smiles. "Do you like it?"

I take a step toward a stunning greenhouse. Unlike the house behind us, the greenhouse looks like someone recently came to take care of it. The spotless glass shines, giving me a good idea of the empty space inside.

I would need to buy hundreds of plants to fill it. Maybe even a thousand.

Declan pulls me against his chest so he can lay his chin on my shoulder. "I thought about letting you pick a place, but when my real estate agent sent me this listing, I knew it was the one. I drove out the same day to check it out and put an offer on it."

"Why?" I croak.

"Because there is nothing I want more than to turn a house into a home with you."

Declan needs to come with a warning sign because I'm susceptible to swooning whenever he is around.

"It's beautiful."

His arms tighten around me. "Want to check it out?"

"Can we?"

He grins as he steps away from me and opens the door. I spend the next five minutes exploring the place, cataloging just how much space I would have.

"I think I'm in heaven." I trail a finger across an empty table waiting to be covered with pots.

"So I take it that you like it?" His confident voice doesn't match the hesitant look in his eyes.

He's nervous.

Anxious Declan is my favorite Declan because it's the version of him no one else knows about. He tries so hard to hide it from everyone else, but around me, he doesn't mind dropping his guard. It makes my chest all warm and tingly to know he trusts me enough to share that part of himself. Because to someone like him who grew up thinking emotions were weaknesses, it probably means so much more than I could ever imagine.

I walk over to him and wrap my hands around his neck. "I love it so much."

"Good. Because if my proposal didn't work, this was my next best option to convince you to marry me."

I smack his wet chest. "You can't buy people's love like that."

His eyes *twinkle*. "I don't want other people's love. I want *yours*."

"You already have it."

He blinks.

I stand on the tips of my toes so my lips hover over his. "*Daisuki.*" I press my mouth against his, and he releases a shuddery breath. "*Szeretlek.*" He groans as I deepen the kiss, only to pull away breathless not a minute later. "*Ich liebe dich.*" I repeat the same three words he whispered to me back when he made love to me.

His eyes shut as if he is experiencing a sensory overload.

"I love you." I finish in English, just to get my message across because I most likely ruined the pronunciation of all the words.

"Say it again." His darkening eyes linger on my mouth.

"I. Love. You."

He kisses the top of my forehead. The pain etched into his face guts me, knowing he spent thirty-six years of his life believing he was unlovable—all because of his shitty, abusive father.

I cup his cheek. "I will always love you. Today. Tomorrow. Forever."

"You say that now…" His voice drifts off as his eyes dart away.

My chest clenches. "And I'll say it every day until you finally believe it."

"It could take forever."

I trace his wedding band with the tip of my finger. "It's a good thing all we have is time."

EPILOGUE

Iris

One Year Later

I s he busy?" I stop in front of Declan's assistant's desk.

"Go on in." He shakes his head with a smile before returning his attention to his computer screen.

I walk up to Declan's office door and knock a fist against the wood like I've done hundreds of times before. His deep rumble of a voice makes it past the door, and I open it before he has a chance to protest.

"I told you I don't want to be disturb—" His voice drops off as our eyes connect. The frown on his face quickly morphs into his signature small smile that makes me weak in the knees.

My legs wobble, and I nearly roll my ankle before righting myself.

He stands and helps me into my chair before I do something unfortunate like land face-first against the carpet. The way he acts ever since I announced I was pregnant makes me feel like he won't rest until I'm permanently protected in bubble wrap.

"I told you to stop wearing those death traps weeks ago." Ever since Declan read one horror story about a pregnant woman and heels, he hasn't let the subject go. I'm afraid I will come home one day to an empty closet and a fireplace burning with all my prized possessions.

"I want to enjoy my shoes while I can still see them." I pat my small baby bump.

"They're dangerous."

"I've been walking around in heels since I was a toddler and discovered my mother's closet. Don't insult me like that."

He presses his lips against the top of my head. "How's my favorite girl?"

I almost correct him but hold back.

Don't ruin the surprise.

"I woke up without running to the toilet, so I count today as a success worth celebrating." I place the takeout bag from our favorite Italian restaurant on Declan's desk.

He laughs as he takes a seat in his chair across from me. "What did the doctor say about your morning sickness?"

"He assured me the constant nausea is temporary and that it should clear up soon if I'm lucky. He said *if*, not *when*. If!"

"What's the point of calling it morning sickness if it lasts all day?"

"Because false advertising works wonders on naive women like me."

Declan chuckles. My heart beats harder against my chest as he grabs the paper bag.

He halts right before opening it, and I nearly groan.

Calm down before he gets suspicious.

Planning a surprise behind Declan's back is hard work. He has made it a point to come to every doctor's appointment, so I had to work my magic with his assistant to book his schedule solid. Poor Jeff had to deal with his anger all morning.

I'll make sure he gets a nice bonus for his sacrifice.

"Did anything else come up?"

I shake my head. "Nope. Everything is all good, although I gained ten pounds already."

His grin widens. My eyes narrow, which only makes him laugh.

"Good to know I've been feeding you well."

"Feeding me? More like spoiling me." Declan comes home by dinnertime every night just to cook me a balanced meal. At first, I thought it was a one-time thing, but he has made it a point to be home by 7:00 p.m. every day.

"Get used to it."

"For how long?" Once he becomes CEO, I doubt he will have time for small traditions like that.

"Indefinitely."

I blink. "Even when you're CEO?"

"Especially when I am. You keep me sane."

"That's a terrifying notion, seeing as I cried during a grocery store commercial just last week."

He shrugs. "To be fair, it was a really good advertisement."

My head drops back as I laugh. When I come back up for air, Declan's gaze is zoned in on me like a spotlight.

"What?"

His bright eyes match the smile on his face. "I miss having you around here."

My chest tightens, and I'm hit with an overwhelming wave of affection. "Jeff is good at his job."

"Jeff isn't *you*."

I stand and walk around his desk. He rolls his chair back and tugs me onto his lap. His hands wrap around me, with one landing on my bump.

The content look on his face does something crazy to my heart rate. He leans forward to kiss me, but my growling stomach makes him pause.

His brows tug together. "Did you eat yet?"

I wince. "No."

He extracts me from his lap before helping me back into my seat. Instead of returning to his chair, he grabs the takeout bag and rips it open.

"This isn't healthy."

I roll my eyes. "Excuse me for being in the mood to celebrate."

"Celebrate wha—" His voice trails off as he pulls out a mini succulent from the bag. The black *I'm a succa for my little girl* stands out against the white pot.

"I thought you could keep it on your nightstand next to the other one."

He turns toward me with wide eyes. "We're having a girl?"

I nod with a smile. "I found out today."

Declan hauls me into his arms and kisses me hard. His arms lock around my body, holding me up while he ravages my mouth. My chest feels close to combusting with the love he showers me in. He doesn't stop kissing me until my growling stomach reminds us of the third little person in the room who is hungry.

He pulls away. I open my mouth to protest, but stop myself as Declan gets down on his knees in front of me.

He kisses my stomach, and I nearly melt from the sweetness of it all. My eyes fill with tears. One leaks out and makes a trail down my face.

"I know I'm going to have my hands full with you, baby Kane, but you'll be worth every gray hair on my head. I can guarantee it."

EXTENDED EPILOGUE

Declan

"R emember what I told you."

"We gots to be quiet." My daughter presses her finger against her lip before giggling. Ilona doesn't know the first thing about using an inside voice, but I don't call her out on it. She is only five after all.

I scan her mismatched outfit from head to toe. "Where's your sign?"

Her small lips part as she sucks in a breath. "I forgot." She runs back down the hall. Her braids swing behind her, making the butterfly beads at the end bounce.

Based on the noises coming out of her room, it sounds like a war is going on in there. I resist the urge to go check on her. Iris says I need to stop being a helicopter parent because she needs to start growing up.

Fuck growing up. I want her to stay five years old forever.

"Got it!" she shouts as she bolts out of her room.

"Shh." I press my finger against my lips.

She giggles, and the sound feels like drinking pure sunshine. Her tiny shoes slap against the hardwood floor as she makes her way back to me.

"Let me have a look." I put on a serious face and gesture toward her poster.

She holds the graduation sign upside down, so I switch it right side up.

hAppy grAbUAtIOn.

Close enough.

"Hmm." I stroke my chin.

She looks up at me with her big brown eyes full of uncertainty. "Do you think Mommy will like it?"

I lean forward and give her a kiss on her chubby cheek. "I think she'll *love* it."

"Yes!" she whisper-shouts to herself, and part of my heart melts at the sight.

"Come on. Let's go get Mommy." I hold out my hand.

She stares at it before running straight toward our bedroom door without bothering to wait for me.

"Ilo—"

Too late. She barrels into our room. "ZERPRISE!"

I'm quick on her heels, not wanting her to get too excited and hurt Iris in the process.

Our daughter jumps on the bed, making the gold dust from

her poster fly all over our white comforter. I hate glitter but raising a daughter with an obsession for arts and crafts means I inhale the stuff like an addict would cocaine.

Iris seems to have the same thought as me as she looks up in amusement. "Care to explain what's going on here?"

Even after years of being married, Iris has a way of incapacitating me with nothing but her smile. I'm filled with longing as I take her in.

After a close call at the ER last month, Iris has been on bed rest for the duration of her pregnancy. The change has been hard on her. She went from being able to go to school and help raise Ilona to being trapped in bed. And although she won't admit it, I know she is still upset about not making it to Dreamland Tokyo's opening ceremony a week ago.

Hence the party. I couldn't let her years of hard work go uncelebrated. It might have taken her longer than most to graduate from college, but we have one healthy kid and two on the way thanks to the sacrifices she made to put family first.

"Daddy planned a grabuaton party for you!"

"A *what*?"

"A graduation party." I stop by Iris's side of the bed and press a soft kiss against her lips.

"Ew!"

Iris laughs. "Are you sure you're ready for twins?"

"Of course. We still have half a minivan to fill."

She shakes her head with a smile. "At this rate, we might need a bus."

"That can be arranged."

She laughs before gasping as I throw the comforter off her.

"Stop distracting me. We have guests downstairs who are waiting to see you."

"Wait! You mean right now?"

"Yes. Let's go."

She looks down at her outfit in horror. "I can't see everyone like this."

"You look great."

"Psst. Daddy?" Ilona waves me over.

"Yes, sweetheart?" I lean down so she can cup her hand over my ear.

"You forgot the hat." She speaks at full volume, completely missing the point.

Iris muffles her laugh with the palm of her hand.

Shit. The hat.

"One second." I rush downstairs and grab Iris's graduation cap off the dining room table without running into anyone. By the time I make it back to the bedroom, Iris has thrown on a casual dress and Ilona is missing.

"What are you doing walking around?"

"I'm on bed rest, not life support. It's good to get some exercise in every day."

I place the cap on the top of her head before bending down to cradle her in my arms.

Her eyes roll. "You're so dramatic."

"I prefer the term *overprotective*." I carry her out of the room and down the stairs. The sound of people talking grows louder as we enter the living room.

"Surprise!" everyone shouts.

Ollie barks before his tongue falls out of his mouth. I can

barely make out his mini graduation hat with all the fur covering his head.

"Oh my God." Iris covers her mouth.

Both of our families are packed into our living room. Iris's mom helped me decorate the place with streamers, balloons, and enough confetti to make my daughter happy.

Iris cups my cheek, and I look down at her.

"Thank you for planning this." Her eyes glisten.

"You deserve it. It's my fault you got pregnant again in the first place."

Her head drops back as she laughs up to the ceiling. "You and that damn private jet. We wouldn't have these issues if we flew commercial."

"Want to bet?"

She smacks my chest with another giggle before I deposit her on the couch.

Once everyone has a glass of sparkling apple cider in their hand, I call Ilona over so we can give our speeches.

Ilona wouldn't tell me what she planned for Iris, but I assumed it would be something short and sweet.

I should have known it wouldn't turn out that way.

She presses a palm against her heart. "I pledges allegiance to the flag…"

Iris cackles as everyone looks around with confused faces before joining in and reciting the Pledge of Allegiance. By the time it's my turn to speak, half the group is already red-faced or teary-eyed from withheld laughter.

Ilona looks up at me. "How did I do, Daddy?"

"Good work, sweetheart. It's going to be hard to beat that one."

She shoots me the brightest smile before running back to her cousins.

Although I'm no longer nervous to speak in public since becoming CEO, I still feel a jolt to the heart when Iris looks at me.

I raise my glass. "Congratulations on this big accomplishment. I never doubted your ability to be an incredible mother, wife, and student, although I know you did. But you persevered despite the doubt and earned your degree to help others just like you. There is not anyone more deserving of this diploma than you, especially given the sacrifices you made to achieve it. You're the strongest person I know and the hardest worker I've ever had the pleasure of collaborating with, and I'm grateful our kids have you as a role model to look up to."

She wipes her eyes.

I finish off with a word just for her. *"Gunnen.*"*

"Was that even English?" Nana calls out from somewhere in the crowd.

"Dutch or German if I had to guess," Rowan offers.

"Why the heck would he say that?"

Iris smiles. "Because we're in love like that."

---

* **Gunnen:** *Noun, Dutch:* to find happiness in someone else's success because that's how much you love them.

Thank you!

If you enjoyed *Terms and Conditions*, please consider leaving a review! Any review, however short, helps spread the word about my books to other readers.

Join my Bandini Babes Facebook reader group for all things romance and bookish updates.

Scan the code to join the group

Also by Lauren Asher

Throttled

Dive into my Formula 1 world with Noah and
Maya, a brother's rival forbidden romance.

Collided

A story about two friends who complete
a naughty bucket list together.

Wrecked

An enemies-to-lovers forced proximity romance
featuring a Formula 1 bad boy and his PR agent.

Redeemed

If you like fake relationship romances with a
grumpy hero, check out Redeemed.

Scan the code to read the books

Also by Lauren Asher

The Fine Print
The first book in the Dreamland Billionaires
series about a fairy-tale theme park, a grumpy
boss, and his infuriatingly sunshiny heroine.

Final Offer
The last book in the Dreamland Billionaires series
about second chances and two people who have no
interest in falling in love with each other (again).

Scan the code to read the books

WHAT'S NEXT FOR THE DREAMLAND BILLIONAIRES?

Final Offer, a second-chance romance featuring Callahan Kane and his mysterious ex.

Acknowledgements

Like Declan with Iris, I'm fortunate to have the best team supporting me with the release of *Terms and Conditions*. Thank you from the bottom of my heart.

To my readers—Thank you. Without your love for *The Fine Print*, this sequel would have never happened. I appreciate each one of you that read, review, and rave about my books to your friends, family, and followers. Your love for my characters and my way of telling stories has changed my life in the best way possible. Feel free to send me an email or a DM whenever. I read every single one.

Mom—Thanks for always reminding me to water my plants while writing this book. They appreciate your dedication to helping them survive while I was deep in the writing cave.

Mr. Smith—You might not be a billionaire, but I love you anyway.

DP—You might be wondering what the hell is happening as you read this acknowledgment in the middle of a bookstore. Surprise! I write romance books. Don't feel obligated to buy this copy though.

Erica—Solely thanking you for editing this book would be an extreme understatement. Your friendship, pep talks, and support during one of the hardest years of my life means the world to me. Thank you for making my days brighter.

Becca—Thank you for believing in me and my story even when I forget to do the same. You push me to be the best author version of myself, and I can't wait to continue growing with you.

Mary—To one of my very first book friends and the person I text most in the world (Sorry, Mr. Smith), thank you. Your talent speaks for itself, and I can gush about your kick-ass graphic design skills for hours, but I'll save it for a voice note.

Kendra—Thank you for helping me bring this book to the next level. You truly are a gem in this book community and I'm grateful to have your support. From sending me song choices to spreading the word about my books, I can't express enough gratitude for everything you've done for me.

Elizabeth T—Thank you for being a part of this project as my sensitivity reader. Your feedback and brainstorming with me really helped bring Iris and her family to life.

My beta readers (Amy, Mary, Nura, Mia, Elizabeth, Kendra)—I appreciate each of you helping me make this story come to life. Thank you for putting up with my tight deadlines, imposter syndrome, and constant questions and revisions.

Jos—Your text messages and voice notes always make me smile, and I'm so grateful to have you in my life. Thanks for putting up with my terrible texting habits.

My Bandini Babes—Thanks for making my group feel like a second home. I enjoy getting to know each of you by name, favorite F1 driver, and book boyfriend you want to claim.

To the whole team at Valentine PR—Thank you for helping me make this release possible.

To those two lines from Taylor Swift's "Illicit Affairs" about a secret language—Thanks for existing. You helped inspire Declan and Iris's word game.

About the Author

Plagued with an overactive imagination, Lauren spends her free time reading and writing. Her dream is to travel to all the places she writes about. She enjoys writing about flawed yet relatable characters you can't help loving. She likes sharing fast-paced stories with angst, steam, and the emotional spectrum.

Her extra-curricular activities include watching YouTube, binging old episodes of *Parks and Rec*, and searching Yelp for new restaurants before choosing her trusted favorite. She works best after her morning coffee and will never deny a nap.